Read what people are already saying about

The Hidden Legacy

'*The Hidden Legacy* is **the best kind of mystery novel** . . . It's a story that's hard to put down – and hard to forget.'
Alison MacLeod, Booker-longlisted author of *Unexploded*

'**I was gripped from page one** by GJ Minett's debut thriller. He approaches a tough subject with remarkable skill and sensitivity. I loved it.'
Fleur Smithwick, author of *How To Make A Friend*

'A thought provoking, subtle novel . . . **Great stuff!**'
Jane Rusbridge, author of *Rook*

'Minett has created **a cast of interesting characters** and there is satisfaction in watching them discover the untruths and half-truths handed down through generations.'
The Irish Times

'**Chock-full of unexpected twists**, it's the sort of book that will keep you staying up far too late.'
Culture Fly

'Gripping, disturbing and heartbreaking, **this thought-provoking book is a must read**. Highly recommended.'
Promoting Crime Fiction

Beautifully handled and **enjoyable to read.'**

Buried Under Books

'Every now and again a book really hits all the individual spots that make a **perfect reading experience** for me. This is one of those books!'

Cleopatra Loves Books

'This is an **intelligent, intriguing** and most of all, well-constructed novel.'

Crime Pieces

'This is **one of my favourite mysteries of the year**, and I'm sorry I waited so long to read it.'

Book Mood Reviews

'This is a book that **I would put ahead of many of the current and recent big names.'**

Clothes in Books

'Minett has written **an outstanding debut novel** in *The Hidden Legacy.'*

Nudge

'**A powerful, memorable opening** to the novel'.

ReviewsRevues

THE
HIDDEN
LEGACY

G.J. Minett studied at Cambridge and then spent many years as a teacher of foreign languages. He studied for an MA in Creative Writing at the University of Chichester, and won the 2010 Chapter One Prize for unpublished novels with the opening chapter of *The Hidden Legacy*.

THE HIDDEN LEGACY

G.J. MINETT

twenty7

First published in Great Britain in 2015 by Twenty7 Books

This edition published in 2016 by

Twenty7 Books
80–81 Wimpole St, London W1G 9RE
www.twenty7books.com

A CIP catalogue record for this book is available from the British Library.

Paperback ISBN: 978-1-78577-014-2
Ebook ISBN: 978-1-78577-008-1

1 3 5 7 9 10 8 6 4 2

Printed and bound by Clays Ltd, St Ives Plc

Twenty7 Books is an imprint of Bonnier Zaffre,
a Bonnier Publishing company
www.bonnierzaffre.co.uk
www.bonnierpublishing.com

For Elaine

PROLOGUE

November 1966: John Michael

It's a quarter to nine when he reaches the school gates. *Ten minutes*, he thinks, *ten minutes*.

He'd have been here earlier, but he had to wait until his dad was safely out of the way. The last thing he needed was awkward questions. *What's with the duffel bag, son? What's wrong with your satchel? What have you got in there anyway?* So he'd waited, kicking his heels in the hallway, counting off the seconds until at long last his dad oh so slowly closed the bonnet of the Austin A40, climbed in and drove off. As soon as he'd watched him turn the corner at the end of the road, he slammed the front door and ran the mile and a half to school, barely pausing for breath – not easy with a heavy bag strapped across your shoulders. He'd lost his footing several times, skidding on the icy pavement.

He takes several deep breaths. His shirt is clammy against his back and the chill of the air is starting to bite through his clothing now that he's no longer on the move. But at least he's here.

It's fourteen minutes to nine. He has nine minutes.

At five-to precisely, Miss Cattermole will emerge from the staff room and stride confidently out to the centre of the playground. She'll ring the bell seven times with extravagant sweeps of her right arm. Always seven times. Always her right arm. The left dangles limply at her side. Permanently useless. Some say it was a war injury, but he doesn't believe it. People just love to make up stories ... and what would someone like Miss Cattermole have been doing in the war anyway? One thing's for certain, she'll never say what really caused it. Waves away questions with the words 'gross impertinence'. Favourite phrase of hers. Everything's 'gross impertinence'. He knows what it means – it means don't ask.

When she rings the bell, everyone will appear from nowhere, as if by magic. They'll gather like ants around a jam jar. In the summer you have to drag them out of their hidey-holes, but when it's this cold they come pouring out, can't get inside quickly enough. The fourth and fifth years will emerge from the walled area by the boiler room. It's their territory because they're the oldest. He hasn't been at secondary school for long, but he knows this much. If you've got any sense, you keep away from there.

The third years will be sheltering in the bike sheds, making the most of their last chance until break for a quick smoke. As for the first and second years, they'll be dotted around what's left of the playground, huddled into groups to protect themselves against whatever the weather and the older pupils might decide to throw at them. They'll be first in the line which will form at the main entrance, waiting for Mr Copeland to unbolt the doors from the inside – first, that is, until the older pupils push their way in ahead of them.

Once Miss Cattermole has rung the bell, it will be too late.

He looks again at his Timex wristwatch. *Ticka ticka Timex.* He has eight minutes.

The playground is a mass of bodies. Seems like everyone's taller than he is. This isn't going to be easy. It's one thing to stand at the gate and spot her as she arrives. Now that he's late, how's he supposed to find her in this forest of arms and legs? He hurries from group to group, trying not to draw attention to himself.

Just another first year going about his business.

Insignificant.

He heads for the bike sheds, then stops. The duffel bag is cutting into his shoulders and he needs to slide it off his back, just for a few seconds. He catches it by the straps and lets it dangle from his wrist, moving stiff neck muscles from side to side. As the bag swings backwards and forwards, he can hear the liquid sloshing around inside the container. He finds the sound reassuring. Then he hears a laugh that works on his senses like a road drill.

Carol Bingham is not the sort of girl his mother would have wanted him to bring home. *Never in a month of Sundays!* She's been in trouble more than once for wearing a miniskirt and make-up to school. She's very common, swears a lot. Calls him 'half inch' and wags her little finger at him. That's very unkind. Her laugh's easy to pick out ... and once he's tracked down Carol, finding Julie is easy. She never seems to stray more than a few feet from Carol's side. Unfortunately.

Until yesterday he thought Julie was the nicest girl he'd ever met. Now he knows better. Maybe she's nice when Carol's not there. Maybe she changes because she's embarrassed in front of an audience. But that's no excuse. And nor is being pretty. *Good manners cost nothing.*

Carol's already spotted him and she's making sure everyone within range knows about yesterday. And the others are all laughing now. Taking their cue from Carol, they're wiggling their little fingers and chanting 'half inch' in high, squeaky voices, clouds of warm breath clinging to them like speech bubbles in a cartoon. He ignores them and stands in front of Julie. *Sticks and stones.* He knows what he has to do.

Things could still change, even now. Julie could turn to Carol and tell her to grow up. She could be nice to him if she wanted. It's her choice. But he suspects deep down that she doesn't have it in her. And sure enough, she rounds on him before he can even get a word in: *Jesus, don't you ever learn?* Tells him to *piss off.* She's picked up that sort of language from Carol, of course. Then, in case she's not made herself clear, she turns her back on him with a toss of her hair and returns to the conversation he's interrupted.

So, he thinks to himself, *that's that, then.*

He rests the duffel bag on the floor, takes off his gloves and loosens the toggle. Julie may have finished with him, but Carol clearly hasn't. She wants to know what he's got in there. Flowers? Chocolates? *Look, Julie – Romeo's brought you a present, ha, ha!* He doesn't answer. He manoeuvres the container out of the bag. It's a tight fit and keeps catching on the strings, just as it did going in. Everyone's intrigued now, pressing forward for a closer look. He finally yanks it free and rests it on the ground. Unscrews the cap of the can he took from his father's garage. Takes the can in both hands, straightens up and swings it in Julie's direction, sending its contents flying out in an arc, backlit by the sun, colours sparkling. The can is heavy and the momentum nearly drags it out of his hands.

Carol and Julie leap back with a squeal. Carol swears – of course, she would do. The two girls hunch their shoulders and glance at each other as if they can't quite believe what's happened. Then they start shrieking. Their clothes. Their hair. And the smell – it's disgusting.

All around him there's silence, followed by nervous giggles as the hangers-on wonder what will happen next. This should be good. Carol is not someone you mess with. She's got a seventeen-year-old boyfriend with a Vespa. No way will she let him get away with this – she'll kill him. So everyone's watching the two girls to see what their next move will be … which is why he has time to take the matches from his pocket, light one and throw it into the pool of liquid gathering at their feet. It's over before anyone realises what's happening. And that brings them to life alright, scattering in all directions.

He throws down the box containing the rest of the matches, turns on his heels and walks through the playground, heading for the school gates. Walks, not runs. Walks away, as if nothing at all has happened. He's calm, in control. 'Unflustered' is the word they'll use at the trial. It's what everyone will remember.

No one moves to stop him. He walks on, hears nothing. He's vaguely aware of Miss Cattermole barrelling out of the school building, heading for the two girls, one arm flapping uselessly like a wounded penguin. But that's all.

Which is odd, really. Should have heard something, they will tell him. You could hear the screams in Rennison Park, several streets away.

PART ONE

THE LETTER

1

February 2008: Ellen

The letter was there on the mat when Ellen came downstairs. She missed it at first among the daily quota of junk mail and local advertising, which she swept up along with the rain-damaged *Independent – mental note: serious word with the paper girl –* and whisked away into the kitchen. It was the light blue envelope that caught her attention; the letters AWL shaped into an elaborate logo in the top left-hand corner. On the reverse side she found the words *Aitcheson, Wilmot and Lowe, Solicitors* printed in full, immediately above an address in Cheltenham, Gloucestershire.

Her immediate response was one of surprise. She wasn't unaccustomed to letters from solicitors – she received more than her fair share, sent on behalf of disappointed holidaymakers, holding her personally responsible for everything from faulty bathroom fittings to the lousy weather. These were always sent to work though, never to her home address. She fanned her face with the envelope, debating whether to open it straightaway. She even got as far as picking up a knife and inserting the tip of the blade into the flap before thinking better of it. She placed it carefully next to her plate on the table. She'd have more time over breakfast. There were more pressing things to see to first.

Early mornings were frantic – invariably. No matter how hard she tried to impose a semblance of order on the chaos, the odds were always stacked against her somehow and today was no different. First Harry, who had to be prised out of bed with a chisel on the best of mornings, decided he was too sick for school. For two or three minutes Ellen probed and he parried, an impasse which was resolved only when he realised that missing school would also rule out Under-9s football practice. Suddenly it was Lazarus all over again.

As for Megan, she was giving full rein to every pout in her extensive repertoire because Ellen was refusing to take Harry and her to the cinema on Friday night, having already invited Kate to dinner. She'd offered to take them both some other time but, for reasons destined to remain beyond her comprehension, this wasn't good enough. Megan came downstairs minus her school sweatshirt, which she was unhappy about wearing because it was too small, *made her look stupid*. Ellen instinctively interpreted this as a euphemism for *overweight* and found herself pressing emotional alarm bells better left untouched for some time yet. *She's only ten, for God's sake! If she says stupid, she means stupid.* She persuaded Megan to wear it for the rest of the week, promising to take her into town and buy a new one at the weekend. The victory felt Pyrrhic at best – she suspected the sweatshirt would be taken off and stuffed into Megan's bag the moment she drove off.

Then, to set the seal on a stressful start to the morning, Harry was unable to find his lunch box. She wasted valuable time searching for it before he remembered leaving it in the back of Shannon's car. Trying not to roll her eyes, Ellen grabbed his sandwiches, banana and carton of apple juice and thrust them into a large freezer bag, saying nothing but knotting it with a vehemence that spoke volumes. *What's the matter with Jack? How long does it take to check they've left nothing behind? Who's the adult here? And what sort of a name is Shannon anyway? What is she – a cheerleader, for God's sake?*

Although they were running late by the time everyone was seated at the table, Ellen vowed not to let it spoil her breakfast. *It's only ten minutes*, she told herself. She'd make it up somehow. She poured muesli into her bowl and reached for the pile of letters, weeding out the junk mail first, which she always binned unopened. Then came the various advertising leaflets and special-offer coupons for things she would never buy, plus the free local paper, which she never bothered to read and which, unlike the *Independent*, was bone dry. Of course.

The credit-card statement and the car insurance renewal form were placed in the centre of the table – she would have to deal with them tonight. The letter from AWL she saved until last.

'Mrs Ellen Harrison', it said in the small window, with not a trace of irony. The last time she'd changed her name, she'd continued to receive letters addressed to Miss Ellen Sutherland for what seemed like an eternity. Presumably she could expect more of the same now in reverse. It occurred to her that she was guilty yet again of thinking about her divorce less in terms of its emotional impact than the logistical and administrative inconvenience it would entail. Kate would be merciless if she knew. *What are you like, girl? Do you ever listen to yourself?* She'd once referred to Ellen as an emotional vacuum, pausing perhaps a fraction of a second too long before smiling to suggest that she wasn't being serious. From time to time Ellen found herself wondering about that pause.

Picking up the sharp knife once more, she sliced the envelope open and teased out the crisp blue notepaper. Unfolding the single sheet, she read it. Then, with a frown, she read it again, more carefully this time.

February 5th, 2008

Re: The Last Will and Testament of Eudora Jane Nash

Dear Mrs Harrison,

I should be grateful if you would telephone me as a matter of some urgency in respect of the above. When calling, please ask to speak with me in person. I look forward to hearing from you.

Yours sincerely,

Derek Wilmot

Senior Executive Partner

None the wiser, she looked again at the envelope, then threw it into the middle of the table with a sigh. Nonsense, of course. No question. Who on earth was Eudora Nash? She'd never heard of her. It wasn't exactly a name you'd forget in a hurry. As for Cheltenham, she'd never been there in her life, as far as she was aware; she'd have difficulty locating it on a map. Whatever was going on here, it was nothing to do with her. Someone had obviously been careless, picking out the wrong Ellen Harrison, and now her time was being wasted. She hated sloppiness.

Slipping the notepaper back into the envelope, she promised herself she'd ring from work and sort it out the first chance she had.

COTSWOLD DAILY GAZETTE

APRIL 12TH 1967

JUDGE REVEALS IDENTITY OF BOY X

In a surprise development on the opening day of the trial of 'the playground killer', hitherto known as Boy X, it was announced that the injunction ensuring his anonymity was to be lifted. The judge, Mr Justice Lawson, said in his opening remarks that he had taken this unusual step under advisement and that the decision met with the approval of both the prosecution and defence legal teams.

Naming 12-year-old John Michael Adams of Churchdown, Gloucestershire, the judge explained that lifting the injunction was the only sensible course of action under the circumstances. The boy's identity has been common knowledge for some time, both in the local area and further afield, and any suggestion that his anonymity might be protected would be little more than hypocrisy. He took the opportunity to condemn what he described as 'the maverick and highly irresponsible behaviour of individuals representing news agencies and media organisations, from whom higher standards of professional integrity might reasonably be expected'.

Mr Justice Lawson also made clear his expectations of anyone attending the trial. He said that it was his duty 'to uphold the process of law and order and to ensure that the proceedings are carried out with the appropriate degree of decorum' and that any unwarranted outbursts would result in the immediate ejection of those responsible.

It is now almost five months since John Michael Adams is alleged to have walked into the playground of Fairfield Secondary Modern School and poured petrol over two 14-year-old schoolgirls before setting them alight. Julie Kasprowicz died in hospital from her injuries. Carol Bingham suffered serious burns to her face and shoulders and, after several operations, is expected to bear the physical and emotional scars for life. The accused watched impassively throughout the 45-minute hearing. Sitting on a raised chair in full view of the court, including members of the families of both victims, he spoke only once, confirming his identity in a quiet voice. Accompanied by a social worker, he smiled from time to time at his father, who sat almost within touching distance. His mother, as has already been widely circulated, committed suicide in July 1964.

The trial continues...

2

February 2008: Ellen

'I'm afraid Mr Wilmot will be in conference all morning. Might I take a message?'

Ellen turned away from her first-floor window, leaving the boys on security to deal with the delivery lorry which had just turned in through the gates. She reached for her coffee and dunked one of her Rich Tea biscuits, watching with satisfaction as the dark stain seeped slowly upwards.

'I don't think so. I'm actually ringing at Mr Wilmot's request. I have a letter here asking me to get in touch as a matter of some urgency. His words, not mine.'

'I see. Might I have your name, please?'

'Ellen Sutherland ... although he'll know me by the name of Harrison.'

'Mrs Harrison – of course. I'll see if I can connect you. Might I ask you to hold for just a few moments?'

Click. Cue muzak.

You might, thought Ellen, then instantly reproached herself for being so pedantic. The girl was only doing her job. When it came to her own staff, she'd take artificial and mannered over rude and aggressive any day of the week.

She eased the soggy half of the biscuit into her mouth, then settled back in her chair and listened to what she tentatively identified as Vivaldi. She remembered, when she was first pregnant with Megan, she'd vowed to find some way into what she saw as the arcane world of music, poetry and art appreciation. She'd even gone as far as sending for a copy of the prospectus from the local college in the hope that there might be a course that would fit the bill. *Bluff your way through the Classics. Culture for the terminally clueless.* Something of that order. But, as with so many other projects aimed at self-improvement, she'd never found the time or the impetus required to move things forward. Then, of course, once the children were born, the idea of evening classes became a non-starter.

She'd pushed the children into learning an instrument at an early age, as if determined to compensate through them. She'd bought a recorder for Megan who, for a while at least, had shown enough interest and aptitude to encourage Ellen to consider possible next steps. Flute? Clarinet? Where might she go for private tuition? She could see now how misguided she was in making her enthusiasm for the project so obvious. Megan was never slow to recognise a button she could press and her interest soon evaporated altogether, much to Ellen's frustration. As for the guitar that Harry had pestered her to buy, she'd caught him last week standing on it to reach one of the shelves in his bedroom. That was more use than it had been put to in the preceding twelve months. It seemed the harder she tried…

'Mrs Harrison? Good of you to ring so promptly. I'm Derek Wilmot.'

Miraculously available after all.

'Not at all,' said Ellen, trying to swallow the rest of the biscuit and free up her mouth. 'I'm intrigued – it's not every day I'm mentioned in a will.'

'Quite.'

'Especially the will of someone I've never even heard of, let alone met.'

'Indeed.'

Ellen paused to allow this to sink in. 'You're not surprised that I don't know this ... Eudora Nash?'

Wilmot sneezed, and excused himself. 'I am sure there are many questions you'll want to ask, Mrs Harrison, but first things first. If you'll bear with me just for a few moments, there are one or two formalities to be observed. I need to be certain that I am indeed speaking to the correct person. Your full name is Ellen Catherine Harrison?'

'It was.'

'I'm sorry?'

'I'm divorced. As of last month.' It occurred to her then, for the first time, that it was actually one month to the day.

'I see.'

'I'm now Ellen Catherine Sutherland again.'

There was a pause, during which she could hear him rummaging through the sheets in front of him. 'I'm sorry to hear that, Mrs Harrison,' he said at length, his tone flat, dispassionate. 'Although I feel bound to point out that, in respect of the matter in hand, this changes nothing. Our immediate concern here is one of identity rather than nomenclature.'

Ellen tried to conjure up a mental picture to go with the voice, came up with cobwebs. Cobwebs and clouds of dust. A Dickensian lawyer, black coat, thinning silver hair, mutton chop whiskers, stooped over his work, trembling quill hovering over the virgin page, desk heaving with piles of dusty ledgers. Not exactly of this world. She tried not to be too offended by his casual dismissal of her personal circumstances.

'Can you confirm your date of birth?'

'September the twenty-second, nineteen seventy-four.'

'Place of birth?'

'Chichester. West Sussex.'

'Indeed.' Another shuffle of papers. She could sense him ticking boxes.

'And your current employment?'

'Excuse me for asking,' said Ellen, 'but is all of this strictly necessary?'

'If you'll just bear with me –'

Ellen took a deep breath and wondered whether or not to pursue the point. She looked at the photos of Sam Balfour which took up most of the wall facing her – one large portrait plus a number of shots of him shaking hands with a variety of celebrities and local politicians – and tried to imagine how he would have dealt with the Derek Wilmots of this world. She suspected he would have given him very short shrift. Empire building didn't allow for social niceties.

'I'm manager of Langmere Grove Holiday Park near Ryhill in West Sussex,' she said.

'And your mother's name?'

Ellen nudged at the coaster on the desk in front of her until it was equidistant from each of the edges forming the corner.

'Barbara Ann Sutherland.'

'And her maiden name?'

'That *is* her maiden name.'

'I see.' Slight clearing of the throat.

'And her date of birth?'

'First of February, nineteen thirty-seven.'

Ellen waited. Taking a tissue from the box on her desk, she dabbed at a few drops of coffee which had spilled over the rim of the cup.

'And ... ah ... your father?'

She screwed the tissue into a ball and dropped it into the bin next to her.

'On my birth certificate it says "Father unknown".' She did her best to keep the irritation out of her voice.

'Indeed,' said Wilmot. If he had picked up on anything defensive or sensitive in her tone, there was nothing in his voice to suggest it. During the ensuing pause, she took a sip of coffee and began dunking the other biscuit, which broke off before she could lift it clear of the cup.

'Well, that would appear to be satisfactory for the time being. I think we can say with some confidence that you are the ... Ellen Catherine Harrison my client had in mind. You will of course need to bring with you documentary evidence as corroboration when you pop in to see us. Your passport maybe...'

'Excuse me?'

'...driving licence, something of that sort.'

'Mr Wilmot,' said Ellen, taking a spoon and scooping the remains of the biscuit onto the saucer, 'you *do* know I live in West Sussex?'

'Of course.'

'In which case, you must be aware that "popping in to see you", as you put it, would entail something in the region of a six-hour round trip.'

'I appreciate that, Mrs Harrison...'

'Ms Sutherland.'

'Indeed. Nevertheless you'll understand that in matters such as these, there are protocols which have to be observed, forms to complete, etc.' Oh so patient. Not quite patronising, but near enough to irritate her intensely. 'If today is out of the question, perhaps we could try for tomorrow morning. What would be a good time for you?'

'Apparently I'm not making myself clear,' said Ellen, pressing her ballpoint pen against the desk and clicking it open and shut, open and shut. 'I have a job. Two children. I'm a single parent. I can't simply drop everything and drive all the way to Cheltenham just like that.'

'I understand the difficulties, Mrs Harrison,' said Wilmot, with the weary indifference of someone who does nothing of the sort. 'I assume however that you will want this whole business to be tied up as quickly as possible.'

'What business? You haven't even told me what it's all about. I don't mean to sound mercenary, Mr Wilmot, but if I've come into money somehow, how much is it? For all I know, arranging for someone to look after the children and then travelling all that distance might leave me worse off than when I started. You take my point.'

Wilmot gave what might have passed for a dry chuckle. 'I think we can safely say you will not regard it as a waste of your time,' he said. 'Perhaps if I tell you that my client has bequeathed to you full title and deeds of a property called Primrose Cottage...?'

Ellen pulled the phone away from her ear and stared blankly at it for a second.

'Excuse me?'

'It's in Oakham ... a rather picturesque little Cotswold village. I don't suppose you know it, by any chance?'

'Did you say ... a cottage?' Ellen gave up any attempt to keep the note of incredulity out of her voice.

'Indeed – although the word "cottage" may give quite the wrong impression as to its size. It's actually more spacious than it looks from the outside – early nineteenth century, old Cotswold stone, three bedrooms, small front garden, larger one to the rear. Also outright ownership of a field which borders the property. I gather the owner before my client was a keen rider and used to keep his horse there although, of course, you might have your own plans for it.'

A sharp squall buffeted the window, picking up a cluster of raindrops in the air and flinging them against the glass. From the comfort of her office, Ellen watched two cleaners struggling to push a trolley from one building to another. A member of the grounds maintenance crew backed an open-top buggy across the courtyard to get it under cover. The driver of a delivery van, parked outside the unloading bay at the rear of the on-site supermarket, tried hard to avoid looking ridiculous as he chased after a handful of papers, which skipped out of range every time he tried to plant his foot on them. A day like any other.

'Mrs Harrison?'

'Yes ... I'm still here. I'm just ... You're sure about this?'

'Absolutely. My client was a very particular lady, meticulous in her preparation. She went to a great deal of trouble to find you. I can assure you, there is no mistake.'

'But I don't even know who she is. I've never heard of her,' said Ellen, ticking off the objections as they occurred to her. 'This can't be right, surely. It'll be contested – I mean, the family aren't going to just sit back and let some total stranger come wandering in and take over their home, are they?'

'There is no family...'

'What ... no one?'

'Well, perhaps it would be more accurate to say that there is no one in a position to make a realistic claim. My client, you understand, was an elderly lady. She was ninety-one when she died. She outlived her husband by more than thirty years. There are no children. There *was* a younger sister, Miss Emily Nash, but she died a few years ago.' More shuffling of papers. 'In June 2001, to be precise.'

'What about her husband's family?'

'My understanding is that relations between my client and her husband's family were no more than civil even while he was alive. Since his death, there has been no contact to speak of. Of course, one can never be sure about these things – such matters do have the unfortunate tendency to draw out the most unlikely claimants. However the will is quite straightforward. Apart from a few personal items, the property goes to you and the money is equally divided between three children's charities. There are no grounds to encourage anyone to contest it and, should they do so, they will most certainly fail.'

There was something very reassuring about his confidence. A thought occurred to Ellen.

'The funeral – when is it?'

'Ah yes –'

'Maybe there'll be someone there who can shed some light on this, someone she confided in. I ought to be there.'

He cleared his throat. 'The funeral was yesterday.'

'Yesterday? But ... when did she die?'

'Monday of last week.'

'Monday? But that's over a week ago.' For some reason she couldn't quite define, Ellen felt culpable in her failure to be there, as if she had let the old lady down somehow.

'My client was most insistent that you should not be notified of her death until after the service.'

'Really? But why?'

'I have no idea,' said Wilmot. 'There were several things my client chose not to share with me. She may, of course, have been less reticent about talking to some of her friends in the village, which is one of the reasons why I thought you might be anxious to visit the property as soon as possible.'

In other words, why don't you just do as I suggested and get yourself over here! Ellen thought this over for a moment.

'So how long will it be before the cottage is legally mine? You mentioned papers I need to sign.'

'Just a few formalities. Everything that does not require your direct participation has already been taken care of. If you were to come here as early as tomorrow morning, the property would be yours by the weekend. If you wish, I could also give the keys to one of my associates and arrange for him to drive you over there so that you might view the property for yourself.'

Ellen was working through the possibilities in her mind. Jack didn't work Wednesday evenings. If he could have the children, she'd be able to make a really early start. Leave at seven, be there by nine thirty. Three hours or so to sort out the formalities and visit the cottage, then back by mid-to-late afternoon to pick up the children. Colin could take care of things at work – no problem there. He was desperate for any opportunity to show

Sam and everybody else for that matter that he could do her job standing on his head. It would all hinge on Jack.

'This village,' she said. 'Oakley?'

'Oakham.'

'How far is it from Cheltenham?'

'Half an hour or so, I would say.'

'And is there anything in the will to say whether or not I'm allowed to sell the property?'

'No,' said Wilmot, a note of disapproval creeping into his voice. 'No, there is no stipulation to that effect. My client did express hopes that you might be so enamoured of the cottage that you would want to keep it. Once the property is legally yours however, you are not bound by any such considerations. You will be free to do with it as your conscience dictates.'

'And property in a Cotswold village...?'

Wilmot paused for a moment, as if choosing his words carefully. 'You appear to be groping your way towards a particular question, Mrs Harrison. Perhaps I might save us both some time by saying that I can tell you with some degree of certainty how much the property is worth.' If there was any ambiguity in his tone before, there was none now. Ellen reached across the desk for her notepad and waited.

'My client arranged for valuations with three separate agencies in the months leading up to her death. They varied by fifty thousand pounds, but the lowest estimate was for seven hundred and seventy-five thousand pounds.'

Ellen slowly lowered the receiver to her shoulder. Clicking the biro again, she flipped open the pad and wrote a seven, followed by another, then a five, a comma and three zeros. She looked at it for a moment, then wrote a dash, followed by an eight, a two, a five, a comma and three more zeros. She placed a pound sign at the front, a large, exaggerated symbol which dwarfed the numbers. Finally she drew a box around it all and underlined the figures three times. It did nothing to make any of it seem more real.

'Mrs Harrison?'

She took up the receiver once more.

'I'll be there tomorrow at nine thirty.'

3

February 2008: Ellen

Jack's rented flat was in a quiet, leafy area of Chichester, to the north of the Festival Theatre and the university. He had the ground-floor rooms of a three-storey Georgian building, which was owned by one of his father's business contacts. The other two floors were divided into flats occupied by various young professionals and an elderly spinster whose imperious manner suggested she might have been there since the house was first built. Jack's arrival had put a few noses out of joint, especially in the case of the young married couple on the top floor, who had been casting covetous glances in the direction of the spacious ground-floor rooms for some time. Whatever understanding they believed they had with the owner proved worthless once Jack's father started calling in favours. It was always the way.

What's more, unless Ellen was mistaken, the timely availability of the flat was not the only reason Jack had to be grateful to his parents. He still spent the bulk of his time at home, pursuing his writing career (or, as Ellen had slowly come to regard it, his *'writing career'* – she found it hard to believe any 'pursuit' could be quite so inert and lethargic). The income he gained from this was negligible and had never come close to matching his outgoings in all the time she'd known him. He did have a proofreading job with a publisher of technical manuals based in Winchester but that did little more than cover his beer money and general entertainment. To Ellen it looked very much as if the Harrisons had come up trumps and bailed out their wayward son yet again. Even though it was no longer any of her concern, she couldn't help feeling slightly irked by the fact that things were always so easy for Jack. He could invariably expect to fall on his feet. Somehow life circled without ever managing to land a meaningful blow.

He came to the front door, wearing jeans and a Sussex University sweatshirt which was in something like its fifth or sixth incarnation. He smiled and leant forward to kiss her. She flinched instinctively, then offered her cheek just as he pulled his head back. He held out his hand to get past the awkwardness of the moment and offered to take the overnight bag, into which she'd hurriedly packed the children's night things and lunches for the following day. She said she could manage, then relented and tried to hand it over just as he gave up and reached past her to shut the front door.

She followed him down the narrow corridor, past the winding staircase which led to the flats upstairs, past the expensive-looking racing bike, which was padlocked and tucked away in the recess under the stairs. The Audi was fine for journeys but Jack needed something more suitable for 'tootling around town', as he put it. Anyone else would have been happy to make do with a pushbike, even a sit-up-and-beg with a basket at the front. Jack had admitted to spending £250 on the bike itself, which in Jack-speak almost certainly meant at least twice that amount. More or less in the same price bracket were the clothing and other accoutrements – flash helmet with wind-channelling vents, garishly coloured Lycra vest and padded shorts, gloves, goggles. It was an investment, he claimed – an investment in his health. He was embarking on a fitness drive which would make a new man of him. The exercise would lend a sharpness to his thinking – *mens sana and all that*. He would thrash his way up over Goodwood and the Trundle, get to know Sussex like he'd never known it before, then settle down and compose the best poetry he'd ever produced. As far as she was aware, he'd worn the gear all of twice. Last time she'd checked the gloves were still in their wrapper.

The door to his flat was ajar. He opened it wider with his foot and stepped aside to allow her into a small hallway, sealed off on all sides by a series of doors. Ellen entered the lounge via the final door and found herself staring at a huge plasma TV screen on the opposite wall, where a number of impossibly beautiful Australian youths, male and female, were agonising over the mysterious disappearance of their drama teacher. Both of her children were totally absorbed by it. Megan was stretched out on the settee, her head supported by a pillow. Harry was lying on the floor on his stomach, elbows protected by a cushion and head resting in his cupped hands. He got to his feet and came over immediately to give her a hug. For her part Megan mumbled something that sounded like 'Hi' and waved a hand in a vague sort of way, needing to be prompted before she sat up and made room on the settee.

Ellen sat between the two of them, an arm around each, and tried not to dwell on the fact that she would not be seeing them for another twenty-four hours. This was their time together and she filled it with the usual questions. *How was Megan's whale project coming along? Had she remembered to hand in the form and the cheque for the residential trip in June? Had Harry thought to check lost property for his missing trainers?* They both answered distractedly, peeling their attention incrementally away from the screen for no longer than it took to answer. This was precisely why they were not allowed to watch any soaps at home. Some of the rubbish they would lock onto, given half a chance, defied belief. It took real willpower not to get up and switch the damned thing off. She forced herself to remember that this was not her home.

She watched for a minute or two. A different character had appeared, this one with slightly crooked teeth and what could only be described as a mullet. She remembered the days when the villains were instantly identifiable because they always wore black. Now you simply looked for the one who was just a shade less than drop-dead gorgeous.

'Best to give 'em ten minutes or so,' called Jack through the serving hatch. 'You won't get much out of them till it's finished.' *In which case, why let them watch it?* 'Come in here,' he continued. 'I'll get you a drink.'

Ellen gave their hair an affectionate ruffle and got up from the sofa (which also wasn't cheap). She squeezed past the children, pausing briefly in front of the mirror and running her fingers through her hair in an attempt to tease it into something more presentable. Then she dropped her hand to her side as she realised Jack was watching her through the hatch. He slid open the partition door and she took a seat at the dining table, cross with herself for a moment's carelessness. Jack never needed an excuse to leap to the wrong conclusion.

'Here, I'll just get those.' He reached across her and plucked the Pizza Hut boxes from the table. He went over to the bin, found it full and thrust them into a corner of one of the work surfaces instead.

'I'd have cooked them something,' he said, opening a cupboard and taking a bottle of wine from it. 'You know, something a bit more nutritious, only with all the short notice and everything ...' *Absolutely*, thought Ellen. Half-ten this morning she'd rung him – how could anyone be expected to rustle up a few vegetables in that time? She reminded herself that he was doing her a favour. Now was hardly the time to take him to task about the TV, their diet, what time they needed to go to bed. *Nine o'clock. Absolute latest.*

'You're not opening that for *me*, are you?' she asked, as he took a corkscrew from the drawer and inserted it into the neck of the bottle.

'Nope.'

'Only ... not for me, please. I can't. I'm driving.'

Jack put the bottle between his knees and gave a sharp tug to free the cork. Then he reached up to one of the overhead cupboards and withdrew two glasses.

'One glass won't hurt you,' he said. 'I'm not offering you the bottle.'

'No, honestly.'

He placed the glasses on the table and poured with an exaggerated raising and lowering motion. Then he handed one of them to her.

'Here,' he said. 'Tell me what you think.'

It was always this way with Jack.

So ... is that a yes or a no?

No.

Was that a yes?

No.

Sounded like a yes to me.

It was a no.

I'll take that as a yes then.

Jack to a T.

Ellen took the glass from him and sipped gently. He looked intently at her, gauging her reaction.

'Mm ... nice,' she said. *Nice!* God, she was such a philistine. Oh to be able to talk with authority of bouquets and vintages and such like. Jack smiled, as if reading her thoughts.

'I should hope so. Cost enough.'

He flashed his grin, the Jack grin, and the years rolled back like waves. She looked again at his Sussex University sweatshirt, which they both knew he would never have worn as a student. He'd have died rather than subscribe to some bourgeois sense of collegiate identity. In those days his T-shirts had been ablaze with provocative slogans and calls to arms. They never hinted or whispered – they screamed. They spat. They assaulted the senses, spraying vitriol and condemnation indiscriminately. Abortion? FUCK THE POPE! Chechnya? FUCK THE KREMLIN! Rwanda? FUCK THE HUTUS! The cause was immaterial. Effect was everything.

When she finished her Business degree, he quit his own Creative Arts course and went with her, even though it had twelve months still to run. If you believed Jack's version, he'd outgrown the course anyway. There was nothing more it could teach him. It was staffed by mediocre wannabes who weren't and never would be, social inadequates who had sold out to the Establishment years ago and were more concerned with tenure than getting out there and *creating* something. He didn't need them.

Only Ellen suspected the truth – that he had jumped before he could be pushed.

'So – this Cheltenham trip. What's all that about?'

Ellen brought him up to speed with the letter she'd received and her conversation with Wilmot. She found herself avoiding any reference to the cottage and its value. Instead she kept things non-specific, playing the whole thing down as much as possible and trying to create the impression that she had no expectations of any great substance. She wondered why this was. Habit? Had evasion and half-truths become so deeply ingrained in their relationship that deception was now second nature to her? Or was it maybe a touch of embarrassment at the timing of it all? One month divorced, all the legal formalities concerning their financial circumstances finalised at last, and then suddenly here she is, with what could reasonably be described as a fortune landing in her lap. How convenient was that? She knew how it would have looked to her, had the roles been reversed. She didn't want to see the counters clicking over in his eyes or the inevitable calculations and suspicion.

Jack, to give him credit, seemed more intrigued by Eudora Nash.

'I'll tell you what,' he said, shaping to top up her glass until she stubbornly placed one hand over it. 'You may not have heard of her but she sure as hell has to figure *somewhere* in that shadowy past of yours. Have you talked to Barbara?'

Ellen arched an eyebrow and he instantly held up one hand by way of apology.

'Oh yeah ... right. Sorry.' He turned his back for a moment and put the bottle on the work surface. 'Still, it's not like she's out of it all the time, is it? I mean, she does have her moments, doesn't she?'

Ellen put down her glass and made a conscious effort to keep her tone as neutral as possible. 'When was the last time you spoke with her, Jack?'

He took a sip from his glass. 'Your mother? Dunno. Not for a while, I suppose.'

'Things have moved on a lot in the last year or so.'

'It hasn't been that long...'

'How many times have you been to Calder Vale?' She waited, enjoying his momentary confusion and confident that the point was hers. She knew he'd sooner take holy orders than visit her mother in a nursing home. 'Half the time, she doesn't even know who *I* am, let alone this ... *Eudora Nash*. She may have her moments, as you put it, but they're getting fewer and further between.'

'Yeah, well –' he said, rubbing at some imaginary mark on his trousers, as the opening for an apology slipped past.

'And even when she's vaguely compos mentis, what makes you think she'd explain herself to *me*? You know what she's like.'

'OK. So what about the Balfours?' he asked, striking out for clearer waters. 'Maybe they'd know something. Have you asked them?'

Here we go, thought Ellen. *How long have I been here? Ten minutes?* Jack rarely needed an excuse to have a go at Sam. She'd never managed to isolate exactly what it was that rubbed him up the wrong way because there were so many possible contributory factors. Jack was a dreamer – Sam preferred to roll up his shirtsleeves. Sam was capitalism personified – Jack liked to think of himself as driven by purer instincts. Sam had conceived and built Langmere Grove from scratch – Jack had built nothing. And much as he liked to sneer about the millions Sam had made and the luxury retirement villa he shared with his wife Mary in Barbados, the envy announced itself almost every time Sam's name was mentioned. Maybe it was that easy: Jack wished he had money – Sam had it.

He was less scathing about Mary Balfour, who had interviewed and subsequently befriended Ellen's mother when she first arrived at Langmere, but then again it would have been difficult to find fault with someone so generous and kindhearted. Unable to have children herself, Mary had spent a lot of time with Ellen during her formative years, even looking after her while Barbara was at work. And if Sam had been the one to sponsor Ellen through university and open doors for her, it was almost certainly Mary who was doing the nudging. Jack seemed prepared to give her the benefit of the doubt but wasn't able to extend the courtesy to Sam. The debt of gratitude which Ellen owed her benefactor clearly stuck in his craw and she'd long since given up on the idea that anything would dislodge it now.

'Sam will be video-conferencing on Friday – I'll ask them then.'

'Ring now if you like – you can use my phone.'

She gritted her teeth. 'No rush. It's not that big a deal. It'll probably all be cleared up tomorrow. Besides, he won't know anything.'

'How can you be sure?'

'I just am.'

'Why? 'Cos it's good old Sam?' said Jack. 'You think he wouldn't keep anything from you?'

Ellen shaped as if to accept the challenge but decided to let it rest. There was no point once Jack got going. Never had been.

'Look, I know he put you through university and all that but I've always said you're too quick to take everything he says at face value,' he continued. 'Me, I wouldn't trust him any further than I could throw him.'

'Yes, well ... you two never did get on.'

'Never gave me much of a chance, did he? He was on my case right from the start. I can understand why you won't hear a word said against him. I get that he's been like a father to you but I tell you – still waters, that man. Still waters. Bit like the swan. Anyway, it's your bed, El. You know what I think.'

Ellen ignored the mixed metaphors, bit her lip and said nothing. She wouldn't rise to it. She didn't need to, not any longer. Those days were long gone, she told herself. Before she left she would sit down and spend some quality time with her children, while she could. Then she'd walk away from it all. Things were different now because she could do just that – walk away. This didn't have to turn into a clash of wills that would dominate the whole evening.

But she made one silent promise to herself. When she got home, she would have a long, hot, relaxing bath and pamper herself with bubble bath and oils of every description. Then she'd make herself a hot chocolate, wrap herself in her dressing gown and curl up on the settee with a good book before grabbing an early night in readiness for the journey. What she would *not* do was brood on Jack's hints about the Balfours. Nor, under any circumstances, would she phone them. She wouldn't give him the satisfaction.

'Hey! So how's my favourite girl, then?'

'Hi, Sam.'

'You fit?'

'I'm fine.'

'And the kids?'

'They're good too. You and Mary?'

'Yeah ... not bad for a couple of old fossils.'

'That's great. Listen, is this a bad time?'

'Never a bad time when it's you, girl. We've just come up from the beach. Mary's rustling up a salad. Here ... I'll just switch you to speakerphone and you can say hi.'

Ellen sank back and allowed the hot water to settle around her shoulders. Sinatra, who had been crooning quietly in the background, now sounded much clearer and Mary could also be heard cooeeing from all of four thousand miles away. Ellen called out to her, summoning up a mental picture of the luxury seafront apartment, still fresh in her mind from her visit four years ago. She and Jack had taken the children for ten days of sun, sea, sand and water sports with accommodation provided and only the flights to pay for. Unfortunately the reality had been more stressful than she'd bargained for. The children's body clocks were all over the place and Jack, with two young children in tow, had found living with two seventy-plus-year-olds somewhat at odds with the beach-bum idyll he'd envisaged. He made a poor fist of disguising his boredom after the first couple of days and the enforced proximity took its toll on what had always been a fragile truce between him and Sam. By the time the ten days were up, the usual expressions of regret sounded more than a little hollow.

Now, of course, the children were that bit older and Jack was out of the picture, and Sam in particular had been pressing for her to come and visit again. She spent a couple of minutes fending him off, assuring him that she and the children would be out there the following year, come what may, for their fiftieth wedding anniversary. Then she answered his questions about the business, talking him through what had happened in the last few days.

'So-o-o ...' he said, the moment she'd finished. 'We nearly there yet?'

'Nearly where?'

'Well, let me see. You're fine. The kids are good. Work's coming along just nicely. So that kind of leaves me wondering what's so important that you've decided to call, when you know we've got a conference call anyway in, what, thirty-six hours or so.'

Ellen chuckled. 'OK. There was something,' she said, scooping up a handful of bubbles with her free hand and blowing gently into them. 'Probably nothing serious but I thought I'd run it past you. Only there's this name that cropped up this morning. It's supposed to mean something to me but I honestly don't remember having heard it before.'

'So what's the name?'

'Nash. Eudora Nash.'

There was a pause, almost imperceptible but there none the less.

'Nash, you say?'

'Eudora.'

Another pause. 'Eudora? That's some name. You don't get many of those to the pound nowadays.'

'Do you know her?'

Sam sighed. 'Aw hell, girl – you get to my age, you have enough difficulty remembering your own name, let alone some-one else's.'

'What about you, Mary?' she called, raising her voice. 'Mean anything to you?'

'She's gone back into the kitchen,' said Sam. 'If you hold for a few seconds, I'll ask her.'

There was a click and Sinatra faded into the distance again. Ellen looked at the handset for a moment, wondering why Sam had decided to take her off speakerphone. She waited patiently for twenty, thirty, forty seconds, then pressed the receiver to her ear and listened carefully to make sure she hadn't been cut off. She was surprised – how long did it take to ask a simple question?

'You still there?' The speaker was open again. She could hear Sinatra telling everyone that Chicago was his kind of town.

'So what did Mary have to say? The name mean anything to her?'

'Aw hell, it's like I said. You get to our age, nothing much sticks any more. With a bit of context, maybe?'

'Context?'

'Like how this name cropped up in the first place?'

Ellen paused for a moment, uncertain as to how to play this. She was surprised that this element of calculation had crept in. A conversation with Sam was usually the most nat-ural thing in the world. They'd always been so easy in each other's company. The suggestion that she might actively seek to keep anything from him and Mary was intrinsically ludi-crous. And yet...

For the second time in a matter of hours, Ellen went over the events of the morning. And, as with Jack, she avoided any mention of the cottage. She gave the gist of the letter and told him she was planning to meet the solicitor in the morning.

Sam heard her out. There was a silence at the other end which Ellen found disconcerting. At last his voice came through, clear and confident as ever. 'Know what I'd do if I were you, girl?' he said.

'Go on.'

'I'd forget all about it.'

'Why?'

'More trouble than it's worth, by the sound of it. Travel all that way, then find all you've got is some vase you don't even want. That's if they've got the right person in the first place. You'd be amazed how often they get that sort of thing wrong. Better off staying put. Waste of a day, seems to me.'

'Be nice to clear it up though, wouldn't it?' she asked, disingenuously. 'I mean, aren't you curious as to why she's leaving me anything at all?'

'Who knows? These widows,' he sighed, clambering aboard one of his favourite hobby horses down the years, 'more money than sense, most of them. They leave millions to their cats, for Christ's sake. Last thing you want is to try working out what's going on between their ears. I tell you, you've got better things to do with your time.'

'And if it's more than just a vase?'

Sam paused before answering, as if weighing up alternatives.

'Tell you what, why don't I make a few calls? I could give Isaac a ring ... ask him to check this firm of solicitors out. What was their name again?'

'I don't remember,' she lied. 'The letter's in the kitchen somewhere and I'm in the bath.'

'So ring me back, OK? Or better still, I'll give you ten minutes or so, then call *you* back – save your phone bill. You let me have their name and I'll give Isaac a ring. He'll take care of everything for you. If there's anything even remotely iffy about it, he'll sniff it out for sure. And if it's all legit, he can give you the good news in person. What d'you say? Save you a lot of trouble.'

Ellen assured him this wouldn't be necessary and thanked him for his concern. Sam persisted for a while but she held firm, made it clear she wasn't about to change her mind. She moved on to other matters as soon as she was able and asked to talk with Mary for a couple of minutes. Then she rang off before Sam could get back on the line and start all over again.

She put the handset on the floor beside the bath and slid down into the water until it covered her head. After a few seconds, she resurfaced and swept her hair back from her face. Then, resting her head on the edge of the bath, she replayed the entire phone call in her mind.

She tried to rebuild the conversation as accurately as possible. She might be wrong, of course. It wasn't as if she'd been paying particularly close attention to what she was saying in the early part of the call, so yes – she might have said something, somewhere along the line, to suggest that a visit to the solicitors would involve a long journey. She *might*. Although she was inclined to doubt it.

But one thing she was sure of and nothing would persuade her otherwise. At no stage had she said anything about Eudora Nash being a widow.

Not once.

COTSWOLD DAILY GAZETTE

APRIL 22ND 1967

EVERY PARENT'S NIGHTMARE

John Michael Adams, aged 12, was yesterday sentenced to be detained at Her Majesty's pleasure for the murder of 14-year-old schoolgirl, Julie Kasprowicz and the attempted murder of her classmate Carol Bingham. Although no actual fixed term was specified, Mr Justice Lawson recommended that he 'should remain in custody for some considerable time'. Legal experts were suggesting last night that it may be 15–20 years at the very least before he will be considered for release. As the verdict was read out, there were cries of triumph from relatives of the two girls, interspersed with angry shouts aimed in the direction of the prisoner, who seemed unmoved by what was taking place. His father, sitting near by, buried his head in his hands as his son was taken down in the company of two social workers.

Mr Justice Lawson, recalling the attack in the playground of Fairfield Secondary Modern School in Churchdown, Gloucester, described it as 'unspeakably barbaric and depraved'. He said that, in his opinion, the jury had discharged its duty honourably and shown 'commendable integrity in wading through the volumes of conflicting and confusing psychiatric reports which had been placed before them.' It was his considered opinion that these tactics represented nothing more than deliberate obfuscation on the part of the defence. There was 'nothing there which either provided a plausible explanation or went any way towards offering mitigation for the tragic events of that morning'. Addressing the prisoner, he went on: 'You are every loving parent's nightmare. You have willfully cut short one young life and ruined several others, yet not once have you shown any remorse for the suffering you have caused. Clearly you represent a major threat to society and I would be failing in my responsibilities if I were to allow you your freedom until such time as we can be sure that this threat has been removed.'

Pages 2 and 3: 'Nowhere he can hide' – the anger of Phil Bingham

Pages 4, 5 and 6: Anatomy of a Child Killer

Page 22: Leader Comment

PART TWO

THE JOURNEY

February 2008: Ellen

Thursday morning dawned cold but clear. When she stepped outside, Ellen was relieved to find nothing more challenging than a light dusting of frost coating the back lawns. What she could see of the sky, above the dull gleam of streetlamps, appeared to be cloudless for the first time in weeks. She made a mental note to remind Jack to make sure Megan wore her sweatshirt.

A thin layer of ice proved troublesome on the minor roads near home, but by the time she'd bypassed Winchester and reached the Berkshire Downs a pale, wintry sun was already fingering its way across the hilltops. She settled back to enjoy the rest of the drive.

She tried to remember the last time she'd taken this road. Her only memory of it was a trip to Snowdonia with Jack, a few months before their wedding. Their first time away together had unfortunately coincided with the wettest fortnight any of the locals could remember. The storms, unrelenting in their ferocity, had practically washed them off the hillside, turning established campsites and well-worn trails into little more than quagmires overnight. The rain came at them all day long in horizontal bands, lashing their faces and giving the lie to their supposedly waterproof clothing.

It was all the same to Ellen. She loved the drama, the thunder echoing off the hills, the insistent tattoo of the raindrops and hailstones on the canvas while she and Jack huddled together, rubbing frantically at each other's hair with permanently damp towels and snuggled inside their double sleeping bag to keep the cold at bay. She would have been happy to make the best of it.

Jack, on the other hand, always had to be doing something. He was stir-crazy after as little as half an hour of crouching inside a small tent with just her for company. He needed others around him, people he could dazzle. For him, there was nothing romantic about being soaked through, frozen and miserable. Even that far back in their relationship, Ellen knew that keeping him on board for the whole fortnight was going to be a delicate balancing act. True to form, he came down with a cold before the first week was out and convinced himself it was pneumonia at the very least, so that was that. They came home a week early. Over almost before it had started.

She remembered asking, as they headed towards Newbury, if this was where *Watership Down* had been set. Jack had laughed – 'European Capital of the Hunt' he called it. 'Wall-to-wall fascists'. Then he slipped seamlessly into one of his tirades against the 'landed gentry' and the hypocrisy which underpinned their supposed love of the countryside. All that was missing was the T-shirt: FUCK THE RABBITS! She smiled at the memory.

She reached the outskirts of Cheltenham at least half an hour earlier than expected but then had to contend with a bewildering one-way system, which seemed determined to show off as much of the town as possible. She found herself being funnelled down a succession of broad, tree-lined avenues, past imposing Regency buildings and expansive municipal gardens. Then she seemed to double back on herself as the traffic snaked its way around the less commercial part of the town before bringing her to a theatre she was sure she'd driven past earlier. When she found Oriel Road at last, she had to drive away in search of a car park, every roadside space having been snapped up, even this early in the morning. As a result, she was five minutes late when she walked through the doors of Aitcheson, Wilmot and Lowe.

The moment she gave her name in Reception, she was shown straight into a light, spacious office where a man introduced himself as Derek Wilmot. It wasn't until he spoke that she made the connection. The voice was unmistakable, even though he was nothing like the dusty old fossil she'd imagined from the other end of the phone. He was at least twenty years younger, trim and dressed in a light grey suit which, if it didn't exactly make him a sharp dresser, nevertheless suggested a certain sense of style. As he stepped forward to shake her hand, he made eye contact and sketched out the vaguest hint of a smile.

He offered her a seat and a cup of tea, which she gratefully accepted.

'Pleasant journey?' he asked, retreating behind the desk and removing a number of documents from a large blue folder.

'Pretty much,' she replied. She offered a few throwaway observations on her day so far, finishing with a light-hearted account of the difficulties she'd had in locating the building and finding somewhere to park. He murmured something vague in response, without looking up from the documents. It sounded like 'Splendid', and she realised that she could have been giving the shipping forecast for all he knew. His question had been a reflex, another tick on the checklist. His attention was already elsewhere.

He took a pair of spectacles from a Specsavers case on his desk and perched them on the end of his nose, tilting his head as he peered at the documents spread out before him. From time to time he mumbled quietly to himself as if confirming that everything was in order. Then, just as she was wondering if he'd forgotten she was there, he looked up, peeled off the glasses and handed over the first sheet for her to sign at the appointed place. Ellen smiled to herself. So much for the social niceties.

She spent the next few minutes, reading and signing documents as they were passed to her. Wilmot came round the desk to stand at her shoulder, constantly nudging the next paper closer for her perusal. He did at least faithfully discharge his professional responsibilities in urging her to read them carefully before signing, but she sensed this was done more for form than anything else. By the time her cup of tea arrived, the formalities had been more or less completed.

'Miss Devonshire,' he said, speaking into the intercom, 'would you please ask Liam to come in? And if Mr and Mrs Coleridge are here, would you tell them I'll be with them shortly?'

Ellen winced as she took a quick sip of tea, burning the roof of her mouth.

'So, is that it, then?' she asked. Although amused by his lack of interest in the social conventions, she was nevertheless a little confused by the stark contrast between his elaborate wooing of her over the phone just twenty-four hours earlier, when she was made to feel that her presence here would be so much appreciated, and the almost indecent haste with which she was now being processed. It felt as if, simply by walking through the door, she had automatically become yesterday's business, slipped inside a folder which was about to be consigned to the depths of some filing cabinet, never again to see the light of day. It seemed to her that some sort of acknowledgement of her efforts wouldn't have gone amiss.

'That's all we can do for now,' said Wilmot. 'It will take forty-eight hours for the documents to be finalised. My client did everything possible to expedite matters. Thanks to her foresight, the property should be legally yours by the weekend.'

'This weekend?' Even though he'd said as much on the phone the previous day, it still seemed remarkably soon. In her experience at Langmere Grove, solicitors moved no more quickly than was absolutely necessary. They liked to ponder, deliberate, eke things out for as long as possible. The whole concept of 'expediting matters' was alien to them. 'So if I were to come up again on Saturday…?'

'Well, Saturdays are not normally part of our business hours,' said Wilmot, checking the temperature of the radiator behind him, 'but I'm often here for a while in the morning. You could collect the keys from me. Do you find it a little warm in here?' Without waiting for any kind of response, he walked over to the thermostat on the wall by the door and adjusted it slightly. 'We can agree a time, if you wish. As for this morning, Mr Sharp will drive you over to Oakham to see the cottage. I'm assuming you would rather be driven?'

Ellen thanked him. After three hours behind the wheel, it would be nice to sit back and leave the driving to someone else.

'He'll have the keys to Primrose Cottage and will be able to show you around. I'm sorry I can't accompany you myself, only I have a number of appointments this morning. I'm sure you understand.'

Ellen waved vaguely to acknowledge the fact.

'One thing though,' he continued, raising a finger as if to emphasise the point. 'Please don't be offended but I am obliged to remind you that the cottage is not legally yours until these papers have been processed. You're not entitled to remove anything from the property until then.'

Ellen nodded. She bent her head to take another sip of tea but had barely drunk half of it before Liam Sharp came in to escort her to his car. Wilmot hovered by the door, as if to make it clear that the meeting was over. As she passed him in the doorway, he offered his hand once more. It felt like little more than a gesture as he led the way back into the reception area, where an elderly couple rose to meet him. His mind had already turned to other things.

Liam Sharp was in his early twenties. Ellen needed all of a minute to classify him as an irritant. Maybe it was the handshake which lasted a little longer than necessary. Alternatively, it might have been his excessive use of hair gel or his restless, fidgety manner, expressed in a series of yanks at the cuffs beneath his jacket and the occasional tug at his trousers. Whatever it was, Ellen's regrets about accepting a lift began long before they reached the shiny black Mazda convertible in the company car park at the rear of the building. She hoped it wouldn't be a long drive.

He opened the passenger door for her and settled behind the wheel, running one hand through his hair as he sneaked a quick look in the mirror. Then he fired up the engine with what struck her as an exaggerated blast of the accelerator and launched the car into the unsuspecting traffic threading its leisurely way through the centre of the town. At the first set of lights, he flipped open his mobile and made a brief call, apparently to someone's answerphone, explaining that he was going to Oakham and would be out of the office all morning.

Ellen sneaked a glance at him, wondering how on earth she was going to handle it when Megan brought home someone like him ... which she surely would do, even if she made clear her disapproval. *Especially* if she made clear her disapproval. If her own adolescence was any sort of yardstick, she could expect her daughter to go through her fair share of shallow, vacuous, self-preening nonentities before stumbling on someone acceptable.

She remembered the little girl in the red sweatshirt, skipping off merrily into the playground on her first day at school and recalled how proud she'd felt that her daughter was so self-possessed and confident, not clinging tearfully to her mother like so many of the others. Now, in what seemed like the blink of an eye, Megan was a teenager in all but chronology and Ellen found herself wishing for a little less of the independent spirit. She wished she could hold on to the little girl in her for a while longer. Her grip already felt a touch too tenuous. For just a moment she caught herself wondering how her own mother had coped with these same doubts all those years ago. It wasn't something she'd ever thought to ask and there wasn't much to be gained from seeking answers now.

Sharp apparently knew only one way to drive, which was to tailgate with excessive use of the horn. All of this was done to the accompaniment of a raucous soundtrack issuing from his speakers.

'Linkin Park,' he said by way of enlightenment.

'Sorry?'

'You like it?'

'Actually,' she said, raising her voice and applying one hand to her forehead for emphasis, 'I've got a bit of a headache. Have you got anything a bit quieter?'

'Quieter? Dunno. I'll have a look.' He reached across and rummaged through a stack of CDs in a compartment in the dashboard. Then he looked up just in time, braking sharply to avoid ramming the car in front.

'Linkin Park will be fine,' she said.

'Cool.' He went back to his arrhythmic tapping on the steering wheel.

The traffic thinned out gradually as they left Cheltenham, which for him represented the ideal opportunity to show what the car could do. They roared through the village of Prestbury and picked up a B-road heading for Cleeve Hill.

'Actually, would you mind slowing down a little? It's making me feel sick.'

'Cool.' He eased down a fraction.

Ellen sat back and closed her eyes, hoping this might somehow convey the impression that small talk was off the agenda. She turned her thoughts to Eudora Nash. In a quarter of an hour or so, they'd be arriving in Oakham and she would get her first glimpse of Primrose Cottage. She'd gone over it all so many times since yesterday morning. She'd been distracted at work, had slept fitfully and then spent most of this morning's journey trying to come up with an explanation.

Deep down there lurked the fear that this might yet turn out to be one huge mistake. She'd half-expected Wilmot to greet her this morning with a rueful expression and profuse apologies. *So sorry to have wasted your time. It was a different Ellen Catherine Harrison after all. Who'd have thought it?* She'd have been angry, frustrated at the waste of a day, but she'd have got over it soon enough. After all, it wasn't as if she'd actually lost anything. It had never been hers in the first place.

But in a quarter of an hour or so, she knew, that would all change. Once she'd seen the cottage, walked around it, taken emotional possession, she suspected the disappointment would be that much harder to take. She knew what she was like.

So for now she clung to the other possibility ... that this was not a mistake. That she was precisely the person Eudora had in mind. And if that was the case, that begged any number of questions which she knew she'd never be able to ignore. She'd want to know everything there was to know about Eudora Nash.

'You can see the racecourse down there,' he said, breaking into her thoughts as they levelled out at the top of Cleeve Hill. 'Behind you – to your left.' By the time she'd manoeuvred herself into a position where she could see behind her, they'd swung right and it was gone. Then a few minutes later he was pointing to an attractive modern house set in splendid isolation.

'An' that's Tony Jacklin's place. Or used to be any rate. Don't know if he still lives there – I still call it Tony Jacklin's place though.' In the absence of any response from her, he turned to face her. 'Tony Jacklin?'

'Who?'

'Famous golfer. You must have heard of him.' He smiled and raised his eyebrows. Clearly her ignorance came as no great surprise. They roared down the hill and into Winchcombe, where he was forced to slow to what felt like a crawl by a queue of drivers, apparently hell-bent on observing the speed limit. She looked on with genuine interest as they threaded their way through the winding main street, past the sign for Sudeley Castle and the church, squeezing between houses which were so close to the road she felt she could step from the car straight into their front rooms. The archetypal Cotswold village, such as she'd seen a thousand times on holiday programmes, scenic calendars and magazine covers. Perhaps that explained why the village looked so familiar to her, even though she knew she'd never been here in her life.

As soon as the opportunity presented itself, Sharp pulled out and overtook the queue of traffic. He smiled as he blew Winchcombe out of his exhaust and threw Ellen back into her seat. A signpost flashed past – still no mention of Oakham. She seemed to remember Wilmot describing it as a half-hour journey. It couldn't be much longer, could it?

'Must have come as a bit of a shock,' he said.

'Sorry?'

'When you heard about the cottage. Bet you couldn't believe it.'

She said nothing.

'You didn't know her, then?'

'No.'

'And you've no idea why she's left it to you?'

She shook her head.

'Sort of thing never happens to me. Lucky lady, I'd say.'

'What about you?' Ellen asked, her curiosity getting the better of her instincts. 'You ever meet her?'

'Miss Nash? Couple of times. Came in by taxi. And then we came to her place just the once – not long before she died. About three weeks ago.'

'You came here?'

'Drove Mr Wilmot out here 'cos he doesn't drive. No skin off my nose – gets me out of the office, like.'

'So what was that about?'

'What – the meeting?' He shrugged his shoulders. 'Who knows? Probably wanted to tie things up, you know? She must have known she hadn't got long left.'

'What did they talk about?'

'Dunno. Sent me off for lunch, didn't he? Moment we got there. There's this pub at the top of the hill, just as you're leaving the village. The Wayfarer's. Said I could chalk it up to expenses and pick him up on the way back, after he'd – Shit!'

He braked suddenly, throwing the car into a right turn that was controlled but a lot sharper than it might have been. They now found themselves in a long lane, darkened by overgrown hedgerows which loomed up on either side. The occasional gate or junction offered a glimpse of fields and farmland but otherwise they were enclosed in a winding green tunnel which stretched away into the distance. It felt as deep into the countryside as she could ever remember being.

'Sorry about that,' said Sharp. 'Missed that turn *last* time. Sort of sneaks up on you.' Even he felt obliged to drive a little more circumspectly now, the high hedges and the frequent bends in the road making it impossible to see any oncoming vehicle until the last moment. They drove over a small bridge, then past a sign announcing that they'd arrived in Oakham.

The outskirts of the village offered up a number of properties of fairly recent vintage, many of them oozing prosperity. Then the road broadened out and swung left into the village itself and instantly they leapt back in time: a cluster of small labourers' cottages around the village shop, dirt tracks leading off to farms which were signposted but not always visible from the road, trails of horse manure and mud, pressed into the surface by tractor wheels. They drove past the evocatively named Old Manor House, then swung right and up a slight incline, past a Norman church and a war memorial, which still displayed a couple of bedraggled wreaths from a few months ago. *Silas Marner* had been one of Ellen's A-level English texts, more years ago than she cared to remember. This was exactly how she would have imagined the setting.

Halfway up the hill he slowed to allow a woman to be dragged across the road by two springer spaniels. Then he drew to a halt outside a property which was bordered by tall, well-maintained hedges. He pulled on the handbrake and switched off the ignition.

'Here you are then,' he said, as if introducing the next act. 'Primrose Cottage.'

'Oh my –'

Ellen stood still, one hand raised to her mouth. She leant back on the gate for support, causing it to swing shut behind her. She stayed there for a moment, taking it all in.

Her mind drifted back to one Saturday evening, shortly before the divorce was all tied up and put to bed. Kate had come round, armed with a Chinese and a couple of bottles of red wine, for what she liked to call a *wallow*. They'd curled up on the settee together, wrapped in blankets, and settled in for an evening of black-and-white movies on TCM. One of them (the name escaped her for the moment) was a classic weepy, with Ronald Colman and Greer Garson living in a country cottage which Kate had laughed off as totally unrealistic. Typical Hollywood overkill. Too beautiful for words. 'Couldn't exist outside a film set.'

Well, Kate…

Ellen took a deep breath. Sharp, a few yards ahead of her, stopped and turned to face her. He followed her gaze to the cottage, as if trying to take it in for the first time through her eyes.

'Not bad, eh?'

'I don't know what to say,' she said with a shake of the head.

He unwrapped a stick of gum and folded it into his mouth. 'Like I said, some people have all the luck.' He looked as if he was about to drop the wrapper, then realised she was watching and thought better of it. Instead he slipped it into one of his jacket pockets and from the other he produced a set of keys, attached to a large wooden fob.

'I'll open up, if you want. Let you have a look around inside.'

'In a minute. There's plenty to see out here first.'

He shrugged his shoulders, tugged at his trousers and went back to the car to retrieve his mobile, which he'd left on the dashboard. Ellen moved to let him through the gate, happy to lose him for a while. She turned her attention back to the cottage.

Shameless, she decided. That was the word for it. *Shameless.* It sat there, basking in all its glory, demanding undivided attention. *Look at me. Love me.* The figures *1805*, worked into the stone above the front door, were faded but still discernible, even from where she stood. It wore them like a badge of honour. The Cotswold stone might have darkened with the years but it had been allowed to age gracefully. No endlessly repeated coats of whitewash here, nothing so undignified as a facelift. Primrose Cottage seemed as comfortable with its moss and its damp patches and its faded colour as it was with the glass conservatory, running the entire length of the left-hand side of the building, designed to catch the best of the sun. Ellen took in the hanging baskets, suspended at regular intervals from brackets in the wall, trying to visualise how they might look a few months from now. They'd be an absolute riot of colour in the summer, along with the honeysuckle and passion flowers which threaded their way in and out of the trellises. It almost took her breath away to think that this was actually hers.

Why?

The path led up to the front door, then broke off left and right, forming a loop which wove its way around the cottage. The raised front lawn was protected by neatly tended borders and a low wall, made from the same Cotswold stone as the path, a golden butterscotch of a very different vintage from that used to build the cottage itself. It was two to three feet in height at the start of the path but melted away in the sunlight, as the lawn sloped down towards the house. She stooped to take a closer look at the unfamiliar plants in the borders and tried to imagine how they might look when they came into their own on a bright summer's day. She trailed a hand through them as she walked towards the cottage, wondering who was responsible for this hard work. Surely not Eudora herself. The grass had clearly been cut throughout the winter months and was immaculately maintained, almost manicured. An elderly woman might conceivably have been able to cope with the borders, but everything else?

She turned left and stepped off the path. The feeble sun had been trailing in her wake all morning but had not yet had time to work its magic on a thin layer of frost covering the grass. The ground crunched underfoot as she left a trail of footprints behind her. She headed off towards a pergola draped in vines, which shielded a sculpted rockery. At its centre a natural spring trickled across the rocks and dropped into a small pool. The surface of the water was flecked with miniature ice floes, which were still holding out against the gradual thaw.

The rest of the world, the life Ellen had made for herself, seemed light years away all of a sudden. She sat down on a wooden bench and tried to get some sense of Eudora Nash. Presumably she must have rested here on this very seat and taken in the same scenery countless times in the past. What was she thinking while she sat here? Was she remembering her husband? Ellen recalled Wilmot saying that she'd outlived him by thirty years or more. Was this somewhere they used to come to sit together all those years ago? Or had she moved here much later, after he'd gone? She wished she'd thought to ask how long this place had belonged to Eudora. Presumably someone in the village would know.

After a minute or so, she stood up and started to retrace her steps. From the pergola she could see Sharp at the side of the cottage, fiddling with his mobile. He reached into his pocket and dropped the chewing gum wrapper into a bin clearly marked 'GREEN WASTE RECYCLING' without even taking his eyes from his toy. She ignored him and followed a twisting path down to the back of the cottage. A patio with table and chairs looked out over a large expanse of lawn, its uniformity broken only by a canopied swing hammock, which faced away from the cottage.

This, she realised, was the only part of the property not pro-tected by high hedges, but it wasn't difficult to see why. From this back lawn she had an uninterrupted view of the frost-covered hills in the distance. A footpath ran parallel with the cottage for a while before climbing and disappearing into a small copse of conifers, which stood ramrod straight and motionless in the breathless calm of the day. A number of farms and cottages were dotted about here and there, few enough to be counted on the fingers of both hands. There was a lane, little more than a dirt track really, which threaded its way in and out of these properties and the surrounding farmland. Other than that, there was nothing. Nothing but fields and hills as far as the eye could see. No wonder Eudora had felt no need for high boundary fences at the back. This place did not so much offer privacy as define it. *Weren't you lonely here, Eudora? Or was it precisely this solitude you were after?*

She walked over to a gate in the far corner, which closed off a small field. Wilmot had said something about the previous owner, the one before Eudora, keeping a horse in it. She wondered what the poor creature had done for shelter in the winter months. Then she thought about Megan, who had been having riding lessons for three years now. How much more convenient was this – a simple stroll across the garden any time Megan wanted to ride? And just the thought of having a horse of her own ... she would just *die.*

She shook her head, dismissing the fantasy almost as soon as it had come to her. After all, it wasn't going to happen. Even if the cottage turned out to be hers, she couldn't keep it. Not with her work at Langmere. They couldn't move here – it just wasn't possible.

The sound of approaching footsteps on the frozen grass alerted her to Sharp's presence, even before he appeared at her side. He put both arms on the top bar of the gate and rested his chin on them. Then he thought better of it, straightened up and wiped at the sleeves of his jacket, which had picked up a greenish tinge from the damp wood.

'Go mental, living here,' he said.

Ellen picked up a low humming sound and scanned the horizon for its source. A small tractor was toiling its way up one of the hills in the distance, its engine labouring as it sought the appropriate gear and leant into the slope. To her right, the sound of Sharp scraping mud from the sole of his shoe against the gatepost sounded abnormally loud. She had never known silence to equal it. Never. It was total. In the summer, of course, there would be birdsong in the hedgerows and the constant drone of insects, but for now there was little to break the spell as winter held its breath. Apart from the tractor, this would have been pretty much what she'd have seen from this vantage point at any stage during the past two hundred years.

'Reckon they could drop a nu-cular bomb on this place and no one'd notice.'

'*Random Harvest*,' said Ellen.

'Do what?'

'*Random Harvest*. It's a film I saw a while ago. I've been trying to think of the name.'

'Cool.' Sharp pushed himself away from the gate and asked if she was ready to have a look inside now. She nodded and followed him round the remaining side of the cottage. Here she found a two-tiered vegetable garden, fairly desolate at this time of year with just winter cabbage, sprouts and broccoli on show but with the soil already turned over in readiness for the spring crop.

'So who looks after the garden?' she asked.

'Can't remember his name. Mr Wilmot did tell me. Drives over from one of the villages around here. He'll be here later. Comes Mondays and Thursdays.'

'How come he still works here? Who's paying him?'

'You are,' said Sharp, grinning as he fished the keys from his pocket once more. 'Comes out of the estate. Least, it does for the time being – till you sell it, like. Then it's someone else's problem.'

He negotiated the two locks and lifted the black latch, giving the bottom of the door a nudge with his foot to help it on its way. He felt around for the light switch and they stepped into a small cloakroom area, impregnated with the smell of old boots and damp rainwear.

'We've still got the utilities then?'

'The what?'

'Electricity. It's still working.'

'Yeah ... right. Electricity. Gas. They're both OK. Phone's gone though.'

'Really?'

'Last week. Not much point in keeping it with no one here to use it. But you couldn't do without gas – boiler needs it for the central heating. Leave that off for a couple of nights and you'd be looking at burst pipes and the place under six foot of water. Front room's through here.'

Ellen stepped back to let him lead the way. 'You seem to know your way around pretty well for someone who's only been here once.'

'Only once while she was alive. Came out last week though. Had to drive the old man to the funeral, didn't I? Soon as it's over, he asks me to bring him here, shows me round and tells me what you'll need to know. Thinks of everything, does Mr Wilmot.'

He walked ahead of her, ducking his head instinctively as he entered the room. 'OK,' he said, both hands plunged deep into his trouser pockets. 'The front room.'

Small, was Ellen's first thought, immediately followed by *cold – very cold*. She wrapped herself more snugly in her cardigan, folding her arms to hold it in place. If Sharp was right about the heating, it clearly wasn't having a lot of effect in here. Presumably it was on timer rather than constant.

Dark too. The room was poorly served by a small window which struggled to make use of the early morning sunlight. Even with the aid of the overhead light, which clearly needed a bulb of a much higher wattage, the room was unable to throw off the gloom. The armchair and sofa were covered in identical faded floral prints and the bare stone walls were forbiddingly cold to the touch. The fireplace, with its open hearth and logs neatly stacked in a small recess, offered the only prospect of comfort in here. Maybe by firelight the room might look more welcoming.

In the far corner of the room, the motionless hands of a grandfather clock stubbornly insisted it was ten past four. Next to it stood a Welsh dresser which looked almost as old as the cottage itself. Ellen stepped over to it and lifted two photographs from one of its shelves, the only ones on display in the room as far as she could make out. She carried them over to the window to get a better look at them. One was a three-quarter-length photo of a good-looking man in early middle age, dressed in a rough tweed suit, the shirt collar tight at the neck and his hair greased down into a centre parting. He was leaning casually against a gatepost, his arms folded across his chest. The photo had managed to capture the merriment in his eyes, a dancing light which seemed to draw her in as she looked at him. The old wooden frame and the fading sepia colouring were not enough to keep his personality in check. Even now, what must be sixty years or so later, it spilled over into the room.

In the other photo, which clearly predated it by a few years, the same man was joined by a young woman. They were framed by the arch of a lychgate, he dressed in a uniform Ellen didn't recognise, she smiling self-consciously and caught in the act of thrusting up a hand to keep her troublesome veil away from her face. A young couple, on the cusp of a new life together. Ellen peered closely at her and smiled.

'Hello, Eudora,' she said quietly.

She put the photos back on the shelf and picked up a vase of chrysanthemums and carnations, which had clung on to life for a little longer than their mistress but not much. The stagnant water did nothing to relieve the dank and oppressive smell which permeated the room. Cold as she was, she had to suppress the urge to throw open the window and every door in the place and let in the fresh air. She wondered briefly about the flowers. Clearly they were not from the garden – not in February.

'This way,' said Sharp, squeezing past her and heading back into the hallway. She followed him into a kitchen which could best be described as functional. No frills or excesses but clean, a reasonable size and fairly well equipped with the essentials. No dishwasher, she noted. Presumably she had no need for one if she was always cooking for herself. Good work surface though. Plenty of cupboard space, microwave, tall fridge with a freezer compartment on top. Certainly adequate.

'Need me to show you round or you OK on your own?' asked Sharp, opening one of the overhead cupboards and rummaging around inside.

'I'm fine,' said Ellen, frowning. 'What are you doing?'

'Thought I'd make us a drink,' he said, moving on to the next one. 'Where d'you suppose she kept the teabags?'

'I thought we weren't supposed to touch anything.'

Sharp laughed at her sense of propriety. 'Don't hear her complaining, do you? Anyway ... two teabags? Who's going to know?'

Ellen thought about it and asked for white with no sugar, then left him to it. She felt happier looking around on her own.

Leaving the kitchen, she opened a couple of doors in passing to see what lay behind them. One was a toilet with a small hand basin, the other a utility room, which was where the washing machine had been plumbed in. There was also a full-sized freezer chest, a vacuum cleaner and a number of cleaning materials, all neatly tucked away in their prescribed places.

At the end of the corridor, she climbed two small steps and walked through a sliding door into the conservatory. This, she knew instantly, was where Eudora would have spent the bulk of the daylight hours. Evenings in the front room, maybe, especially on cold nights with a roaring log fire. The days though would have to be spent in here, especially when the sun hit the glass and poured into the room like liquid honey. A cream-coloured sofa with off-white throws was strategically placed to take in the pergola and the rock garden at the side of the house. In front of the sofa was a glass-topped coffee table, a copy of *Country Life* lying open, presumably at the page where Eudora had left off reading for the last time. A pair of spectacles lay next to it. Ellen moved as if to close the magazine, then thought better of it.

Over by the window was an old rocking chair which wouldn't have looked out of place on an Adirondack back porch. She decided to try it out. It creaked ominously the moment she started to ease it back and forth and she jumped up quickly, cursing those extra pounds. Some day she really would get around to doing something about it. In the corner was a small cabinet, which supported a record player with a Perspex lid. Tucked away in the shelves were a number of LPs which, judging by their covers, had seen better days. She flicked idly through them: *Carousel, The King and I, South Pacific*. Eudora had loved her musicals, then.

At the far end, where the conservatory joined the rear of the cottage, a writing desk faced out over the back lawn and provided the same view of the hills that Ellen had been enjoying a few minutes earlier. She walked over to take a closer look at the laptop which was out of its case and set up ready for use. *Good for you, girl*, she thought. Her mother, although twenty years younger than Eudora, had always been intimidated by new technology. Barbara had picked up the little she needed to know during her time on Reception at Langmere Grove, but the idea of her going anywhere near a computer for personal use would have been laughable, even before the dementia set in. Eudora had clearly found for a use for it.

Her hand hovered over the 'On' button and paused there. It wasn't her laptop – not for another couple of days, at any rate. She was a little uncomfortable about the idea of prying into Eudora's personal affairs within ten minutes of crossing the threshold. It was bad enough that she was traipsing through the cottage like some insensitive tourist. It felt like an intrusion, however much she tried to convince herself that this was what

Eudora had intended. Logic dictated that the laptop would not have been left there if it contained anything she wasn't meant to see, but even so. It just didn't feel right.

Her thoughts were interrupted by the sound of Borat's voice coming from the kitchen, Sharp's customised ringtone. She decided she'd forget the laptop for now and satisfy herself with a quick check of the desk drawers. To her disappointment, they were all locked. She looked around briefly for the keys but couldn't see any. She added it to the mental list of things to ask Wilmot when she next saw him. Already she was beginning to attune herself to the idea of a return visit at the weekend.

She left the conservatory and went upstairs to look at the rest of the cottage. The staircase was narrow and steep, twisting back on itself, and she was grateful for the rope banister, which she used to haul herself up. It was a short but demanding climb, even for her relatively youthful legs. Eudora must have been so grateful for the downstairs toilet. You wouldn't want to do this more often than you had to.

The wooden floor of the landing was covered at intervals by rugs, which did little to prevent the boards from creaking every few paces. She took a quick inventory of the rooms. Bathroom – on the small side, certainly not as big as the one she was used to at home, but serviceable and (predictably) spotless. Bedroom one – single bed, old teak wardrobe, small bedside table with a clock radio and a copy of the Bible. Bedroom two – small, used principally as a storage room. Double bed (which must have taxed the imagination of those charged with getting it into the room in the first place). Small chest of drawers. Every available bit of floor space (and most of the bed for that matter) occupied by large crates such as those used by removal companies. A quick check inside one of them revealed clothing (male). Another contained books (Dickens, Austen, the Brontës). A third held documents and loose papers. Presumably not many visitors came to stay at Primrose Cottage.

The third bedroom was obviously Eudora's. Large double bed. Kidney-shaped rosewood dressing table, polished to within an inch of its life, supporting a lavender-coloured jewellery box and a brush-and-comb set. Bedside table holding spectacles case (empty) and copy of *Return of the Native*. Reading lamp perched precariously near the edge. Ellen walked over and moved it into the centre. Oak wardrobe with sliding doors. She took a quick look inside and decided that whatever vices Eudora might have enjoyed, shopping for clothes was not one of them. There was an abundance of woollen cardigans and jumpers but only a couple of nice dresses. For the rest, the emphasis seemed to be on the practical – tweed, made to last, nothing extravagant or showy. There was certainly very little here to suggest ninety-one years of self-indulgence.

Ellen placed one hand on the dressing table and rubbed at the bedroom window to remove the condensation. Peering through it, she tried to make out the tractor she'd seen earlier but there was no sign of it now. She could see the woman with the two springer spaniels though. She was now on the footpath which ran parallel with the end of the garden, heading towards the copse and tugging frantically at the leads in an attempt to exert some sort of control over the dogs. Clearly she wasn't sufficiently confident to let them run loose. It was far from clear who was walking whom.

A sudden movement caught her eye and she craned her neck forward to see Sharp on the patio below her, mobile pressed to his ear. He was hunched over, clearly feeling the cold, and she wondered briefly why he'd opted to take his call outside. Girl trouble, she told herself with a smile. That was something he'd want to keep to himself. He couldn't afford to be seen to care. Far from cool. He looked up and saw her at the window. Pausing for a moment, he waved sketchily, then turned his back and ended the call abruptly.

He was in the kitchen once more by the time she'd finished looking around upstairs. He held out a cup of dubious-looking coffee.

'No milk – least, none you'd want to put in your drink. Came out in lumps. No teabags either. There's a jar over there with "TEA" on it but it's all loose, like.'

'Coffee will be fine,' she assured him.

'Couldn't remember what you said, so I just put the one spoonful.'

Ellen thought about making another but decided to spare his feelings. She took her drink into the conservatory and rested it on the coffee table before easing herself onto the sofa, which seemed to stroke and cosset her as she sank into it. Sharp followed her but stayed on his feet, wandering aimlessly from one side of the room to the other. He checked his watch, then picked up a biro and tapped the lid of the laptop several times, as if tuning in to some silent rhythm only he could hear. Then he wandered over to a Vettriano calendar which was hanging from the back of the door and flicked through the pages, looking at the pictures. Ellen watched him take a sip from his drink. He walked over to gaze out of the window for a few minutes before checking his watch again.

Eventually he came over, put his cup on the table next to hers and sat down on the sofa, careful to leave a respectful distance between them.

'Alright then?' he said.

'I'm sorry?'

'The coffee.'

'Oh ... yes. Fine.'

'Thought so. I'm good with coffee. Long as it's instant.'

She leant forward and picked up Eudora's *Country Life*.

'If you fancy a walk after –' he said.

'A walk?'

'After you've finished here, like. I was thinking ... that pub I was telling you about. The Wayfarer's? It's only just up the road. They do nice food there.'

'Oh, I don't think –'

'Sausage, egg and chips. Ham, egg and chips. Steak and kidney pie. All good stuff. I was thinking, we could nip up there and have a drink, maybe something to eat before we go back. My shout, like.'

Ellen laughed. 'It's only just gone eleven. Besides, I brought lunch with me. I'll eat it in the car on the way home.'

'Cool.'

It wasn't just her lack of inclination to spend any more time with him than she had to. He might be anxious to come up with an excuse for getting back late to the office, but she preferred to set off as early as possible. She knew that if she were to get back to her car and leave Cheltenham by midday, there was a reasonable chance she might be home in time to collect Megan and Harry from school. Maybe they could go swimming at the Leisure Centre. Harry in particular loved it and she'd been promising for ages but never quite found time for it. As an alternative, lunch with Liam Sharp didn't even come close, however much she might have liked to see the local pub and maybe meet a few of her new neighbours. Not that they would be, of course. Neighbours.

'Still ... no rush, eh?' he said, taking a sip from his drink and making a series of whooshing noises as he realised how hot it was. 'Plenty of time to enjoy your coffee. You reckon she kept any biscuits in there?'

'Not for me, thanks.'

'I'll see what there is. You never know.'

He got to his feet and headed back into the kitchen. Ellen flicked through the magazine, wondering if she might be able to learn something about the area. She'd never been to the Cotswolds. There'd been no time or money for holidays when she was young. As soon as she was old enough, the six-week summer break from school was given over to working at Langmere Grove, first of all in the supermarket, then helping her mother in Reception. What holidays they had were usually spent at home, in the rent-free caravan they were allowed to use on site until they finally had enough money for a small semi-detached house in Middleton. Why go away and waste money, with the beach at West Wittering practically on your doorstep?

She and Jack had broken the mould to a certain extent. After the debacle in Wales, they'd honeymooned for two weeks in Goa, spending the best part of the next twelve months paying it off. And now her holidays were geared around the children – Center Parcs in Belgium last year, Disneyland booked for the summer.

But there were large areas of this country which were still completely unknown to her. It occurred to her that she probably knew Barbados better than she did the Cotswolds.

Sharp's voice came floating in from the kitchen.

'You get to choose. Custard creams or digestives. Bit soft but I think they're OK.'

'No thanks.'

'Sure? Probably just as well. This one's got –'

Ellen jumped as three sharp raps resounded throughout the cottage. The door knocker had clearly lost none of its effectiveness over the years.

'Want me to get that?' called Sharp.

'No, I'll go.' Ellen hauled herself out of the depths of the sofa and headed for the front door, straightening her skirt as she went. The latch was stiff and she fiddled with it for a few moments before opening the door. It swung back to reveal a tall shambles of a man, dressed in a suit that had clearly seen better days and an unbuttoned raincoat that should have been discarded years ago. His age was difficult to assess accurately. He looked to be in his late sixties, but the excess weight he was carrying might well have inflated that estimate by several years. He removed a battered trilby from his head and smiled, holding up a fifty-pence coin for her perusal.

'Found it on the path – by the gate,' he said, his voice pitched an octave higher than she'd been expecting. It sounded odd in such a large man. 'Don't know whose it is.'

'Oh. Thank you.'

'Is she ready?' He peered over her shoulder.

'I'm sorry?'

'Eudora. Is she in? I've come to collect her.'

December 1973: John Michael

The professor's here today.

First visit for nearly two months. Time was, he came at least once a week but the book's published now. The interviews are over. The tape recorder's been put away. The professor's got a new project, a six-part series for the BBC on the decline of family values in Britain in the Fifties and Sixties. Or should that be *F-Fifties and S-Sixties?* Filming's already under way. Busy man, everyone wants a piece of him. They reckon he'll get something in the Honours List for services to the Arts, despite his unfailing and controversial support for the boy known as 'Every Parent's Nightmare'.

When he does come, he brings a present to make up for the gap between visits. Never anything exciting – usually a book of some sort, something designed to *improve the m-m-mind.* There are rules about what he can bring in, mind you. Sometimes, on a good day, he'll bring a bag of frosted doughnuts and he'll sit there in the visitors' room, licking the sugar from his fingers while he talks about how things are progressing. The professor likes doughnuts.

It's difficult to get excited about these conversations now. It's not like it was eighteen months ago, when things were moving so swiftly. That kind of momentum doesn't last. John Michael knows that now. Seems like all he's heard lately are the same phrases over and over again: *groundswell of public opinion; petition to the Home Secretary; letters of support from leading academics, actors and theologians.* Blah-di-blah. They all start to blend into one big letdown and he's had to learn to cope with it or go under. It's such a load of crap. There was a time when the words 'wind in our sails' appeared in every other sentence. Now it's all 'inching our way forward' and 'getting there bit by bit'.

Getting where exactly?

The professor's brought another book today. No doughnuts though. This time the book is *The Ascent of Man* by Jacob Bronowski, signed by the author with a brief message of support which looks suspiciously like the professor's handwriting. He can forgive him for that. His heart's in the right place. He may be a bit of a bore but at least he still comes. Hasn't given up on him.

That's why he's managed to get closer than all those psychiatrists they kept putting in front of him. Waste of time that is ... theirs even more than his. At least he got a few laughs out of it. He doesn't feel remotely bad about the crap he's fed them over the years – perfect upbringing one day, childhood from hell the next. They didn't deserve anything better. It wasn't for *his* benefit they were here. They had one thing in their minds and that was to confirm whatever crackpot theories they brought into the room with them. Pretty clear from the outset that what they really wanted was to hear all about *her*. They seemed to think that because they were dealing with a young boy, he was just going to roll over for them. But he's always known how to keep things covered up. The things they wanted to hear, they were never going to get from him. Never.

But with the professor it's always been different. Least he listens. There doesn't seem to be any hidden agenda with him. He just wants to help. He's looking for answers which might win round the doubters and move the campaign forward. That's always the bottom line with the professor. He can take the two-hour train journey, the lengthy wait, the frisking, the stale air and clanging of doors, the shouting and banging and this shitty room, almost entirely stripped of colour – he'll take it all and come back time after time 'cos the only thing that matters is getting John Michael Adams out of there.

So now the professor knows things he's never shared with anyone else. Things he never even told his dad. Like the one about the ants – that time they invaded the kitchen cupboard. And she didn't lose her temper, like most people would. She just calmly emptied the cupboard and scrubbed it from top to bottom. When she'd finished, she picked up a half-empty jam jar, took him by the hand and led him into the back garden. Then she scooped out what jam was left and made a little trail of it, leading from the jar back down the path. It looked like a long, red snake, he remembers.

She went inside and made lunch. Sausages and mashed potatoes. With ketchup. An hour or so later, she took him back out into the garden and pointed out the stream of ants, marching in columns from a gap under a paving stone, leading to the jar and back. She smiled and put a finger to her lips, like this was their little secret, the two of them. Then she took a small container from her apron pocket, squatted down and poured it over the ants. He can remember kneeling down and looking at them closely. Some of them lay still, as if stuck to the path. Others either scurried off in all directions or lay there, legs flailing feebly.

She told him to stand back. Then she put the container on the floor for a moment and took a box of matches from the same pocket. Taking one from the box, she struck it and dropped it into the puddle. He wasn't sure how he was supposed to react, waited to see what she was expecting, as the blue flame sped along the trail and scorched everything in its path. When she smiled, he knew she wanted him to clap. And she hugged him.

He's told the professor other things too, things he remembers from long ago. Or *thinks* he remembers. That's the problem with having to be inventive all the time. After a while things tend to get blurred until it gets to the point where he's not sure any more whether they happened quite the way he's described them. Some are clear enough. Like the car door. He didn't make that up. He's not sure he's ready to tell him about that, nor about that afternoon in the park – not just yet. But he might tell him about what she did to Mrs Watson's cat. The professor will like that one, and it's a true story – well, most of it. He's pretty sure it is anyway. Maybe he'll tell him that one.

Only not today.

He'll save it for another time, maybe when the professor brings d-d-doughnuts.

February 2008: Ellen

Trevor Bassey looked like a man in shock.

Ellen felt the least she could do was invite him inside for a few minutes to give him a chance to recover. She sent Sharp into the kitchen for a glass of water and led the way into the conservatory, where Bassey slumped into the sofa like an oversized rag doll.

'I'm so sorry,' said Ellen, sitting next to him. 'This must be awful for you.'

He nodded and tried gamely to muster a smile from somewhere.

'I can't believe it. It's so –' He ran his fingers through his thinning grey hair. 'My God, how on earth am I going to tell Sarah?'

'Sarah?'

'My wife. She was going to travel with me but she didn't sleep too well last night and wasn't really up to it. She stayed at home to do some shopping for the weekend, give the place a last-minute once over, you know? This ... she's going to be devastated.'

'I'm so sorry,' she said again, patting his arm. 'Where do you live?'

'Bude – in Cornwall, you know?'

'And you've driven all that way this morning?'

'Yes.' He nodded his thanks to Sharp and took several gulps of water before continuing. 'I generally set off early so as to get here before lunch. That way I can have a bite to eat and rest for a couple of hours before we start the return journey. I always prefer it if we can get back before the light starts to go. Sarah worries about me driving after dark.'

'So Eudora was supposed to go with you then?' asked Ellen, recognising an opportunity to learn a little more about her. He nodded, squeezing his temple with thumb and forefinger.

'For a week. We do this three or four times a year – either Sarah and I come and stay at Primrose Cottage or we take her back to our place. We were here for a week in October, so it's our turn to play hosts.'

'You must be very close.' Ellen winced inwardly at the inappropriate tense but decided she would feel a whole lot worse trying to correct it. 'How did you come to know each other in the first place?'

He drained his glass and struggled to reach the coffee table. He had to rock backwards and forwards a couple of times to gain enough momentum to do so.

'We met on holiday – must have been, what, fifteen years ago? Something like that. Anyway, it was Eudora's first holiday of any sort since her husband died and he'd been gone for quite some time – I remember that much. She and Sarah got on so well, even though there was quite a big age difference, so they swapped addresses at the end of the week. It all took off from there, really. God…'

His face crumpled again and he took a large, monogrammed handkerchief from his pocket to blow his nose. Ellen waited patiently, unsure of what to do. Naked shows of emotion made her feel a little uncomfortable and she always worried that she might say or do something that would make the situation worse. She found herself staring at the handkerchief, the initials FOH prominent in one corner.

'You know what I've just realised?' he continued after a while. 'I rang her last night, like I always do when I'm coming up here … just to let her know what time I'm hoping to arrive. And when she didn't answer, I assumed she'd gone to bed early – you know, to get ready for the long journey. Can you believe that? I sat there listening to her voice on the answerphone, and she'd already been dead for, what … a week, you say? How terrible is that?'

'I'm sorry,' said Ellen, switching her attention from the hand-kerchief to him. 'Did you say you phoned her?'

'Yes.'

'Last night?'

'Well, not her, obviously. Like I say, it was her answerphone. Actually, do you think I could trouble you to fetch me another glass of water? I still feel a little faint.' He smiled at Sharp, who sprang forward to pick up the glass and disappeared once more into the kitchen.

Ellen studied him closely while he refolded the handkerchief and blew his nose once more. Then she looked down at the arm of the sofa, where her fingers had been snaking in and out of the patterned hem of the throw. She extricated them, then straightened the material and stroked it flat. Slowly.

'I'm sorry, you did say your name was Bassey?'

'Please – call me Trevor.'

'And your wife,' she said at length, 'Sandra, was it?'

'Sarah.'

'Sarah. Are you going to phone her now to explain?'

'I don't think so,' he said. 'I think it's best if I tell her in person.'

'Are you sure? You're very welcome to.'

'I think I'd rather be there when she hears the news.'

'If you're sure.'

'Actually,' he said, shaking his head as if waking from a daydream, 'it's only just occurred to me, what with everything that's happened – I don't even know who you are or why you're here.'

'I'm sorry,' said Ellen. 'This is Mr Sharp, who's here on behalf of Aitcheson, Wilmot and Lowe. They're the executors for the estate.' She extended an arm in Sharp's direction as he came back from the kitchen. He stepped forward to offload the drink and offered Bassey his hand.

'And you are...?'

'Ellen. Ellen Sutherland.'

'And you're with the same firm as Mr Sharp?'

'No.'

'Then you're here –'

'Ellen paused. 'I'm here to view the property.'

'An estate agent?'

'No.'

'I see.' He waited for her to elaborate. Ellen gave no sign of doing so.

'So am I to assume that the property is on the market already?' he asked tentatively. 'That seems rather soon.'

'No. It's not on the market. At least, not yet.'

'Then how did you come to hear about it – if you don't mind my asking?'

'Perhaps I might ask *you* something,' said Ellen. He spread his hands as if to say *by all means*. 'In all the time you and your wife spent with Eudora, did she ever talk about her plans for this place?'

'Her plans? How do you mean?'

'Her will. Did she ever discuss who might inherit the cottage after her death?'

He pursed his lips, as if giving the matter a great deal of thought.

'I'm not sure the subject ever came up.'

'Never?'

'Well, it's not the kind of thing you talk about, is it? I mean, that sort of conversation is one you tend to avoid once you reach a certain age.'

'But she didn't say anything about someone from her past? Someone important to her?'

'No. Are we talking about someone in particular here?' He paused for a moment and looked more closely at her. 'Has Eudora left the cottage to you?'

When Ellen didn't offer an immediate reply, he waved the handkerchief in front of his face by way of apology. 'I'm sorry,' he said, 'you must think me awfully rude. It's just that Eudora led us to believe she had no living relatives.'

'As far as I'm aware, she hadn't.'

'You weren't related?'

'No.'

'So how did you two know each other?'

'We didn't.'

'You didn't?' He frowned. 'I don't think I understand.'

'Look, I'm sorry,' said Ellen, looking pointedly at her watch. 'I had no idea it was as late as this. I certainly don't want to rush you, given the shock you've had, but –' She was anxious all of a sudden to bring the conversation to an end.

'Of course, of course,' he said, putting the second glass down untouched and managing this time to reach the table at his first attempt. 'I'm keeping you.'

'It's just, I have rather a long journey myself...'

'I'm sorry.' He hauled himself to his feet. 'My wife is always after me for talking too much. I hope I haven't caused any offence. Ah – there is one thing though.' He raised one finger as if to suggest that the thought had just occurred to him. 'If it's not too much to ask, that is. I wonder if I might ask you a small favour?'

Ellen handed him his trilby and waited to hear him out.

'Last time we came here, Eudora took us through some of her memorabilia. You know the sort of thing, photos of holidays we had together, letters we exchanged. She'd only managed to find a few of them but she said she knew she had lots more tucked away somewhere. She promised she'd look them out.'

He shot the quickest of glances in Sharp's direction, then turned his smile on Ellen once more.

'Anyway, to cut a long story short, Eudora rang a while ago to say she'd managed to find all sorts of little mementoes –'

Ellen remembered the books and papers stacked in numerous piles in one of the bedrooms upstairs and imagined this was where he might find what he was looking for.

'So I was wondering, do you think it'd be alright for me to have a quick look around for any photos and documents that –?'

'I'm really sorry. I'm afraid that won't be possible,' said Ellen.

He smiled patiently.

'I'd be quite happy for you and Mr Sharp here to vet everything I take with me.'

'I'm sorry. For one thing, as I explained, I'm a little pushed for time –'

'I'd be very quick.'

'And for another, one of the reasons Mr Sharp is here is that the final legal details are still being processed. Until they've been completed, nothing can be taken from the property.'

Bassey spread his hands. 'But surely a few papers and photographs –'

'I wish I could help.'

Again he shot a glance over her shoulder as if seeking support from Sharp. There was a momentary flash in his eyes that might easily have been more than mere disappointment. Then he relaxed and slipped back into the weary, resigned expression that seemed made for those heavy features and the perpetual slump of the shoulders.

'Of course. Forgive me. I'm a little tired after the journey and then, what with everything else...'

'I'll tell you what I *will* do,' said Ellen. 'Once I've had a chance to go through it all, I'll make a pile of everything I come across that looks as if it relates to you and your wife. If I find anything, you're welcome to it.'

'Thank you,' he said. 'That's most kind. Perhaps I might leave you a contact number?' He reached into his jacket pocket and produced a card, which he gave to her. She turned it over and noted that his job was listed as *Insurance Agent* with a company in Bude.

'My mobile number is printed there at the bottom,' he said. 'And please remember – it's going to be quite a task, going through everything Eudora's accumulated over the years. If you're pushed for time and want another pair of hands, I'd be quite happy to come back and help.'

'Isn't that rather a long drive, all the way from Bude?'

The sorrowful expression was back in place.

'It would mean a lot to Sarah. I suspect she's going to need something of a pick-me-up. If you're worried about being here alone with a relative stranger, perhaps AWL could spare Mr Sharp here as well to keep an eye on things, as an independent third party.'

Ellen hesitated for a moment, as if weighing up what he had said.

'I'll let you know,' she said eventually.

'Thank you. You've been very kind. Ah ... before I go, do you think I might just use the facilities?'

'Of course.'

He shuffled over to the doorway, hovering there for a few seconds before Sharp took his cue and escorted him down the corridor to the toilet. Ellen stood by the window, watching a vapour trail inch its way across the sky. She drummed her fingers on the desktop to keep her hand from shaking.

Sharp came back in and adjusted his tie, using his reflection in the glass to help him.

'Poor old sod,' he said, switching his attention to his cheeks, as if checking for areas he had missed when shaving. 'Thought we were going to have to send for an ambulance at one stage. Still, must have been quite a shock.'

'Yes,' said Ellen, still trying to think things through. 'Quite a shock.'

'Shame we haven't got time to help him look for those photos though. I mean, it might help cheer his wife up a bit.'

'Actually,' said Ellen, 'do you think I could borrow your mobile for a moment?'

'My mobile?'

'I need to check in at work and I've left mine in the boot of my car.'

'Sure.'

'I promise I'll be quick.'

'No sweat. Take as long as you like.' He took it out of his pocket and handed it over to her. He unlocked it for her and offered to dial the number, but she turned away and walked to the other end of the room. A short while later, she flipped it shut and returned it to him, just as Bassey walked back in.

'Engaged,' she said. 'Maybe I'll try later.'

'Cool.'

Bassey made one last effort to persuade Ellen to let him have a quick search, then relented and thanked her for her hospitality. They accompanied him to the door and along the path, waiting at the gate while he fumbled in his pockets for his car keys. He squeezed himself into the front seat of a dark blue Escort and drove off in the direction from which they'd arrived earlier. Ellen watched him all the way until he'd turned the corner. Once he was out of sight, she took a deep breath to compose herself and turned back towards the cottage.

'Seen enough then?' asked Sharp, blowing into his hands. What sun there was had disappeared behind a bank of clouds and it was noticeably colder now than it had been earlier. 'You ready for me to lock up?'

Ellen walked on into the cottage without answering. She turned left down the corridor and headed for the conservatory once more. Sharp followed her, pausing to pick up the keys to the cottage, which he'd left in a dish near the front door.

'We off then?' he asked again, stepping into the conservatory.

Ellen turned to face him, arms folded. 'Off?' she said. 'No. I don't think we are.'

Sharp picked up on the change in her mood and gave an awkward half-smile.

'Fair enough ... only, I thought you were in a hurry to get back.'

'I am,' said Ellen. 'But we're going nowhere just yet. Not until you and I have had a little talk.'

January 1974: John Michael

David Vaughan.

He lies back on the bed and rolls the name around on his tongue, trying it out like he's sucking an unfamiliar sweet. *David Vaughan. Hi – I'm David Vaughan. Have we been introduced? The name's Vaughan – David Vaughan.*

No middle name any more – just plain David. Best to avoid a middle name, they reckon. Play safe. When there's hardly a person in the country who hasn't heard of John Michael Adams, it's best to keep it simple. Avoid drawing attention to yourself.

The *Vaughan* speaks for itself. His dad's been Peter Vaughan for years now, ever since he decided enough was enough and took them up on their offer of a new identity. Could only take so much crap from his neighbours. Lives somewhere on the east coast now, new job, new life. Comes to visit every month or so, regular as clockwork – secret visits, planned like military operations in case anyone's watching. They've both been warned, as if they couldn't have worked it out for themselves, that when he finally gets out the world and its mother will be trying to track him down. The reporter who finds John Michael Adams will be able to write his own cheque, so any visit is a potential problem. His dad's the obvious starting place for anyone on the lookout. Find the father, find the son.

Smartest thing would be to ditch him altogether. Cut off all contact. He's done it before, after that article came out, the one where he tried to put all the blame onto her, when she wasn't even there to defend herself. Refused to see him, wouldn't even read his letters. Three years he kept it up, till the professor persuaded him to back down. Great believer in the family, the professor. Didn't like the idea of him being on the outside some day with no support. Lots of talk about burning bridges, rudderless ships and the need for life to have the sort of f-f-focus a f-f-father might provide.

So he's given way, allowed him the chance to explain himself. He *is* family after all. He may not be much, but he's all there is. And maybe John Michael hasn't forgiven him completely but he keeps coming back to something she said, just before she went away. She said you don't pick your family – it picks you. It is what it is. You learn to live with it.

And that's what he'll do. Live with it.

February 2008: Ellen

'Talk about what?'

'Oh, I don't know,' said Ellen. 'Let's start with our friend Mr Bassey, shall we?'

'What about him?'

'Well, I'd like to know who he is for one thing.'

'What do you mean?'

'Not difficult, Liam. Who is he? What's his real name? And what was that touching little performance in aid of?'

'I don't know what you're talking about.'

Sharp's face was a picture of wounded innocence and anxiety, the latter gaining territory with every passing second. He did his best to meet her gaze but couldn't sustain it. Hands thrust deep into his pockets, he looked at the floor, nudging the base of the sofa with alternating feet. He was so much more articulate physically than verbally. Ellen almost felt sorry for him.

Almost.

'That phone call last night? When he says he rang here and listened to her voice on the answerphone?'

'What about it?'

'There's no phone connection, remember? You told me yourself it was taken away.'

'So?'

'So how does he get her answerphone?'

'God, I don't know,' he said, tugging at his tie and loosening the top button. 'Maybe it wasn't last night. Maybe it was earlier in the week and he got confused or something.'

'Confused?'

'Yeah.'

'Just like he was confused about the toilet, you mean?'

'What?'

'He and his wife have stayed here all those times and he needs you to show him where the downstairs bathroom is?'

'Oh, come on –'

'AWL.'

'What?'

'He said you worked for AWL.'

Sharp frowned. 'That's because you told him, remember?'

'No. I told him you worked for Aitcheson, Wilmot and Lowe.'

'So what? It's the same thing.'

'I work for Langmere Grove Holiday Park, Liam. What are the initials?

'What?'

'Initials, Liam.'

'I don't know – La ... what was it? Langmere Park –?'

'My point exactly. People don't listen that closely in casual conversation. He'd have struggled to get the name right, let alone work out the initials.'

'Jesus, what are you – Columbo?' He laughed, recovering a little of his composure. 'That's so pathetic. How does that prove he's lying?'

'It doesn't. I didn't say it proved anything.'

'There you go then – what's your point?'

'My point is, it seemed a bit odd to say the least. Which is why I borrowed your mobile.'

The smile disappeared from his face.

'My mobile?'

'Press the redial button and the name O'Halloran comes up. If I were to check the number against the one on the card our Mr Bassey just gave me, you reckon they'd match up? And those initials FOH on the handkerchief he kept waving about – that's a coincidence too, right?'

Sharp looked almost offended. 'You said you needed to phone your office,' he whined.

'Well, aren't I just the sly old shifty-boots? Are you ready now to tell me what you know, or do I pay your Mr Wilmot a visit when we get back?'

He tried briefly to hold it together, forcing himself to look her in the eye while he desperately cast his net in search of options. When none sprang to mind, he slowly linked his hands behind his head and squeezed his elbows forward, as the reality of his situation struck home.

'Shit,' he sighed, screwing his eyes tightly shut and flopping into the armchair. 'Shit!' He buried his head in his hands while Ellen waited patiently. When he looked up, there was a look of resignation written large across his features.

'I'm fucked,' he groaned. 'If O'Halloran finds out you know, he'll think it was me who grassed him up. He'll go straight to Wilmot and tell him everything.'

'You seem to be missing the obvious,' said Ellen. 'If you don't tell me everything in the next five minutes, *I'll* be there long before your friend O'Halloran. Trust me, he's not the one you should be worrying about.'

'Shit!'

Ellen perched herself on the arm of the sofa and waited for him to do the maths. The day she couldn't handle someone like Liam Sharp would be the day she'd give up. She watched as he picked up the untouched glass of water and took a couple of sips for himself before replacing it on the table. Then he took a deep breath as he sank back into the sofa, furiously rubbing at the corners of his eyes as if trying to clarify his thoughts.

'His name's Frank O'Halloran,' he said at length.

'OK.'

'He's a reporter. *Cotswold Daily Gazette* … so he says. Although he does a lot of stuff on his own. Freelance, like.'

'How do you know all this?'

'He told me. Anyway, says so on his card.'

'And the one he gave me said he was an insurance agent.'

'I know. He's got tons of 'em, all different. Prints them off as he needs them. Likes to think he's got one for every situation. But he's a reporter alright.'

'So how do you know him? How did you first meet?'

'Came to the office,' said Sharp, recovering a little of his composure.

'When are we talking about?'

Sharp gave it some thought. 'Dunno. Last summer some time. May? June? Anyway, he came to see the old man. Had all these questions he wanted to ask about Miss Nash. Seemed to think he could just turn up and Wilmot would tell him everything he wanted to know – like *that's* going to happen! I don't think he was in there more than five minutes.'

He grabbed his phone which had started to ring and switched it off without even checking it.

'Anyway, same evening I stopped for a drink on the way home and he's only followed me there, crafty old sod. Offers to buy me a drink and comes straight out with it. No bullshit or anything. Gives me the old spiel about how it must be hell working for someone like Wilmot. Then he asks me how much I earn and tells me it's nowhere near enough, which is spot on as it happens. So he asks if I fancy picking up some easy money on the side, like – in exchange for bits of information every now and then.'

'What sort of information?'

'Anything, long as it had something to do with the old girl. Whatever I could get my hands on. Even if it didn't look like it was worth much. He said he'd be the judge of that.'

'Did he say why he wanted it?'

'No. I did ask once and he jumped down my throat. Said it was none of my business, so I didn't bother asking again. As if I give a shit as long as I get paid.'

'So what did you pass on to him?'

'Nothing really – that's the big joke. I told him straight up. I can't get at most of the documents and stuff. They're all in files in Wilmot's office or on his computer and there's no way you'll ever get in there. He's got this thing about security. It's like Fort bloody Knox, he's got that many keys and alarm systems. I copied the things that were on the network, like – admin things mostly. That was easy enough – things like his appointment schedule and background information on the clients. I thought O'Halloran'd chuck it back in my face when I offered it to him but he took out two twenty-quid notes and gave them to me like it was loose change. Said there was more if I came up with something worth looking at. I couldn't believe it, you know? Easiest money I've ever earned in my life.'

'So what else did you give him?' asked Ellen.

Sharp's expression darkened at this. 'That was the problem. I couldn't get my hands on anything else. At first he said no sweat. I just had to keep my eyes open and let him know the moment she got in touch with us again. Then finally I had this stroke of luck for once.'

He leant back in the chair and crossed his legs, relaxing into his new role.

'Past couple of years or so, we've been computerising all the old records whenever we get dead time at work. I'd got this batch of files for 1998–2002 and had to scan these documents from some agency or other onto the network. You know, some private-investigation firm? Usually I don't bother reading the stuff we scan, but I had a quick look at this one, 'cos we don't use investigators all that often. And then I saw her name on the file.'

'Eudora's?' He definitely had Ellen's attention now.

'Yeah. Miss Eudora Nash – Wilmot had written it on the file in pencil.'

'Wilmot was investigating her?'

Sharp laughed. 'No, she was the client. She wanted them to find someone. Wilmot was just the middleman between her and the agency.'

'Wait, just a minute,' Ellen said. 'Let me get this straight. When did you say this was?'

'March 2000, the letter was.'

'And Eudora wanted to find someone? Did the letter say who?'

'No. It got O'Halloran in a right state though. He went mental when I told him about it. He wanted a copy of it so he could read it for himself. It didn't say who she was trying to find but it was definitely a woman, I can tell you that much.'

Ellen's heart leapt. 'A woman? How do you know?'

'The letter kept referring to *her* and *she*. Called her *the subject* the rest of the time.'

'But you never found anything that said who this woman was? There were no other documents?'

'No. Well, there might have been but if there were, I never found them.'

Ellen's mind was racing as she tried to assimilate all of this new information. For every question he answered, another twenty presented themselves. She was anxious not to miss anything.

'You say O'Halloran wanted a copy. Did you get him one?'

'Forty quid on offer? What d'you think?'

'Can you get *me* a copy of it?'

'How much is it worth?'

'Oh, I don't know, Liam,' she said, investing the words with enough sarcasm to make her point. 'What's the going rate just now for stacking shelves at Waitrose?'

'Jesus,' said Sharp, shaking his head at the unfairness of it all. 'Yeah, of course I can get a copy. That's the whole point of a network. It means we can all access it.'

'Good. You can run one off the moment we get back to the office. Now let's get back to O'Halloran. When was it you found the document and made a copy for him?'

'Dunno *exactly* – two, maybe three months ago?'

'And when you gave it to him, did he read through it in front of you?'

'Yeah.'

'So how was he? Did he say anything? Was there anything you can think of that might offer a clue as to what this is all about?'

'I dunno, do I?'

'I'd think hard, Liam, if I were you.'

'I dunno, right?' he said indignantly. 'I was busy putting the twenties in my back pocket. It's not like I was really interested in the letter. Although ...' He paused for a moment, as if suddenly remembering.

'Although?'

'Well ... it wasn't so much what he said after he'd read it. It was before then, when I first told him about the letter. He wanted to know if his name was in there at all. He said even if I'd only skimmed through it, I'd have recognised his name, wouldn't I?'

'And was it?'

'No.'

'But he obviously thought it might be?'

'Yeah. S'pose. He was a lot happier once he'd read it and checked for himself. *He* didn't trust me either,' he added pointedly. 'Then, of course, he wanted the report. You know? The final one from the agency, once they'd finished the investigation.'

'And did you give it to him?'

'No way. Can't get near it. I never should have seen *this* letter – I just got lucky. The final report will be where it should be, which is in her file in Wilmot's office and there's no chance of getting even a sniff of that, let alone a copy. O'Halloran got really narky about it but luckily the old girl came to the rescue.'

'Eudora? How?'

'She got in touch again – asked Wilmot to come out and see her. Three ... four weeks ago.'

'And you told O'Halloran?'

'Too right. Suddenly I was golden boy all over again. When I told him I was driving Wilmot out here and would be at the cottage, he almost wet himself. Said I was to be his eyes and ears, listen carefully and take in everything they talked about.'

'But I thought you said you weren't at the meeting.'

Sharp laughed. 'Like I'm going to tell him that. *Sorry, Frank. No idea what they talked about but I can recommend the steak and kidney pie at the Wayfarer's.*'

'So what *did* you tell him?'

'Made it all up. Told him she was pissed off because she couldn't find the report anywhere – you know, the one the agency must have sent once they'd closed the case – and she wanted to know if Wilmot still had a copy on file. I said he offered to mail one to her as soon as he got back. You should have seen O'Halloran's face. Couldn't get the notes out of his wallet quick enough.'

Sharp looked very pleased with himself.

'Then she died a few days later and I didn't know whether to be pleased or pissed about it. I mean, one way of looking at it was, it probably meant I wouldn't see much more of O'Halloran so I wouldn't have to keep worrying about him costing me my job. But it also meant I'd be losing a good little earner.'

'So when did you tell him I was coming here?'

'Yesterday afternoon. He said I was to ring him and let him know when we were setting off and he'd meet us here. No way was I to let you leave until he turned up. Then, of course, ten minutes after we got here he texts me to say there's an accident just outside Toddington and he's stuck in traffic. I've been going mad, trying to think of ways of keeping you here. I was worried you'd think I was hitting on you or something.' He laughed to emphasise just how ridiculous a notion that was.

'Do you know where he lives?'

'Well, I haven't got an address, like, but he's local, that's for sure. Dunno what all that Bude crap was about.'

'And did he say why he was so keen to meet me?'

Sharp smiled. 'Pretty obvious, I'd have thought. It's probably the only thing he was honest about the whole time he was here. He wants to look through her papers and things.'

'Because he thinks this report will be there?'

'That's what I reckon. He's going to be so pissed at you sending him away like that. You've no idea what he's like. I wouldn't imagine you've seen the last of him, if I were you.'

'Oh, I'm sure Mr O'Halloran and I will be seeing more of each other,' said Ellen, getting up from the arm of the sofa. Her foot had gone to sleep and she walked over to the window to get the circulation going again. 'In fact, I think I can guarantee it.'

She turned and looked once more at the laptop.

'So O'Halloran is desperate to see this report?'

'Yes.'

'But you've no idea why?'

'Not a clue.'

'And you don't know how he's linked to Eudora in the first place?'

'No.' She looked at him closely. 'Honest,' he added. 'And I don't know who she was trying to find either.'

Ellen walked over to the laptop and picked up the case which was on the floor next to the desk. Sharp realised what she had in mind and looked as if he might be about to object, then thought better of it. As she unplugged the power lead from the wall, she caught sight of her reflection in the glass. She stared hard, imagining for one fanciful moment that she might see Eudora smile back at her.

'Oh, I think we know who she was looking for,' she said, tucking a lock of hair behind her ear. She ran the zip around the edge of the case, securing the laptop.

'Now what I need to know is why.'

5

February 1974: Peter Vaughan

The rain's not a problem. Not really. Maybe there's a little more surface water than he'd have preferred, but as long as the puddles on the unlit back roads don't turn into a series of mini-lakes, it can rain as hard as it likes. He's run in worse than this. Given the choice between a downpour and those steamy days you sometimes get up in the fells, he'll take the rain any time. He's been in races with the temperature in the nineties, running with a map, kagoul, waterproof overtrousers, hat, compass, whistle, plus food and drink for the day, with no more than the occasional puff of air for relief, and insects flying kamikaze-like into every opening they can find. Days like that, you'd kill for a drop of rain, so he's not about to complain now.

No, the real problem is the wind, which has been picking up steadily for the past four or five miles. Running along the shore with a gale at your back is one thing. Ease off, offer yourself up to it and it sweeps you along like a ball of tumbleweed. But now he's cut away from the coast road, it's payback time with a vengeance. He feels as if he's treading water as the full force of the wind squares up to him. There's nothing for it but to duck his head, chop his stride and get his shoulders working.

This long, country lane is like an old, familiar foe – he knows every pothole, every shift in the camber as it winds its way up to the village of Ashbury. It's an unforgiving, uphill slog all the way to the bend near Yabsley's Farm, followed by a sharp drop for the last three to four hundred yards, both of which mess up the rhythm and test screaming muscles to the limit. He used to look forward to the challenge – these last two miles are the only part of the six-mile run which isn't as flat as a pancake, the only stretch that comes even close to offering the kind of challenge his body has come to expect. Now he just finds it tough. Really tough.

He wishes he could still compete at the level he reached a few years ago but knows those days have gone. It's not so much his age. Forty is nothing for a fell runner. Joss Naylor bagged sixty-three peaks in under twenty-four hours not that long ago and there's no real age difference to speak of. But he can't put in the hours any more, and when he does manage to train, there's nowhere around here that can replicate the fells. During all those years in the Cotswolds, all he had to do was pull on a pair of running shoes and within minutes of leaving the back door he had a choice of five or six suitably challenging routes available to him. It's only since he came here, to this unremittingly flat and featureless landscape, that he's realised how lucky he was to have everything he needed right there on his doorstep.

Whenever his carefully choreographed, hush-hush visits to John Michael – to David – take him back to the West Country, he always makes a point of fitting in a training run across Cleeve Hill, telling himself it's not just nostalgia. And although going full time at the inn has made it harder to get away for training weekends in the Peak District or Grasmere, he still manages it every now and then, working his backside off to keep the illusion alive. But the few competitions he's managed to get to in recent years have gradually eaten into his confidence. He knows he can't really consider himself a fell runner now, even if he still feels the need to get out there. After all these years, his body still demands it of him.

He's halfway along Ellesmere Lane now, just under a mile to go. Somewhere up ahead of him, he can hear a car engine and the headlights swing into view seconds before a dark shape bears down on him. Peter hugs the extreme left-hand side of the lane and is drenched by a shower of water, which flies up from a puddle as the driver flashes past. He shrugs it off and pumps furiously with both arms as he reaches the sharpest part of the climb, just below the gates to Yabsley's Farm. He looks up and tries to locate against the darkening skyline the familiar slate roof of the old farmhouse, which represents the highest point of the climb. Even from close range, he can hardly see it through the slanting rain which stings his eyes and causes him to stagger momentarily. Furious with himself for this loss of concentration, he hunches his shoulders once more, anxious to get this over with. He drives on towards the top of the hill, counting off the paces until he reaches the entrance to the dairy farm.

It's at this point that he usually launches into the painful final sprint, a headlong dash downhill to the New Inn, as the earth seems to drop away from him. Today though, as he passes the farm, he eases down into a steady jog, then slows to walking pace. He hears something like a sigh inside. It feels like an ending of sorts.

The inn sits back from the road, separated from it by a gravel drive and a designated parking area. He crosses the courtyard and follows the path round to the rear entrance. Pushing open the huge oak door, he removes his trainers on the coir doormat before stepping inside. He closes the door behind him, making a mental note to see to the stiff latch when he gets a moment. As he crosses the hallway, his stockinged feet make a slapping noise on the flagstones and leave a trail of damp prints along the corridor leading to the staff rooms.

His is one of two, both of them on the ground floor at the rear of the hotel, looking out onto the side alley. The other is unoccupied and has been used as a storeroom for as long as he's been here. His own is small, far too basic to be rented out to guests, but more than adequate for his needs. There's room for a bed, a bedside table, a writing desk and chair, a chest of drawers and an armchair which has lost its springs, not to mention a great deal of its covering. There's also a wardrobe with a door that has defied his every attempt to get it to hang properly, and resting on the writing desk is a black-and-white TV with a small screen and a plug-in aerial. The reception is poor and there's a problem with the horizontal hold, which keeps slipping, but he watches so rarely it hardly seems to matter. There are no posters or pictures on the walls and no photos by the bedside, just a plain, simple wooden cross which was there when he arrived and which he didn't feel entitled to take down.

It's not much, he knows. The flat they found for him in town, when he first came here, was much more spacious. The job at Allingham's went with it though. It was a package of sorts, and working nights as a security guard wasn't for him. He much prefers it here. He works hard and likes the fact that his efforts are appreciated. He's responsible for general maintenance, keeping the grounds tidy, a bit of bar work and filling in on Reception as and when needed. A bit of everything, really. He takes a pride in what he does, and they've increased his hours now, which makes the decision to move in here even easier. He has three meals a day, a roof over his head and a bathroom and toilet just down the hall which no one else uses. The other employees live locally and keep more or less to themselves. They're friendly enough to be good company in small doses but at the same time they recognise his need for a little distance and are happy to respect it.

He peels off his socks and throws them into a laundry bag. Then he goes down the corridor to run a hot bath for himself, stretching gently and massaging his calves while he waits for it to fill. There's a stiffness in one of them that has been troubling him for a few days now. Another sign of age, he supposes.

In the bath, as the steam swirls around him, he slides his shoulders under the water and wonders if she'll come to his room tonight. It's been over a week now, which is as long a gap as there's been since that first time, the night of the staff Christmas party. He wonders if he's said or done anything to upset her. If he has, he can't imagine what it is. He understands that picking up on other people's moods has never been a strong point with him but there's been nothing out of the ordinary that he can think of.

Her attitude towards him, whenever their paths cross during the day, is not likely to offer any significant clues. She's made a point, right from that very first time, of not seeking him out in public or starting up any conversations that might arouse suspicion. A shy smile, a quick hello – nothing to alert anyone to what happens when they're alone together at night. The past few days have been no different, as far as he can see. Maybe it's nothing. Maybe she'll come tonight.

He remembers that first time and smiles as he recalls the heady mixture of astonishment and anxiety he'd experienced when she slipped into his room and, without a word, drew back the sheets and slid in to join him. For one thing, there had been nothing he was aware of to suggest that anything like this was about to happen. In all the time he'd been working there, she'd shown no great interest in him as far as he could tell. If they'd spent quite a bit of the evening together, it was because each of them recognised in the other a kindred spirit. When it came to the loud excesses associated with staff parties at Christmas, they were both happier talking over a quiet drink than throwing themselves around an improvised dance floor and making themselves look faintly ridiculous. And yes, they'd kissed under the mistletoe and had a few drinks but then again, so had everyone. It was one of those things you were expected to do and you were more likely to attract attention if you opted out than if you went along with it. But it was quite a leap from that sort of innocent, ritualised contact to what happened just a few hours later.

The anxiety had stemmed from a number of sources. For one thing, he liked his job and was grateful to the old man for giving him a chance. Sleeping with his daughter, even at her instigation, and even though she was more than old enough to make up her own mind, didn't exactly seem an appropriate way to pay him back for his kindness. He'd managed to keep any such worries at bay while she was there with him, but the moment she left they'd come flooding in, and he'd spent the next twenty-four hours promising himself it was a one-off mistake he wouldn't be repeating. Then she'd returned to his room the following night in the small hours and all such resolve had simply vanished into thin air.

He'd also been troubled to some extent by the … *unconventionality* of it all. He'd heard a lot of talk about the sexual revolution, but he thought it was more or less the preserve of the young, the hippy generation, and he was neither. The same could be said of her too – he'd never actually asked her age but he suspected she wouldn't see thirty again and supposed there wasn't a huge difference between hers and his. And besides, he'd never supposed for one moment that these new attitudes had anything to do with him. He certainly didn't see himself as attractive to the opposite sex. He was more sexually moribund than active. It was ten years since Jennifer had gone and there'd been no one at all since then – and no one to speak of before, if it came to that. His embarrassment and self-doubt almost crippled him that first time.

When she left, just a few minutes after it was all over, complaining she was feeling cold, he was convinced it was an excuse and that he'd been found wanting in some way. It was almost a relief at the time. He half-expected her to avoid him the following morning but when they bumped into each other in Reception, she gave the same quiet smile and that evening, when he returned to his room, there was a pile of extra blankets at the foot of his bed. And she *had* come back.

As he reaches for the soap and lathers both arms and legs, he realises there's a subtle change taking place in the way he thinks about her. Until now he's always viewed all this as more of an arrangement than a relationship. It's like an accommodation, something that's brought together two people who need to forget the real world for a few fleeting moments.

Lately though, she's stayed a little longer each night and they've started to talk. Nothing significant, but he knows she's been divorced for some time, even if he doesn't know why. He knows she's anxious about her relationship with her father and resents the fact that he seems to blame her mother's death on her divorce and the anxieties it caused, even though the illness wasn't remotely stress-related. He knows she has a thing about Toblerone and Jaffa Cakes and has given up smoking for the fourth time but doesn't seriously expect to be able to hold out for much longer. She's told him she was considered one of the brightest children in her class, university material even, but she gave up on that because she knew her father would never allow it. Now it's years since she aspired to anything. He knows she feels trapped in this small village with her life racing away into the distance while all she can do is gaze wistfully after it.

In return, he's managed to tell her he too was once married and has hinted at the fact that it ended badly but not much more than that. How much more can he say? And this, it occurs to him, is going to be something of a problem if they are going to make the leap from arrangement to lasting relationship. Until now she's been happy to live with his evasions. She respects his privacy and takes his training weekends at face value, even though some of them have been cover stories for his visits to John Michael ... *David*, damn it. *David*.

She doesn't even know he has a son. It hasn't been a problem before now.

He scrubs at his face with the flannel, as if trying to drive the thoughts away. Then he takes hold of the chain attached to the rubber plug and gives it a sharp tug to let the water out. He picks up his watch from the rim of the bath and realises he's been lying here longer than he'd intended. They'll be expecting him for dinner before long.

In his room, he pulls on a pair of jeans and a lumberjack shirt. He picks up a heavy-knit sweater, then decides against it. They'll have the log fires going in the bar. If it's busy and he has to eat in the alcove at the back of the kitchen, it'll be no less warm in there. He's putting it back in the drawer when the phone rings. The new boy on Reception – Mark, is it? – is ringing to say that someone in the bar's been asking for him. Wants to buy him a drink. Doesn't know who it is. He says he'll be right there and hangs up.

It'll be Bill Hayden, he thinks with a sigh. Yesterday he helped him get his son's car out of a ditch in Titmus Lane and old Bill insisted on buying him a drink to say thank you. He protested it wasn't necessary but knew at the time he was wasting his breath. That's how things are around these parts. You recognise your obligations and settle them. It's a bit of a nuisance actually. He doesn't really want a drink right now. He'd rather have his dinner and besides, with old Bill there's no such thing as a quick drink or a short conversation. Maybe he can use his meal as an excuse for cutting it short.

He shuts the door behind him and walks down the corridor that leads to the front part of the hotel. He nods at the lad in Reception who points to the bar, as if he needs to be shown the way. He can hear, even before he enters, that it's busy already. He'll probably be needed later to help out. He's happy enough to do that. It's better than sitting in his room, watching a TV screen that refuses to settle.

He smiles at some of the locals who have already taken up their regular places at the bar and looks around, trying to pick out Bill Hayden. He can't see him and is just starting to wonder if the lad on Reception has sent for the wrong person, when a figure sitting at a table over by the window catches his eye. He looks more closely and in that moment it feels as if he has swallowed a hand grenade.

The man half-rises from his seat and smiles, one hand outstretched to indicate the vacant chair he's been saving for him. The temptation to turn round, leave the bar and run ... and keep running ... is almost irresistible, but he knows it's pointless. Apart from anything else, where exactly would he run to?

He crosses the crowded room, grateful for the fact that no one seems to be taking any interest in him. No one, that is, except the man at the table by the window.

'Hello, Martin,' says O'Halloran. 'Long time no see.'

February 2008: Ellen

Kate looked up from the sheet of paper and frowned.

'Inverness?'

'Mmm ... I know.'

'So who do you know up there?'

'No one. Far as I'm aware.'

'What about this – Ashbury?'

'Nope.'

'You've never been there?'

'Not that I remember.'

'How weird is that?'

'I know.'

Kate helped herself to a poppadom from the pile that Ellen had stacked on a plate and dipped it in her tandoori sauce.

'You don't think he's holding out on you?'

'My friend Liam?' Ellen reached into one of the bags and removed another container, from which she peeled the foil lid. She smiled to herself, recalling the look of desperation on Sharp's face as he handed over the photocopy earlier that afternoon. One solitary sheet, which was no help at all really. He must have known she'd be disappointed and feared the worst.

'No, I don't think so somehow,' she said.

Kate took a bite from the poppadom and picked up the sheet again. The letter, on headed notepaper from 'The SJM Agency', was dated April 2nd, 2000. Addressed to Derek Wilmot, it contained confirmation of arrangements made in a phone conversation earlier that same week. There were no specifics as to what those arrangements might be, other than a suggestion that it was time to switch the focus of the search from the north of Scotland to a village on the east coast of England. There was no explanation as to why and no names were mentioned although, as Sharp had suggested, it was clear that the person they were seeking was female. The letter was signed by a Stuart Mahon.

Kate sighed and let the sheet fall onto the kitchen table. 'God, never a dull moment with you,' she said. 'How come these things never happen to me?'

'I know. Your life is so boring.' Ellen poured the steaming chicken korma over a portion of mushroom-fried rice, running a finger round the edge of the plate to prevent it from spilling over.

'Here,' she said, sliding the corkscrew across the work surface. 'Make yourself useful.'

Kate took two glasses from the overhead cabinet and saw to the wine. She took a sip from one of them and topped it up again before carrying the drinks through to the lounge. Then she returned to collect the food, which Ellen had loaded onto trays. She smiled to herself at the korma. Always the same, week in, week out. For Ellen, an Indian was a korma and mushroom-fried rice. A Chinese meant sweet-and-sour chicken balls and egg-fried rice. An Italian was a build-your-own pizza, mushroom, ham and olives or as many of them as were available. The spice of Ellen's life was anything but variety. Kate no longer bothered to comment on it. If nothing else, it made the whole business of ordering a takeaway for the two of them a lot easier.

She transferred everything to the coffee table in front of the TV and snapped off a chunk of poppadom while Ellen disappeared upstairs to check on the children. Remembering the DVD, she reached into her bag and brought out a copy of *The Hours*. She remembered going to Cineworld to see it when it first came out. Mark it would have been in those days. Mark the estate agent. She wondered what he was doing now.

Ellen broke in on her thoughts as she came back into the lounge.

'Megan says to thank you. They're so excited about going to the film tomorrow night.'

'Bless.'

'You sure this is OK, switching nights on you at the last minute?'

Kate picked up a glass and held it out for her.

'Thursday, Friday ...' she said, shrugging her shoulders. 'Adam's in Madrid anyway so it's not like I had to cancel anything. Besides, you don't think I'd want to miss out on something like this, do you?'

Ellen knew she wasn't referring to the DVD. She smiled and reached for her plate.

'I could have done with you there. At the cottage,' she added by way of explanation. 'I'd have pushed O'Halloran for answers if I'd had you there to back me up. I hated letting him just wander off that easily.'

'So why did you?'

'Easy for you to say. I was out there in the middle of nowhere. I wasn't that worried while it was just Liam, but the two of them?'

She snatched quickly at her fork as it slipped from her plate and, in doing so, allowed some of the sauce to slop over the edge and onto her lap. She tried a few ineffectual dabs at her skirt with a tissue from a box on the table, then put her plate down and went into the kitchen for a damp cloth.

'So this reporter –' Kate called after her.

'O'Halloran.'

'Right. O'Halloran. What do you know about him?'

'Nothing. Or as good as. Just what Liam told me.' Ellen rubbed frantically at her skirt with no more than moderate success, but decided it would have to do for now. She could change later, after she'd eaten.

'You've no idea what he's up to?'

'None at all.'

'And you haven't tried Googling him or anything?'

'When, exactly?' laughed Ellen, more amused than exasperated. Never having had children of her own, Kate seemed perpetually bemused by the idea that substantial chunks of Ellen's day were automatically accounted for.

'So you don't even know he's a reporter – not for sure?'

'No,' said Ellen. 'Not really. That's what he told Liam, but how much that's worth –'

'And his name might not even be O'Halloran?'

'God, I hadn't thought of that. No. I suppose not.'

She went back into the lounge and sat next to Kate on the settee. She nudged the DVD to one side to make room for her wine glass.

'What about the laptop?' Kate asked, pointing with her fork at Eudora's case which Ellen had brought back from the cottage.

'Don't know yet. I was going to have a look before you got here but –'

'Yeah, I know. Busy, busy. So basically, what you *do* know is this woman you've never met hired a private investigator to find you – and now she's left you some cottage worth a small fortune in a village you've never visited in your life. But you haven't got a clue as to why.'

'Right.'

'And you've no idea why they were looking in Scotland and East Anglia.'

'No.'

'Where you've also never been.'

'No.'

Kate reached forward and took a sip from her wine glass. 'And you're going back up to the cottage when?'

'Saturday. First thing.'

'What about the kids?'

'Jack's taking them to his parents for the weekend. Grandad's birthday.'

'So you're what … coming back Saturday night?'

'Actually,' said Ellen, raising her fork as she paused to swallow another mouthful, 'I was thinking of staying up there for the weekend. I'm guessing I'll probably need as much time at Primrose Cottage as possible. There's a whole pile of stuff to wade through in the spare room alone. I'll have the keys once I've met Wilmot. I can always stay there.'

'You *are* kidding?'

'Why?'

'Hello – just now it was *Straw Dogs* and duelling banjos, now suddenly it's the Waltons. What happened to creepy cottage?'

'It's O'Halloran who was creepy. The cottage is …' She searched in vain for the right expression. 'I don't know – there's just something about the place. I can't explain it.'

'OK then,' said Kate, leaning forward to pick the DVD up from the table. 'A couple of suggestions, right? If you don't like them, just ignore me.' She waited for some sign of approval from Ellen. 'OK then. First – this film. How badly do you want to watch it tonight?'

'I'm easy either way. Why?'

'We need to have a good look at her laptop and see what's in there. I mean, you might get lucky and find something which explains the whole thing in one go. Maybe she's left you a letter or something, in which case – great. But if not, seems to me you've got some work to do.' She put the DVD back on the table, as if its redundancy had already been established. 'I'd say the biggest problem this morning was you went in there blind. You didn't know the first thing about any of these people – still don't, in fact. We could spend a couple of hours this evening, making a list of things you need to do. If we don't get anything else done, at least we can make a start on Googling everyone whose name's come up so far. Yes?'

'OK.'

'Soon as we've finished eating, you can bring a pen and paper over here and we'll make a start on it.'

'And the other suggestion?'

'You fancy some company this weekend?'

Ellen paused in the act of bringing the wine glass to her lips. 'Serious?'

'I'm driving though. I'm not going all that way in a crappy Fiesta.'

'What about the salon?'

Kate shrugged her shoulders dismissively. 'Told you before – weekends are mine. Not much point in being your own boss if you can't come and go when you feel like it, is there?'

'But Adam ... when does he get back?'

'Sunday morning. But if he can piss off to Madrid without me, I don't see why I should be sitting here, waiting like a good little girl when he gets back. So, what's it to be? You want me to come or not?'

Ellen could see in Kate's eyes that same glint that had been there on the top deck of the bus, all those years ago – that beguiling mixture of amusement and challenge. They had shared the same journey home from school on countless occasions without ever exchanging so much as a glance. But then, one afternoon, three older girls had taken it into their heads that the freaky little creature sitting on her own on the top deck was more than fair game. They'd surrounded her, and barely got into their stride before Kate slowly rose from her seat and came over to sit next to her. She said nothing to the girls and yet somehow the fact that she was there, talking to Ellen like an old friend, seemed like a challenge. It was certainly enough to signal that the game was over.

Ellen imagined Kate taking on O'Halloran. She smiled.

'I'd love you to come,' she said.

February 1974: Martin Adams

'How did you find me?'

'Nice to see you too, Martin.'

'It's Peter,' he says, casting an anxious glance over his shoulder, 'My name is Peter.'

'Relax,' says O'Halloran. 'I don't think anyone's really interested in us, do you?' He seems amused by the situation. 'Two old friends, having a chat? Catching up on lost time?'

He doesn't share O'Halloran's obvious high spirits. He says nothing – doesn't feel it deserves a response. Taking the chair he's been offered, he risks a quick look around the bar. As O'Halloran has suggested, no one seems to be paying any attention. The fact that the room is unusually crowded for this time of evening is working in his favour, he decides. Safety in numbers.

'Have a crisp,' says O'Halloran, tearing the packet open on three sides and nudging it across the table towards him. 'Salt and vinegar.'

He ignores the offer and looks closely at the man opposite him, taking stock of the changes that seven years have wrought in his physical appearance. He's filled out, he decides. He was always tall but now he's big and the extra weight is hanging from him – there's no muscle definition to speak of. He can't be more than thirty, but for a relatively young man he's in poor shape. His complexion is pock-marked and he's got the pasty look of someone who needs to get out more often.

O'Halloran is at least willing to look him in the eye instead of looking away. Memories of him from seven years ago are hazy but he senses there's a confidence in this man, a cockiness even, that wasn't there before. He's not entirely sure he should view this as a positive.

'How did you find me?' Peter asks again.

'I'm an investigative reporter. It's what we do. We investigate.'

'That's a joke, I presume.'

'You think so?'

'You couldn't find your way out of a paper bag.'

'And yet here I am, Martin.'

'Peter.'

O'Halloran smiles. 'And yet here I am, Peter,' he says, placing unnecessary emphasis upon the name.

And he doesn't know what to say to this at first. They assured him this couldn't happen, that as long as he was careful (and he has been *so, so* careful) he was perfectly safe. *Fingers on one hand*, they said. *Need-to-know basis. No chance of a leak.* And yet, despite all their promises that only a handful of people would know his new name, let alone his whereabouts, O'Halloran has managed to track him down. If they can't hide *him* away from the public, how on earth are they going to protect his boy?

He looks closely at O'Halloran, wondering if maybe he's been too easily sidetracked by the shambling appearance. It would be so easy to underestimate him.

O'Halloran drains his glass, holds it up to the light and waggles it in front of his face.

'A drink would be nice', he says. 'Since you're offering...'

'You haven't answered my question.'

'I'll stick with the JC, I think – don't want to change boats in midstream, eh?'

He doesn't move. This feels like a trial of strength. There's a stand-off for a few seconds, while he takes the measure of O'Halloran, who's holding his glass out in front of him, unwavering. There's an element of mockery in the gesture, the smugness of a man who's sure he holds all the cards at present. It would be nice to do something to shake that complacency, to take the glass from him and thrust it into his face, but it's not a serious option and he knows it. If O'Halloran looks sure of himself, it's for a good reason. The last thing Peter can afford is to draw undue attention to himself. He takes the glass and gets to his feet, unable to shake off the uncomfortable feeling that round one has already been conceded.

When he reaches the bar, he's surprised to see her serving there. She often helps Jerry out if things are getting busy but he didn't notice her when he came in and feels unaccountably anxious that she might have been watching him while he talked with O'Halloran. He waits patiently while she serves some of the local football team, who are meeting up here before a night on the town. She gives no indication that she knows he's there but as she finishes dealing with the customer in front of him, she reaches for a straight pint glass, without looking up, and fills it almost to the brim with lemonade. Then she tops it up with lime juice, drops in a couple of ice cubes and puts the drink in front of him with a shy smile. She allows her fingers briefly to brush against his, an innocent, childlike gesture in a woman of her age but one which she would never have ventured even a few weeks ago.

She looks up in surprise when he nudges O'Halloran's empty glass towards her and asks for a pint of JC as well. She gives the pump handle a sharp tug and looks casually round the room, tilting the glass to keep the foaming head under control. Her glance settles eventually on O'Halloran in the far corner.

'Old friend?' she asks

'Not really.'

She nods, and he sees the shadow fall across her face. He wants to expand on what he's said. He's been too brusque.

'Just someone I used to know,' he says.

She puts the drink on the counter and takes the money from him. She brings the change back, and there are the fingers again, lingering a little this time. She asks if he'll be happy to do a stint behind the bar later if needed. She's taking over from Jerry at nine thirty and may be glad of some help. He says that'll be fine, forces a reassuring smile and carries the drinks back to the table. He can feel her questioning eyes on his back all the way there.

O'Halloran has been amusing himself with a pile of beer mats, flicking them into the air from the edge of the table and catching them in the same hand. He spreads them out on the table and accepts his drink, taking three slow draughts before he puts it down. He wipes some of the foam from his upper lip, then reaches past his own drink to pick up the other glass. He holds it up to the light as he peers at its contents.

'Jesus,' he says, screwing up his face in disgust. 'What *is* this?' He sniffs it, then replaces it on the table, pushing it away from him. 'Sworn off the demon drink, are we?'

It's tempting to say he's careful about who he drinks with nowadays – once bitten, twice shy. Already his mind has made the involuntary leap back to those weeks just after the trial, the only time he's ever allowed drink to get the better of him. For just that brief window of time, he was desperate for its analgesic qualities and utterly unprepared for how susceptible it made him to the seductive whisperings and silvery tongue of the gangly young man who'd slipped onto the bar stool next to him. Vulnerable was no fit state in which to encounter someone like O'Halloran.

He keeps his thoughts to himself. O'Halloran takes a final handful of crisps, and stuffs them into his mouth. Then he makes a funnel of the packet, tips his head back and pours the remaining crumbs down his throat.

'Should've asked you to get another couple of these while you were up there,' he says, screwing the packet into a ball and wedging it into the ashtray. The moment he lets go, it springs back into shape. 'Talkative sod, aren't you?' he says, chuckling to himself. 'Hardly get a word in edgeways.'

'What do you want, O'Halloran?'

'Frank.'

'How did you find me?' he asks for a third time.

'Ah, well now. I've been thinking about that.' O'Halloran slumps back in his chair, wiping the salt from his hands on his sleeve. 'I mean, I can see why you'd want me to explain it but ... well, seems to me, if I do, I'll be tossing away the one big advantage I have over you. First thing you'll do is make sure it can't happen next time, am I right?'

'You think I'll disappear again?'

O'Halloran picks up one of the beer mats and turns it in one hand, tapping alternate edges against the table.

'You saying you wouldn't?'

'I'm not going anywhere,' he says, sounding more resigned than defiant. A burst of raucous laughter tumbles down from the bar where the footballers are starting to get a little rowdy. O'Halloran glances across briefly, then turns back to face him.

'Yeah, well – you'll excuse me for not putting too much faith in any assurances from you after the way you upped and legged it last time.'

'You think I had a choice?'

'People always have a choice.'

'Easy for you to say. You didn't have people spitting at you in the street or making crank calls every ten minutes. Try having a patrol car outside your house at night to deal with the local yobs, then tell me I should have stuck it out.'

He pauses, aware that he's started to raise his voice. A woman at the next table seems to be taking an interest in the tone if not the substance of their exchange. She flashes a quick smile when he meets her gaze, then returns to her magazine.

'If it hadn't been for that article...'

'Hey,' says O'Halloran, throwing his hands up in a defensive gesture. 'I was just the messenger, remember? It's not like I made it all up.'

'You twisted everything,' he hisses.

It seems such a long time ago. He doesn't remember the evening too well in detail. He knows that at some stage, after many more drinks than he'd ever had before, he went back to O'Halloran's and opened up, *truly* opened up, for the first time. He'd stayed well clear of the press until then but this doe-eyed, serious young man was the first person to show any interest in him since the whole thing started. He seemed anxious to listen rather than condemn him, as if he actually understood, sympathised even. Said he wanted to put things in their true perspective, show another side to this story that needed to be aired. It's almost embarrassing now to recall how naive he'd been.

He accepts he probably said most of what finally appeared in print. He recognises much of it from private rants born of a genuine sense of grievance, outbursts he'd always kept to himself. In context, within the general picture of a grieving husband and desperate father, these lapses might be understood. Out of context, and especially in print in the cold light of day, they were lethal. He might have survived the photos of himself, staggering down the steps and struggling to get into a taxi in the early hours of the morning. He might even have got away with the heavy-handed hints that his boy had always been too easily influenced by his mother, with her bigoted religious convictions and rigid moral code. What really did for him though was the comment that anyone who did what those two girls had done to his boy deserved whatever they got. He knows he's capable of blurting out such things in a fit of anger but no way would he have meant it. Not like that. No one could ever mean it literally.

O'Halloran seems unimpressed. 'Twisted everything? Bit dramatic, wouldn't you say? I'd call it journalistic licence. You've got to expect a bit of that.'

'You lied to me.'

'Hey,' laughs O'Halloran, almost choking as he takes another mouthful from his glass. 'A bit of revisionism never hurt anyone, but let's keep at least one foot in the real world, shall we? The only reason you were talking to me is because you thought you were dealing with some novice who might be easy to manipulate. You wanted someone to put your side of the story, right? I spent hour after bloody hour, listening to one long, dreary, never-ending, self-pitying *whine*, while you droned on and on about how unfair life was and how you never got a fair shake of the dice, like you were the only person who'd ever had a bit of bad luck. You think that was going to win anyone over? I'll tell you this much, you did *not* want an accurate transcript of that tape to appear in the papers. If I was a bit creative in places, I was doing you a favour, trust me.'

'Trust you?' He shakes his head and reaches for his drink which he has not touched until now. He realises suddenly that Jerry is at a nearby table, wiping it with a cloth and collecting the empty glasses. He forces a quick smile and Jerry pulls a face, nodding in the direction of the footballers. He knows it's all for show really – Jerry prefers to be rushed off his feet, hates it when there's hardly anyone in the bar.

He waits until he feels it's safe to continue.

'So why are you here?' he asks eventually. 'Another big exclusive? The man who tracked down ...' He leaves the sentence unfinished, unwilling to resurrect the name he believed he'd buried for good. 'I'm not going anywhere,' he says again. 'Not this time.'

'Really?'

'I've got a new life here. I've got friends, people who respect me for the work I do. I'm not going to throw it all away by running like last time.'

O'Halloran sits back in his chair and takes this in, as if surprised by what he's heard.

'I'm glad to hear it, Martin,' he says eventually, and it's difficult to decide whether the use of the incorrect name this time is a deliberate provocation or a mere slip of the tongue. 'No, really – I am. I think it's great you've managed to settle down and create a little something here for yourself. Mind you ...' He pauses to take another mouthful of beer. 'If we're going to be picky about things, it's not actually you who's done it, is it?'

'What do you mean?'

'I mean, it's Peter Vaughan, right? He's the one everyone thinks is Mr Reliable. It's Peter Vaughan that girl behind the bar seems so keen on, judging by the number of times she's looked this way. Nice-looking girl too – and why wouldn't she be impressed by someone like Peter Vaughan? Of course ... she might not feel the same way about Martin Adams.'

'OK, you've found me,' he says, tired of the constant baiting. 'So what happens now? You think there's that much mileage in a story about me? After all this time?'

O'Halloran reaches out and puts a calming hand on his to alert him to the fact that he's again in danger of attracting attention to himself.

'Martin ... Peter,' he corrects himself. 'I don't want to write an article about you – not unless you leave me with no choice.' He pauses and takes a look around the room before resuming. 'I don't see journalism as the way forward for me now. No one seems that anxious to snap me up full-time so I don't see why I should hand over something like this when it's me who's done all the donkey work, know what I mean?'

Peter frowns. He hardly dares to hope. Experience has taught him better than that.

'I don't understand. You say you'd rather not go to the press unless I leave you no choice, but what does that mean?'

'Easy,' says O'Halloran, looking around him and then leaning forward again, as if to make sure they can't be overheard. 'It means you're going to take me with you to see John Michael.'

February 2008: Ellen

Eudora's laptop proved to be something of an anti-climax. No sooner had they powered it up than they were denied access by a password request. Kate was resolutely optimistic at first. She fully expected the door to swing open for her after three or four guesses – this was after all what usually happened in films. Unfortunately any attempt to find words that might be personal or significant for Eudora was seriously hampered by the fact that they knew next to nothing about her – the reason they were trying to gain access in the first place. Eventually, after she'd tapped in a series of combinations involving Eudora's name and initials, the system picked up on what was happening and timed them out anyway.

Despite her initial frustration, Ellen was mildly encouraged by this turn of events. Would Eudora have gone to the trouble of finding out about password protection just for the sake of it? If nothing else, it at least suggested there might be something on the hard drive that she wanted to keep away from prying eyes.

'Not a lot of use to us if we can't get in though, is it?' sighed Kate. 'What about the lawyer you met? Maybe she's left that sort of information with him?'

'I'm not even meant to have the laptop yet. Besides, I can't imagine she'd leave a password with her solicitor – why would anyone do that?'

'Well, if we can't get in through the front door, we need some sort of IT geek who can get us in through the back.'

'I suppose I could ask Alan … who is fifty if he's a day,' she added, catching the glint of amusement in Kate's eye.

'Nothing wrong with fifty.'

'…and wears a hoodie and baseball cap. Back to front.'

'Nice. So this guy's your techie?'

'Groundsman, actually. Looks after the pitch-and-putt course. Long story. But if he can't get into it, he'll put us on to someone who can.'

They agreed she would take the laptop into work with her the following day. If Alan thought he could do something with it, she'd free him up for the day to work on it.

On her own computer, she tried Googling Eudora Nash and came up with 43,800 results, many of which seemed to relate in some way to an American author neither she nor Kate had heard of. They waded through them for a while, then tried to refine the search by adding Oakham to the search but met with no success at all.

The private-investigation agency was a disappointment as well. They managed to track down a press announcement from a company called 'The Beresford Management Group', which had apparently taken over SJM just over two years ago. They checked their website for any reference to a Stuart Mahon but found none. They rang the listed phone number but, as expected at that time of evening, it went to voicemail, giving details of the normal office hours. Another task for tomorrow.

Googling O'Halloran did at least bring some success. This time there were 140,000 results but once they'd skipped through the early pages, which were dominated by some insurance executive of the same name, they found a handful of newspaper articles from the *Cotswold Daily Gazette*, most from just the last few years and carrying the byline: Frank O'Halloran. Sharp had been right about that much, at any rate.

The focus was all local interest – an interview with a parish councillor who was about to withdraw from local politics, a look behind the scenes at the annual Cheese Rolling at Coopers Hill. It was low-key, anodyne material which offered nothing that might explain his interest in Eudora. It did however open up the *Cotswold Daily Gazette* as another way forward.

The newspaper's website provided them with a phone number, which switched straight to an automated system with a number of options. They tried the newsroom, where a polite but weary voice explained that only a skeleton crew operated through the night. If Ellen wanted to speak with the editor, she'd need to ring again in the morning. On the off chance, she threw in O'Halloran's name and asked if he still worked there but was told that if she wanted information about employees, she'd have to talk with the editor. The woman's tone suggested she didn't expect Ellen to meet with much success.

At 10.30, they called a halt. Their efforts might not have shed any more light on Eudora but at least Ellen had a clearer idea of where to go from here. If all else failed, there was still her Friday-afternoon visit to Calder Vale.

It wasn't often she looked forward to seeing her mother.

February 1974: O'Halloran

O'Halloran hunches his shoulders and scuttles across the road, groping frantically inside his coat pocket for the car keys. He unlocks the door and wrestles it open despite the best efforts of the wind, which is sending the rain scudding along the promenade, singing in the wires and whipping the darkened sea into a frenzy. Safely sheltered from the elements, he slams the door behind him and deposits the sheets of newspaper containing his pasty and chips on the passenger seat while he does his best to wriggle out of his raincoat. The lack of room to manoeuvre almost defeats him but, after a brief struggle, he settles back and unwraps his meal, which he originally intended to eat on the sea front. The cold he could have coped with but not the downpour, which has appeared out of nowhere.

Between mouthfuls he reaches into a compartment in the dashboard and removes a notebook and biro. He wants to make notes as soon as he can, while everything is still fresh in his mind

– how Adams looked, what he was wearing, what was said. Exact quotes are going to be difficult to recall but that's not a problem. The important thing is to get the gist of it down. He can always improvise later when typing it up. He rests the notebook on the dashboard, which picks up enough of the street light for him to work by, and starts to write.

He's surprised at how well things have gone. The cover story's in place now. He thinks it will hold. The key to it all was patience. He could have confronted Adams some time ago, but he understands the importance of biding his time. Others leap in without taking a good look round first and that's why he's found Martin Adams and they haven't. And it's why he'll get first crack at John Michael as well.

He's been here for a while now, sniffing around and asking questions as discreetly as possible so that word won't get back to the wrong ears. He's done his best to keep a close eye on Adams. It's clear he's still something of a home bird. Apart from his evening runs, he's left the New Inn just twice in the past couple of days and the second of those trips has paid off. If the helpful and greedy lad behind the railway ticket office window is to be believed, Adams has been asking about times for a weekend return to Inverness. No ticket bought, just general enquiries about the weekend after next. Quite specific about that – going up on the Friday, back on the Sunday.

His instincts told him straightaway Inverness has to be significant. It's too far for a weekend training camp and if he's not training, who's he planning to meet? Why travel all that way? And then there's the timing of it all. It's the world's worst-kept secret that John Michael Adams is out already. It's safe to assume they'll be getting together first chance they get. And here he is, planning a trip to the north of Scotland. Could be nothing – could also be something.

So it was worth at least a casual mention, just a quick suggestion that it wouldn't be in anyone's best interests for Inverness to become public knowledge. He simply picked his moment and lobbed it into the conversation to see what the reaction would be, then sat back and watched it explode all over the poor sod's face. Couldn't have had more of an effect if he'd walked in with John Michael on his arm.

Now Adams is more convinced than ever that he has some sort of inside contact who's keeping him one step ahead all the time, which is ironic, really. Truth is, he wouldn't mind a bit of credit for all the hours he's put in, because it's been bloody hard work. When Adams first disappeared, he tried everything he could think of to track him down. Even with his contacts and resources at *CDG*, he came up against one brick wall after another. The block was well and truly on.

Then there was that evening last July, when he was sitting in front of the TV, flicking idly through the channels in search of something worth watching, wondering as he often did what Adams would be doing with himself at that moment. He decided he'd probably be out running, 'cos apparently that was all the sad bastard ever did with his free time. If he mentioned it once on those bloody tapes, he said it a thousand times – how he doesn't usually drink because of his training. Shouldn't be up this late because he's got to train tomorrow morning. Couldn't possibly manage a takeaway – how would he run it off? Every other sentence was training, training, bloody training.

And there was this one race he talked about like it was some sort of Mecca for fell runners where they all came together once a year. The Lake District Mountain Trial – a hundred and fifty silly sods running twenty miles up and down mountains. He made it sound like some sort of religious festival, which begged the question: did he still feel the same way? There was no way of knowing whether he was still competing but even if he'd given it up, might he still go there as a spectator? For the first time O'Halloran found himself considering what it must be like to uproot yourself from everything you've known and start again. Can you do that? Can you cut yourself off completely or do you always take a little something with you into your new life?

So he did his research, and in September he was there at the Traveller's Rest Inn, Grasmere, for the twenty-second running of the event. He was as near to the finishing line as he could get, watching as number 132 came staggering over the line towards the rear of the field, far too exhausted to pay any attention to anyone who might be taking an interest. He almost didn't recognise him – the beard was gone and the hair was a lot longer and much darker. He had to look several times to make sure, but it was him alright. No question.

So now it's time to cash in, to reap the rewards for all that work. A small part of him is worried that Adams might make a run for it even now. He has *previous*, as they say. It would be just like him to panic and take off rather than stick it out. But there are plenty of reasons to suppose that this time will be different. For one thing, he sounds convincing when he says he's got things pretty much together here – he won't want to leave it all behind and start up again somewhere else unless he absolutely has to. And that's where the cover story comes in.

He knew going in that hope would be the key. There has to be just a smidgen, enough for Adams to cling on to. He can't afford to box him into a corner where he'll have nothing to lose. But paint the Doomsday scenario, then offer a way out, and you've always got a chance.

That evening he'd sat there and watched Adams closely as he fed it to him line by line.

He thinks he's bought it.

February 2008: Ellen

It was a quarter to eleven by the time Kate left. Ellen tidied a few things away and prepared for the following morning – another school run. Only then, as she activated the alarm and headed upstairs, did she realise how tired she was. On reflection she might have been better served by an early night but, as she slipped beneath the duvet and reached up to turn out the overhead light, she was confident that at least she'd have no difficulty in going off to sleep.

As she lay there in the dark, she gradually became aware of a purring sound. It was very quiet but there on the edge of her consciousness, demanding to be investigated. She switched the light on again and it took a few seconds for her to realise that what she could hear was the dialling tone from the phone, which she must have inadvertently dislodged from its base when she first got into bed. With a groan, she reached over to the bedside table and gave it a nudge, so that it shifted into place. Then, as an afterthought, she picked it up again to check for messages.

There were three ... and another five missed calls. One was from a call centre, suggesting she get in touch for an unbeatable quote on her household insurance. The others were all from Sam Balfour. She listened to them, then reached into her bag and pulled out her mobile, which had been switched off all evening. Similar story there – this time, two messages and another four missed calls.

The messages themselves were all brief and to the point, variations on the same theme. *No need to call back. Nothing important. Just ringing to make sure you and the kids are OK. Wondering how things went with the lawyer today. Will try again later.* The final message on the extension phone was to tell her he and Mary were going out and that he wouldn't ring again tonight in case he disturbed her. *Don't want to be a pain – just curious about how it went.*

Ellen put the phone back on its base and her mobile in her bag. Then she turned out the light again and flopped back onto the pillow. She didn't want to think too much about it all now – better to wait until the morning. But, tired or not, she found she couldn't let it go that easily.

Sam Balfour was the one reliable male presence in her life, a father to her in everything but name. The very idea that she shouldn't trust him seemed somehow to go against the natural order of things. But whichever way she looked at it, there *was* something about all those calls tonight that was unsettling. It seemed excessive. If he wanted to talk, they had a conference call booked for 1.30 the following afternoon. Why the almighty rush? What did he know that he wasn't telling her?

She knew him well enough to be sure there'd be no point in confronting him with her suspicions. Nothing was more likely to get his back up. Sam didn't do arguments. Things were done his way or not at all. If she pushed him on this, he'd simply throw up a smoke screen, creating an uneasy atmosphere between the two of them. And besides, if he was keeping something from her, he'd have what he believed to be her best interests at heart. Wouldn't he?

Tomorrow, she promised herself. Tomorrow she'd decide how much she wanted to tell him about the trip to Cheltenham and the business with Eudora and the cottage. Somehow she needed to come up with a version that would satisfy an old man and his curiosity.

6

March 1974: Josef

I should be on my way, he thinks.

He puts down his cup and removes his gloves from the radiator next to his table with some reluctance. He's comfortable here and warm, which makes the prospect of pulling on his overcoat and heading outside less than appealing. There were vague flurries of snow in the air when he came in and the temperature was dropping at an alarming rate, so he knows what to expect out there. But the clock on the wall seems to be laughing at him as it skips nimbly from one minute to the next and he knows he can't afford to leave it much longer. He needs to find somewhere to stay the night. That shouldn't present much of a problem, given the surprising number of B&B signs he passed on the road into Inverness, but it would be nice even so to know he has somewhere to return to later. Maybe he'll feel better when he has some sort of base for himself.

It will be dark soon. He hopes he won't have any difficulty in finding the Prince's Arms. Mr O'Halloran's directions seem very clear on paper but it's one thing tackling unfamiliar roads in daylight, quite another stumbling around in the dark and with the weather closing in. He'd feel happier if he'd done a dummy run earlier but by the time he'd finally made it to Inverness his legs had almost seized up completely. Getting out of the car seemed more important than anything else – that and getting a meal inside him. He hadn't eaten since first thing. Dorrie insisted on making him a cooked breakfast and he didn't want to raise suspicions by refusing it, even though he doubted he'd manage to keep anything down for long. Sure enough he was forced to pull over about an hour into the journey, suffering under the censorious gaze of a woman and her young family as he brought it all back up in a lay-by.

That experience made him reluctant to stop for lunch a few hours later, so between then and late afternoon he'd had plenty of coffee from his Thermos but nothing solid at all. By the time he finally entered the outskirts of the town, the all too familiar nausea was accompanied by a slight dizziness, which made up his mind for him. He needed something to eat, preferably something hot.

Now, an hour or so later, the Roadside Lodge has warmed and fed him, and he's tempted to order another hot drink as an excuse to delay his departure just that bit longer. The strength of purpose which drove him from his bed before daybreak and brought him all this way is being strongly challenged by his body's desire to soak up the warmth for as long as possible. He smiles grimly at the thought. He's been increasingly aware in recent years of the change in his attitude towards cold weather. In Poland, in his youth, he embraced it. He remembered his father working out in the fields from before dawn until way beyond dusk, in temperatures that would make this seem like a mild spring day. *You have to tackle it head on*, he would say. *If you admit to yourself that you're cold, you will be. Never give in to it*. He'd taken his father at his word and even as recently as a few years ago, he was happy to walk to the local shops without a coat on the coldest of mornings, drawing puzzled frowns of concern from passers-by. Now he seems to feel the chill as much as the next person, if not more so.

His legs and back offer a token protest at the thought of being disturbed. He takes the heavy overcoat from the back of his chair and slides his arms into the sleeves. His fingers struggle with some of the buttons as if aligning themselves with the prevailing mood of lethargy. His gloves are so soothingly warm to the touch that he can't resist the temptation to slide his hands inside them, even though he knows he'll have to remove them in a moment to pay. Then he stands for a while with his back to the radiator, pressing his legs against it, as if storing up units of warmth for future use, like a camel taking on water.

The girl behind the counter sees what he's doing and smiles – pretty girl, maybe early twenties, somewhere around the age Julie would have been now. She calls out to him, something cheery in an accent as thick and impenetrable as black treacle, and he gives a non-committal smile in return, hoping maybe this will persuade her that he's understood. A thing of wonder, the Scottish accent. All those rolled Rs, the rising intonation, the guttural enunciation that seems to draw on a thousand years of history in every syllable. Bunny Warren, a maintenance engineer with 302 squadron at RAF Duxford, had given him his first experience of it. He used to say (only half in jest, he suspects) that he and his fellow Scots always made a bit of an effort with the Poles. If you wanted to hear the Scottish accent in its purest form, you should hear the extra reserves of phlegm that were saved for conversations with the English. Dead now, of course, Bunny. Like so many of them.

He walks over to the counter, removes one of the gloves and takes his wallet from his back trouser pocket. She tells him how much he owes, then repeats it more clearly when he shows signs of uncertainty. He counts out the coins, which are no more familiar to him now than when decimalisation first came in. It's been three years but he still does the mental maths, automatically converting back into 'real money'. He's never quite managed to overcome the suspicion that he's being taken advantage of in some way, unable to forget how his favourite pie and chips, a monthly treat from the fish and chip shop at the end of the road, went overnight from two shillings and nine pence to 29p, an increase of 100 per cent. Yet another sign that he's getting old.

He asks the girl where the nearest phone box might be, then realises in the midst of her detailed and for the most part unfathomable explanation that he doesn't need to know. Dorrie will be on her way to the cinema by now, if she hasn't arrived there already. Saturday-night film club – just about the only pleasure she seems to allow herself these days. He wishes he could share this passion with her, the enjoyment she derives from escaping just for a couple of hours from the reality of this world. He tried, way back in the dim distant past, but it never worked for him. Where she sees wonder, he sees fairy tales. What she finds uplifting, he views as chicanery. Perhaps that says it all.

He wonders if she suspects anything, anything at all. Not about today – he's sure he's in the clear in that respect. If she had even the faintest inkling as to where he is now or why he's here, she'd have to say something about it. He's pleased with the plausible alternative he managed to come up with. As far as she's concerned, he's in Manchester at a 302 squadron reunion. He's spending the afternoon on a coach trip, visiting museums and wartime aerodromes with old friends and colleagues, and then attending a formal dinner in the evening. It's convincing enough as alibis go. These reunions take place all the time, so she'll have thought nothing of it. Her only concern was the fact that he would be driving as far as Manchester, which she felt was ill advised at his age, especially with the weather so unpredictable at the moment. If she knew he was now in Inverness, having driven almost all day without a break, he'd never hear the end of it. If she knew he was going to be meeting up with Mr O'Halloran, she'd probably have a fit.

No, he's sure she knows nothing of his true movements today but he does wonder just how much she suspects about the illness. She'll know something is wrong, for sure. You can't live that long with someone and not learn a little bit about him. She'll have noted the loss of appetite, heard the unmistakable sounds from the bathroom, maybe even smelt it on him. She's commented on his lethargy and the pallor of his complexion, asked several times if he's absolutely sure he's alright. If they were as close, as intimate as was once the case, she wouldn't need to ask. She'd have been able to make out with her fingertips the contours of the concentration of corrupted cells that has been building up over a period of time, eating away at whatever vitality he's managed to cling to since Julie died. But they've not been that intimate for some time now. They lead lives that are as separate as possible for two people under the same roof. They're independently dependent on each other, if such a thing is possible. She has no way of knowing it's there.

She *has* urged him to go to the doctor. Despite their gradual estrangement, he doesn't think *urged* is too strong a word. She does still care for him and is convinced he needs sometimes to be protected from himself and his own mulish disposition. He's dug his heels in. It's the Pole in him, she says, and his recalcitrance merely increases her frustration, driving the wedge between them even deeper. He regrets this but can't help himself. He has no intention of going to any doctor. There's nothing he needs to be told. He certainly has no intention of undergoing invasive treatment which will strip him of any dignity he has left. If this is his time, if circumstances (even now, he cannot bring himself to acknowledge her precious God) dictate that this is the beginning of the end, then so be it. He's lived a long time, longer than many of the young men who flew with him all those years ago. In a sense, he can even be said to have lived *too* long. No father should have to bury his own child and then live with it. He feels no desperation, no desire to cling to a life that has moved the goalposts and left him behind. He'll take whatever comes and, when he can't take it any more, he'll walk away without a backward glance. It's not been a hard decision to take. There's no pressure here. Pressure is a Messerschmidt on your tail, anti-aircraft fire strafing you, a parachute that catches fire as you struggle to open it. This will be the quiet, dignified, undramatic exit which was denied to others less fortunate than he.

But he's not quite ready. Not yet.

The wind hits him the moment he opens the door to the café and his instinctive reaction is to duck back inside. He turns up the collar of his overcoat, counts to three, then opens the door once more and steps out into the snow, which looks as if it's been falling thickly for some time now. A layer has already settled in the car park and he treads carefully as he picks his way, head bowed, across to his car. He has to remove one glove again to locate the keys in his pocket and takes ages to select the right one and slot it into the lock. The wind catches the door and wrenches it from his grasp. He takes a painful blow to the knee before he is finally able to slide into the front seat and wrestle the door shut.

It's cold in here, almost unbearably so, his breath instantly fogging the windscreen. The heater in his car won't take effect for a few minutes yet. He starts the engine and reaches across to pick up a sheet of paper, which is lying on the front passenger seat. He studies it briefly, familiarising himself with Mr O'Halloran's directions. He looks at his watch – he still has two hours to find somewhere to stay and then make it to the Prince's Arms. If the notes are accurate, he's no more than twenty minutes or so away at present. He wants to be there early. He's thought this through so many times, has thought indeed of little else since Mr O'Halloran first contacted him. He wants to be there when the boy arrives, wants to see him in the flesh for the first time in years and then take stock before he confronts him.

He switches on his headlights and puts the car into gear. Then, with exaggerated care, he edges forward and leaves the car park.

February 2008: Ellen

The first thing Ellen did when she arrived at work was to send for Alan Wharton. Eudora's laptop, still in its case, lay there on the desk between them, ignored for the time being while she used Langmere business to ease her way into the conversation. She always felt the need to do this with him. He was not someone who relaxed easily.

He'd been there for more than six years now and she felt she barely knew him. He'd arrived, armed to the teeth with glowing references and testimonials from the council in Ballymena, where he'd worked for several years for the Parks and Gardens department, but it was his work rate and his calm, unflustered approach to any task put before him that ultimately convinced his new employers that he was the man to take forward the development of the pitch-and-putt course. Everyone knew it would be in safe hands.

The real bonus however was his obsession with and proficiency in the arcane world of information technology. No one knew anything of this extra string to his bow when he was first taken on, but his ability to get the network back up and running had proved invaluable on more than one occasion. Ellen had recently asked him to carry out a detailed review, seeking out weaknesses in the system. She listened now while he fed back his initial findings, then thanked him for the work he'd done so far. As he half-rose, expecting to be dismissed, she cleared her throat and nudged the laptop across the desk towards him.

'There was something else,' she said tentatively. 'I was wondering... could I ask your advice about something? It's personal, not business.'

He sat down again, waiting patiently for her to elaborate, and she was struck once more by just how passive he was in conversation. He only ever seemed to speak in response to direct questions.

'I'm not even sure you'll be able to help,' she continued. 'The thing is, I have this laptop and I can't get into it because it's password-protected.'

She gave the laptop another nudge, as if inviting him to pick it up. He looked questioningly at her.

'It's OK,' she assured him. 'I promise I wouldn't ask you to do anything illegal. It's actually *my* laptop – well, it will be tomorrow.' She laughed, realising how bizarre it must all sound. 'It's a bequest ... you know? In a will? Only it's no use to me if I can't even get into it and I haven't got a clue where to start.'

Wharton still didn't move. He switched his gaze briefly to the laptop case, then back to her. She felt the need to break the silence once more. Damn, he was hard work.

'It's not a problem if you'd rather not,' she said. 'Or if you don't know how to. I mean, you see these things in films and so on, but I don't know how true to life that is. I imagine it's a lot more difficult in the real world, only I don't know who else to ask.'

'It's not difficult.'

'It's not?'

He shook his head. 'It's like anything else – if you know what you're doing. There are programs you can buy that will retrieve passwords from just about any system. Depends on what level of access you want and what you're hoping to do with it.'

'So have you done this before ... this sort of thing?'

'Like I said, it's not difficult.' He began to relax a little, as if more comfortable with solid ground beneath his feet. He talked about forums and downloads, using initials and abbreviations that meant nothing to her and served to obscure meaning rather than reveal it. She tried to follow him for a while but gave up, allowing herself instead to take a closer look at this strange little man, whom she knew to be her elder by a good few years but whose preferred style of dress was more that of a wayward adolescent. The hoodie, jeans and trainers, while eminently practical for outdoor work at this time of year, must be desperately uncomfortable in June and July, yet he wore them all year round, as if fearful of losing part of his identity in their absence. The skintight black glove on one hand, which tended to highlight rather than conceal the loss of a finger in a work accident back in Ballymena, and the New York Yankees baseball cap, which he always removed on entering the office but otherwise wore back to front, suggested he wasn't overly concerned with creating the right impression. He dressed to suit himself, not anyone else, and was happy to be judged on his work.

Computers were clearly the love of his life. This was as close to animated as Ellen had ever seen him. She tried to tune back in and make sense of what he was saying but gave up at the first mention of the word *protocol*. She waited patiently for a pause in the flow.

'So what are we looking at here?' she asked eventually. 'How long would something like this take? Assuming you're happy to have a go, that is.'

He puffed out his cheeks, then let the air out slowly.

'Depends.'

'On what?'

'On how much the previous owner knew about computers for one thing.'

'Not a lot, I wouldn't have thought. She was in her nineties. Then again, I wouldn't have expected her to be using a laptop in the first place, let alone know anything about passwords and usernames.'

'Unless she got someone else to do it for her?'

'I suppose so.' Ellen cast her mind back to the only picture she'd ever seen of Eudora, the wedding photo in the cottage, of the demure-looking young girl on the threshold of a new life. She tried to envisage her as an elderly woman, sitting at the keyboard of a machine that would have been unimaginable back in those days. She couldn't do it.

'Assuming it's straightforward though,' she said, 'how long do you think it would take you to get access to it? What are we looking at? A week? Two weeks?'

He reached across and pulled the laptop from the desk, the first indication that he might be prepared to help her. 'I'd say ... three, maybe four hours. As long as no one's built in other layers of protection, that is.'

'Three or four hours? That quick?'

He smiled. 'It's a laptop, not the Pentagon.'

'And you'd be willing to do this for me? I mean, I'll pay you obviously.'

'When would you want it?'

'Well, I have to go to the Cotswolds this weekend so I was thinking of leaving it with you then but –' Ellen broke off as a new possibility occurred to her. 'I didn't think for one minute you'd be able to get it done so quickly. If there's any chance I might have a look at whatever's in there before I go, that would be fantastic. It could save me a lot of time and trouble once I'm up there.'

'So you want me to have a look today?'

'I'll tell you what,' said Ellen, 'have you got anything on this morning that's desperately urgent? Anything the others couldn't handle between them?'

He shook his head.

'OK – so how about this? I'll get cover for you and get you set up in one of the business lodges. They've all got wireless access. You take as long as you need and do what you can to get me into this machine by, say, five this afternoon, and I'll still pay you the going rate on top. What do you say? You think you could do that?'

He raised one eyebrow in surprise.

'You want me to do this on company time?'

Ellen smiled, recalling Kate's comment the night before to the effect that there's not much point in being your own boss if it doesn't bring a certain amount of independence.

'I won't tell if you don't,' she said.

Much to her frustration, the rest of Ellen's day was less productive. The editor at the *Cotswold Daily Gazette* wasn't remotely helpful and seemed more curious about the reason for her interest in O'Halloran than anything else. He made it clear from the outset that he wouldn't be giving out any information on employees without a clear understanding of the reasons for her phone call and wanted to ask twice as many questions as he was prepared to answer. All she managed to wring from him was confirmation that Frank O'Halloran was an occasional contributor, on a freelance basis, and an offer to pass on her details, so that O'Halloran himself might get in touch personally, should he wish to do so. Ellen hung up without offering anything approaching an explanation.

The Beresford Management Group were more forthcoming but no more illuminating. A receptionist was quick enough to put her through to a softly spoken man with a strong Welsh accent, who was happy to confirm that SJM had indeed been bought out two years ago. Stuart Mahon, the owner of the agency, had taken early retirement and emigrated, as far as he was aware, to New Zealand. He himself had no knowledge of any cases SJM might have worked on before the takeover and the name Eudora Nash meant nothing to him. As for old records, Mahon had arranged for the removal of all of his paperwork once the takeover had been finalised, but whether he'd kept it or made himself a nice bonfire the moment he got home, he couldn't say. He was sorry – he'd love to help and would be happy to take on the task of tracking Mahon down, if she wished to make use of his professional services. She'd thanked him and assured him that wouldn't be necessary.

At least the video-conferencing went well, although today Ellen was aware for the first time of a certain edge to it all. It was one thing to watch Sam reel people in and tie them up on her behalf. It was quite another to process the idea that those skills might have been used against her at some stage on a personal level. For the first time, heretical though the thought might be, she found herself wondering exactly who the real Sam Balfour might be.

He asked for the link to be kept open, once the meeting was over, so that he and Ellen might have their weekly review. True to form, once they'd covered more mundane business matters, in what seemed to her to be an unusually hasty and superficial manner, he worked his way around to her visit to the solicitor and *that lady with the funny name – what was it again?*

Ellen played along, having decided overnight that she would tell him what he wanted to hear, that she'd taken his advice and phoned Wilmot rather than travel all the way to Cheltenham. She'd been left a small sum of money, for some reason. No idea why. Bit of a mystery but the whole thing seemed like a lot of fuss about very little – over and done with. Forgotten.

She wasn't sure, when it came to it, exactly how convinced Sam was but she had no intention of hanging around any longer than necessary to find out. Bringing forward her visit to her mother by a couple of hours, a laudable excuse of which she knew Sam was bound to approve, she brought the session to an end before he could question her further.

She was putting on her coat, ready to leave, when Angela buzzed to let her know that a Derek Wilmot had phoned twice and was anxious to speak to her the moment she became available.

'He said it was *of the utmost urgency*. Called me *young lady*,' she said.

Ellen rolled her eyes and asked her for the number. She dialled and waited patiently for Wilmot to answer.

'Miss Sutherland,' he said, when she identified herself. 'Good of you to call.'

Ellen apologised for not getting back earlier. Wilmot cleared his throat, the prelude to a prolonged bout of muffled coughing. When he came back, there was a catch in his voice which suggested another episode might not be far away.

'So sorry,' he said, at length. 'Dreadful thing. Started yesterday and I haven't found anything yet that will shift it. Not that you want to hear about that. I'm ringing about the cottage.'

'The cottage?'

'Yes – you've heard the news, I take it?'

'What news would that be?'

'Dear me, I was under the impression they were going to contact you in person but ... of course – that would be it. I *did* inform them that the property is not technically yours until we exchange tomorrow, so maybe they decided –'

'Mr Wilmot –'

'My apologies. I'm afraid there's been a break-in. I was contacted this morning by the police who informed me that an intruder was interrupted early yesterday evening by a neighbour of yours, a Mr Woodward. His wife notified the authorities but unfortunately the intruder was long gone by the time they arrived. We were contacted as solicitors for the previous owner and I was driven out to the cottage. I've been trying to contact you since I returned to the office.'

'This is ... this is awful,' said Ellen. 'Do you know if anything's missing?'

'As far as I can see, the intruder, whoever he was, did not get much further than just the one room. Everywhere else was tidy, just as my client had left it but there had been some sort of disturbance in the conservatory. I don't know if you recall, but there is a desk in there and the locked drawers have been forced open and emptied, I regret to say. There was also a laptop which has been removed, which is intensely irritating for you, I'm sure, but I am not aware of anything else that has been taken. The rest of the cottage seemed untouched. It could have been a lot worse.'

Ellen thought for a moment, wondered if she might be able to get away without saying anything, then decided that the police involvement left her with no choice.

'About the laptop, Mr Wilmot,' she said, pausing to allow another fit of coughing on the other end of the line to subside. 'There's no need to worry. I have it.'

Wilmot's response, when it came, sounded cautious.

'*You* have it?'

'Yes. I brought it home with me when I visited the cottage yesterday.'

'But I thought I made it quite clear –'

'You did, yes. I'm sorry. I was hoping to find something in there that would explain exactly why the cottage has been left to me and I couldn't wait until the weekend. I know I had no right to take it and I apologise but at least you don't need to worry about it. It's quite safe here.'

Wilmot let her know that this was hardly the point and asked if Liam was aware she had taken it with her. She lied and said she'd sneaked it out of the cottage while he was otherwise occupied. She suspected the boy was going to have a tough enough time of it as things stood, without having to explain why he'd seen fit to collude with her.

'So this intruder,' she said, changing the subject. 'Did the neighbour manage to get a look at him? Do the police have a description of some sort?'

'Unfortunately not,' muttered Wilmot, sounding none too appeased. 'I understand that an unfamiliar car was parked towards the foot of the hill, just opposite the church, at around that time. One of the villagers saw it there and assumed it was someone who was calling in at one of the Mews cottages opposite or maybe visiting the churchyard. It was a dark colour by all accounts but that is not likely to be of much assistance.'

Maybe not, thought Ellen, recalling O'Halloran's dark blue Escort. *And then again...*

She thanked Wilmot for putting her in the picture and apologised once more for having taken the laptop. She asked if the break-in had changed anything – would it still be OK for her to take possession of the cottage and stay there that weekend? He told her there would be no problem from a legal point of view but queried the wisdom of staying overnight, given recent events. He was making arrangements for the broken window to be replaced but that hardly made it any safer.

She assured him she wouldn't be staying there alone and thanked him again. He finished by saying that, as she was not yet in full legal possession of the property, he would take it upon himself to contact the police and explain the missing laptop.

The note of censure in his voice was difficult to ignore.

March 1974: O'Halloran

He's aware of the waitress hovering at his shoulder. Without turning his head to acknowledge her, he removes the road map from the table to make room for the tray she's carrying. While she unloads the contents – steak and kidney pie and chips with a side order of onion rings and two thick slices of farmhouse loaf – he refolds the map to fit what little space is left on the table. Then he spears a couple of chips and takes a bite from them while his eyes roam across the multicoloured lines representing the roads of Inverness and the Black Isle.

He's glad he decided to make a weekend of it – good move, that. Yesterday was a pig of a day, all that fog and ice on the roads. If he'd left it till this morning to set off, he'd have been shattered by now ... not exactly the best preparation for his big evening. Doesn't bear thinking about. The only time he's ever travelled this far north, he couldn't have been more than six or seven years old and it was his father behind the wheel, trying to find a way past a succession of caravans and lorries on the roads around Loch Lomond. Not very big on dual carriageways, the Jockos. Crawling along past even the most spectacular scenery can lose its appeal after a while, especially if you can't see half of it for mist and sleet and you've got the windscreen wipers on the whole way. By the time he arrived yesterday evening, he felt so sick and tired he opted for an early night without dinner.

He's made up for it today though. A good night's sleep worked wonders and after a big fry-up for breakfast he was fit and raring to go. He's had a look round the Black Isle – neither black nor an island, as the woman on Reception felt obliged to point out. The tourist pamphlets in his room suggested dolphins might be seen from somewhere called Chanonry Point, just beyond Avoch, but even though he stood there like a dummy for half an hour with a coach party of Japanese tourists he hadn't got even a sniff of them. He did get some photos of the Moray Firth, although he wasn't sure how they'd come out with the weather as filthy as it was. Amazing to think people actually chose to live here.

Next he drove south to have a look at Castle Urquhart and grabbed a sandwich and a coke from a café in Drumnadrochit before driving back with Loch Ness to his left and picking up the coast road along to Nairn, where his parents rented a cottage all those years ago. He spent the best part of the afternoon there, reliving childhood memories and freezing his backside off, before driving back to the hotel for dinner. He knows he hasn't got long before he'll need to head off for the Prince's Arms but there are no guarantees he'll be able to get a decent meal there and no way is he missing out on dinner.

He empties three spoonfuls of sugar into his tea and drags the spoon through the liquid. Taking a sip, he wonders where Martin Adams is right now – or Peter Vaughan as he insists on being called. By all accounts he's managed to scrounge a car from somewhere so he'll be driving up instead of taking the train, which was the original plan. Ironic really – if Adams hadn't gone to the station that morning to check on train times, this whole Inverness business might have remained a secret between him and his son.

He talked with Adams last night on the phone. Apparently he could only get the weekend off work so he had to delay setting off until this morning. Up today, back tomorrow, poor sod. He looks at his watch – getting on for 6.30 – and decides he can't be far away now. Not if he's going to be there by 8.00.

Old man Kasprowicz too. It won't have been easy for him. He's no spring chicken. He's glad he chose Josef in the end. It would have been easy to go for Phil Bingham. Many would have seen him as the obvious choice, because with someone like Bingham you're guaranteed a bit of a scene, something dramatic. In the end though, that's what counted against him. The problem with the Binghams of this world, him and that gobby wife of his, is that they're just too much after a while. They're too obvious. They might have been flavour of the month for a while, rent-a-quote, instant copy to be wheeled out at the drop of a hat, but overexposure can soon turn you into a caricature. Between them they've managed to turn a groundswell of heartfelt support into one big yawn and, given what happened to their daughter, that's some achievement.

Josef Kasprowicz though is something else. There's something compelling about the man, a certain ... *dignity*. O'Halloran has no children of his own so maybe he's not the best judge, but it seems to him that the Binghams have been claiming more than their fair share of moral outrage. For all they've suffered, they do at least still have *their* daughter. And yet, since the news first broke to a disbelieving world, Kasprovicz and his wife have shunned the limelight as assiduously as the Binghams have courted it, which is why Josef will prove to be the right choice for this evening.

He wonders what they're doing right now, Kasprowicz and Adams – what they're thinking. Two solitary travellers, each utterly unaware of the other, following the threads he's woven and drawing ever nearer to the centre of the web. The maps he has with him at the breakfast table show the area around Inverness and the Black Isle – they go no further south than Perth. He puts them on the floor beside him to create a little space on the table. Then he takes the salt cellar and gradually empties it, using its contents to sketch an improvised outline of England and Scotland on the table.

When he's finished, he draws a diagonal wavy line from east to west to represent the border between the two countries. He takes another sip of tea and thrusts his fork into the steak and kidney pie while he admires his handiwork. Then, having done the necessary calculations, he takes the salt cellar and places it below the border somewhere in the east, where Adams would have started his journey. Kasprowicz is represented by the pepper pot, which he puts in the west.

As an afterthought, he scoops up a chip and drops it somewhere in the north-east of Scotland. He has no idea where John Michael Adams is at present – even his father can't (or won't) say where – but he assumes it has to be somewhere vaguely near Inverness, otherwise why drag his old man all that way up here for their big reunion? Yes, he won't be far away, that's for sure.

He sits back and studies the map. For a moment he thinks he has a sense of what it must have been like to be a general during World War II, standing on the balcony in the War Office and looking down on the troop deployments on the large-scale maps below. Then, taking hold of the salt cellar and the pepper pot, he slowly nudges them further north, through the border and into Scotland.

At some stage this evening, they'll all be together: salt cellar, pepper pot and chip will all have converged on the Prince's Arms. And he'll be there, waiting. John Michael is expecting only his father. Martin Adams knows O'Halloran will be there but has no idea about Kasprowicz. And in a couple of days from now, everyone this side of Pluto will want to talk to the man who single-handedly choreographed the whole thing, the only one capable of putting it all together. The wailing and gnashing of teeth at the *Cotswold Daily* Fucking *Gazette* will be something worth hearing. He smiles as he wonders who they'll send over the top to talk to him about it. Poor sod.

The waitress is clearing another table and has noticed his unorthodox use of the condiments.

'Is everything OK?' she asks.

'Fine,' he replies, picking up the chip and flipping it into his mouth. 'Everything's just fine.'

February 2008: Ellen

Ellen had been coming here for almost three years now. When asked for her impressions of Calder Vale, she was never less than effusive in her praise. The staff were remarkable – she could not speak highly enough of their dedication, their professionalism, the unlimited reserves of patience they brought to their work and, above all else, the genuine affection in which they seemed to hold those entrusted to their care – as if these were not patients but friends or relatives in need of their support. She had no idea how they did it. Mild irritation seemed to be the worst they could run to, whatever the provocation.

As for the location, only the most churlish of dispositions might find grounds for complaint. When her mother's dementia was compounded by a stroke and her need for round-the-clock supervision became irrefutable, Ellen and the Balfours had done extensive research to ensure that they came up with the right place. They looked at Calder Vale online initially and it was the beauty of the physical surroundings, the swathes of lawn sweeping down to the shore that persuaded them to investigate further. They were already half-sold on the place before they'd even been there in person.

The moment they turned off the access road and in through the imposing gates, their first glimpse of the house set the seal on things. It was a particularly bright late April morning and the sun seemed to pick out each of the huge banks of windows at once, lighting up the building like fireworks against a clear night sky. The poplars lining the approach to the front of the house were swaying in the breeze, as if nodding in the direction of the building, waving them forward. As they pulled into one of the parking spaces and crossed the shale-covered area leading to the entrance hall, Sam pointed out the closed-circuit cameras that followed them every step of the way. She found it immensely reassuring. Her mother would be safe here.

She couldn't point to any one occasion and say that was it – that was when her feelings about Calder Vale started to change. Presumably it was a gradual process, this insidious erosion of her reserves of optimism. Maybe it was inevitable, given the uncertainty in which everything in her life seemed to be shrouded. The past three years had been such a drain on her energy; first Barbara's dementia, then the stroke, and finally the realisation that she was going to have to face it all without Jack. In some respects it was like living in a cryogenic state, waiting for some unspecified moment in the future when it would be OK to surface and resume a normal life.

All she knew for sure was that now, every time she turned in through the gates and the house came into view, she felt weighed down, assailed by a sense of unease for which she had no rational explanation. It had nothing to do with any doubts concerning the quality of care, nor any reservations about the comfort of the accommodation. Nothing substantive had changed since that first visit and yet somehow it was *all* different. The poplars lining the drive slid past her now like bars on a cage. There was something unsettling, something almost Orwellian about the way the camera seemed to single her out, locking onto her the moment she stepped from the car and logging her every move. The windows were dark and gloomy, with so many shades drawn it was difficult not to imagine several pairs of eyes peering out at her from behind them, noting the length of time since her last visit.

In the early days, Jack and the children used to come with her, at least at the weekend. Then, for obvious reasons, it had been just Megan and Harry. Now, as often as not, she came alone. For a while she'd insisted they come at least once a week on the grounds that this was their grandmother and there was no way of knowing how much longer they'd have the chance to see her. She didn't want them to regret missed opportunities.

The relentless deterioration in Barbara's condition however had eventually taken its toll on the children as well. They would arrive to find their grandmother almost totally unresponsive, staring out of the window or gawping at the TV screen in the corner of the Day Room. Even when she was at the peak of her powers, she tended to drift in and out, unsure who her own grandchildren were without frequent reminders. They found it disconcerting when she asked questions they'd answered in detail only a few moments before, or retold the same anecdote three or four times in quick succession.

Harry in particular was anxious too about the physical changes brought about by the stroke. He flinched when prompted to kiss her cheek. Her lopsided smile and frozen features confused and upset him, as did the fact that most of the time he found it difficult to understand what she was saying. In the car afterwards, he tended to be subdued while Megan was more likely to give voice to her frustrations. It was all so *boring*. She could have been spending the afternoon with friends, watching this or that programme on television – and *anything* could have been happening on Facebook while she'd been away from it. Why did they have to come to this stupid place? Ellen took a deep breath, forced herself to look beyond the obvious and decided one evening that she wouldn't make them visit any more unless they chose to. She only had the energy to fight on so many fronts at once and besides, maybe they were right. Maybe it was just too much to ask of children of that age.

So now she came alone, three times a week for a couple of hours or so – Tuesdays, Fridays and Sundays – while Jack looked after the children. If something unforeseen made the visit impossible, she always made a point of phoning, so that someone could let her mother know not to expect her. She understood this was hardly necessary – most of the time Barbara didn't even recognise her when she walked into the room. Even on her better days, Ellen strongly suspected her visit would be forgotten almost before she was out of the door. But she never knew for sure, from day to day, which version of her mother would be there. *Maybe today will be better*, she thought to herself, as she pulled into a parking space in the designated area. *Maybe today.*

She stepped out of the car and shaped as if to shut the door, then changed her mind. Reaching in, she picked up a blanket from the footwell and draped it across the laptop, which was lying on the passenger seat. *Better safe than sorry.* Alan Wharton had brought it over to her, just a couple of minutes later than the agreed time, full of apologies for having taken so long. He'd managed to do what she needed and had reset the password to 'Langmere' to make access easier for her. He offered to take her through what was in there but she was conscious of the time and worried that she might hit the heavy traffic around Chichester if she delayed much longer. She'd have to take a look at it later tonight, when she and the children arrived back home after the film.

She thanked him and asked how much she owed, offering to pay in cash if he preferred. He shook his head, wasn't having any of it. He'd enjoyed himself, spent the day doing what he loved best. He wasn't about to take her money. She wanted to protest but accepted this was a discussion that would have to wait. If all else failed, she'd find out the going rate and simply add it to his pay at the end of the week.

'What *was* the password, by the way?' she suddenly thought to ask as he was leaving.

He paused in the doorway and turned back to face her.

'Primrose82,' he said.

She smiled. Eudora certainly loved her cottage.

Jacob was doing a stint on Reception when she walked into the entrance hall at Calder Vale. She liked Jacob. He had a soft spot for her mother. Every chance he got, he was slipping her extra Jaffa Cakes with her afternoon tea, plumping up her hair or checking whether she needed another pillow in her chair. He made great show of professing total disbelief that she could be as old as she claimed – *surely there must be some mistake*. Somehow he managed to make the obvious flattery sound convincing.

He smiled and waved a pen at Ellen as she crossed the marble floor towards the desk. She took it from him and signed in. *Ellen Sutherland*. As if the last twelve years counted for nothing.

'How is she today?' she asked. He waggled a hand as if to say *so-so*.

'She was pretty good this morning,' he said, and this told her all she needed to know about how she would be right this minute. In Calder Vale speak, what was left out was always worthy of serious consideration.

She handed the biro back to him and headed for the Day Room, where she knew Barbara would be at this time. On a

Tuesday she was often in her own room, if the OT and physio sessions had taken a lot out of her. Fridays however she was wheeled down to the Day Room to be with everyone else for a couple of hours before dinner. There were a dozen or so residents in there when Ellen walked in. Some were watching the large flat-screen TV, listening as Anne Robinson sniped at quiz contestants. Others were chatting in small groups or dozing quietly.

Barbara was in a corner, facing a darkened window with her back to everyone else. Pausing for a moment to look at her, Ellen was struck yet again by how difficult it was to equate this frail, damaged creature with the forceful woman who had seemed so indomitable, so self-sufficient when she was younger. Their relationship had always been a troubled one, especially during Ellen's teenage years. There was an emotional distance between them, which she was quick to blame on her mother's reluctance to talk about the past, a barrier she'd never managed to break down. Her relative independence at university and then with Jack had given her a clearer sense of perspective, including an appreciation of the sacrifices her mother must have made on her behalf. She could see that if Barbara's feelings for her were not always obvious, it clearly wasn't because they didn't exist. Understanding this was one thing. Establishing a genuine connection was another.

She crossed the room, picking up a visitor's chair as she went. She stooped over the back of the armchair and was about to offer a kiss on the cheek before realising Barbara was asleep. The motion was enough to disturb her though and she flinched as she opened her eyes, blinking rapidly while she tried to process what was happening. She frowned, as if uncertain about the identity of the woman who had just positioned a chair opposite her.

'It's OK,' said Ellen, placing a hand over hers on the armrest. 'It's only me.' And she was rewarded with that half-smile, hinting at recognition. The moment of concern had passed and there was a certain amount of clarity in her expression. Maybe the sleep had done her some good.

'How are you feeling today – OK?'

'Not too bad.' *Hot hoo vad.* Her speech now was breathy, a collection of aspirates and softened consonants which still lay within the compass of her frozen facial muscles.

'Can I get you anything? A drink?'

Barbara closed her eyes and sank back into the armchair. She slipped her hand from beneath Ellen's and waved it in the general direction of the table beside her. Next to a glass stood two large bottles, one containing mineral water, the other lime juice, her favourite drink which always seemed to be there. Jacob's work again, she was prepared to bet.

She poured the right mixture – her mother always preferred it so strong it set Ellen's teeth on edge when she tried it – and handed the glass to her. Then she began the ritual of bringing her up to date with what had been happening since her last visit. The routine never varied, irrespective of Barbara's condition. Sometimes she was able to make her own contributions and help to keep the conversation moving along, but even when she appeared to be out of it, her mind flitting from one version of reality to another, Ellen still talked to her ... and talked ... and talked. Anything to pass the time. Anything to fill in the silence that had haunted every conversation between the two of them.

There had been a time when Ellen dealt exclusively in questions. As a child she'd pressed her mother for details about the father who existed for her only as an absence. The fact that he'd died before she was born brought with it a whiff of the exotic that she was able to use as emotional currency whenever friends asked where her daddy was. She invented lives for him, struggling to remember exactly which version she'd told to whom. At various times he'd been a pilot, a doctor, a soldier. He'd died in a car crash, succumbed to an incurable disease while helping children in Africa, drowned trying to save a little girl who'd been swept out to sea. But there would have been no need for these elaborate flights of fancy if her mother had just been able to sit down and talk to her about him for one evening, even just half an hour. All she needed was an outline, a shadow she could fill in. Her imagination would do the rest.

But the conversation had never got past first base. She only had to mention her father and the door slammed shut. Her mother never yielded an inch. Whenever Ellen went to stay with friends for a sleepover, she was always amazed, and not a little resentful, to see just how easy-going and approachable a mother could actually be. There was nothing easy about her relationship with Barbara. Intimacy was a foreign country.

So she learnt not to ask. It was easier that way. Instead they talked *at* each other. Whenever they were together, Ellen poured out details about her day, about the children, about Langmere Grove where Barbara herself had worked. And until her condition worsened Barbara did the same, their respective monologues passing on different tracks like trains in the night, heading nowhere significant. And now there was just the one train: she did the talking for both of them. Anything to fill the silence.

So she brought her mother up to speed on everything at home – the children, how things were going at school, Harry's football training, Megan's invitation to a disco, the film they were all going to see as soon as she'd picked them up from Jack's that evening. She grumbled about Megan's mulish refusal to wear her school jumper – *was I ever that bad?* Even Barbara's ambiguous response – a snort and a slight tilt of the head – was encouraging. They were touching base. It was almost like having a genuine conversation.

She moved on to Langmere, inventing messages from old friends who still worked there and remembered Barbara. Some did in fact approach her from time to time and ask for best wishes to be conveyed but nowhere near as frequently as she suggested. A harmless enough deception, she felt. True in spirit at least.

She was about to mention that Kate had come round for dinner the previous evening when Barbara leapt in first, her face brightening all of a sudden.

'It's Friday today,' she said, holding her glass out for Ellen to take.

'That's right.'

'My daughter's coming this afternoon.'

Ellen swallowed and took a deep breath. She took hold of her mother's hand and patted it gently.

'I'm here now,' she said. 'It's me, Ellen.'

Barbara's voice barely skipped a beat.

'She's bringing my grandchildren with her,' she said. *Hand hildren.*

'Not today, Mum. They're at Jack's – you remember Jack?'

'Jack?'

Ellen leant forward to put her face directly in front of Barbara's. The eyes gazing back at her seemed distant somehow, as if focusing on something beyond her. She opened her mouth to continue, then changed her mind, plucking instead at a few stray locks of hair that were trapped inside her mother's collar and teasing them free. She put the palm of her hand to the side of her face and stroked it, the skin dry to the touch, almost like paper.

'That will be nice for you,' she said eventually, giving her a quick kiss on the cheek. She reached over to put the glass back on the table, then sat back in her chair.

She didn't talk for some time, allowing Barbara to rest instead. She walked over to a magazine rack and helped herself to a fairly recent copy of *House and Home* – anything to help pass the time. Jack wasn't expecting her to pick up the children for another hour at least, so she was in no hurry to leave just yet.

One of the other residents came over at one point, an elderly woman who was never short of a word or two but who meant well. Then a care assistant brought tablets for Barbara, which she washed down with gentle sips from her drink. When the six o'clock news came on, Ellen put the magazine to one side and turned Barbara's chair to face the TV set. She picked out occasional items that she thought might interest her mother and slowly, slowly the hands on the large clock on the wall crept round towards 6.30.

The one subject she hadn't raised was the letter from Wilmot. She didn't want to enter into any complicated account of her visit to Cheltenham and the cottage that had so mysteriously come her way. Lengthy explanations of any sort were a waste of time. Even at her most alert, there was no way Barbara could cope with anything like that. A simple question-and-answer routine, short and to the point, was the only way she might learn anything about her connection to Eudora, if one existed.

She wished now she'd raised the subject a while earlier before her mother drifted out of range. She'd been reluctant to dive straight in for fear of giving the impression that this was the principal reason for her visit. Also there was always a chance that merely raising the subject might re-open old wounds and she had no wish to ruin the entire visit before she'd even made herself comfortable.

So she waited, putting the moment off in the hope that an opportunity might somehow present itself even now, an indication that her mother was responding with some degree of clarity. When the time came for her to stand and put on her coat in readiness for her departure, she decided it was now or never.

She moved her chair back a little and squatted down on her haunches in front of Barbara. Then she picked up each of her hands in turn and held them in her own, resting them in her mother's lap. She looked her in the eye, anxious not to miss anything significant.

'I nearly forgot,' she said. 'There was one more message for you. This woman … I don't know who she is but she asked to be remembered to you.' She paused, watching for the slightest reaction.

'Her name's Eudora? Eudora Nash?'

The hands seemed to clench slightly under hers. There was something of a twitch maybe at the corner of one eye but that could easily have been her imagination. Ellen said nothing for a few moments, waiting to see if her mother had anything at all to say. Again, there was no reaction to speak of.

'So who is she, Mum?' she persisted. 'This Eudora Nash – how do you know her?'

Still nothing.

'I'm probably going to see her some time next week,' she improvised, looking away briefly so that the lie wouldn't register in her eyes. 'Do you want me to say hello from you? Have you got a message for her maybe?'

Her legs were starting to cramp up. She stood up to straighten them.

'I'll do that then, shall I?' she asked, giving it one last try. She watched closely, then bent over and gave her mother another kiss on the cheek. She said goodbye, gave the usual assurances about when she'd next visit, aware as she did so that a lot would depend on what time she and Kate decided to leave Oakham on Sunday. Maybe she'd have to leave it until the evening before coming back here.

She picked up her mother's glass and put it back in her hands once more before patting her on the shoulder. Then she turned and walked towards the door, where she realised that Jacob had been watching her. He asked how it had gone and they were swapping notes when she heard a cry and the sound of breaking glass.

Jacob was the first to react. He called out to one of the other assistants for help and was by Barbara's side before Ellen had even worked out what was happening. He whispered soothing words into her ear as he carefully prised her fingers apart and plucked at the remaining tiny fragments of glass. Ellen looked around desperately for a cloth of some description, horrified by the deep cut that now creased the palm of her mother's hand.

The blood was flowing freely, dripping through her fingers and onto her lap.

'Not very clever now, was it?' Jacob cooed, keeping the tone light and aiming a mock frown in Barbara's direction. Two other assistants arrived swiftly with a couple of cloths, a towel and a bowl of water. Ellen stepped back momentarily to allow them room in which to operate. As she did so, she looked in surprise at her mother, wondering at the force she must have exerted to break a glass by squeezing it like that. She'd never have believed she had it in her.

The moment there was room, she moved closer and put her arm on Barbara's shoulder to comfort her. As she did so, she realised she was mumbling something, which she couldn't quite make out. Leaning forward, she asked her to repeat it. The voice was quiet, but steely in its determination. The words, no matter how slurred, were unmistakable this time.

'You stay away from my daughter,' she heard. 'Leave her alone.'

March 1974: Josef

The snow is heavy now, coming down like a white blanket, blotting out his vision so quickly that each sweep of the wipers from right to left is barely enough to clear the windscreen. In Inverness itself and the built-up area around it, the snow was settling on driveways and pavements but there was enough traffic to keep the road itself relatively clear. Out here things are very different. He's seen no more than a handful of cars in the last quarter of an hour and the road surface is worsening by the minute. Already, on a couple of occasions, he's felt the rear of the car start to drift at the slightest touch of the brake pedal.

This country road seems to be going on for ever. What's worse, it's unlit and so narrow here that it's not too difficult to imagine it petering out into a dead end before long. If that happens and he has to do a three-point turn in the dark, he could easily end up in a ditch or stuck on a grass verge, unable to get any traction. This is no place to be stranded – it's some time now since he remembers passing a phone box or building.

He hopes it's the right road. He stopped a while ago and asked for directions. A man, who'd ventured outside to cover his windscreen and bonnet with a layer of blankets, told him he needed to take the first left at the crossroads, assuring him that the Prince's Arms was no more than two, maybe three miles from there, just the other side of the village of Lachlie. *Dead straight*, he said. *Cannae miss it.* He's been driving down that same road now for what feels like a quarter of an hour at least, with no sign of the pub and not one road sign to reassure him he's at least heading in the right direction. Even allowing for the fact that he's playing it safe, barely climbing above twenty miles an hour, how long can it possibly take for him to cover a couple of miles? He removes the now redundant directions from the passenger seat and screws them into a ball in his frustration.

It's the diversions that have thrown him. In a lighter moment, he might appreciate the irony of it all. He's travelled nearly 400 miles and reached Inverness with hours to spare and barely a problem worthy of the name, give or take a little ill health. He's allowed himself plenty of time to find a bed and breakfast and has come across one which suits his purpose just perfectly. The owners, a retired couple more or less his own age, were dismayed to hear that he planned to go out again so soon after such a long drive, especially in view of the weather forecast for the area. When he explained he'd come all this way to meet someone, they urged him at least to bring his case in and maybe have a cup of tea with them before setting off again but he politely declined their offer. He wanted to be absolutely sure he was first there, to be in position to watch the others as they arrived.

But within minutes of setting off again he hit the first diversion – a police car was blocking off the road because of a multiple pile-up and sending everything back the way it had come. He followed the rest of the traffic as it threaded its way through a network of unfamiliar streets, hoping they would eventually lead him back onto the road he'd been forced to abandon. Every so often the queue of traffic ground to a halt again, for no reason that was immediately apparent, and on one occasion a policeman on a motorcycle drove past, stopping at each car window to explain that this road too would be closed for another ten minutes or so – presumably another collision.

By the time he'd cleared the outskirts of the town, there was no way he was going to arrive at the Prince's Arms as early as he'd been hoping. By his reckoning, he was several miles west of where he needed to be. Rather than waste time trying to regain the original route, he decided he'd be better off using his AA road map and coming into Lachlie from the opposite end. It had seemed like a good idea at the time. Now he's just hoping that this is indeed the right road and that he cannot, as the man said, miss it.

He passes some lights on his left, the first sign of habitation for several minutes. It's a farmhouse, he realises, as he draws nearer. He's tempted to stop once again and ask for directions but decides instead to give it another two minutes. At least he has somewhere he knows he can return to in the event of an emergency. And he's rewarded for his persistence when, just a couple of bends later, lights suddenly appear out of nowhere as the lane broadens before forming a junction with a major road. Away to his right is a sign welcoming him to Lachlie. He's here at last.

He knows he's come into the village from the wrong side and will have to drive through it to find the Prince's Arms. Now that he's back in the arms of civilisation the snow seems less threatening somehow, as if the lights and the buildings have stripped it of its elemental force. A touch of tailspin, as he turns onto the main road, reminds him that this is no time for complacency.

The Prince's Arms is easy to find from here. It lies in a deep hollow, just the other side of the village. As he approaches, he can see there's no point in trying to find a space in the car park, which is nowhere near large enough to cope with the number of vehicles that seem to have been attracted here this evening. Instead he drives another 50 yards down to the pub itself, then beyond it, continuing up the hill, past a line of cars which have parked on the verge, presumably confident they'll be able to drive off again later in the evening, whatever the conditions. The slope is much steeper by the time he reaches the end of the row. He pulls over but then drives on for a hundred yards or so as an afterthought, making use of a lay-by to turn the car before returning to park it. Now he's facing down the hill approximately sixty yards or so from the entrance to the pub. The overhanging trees give just enough shelter from the snow to suggest that from here he ought to have a more or less uninterrupted view of events as they unfold.

It's almost eight o'clock and he's later than planned. There has to be a chance they're already inside by now. Mr O'Halloran wants the father and son to have some time together before he springs his surprise, so he still has half an hour or so before he's due to make his entrance, but he hoped it might settle his nerves to watch them for a while before they're even aware he's here. It feels like a missed opportunity, as if he's lost some element of control by arriving so late. Then it dawns on him that if he's been delayed in Inverness, they may well have been too. Not knowing for sure either way is unsettling.

Fortunately the whole area around the front entrance to the Prince's Arms is floodlit. He can see not only who's going in and out but also anyone approaching the pub, the moment they come within fifty feet of it from either direction. He's satisfied he has the perfect spot here – as long as they're not already inside.

There's only one way he'll be able to put his mind at rest. He'll need to be careful, obviously. The last thing he wants, after Mr O'Halloran has gone to all this trouble, is to go blundering in there and give the game away. He'll need to make sure there's no way he can be recognised. He doesn't think there's that much of a risk. They only know him from the trial after all, and it's been almost seven years since then. Seven years of standing still and holding his breath. Holding his breath because there's nothing worth saying until he has the chance to say it to the right person. Tonight has been a long time coming.

He steps from the car, fastening his coat to the throat. Then he opens the boot and takes out his hat, which he wears during the long, solitary walks in the countryside that have become part of his routine now. They used to walk together. Now he honestly thinks he prefers the solitude.

He pulls the hat down firmly so that it all but covers his eyebrows. Then he takes a tartan scarf and wraps it round the lower half of his face, only partly to protect himself from the cold. He stoops to take a quick look in the wing mirror and decides there's so little of his face visible, he has nothing to worry about. Not even the boys from the 302 would recognise him now.

The temperature has dropped several degrees since midafternoon. The conditions underfoot are icy and the slope makes things difficult for him as he picks his way carefully down the hill. *Like an old man*, it occurs to him. It doesn't seem like so long ago he'd have been running down here, like those two young lads up ahead who've just leapt from a car. They've grabbed handfuls of snow from the verge and are bombarding each other, so sure-footed and fearless as they race down the hill towards the entrance. The invulnerability of youth. He envies them their blind, unsuspecting faith in a future that belongs to them.

He's still several yards from the pub when a door opens and the reason for the large number of cars becomes obvious. Gaelic music, fiddles, accordion and a woman's voice leak out into the cold night air. On a board at the roadside is a sign advertising *Avoch in Concert* with today's date beneath it. The music increases in volume as he opens the door and steps into a hallway, with doors right and left leading to Public and Saloon bars.

The music is coming from the former so he tries the Saloon first. He puts on his glasses and peers round the door, trying to be as inconspicuous as possible. There are several tables in here, most of them occupied already. Some people are drinking at the bar, a few have gathered round a huge log fire, making a fuss of a pair of black Labradors stretched out in front of it. He doesn't need long to establish there's no one in here he recognises. He walks further into the room to make sure he's not mistaken, then turns round and heads for the Public Bar.

This is a much larger room than the Saloon but it's heaving, so much so there's no way he can hover near the entrance and hope to run his eye over everyone in here. Quite apart from anything else, he'll be battered by the door every time it opens, which seems to be every twenty seconds. He nudges his way forward, apologising every time he jogs someone as he tries to negotiate a path through to a vantage point where he might have a better view. He follows a woman who's juggling four baskets of chicken and chips, calling out the number of the order at the top of her voice and barely making herself heard above the music and conversation. Eventually he finds a place in the corner near the large bay window where he can relax a little.

At the far end of the room, on a makeshift stage, is the group, a six-piece band who seem to his untrained ear to have at least some idea of what they're doing. It's not his sort of music but some of the instrumentals are quite complex and the girl's voice is melodic enough. He just wishes they weren't so loud.

Several people are standing in front of the stage, watching the musicians perform. A couple are dancing – he assumes they're not part of the act – and it's not too difficult to imagine others joining in once they have a few drinks inside them. The crowd at the bar is several rows deep and every table appears to be taken. There's no fire in here, nor any need for one. There are so many people, he feels uncomfortable in all these layers of clothing.

Safely tucked away in his corner, he lets his gaze strafe the room in search of anyone he might recognise. He's relieved to pick out Mr O'Halloran almost immediately. He's sharing a table with two young couples, although he doesn't appear to have anything to do with them. He has a newspaper open in front of him but it looks like it's more for show than anything else. He's looking up every so often, his attention never very far from a table just two away from his. It's occupied by a young couple and a middle-aged man, who's sitting slightly apart from them. The latter looks uncomfortable, on edge. He has a drink in front of him, what looks like lemonade, and every so often he takes a quick sip, then puts it back on the table while he concentrates on the door, as if checking everyone who comes in. He looks so different now, so much older, despite the longer hair and the absence of the beard, which always looked so untidy. He probably wouldn't have recognised him if it hadn't been for Mr O'Halloran's obvious interest. *So*, he tells himself. *One of them has made it, at any rate.*

The shock of recognition makes him take a step back. He drops into a window seat to take the weight off his legs which seem intent on betraying him. Fortunately no one seems to notice anything untoward. Neither man has paid him any attention since he came into the room. Each seems locked into his own thoughts to the exclusion of everything else.

He's surprised by the strength of his reaction. He's been imagining this moment for so long, never quite daring to hope he'd ever have the chance to experience it. Now, since Mr O'Halloran got in touch and told him about Inverness, he's been planning it down to the last detail. He knows word for word what he's going to say. He's rehearsed it until each sentence is deeply ingrained in him. He could be shaken awake in the middle of the night and still reproduce it without a moment's digression or hesitation. And yet here he is, shaken to the core when the moment finally arrives, not even sure he's up to standing on his own two feet, let alone delivering his lines.

And this is *Martin* Adams, he reminds himself. This is just the father. If his reaction to seeing *him* is this extreme, what will he be like when his son walks in? All of a sudden he's desperate to regain the sanctuary offered by his car. He'll need time to compose himself before he's up to something like this.

Pushing himself away from the window seat, he keeps to the edge of the room, trying not to draw attention to himself. He scans the faces at the bar as he passes them, in case the boy's already there. It's seven years since he's seen him, of course. His features will have changed significantly since then but he has no fears that he might not recognise him. He's seen that photo more times than he'd care to remember and besides, those awful days in the courtroom are seared into his brain. Whatever else may have changed with the passage of time, he knows he's not going to have forgotten those eyes. *Every Parent's Nightmare,* they used to call him, as if desperate to claim a share of the agony and loss for themselves. He'll recognise him, alright.

The boy's not here now, that much is certain. He mumbles more apologies as he squeezes his way to the door, leading to the foyer. Another order of chicken in the basket drifts past, the smell combining with that of the all-pervasive cigarette smoke to unsettle his stomach yet again. He steps through into the hallway, allowing the door to swing shut behind him, and takes a deep breath, grateful that at least it's a little quieter. He clearly looks as bad as he feels because the waitress, on her return trip, takes the trouble to ask if he's OK. He thanks her for her concern, then takes the scarf which has unravelled and wraps it around his face again.

As he reaches out for the door, it swings open, catching him on the shoulder. A blast of cold air rushes in, carrying with it a few flakes of snow, and a man and a woman come crashing through, desperate to get out of the snow. They both apologise and while they're making sure he's OK, a figure in a yellow kagoul slips past them. Josef just has time to register the incongruous picture of a large grinning face on the back before the figure pulls the waterproof top over his head. He turns round, just for a moment, as he shakes the damp from the kagoul and folds it carefully. Then, without paying any attention to the others in the hallway, he opens the door to the bar and disappears inside.

And now Josef knows he was right. Even after all these years, there is no way he could ever have mistaken those eyes.

7

February 2008: Ellen

'You're kidding, right. Nothing?'

'As good as. Nothing that helps us, at any rate.'

'So what's with the laptop, then?' asked Kate. 'I mean, I know she wasn't exactly short of money but it's not like they're cheap, is it? You'd think if she was going to buy one, she'd at least use the thing.'

'I didn't say she didn't use it.' Ellen cradled the handset between ear and shoulder as she reached into the fridge for the tub of margarine. 'There's emails and a handful of Word documents, just nothing that seems to take us any further forward, that's all.'

She lifted the crumpets out of the toaster and fetched a knife from the drawer.

'You sure?'

'Positive.'

'So who are the emails to?'

Ellen spooned raspberry jam onto the crumpets while she talked Kate through what she'd found, which was significantly less than they'd been hoping for. She'd barely taken in a word of the film that evening. The children had loved it, which was the main thing, but she'd been too preoccupied with thoughts of what the laptop might reveal to pay any great attention to what was happening on the screen. Then, having driven home and put the children to bed, she'd turned it on and typed in *Langmere* as instructed, only to find next to nothing there. It took her no more than ten minutes at the outside to conclude that this was yet another dead end.

It appeared to have been bought with one purpose in mind. Almost every email dealt with Parish Council business. Most were exchanged with someone she addressed as Rowan, who appeared from the contents to be the vicar, not only for Oakham but for two other villages as well, which surprised her. She wasn't aware it was customary for members of the clergy to be shared around in this way. She decided he was someone worth looking up in the next couple of days. If nothing else, he clearly had regular contact with Eudora. Ellen was amused to discover from the hotmail address that his surname was actually Williams. Reverend Rowan Williams. She imagined the nepotism jokes must be wearing a bit thin by now.

The Word documents were divided into three folders. One contained copies of a monthly church newsletter, which offered nothing that was likely to be of much help or interest to her. The second was used for the minutes of Parish Council meetings and was no more illuminating. The list of officers, printed as part of the heading, identified Eudora as the Minutes Secretary. She seemed content to take a back seat during discussions, her name coming up in business items only when volunteers were listed – the annual church fete, coffee mornings, a trip to Salisbury Cathedral in December 2006, Prinknash Abbey a few months later.

The third folder, labelled *Miscellaneous,* was no more than a collection of shopping lists, an improvised address and phone book, emergency contact names and numbers – plumber, electrician, gardener. Whatever hopes Ellen might have had of the laptop and its contents, she was left with little more than snapshots of a quiet, uneventful life. There was nothing there to shed even a speck of light on Eudora's past or, more specifically, how their lives had come to overlap.

'How about her web browser?' asked Kate, reluctant to let go. 'Anything in her Favourites?'

'Nothing. Practically the only thing in the History section is Tesco online shopping. Trust me, there's nothing there. Shit!' She stooped to pick up the knife which had slipped from the work surface to the floor. 'I'll bring it with me tomorrow and you can have a look for yourself, if you like. Bring plenty of Valium though, in case the excitement gets too much for you.'

She nudged the fridge door shut with her knee and went through to the lounge, where she dropped wearily into an armchair, resting the plate in her lap.

'I don't get it,' said Kate. 'It doesn't make sense.'

'What doesn't?'

'Well, why go to the trouble of password-protecting? How old was she – ninety?'

'I think Wilmot said ninety-one.'

'There you go then. You think she did that herself? Someone else *has* to have set it up for her, and if she went to that much trouble, there must have been something she wanted to hide. And even if I'm wrong, even if she was savvy enough to do it herself, why bother if all she's got in there is minutes of church meetings and newsletters – what's the big deal exactly?'

'I don't know,' Ellen admitted.

'Exactly. There's got to be something, Ellie. And if it's not on the hard drive, there's a back-up somewhere – you know, a memory stick, or maybe one of those external hard drives you can plug in and go. Maybe she saved things to disk. Are there any in the case?'

'Already been there. There's nothing like that. Anyway,' Ellen continued, wiping away a trickle of jam that had seeped from the corner of her mouth, 'I thought the whole point of a back-up is to make a copy of what's already on the hard drive.'

'So maybe she typed it straight onto the memory stick.'

'But if she did that, we're back to square one, aren't we? Why password-protect the laptop if this mythical document was never on it?'

There was a pause while Kate digested this.

'Damn, this is weird,' she said eventually.

'Isn't it just?'

'And you didn't get anything from Barbara, you say?'

'Not really. There's something there alright, I'm sure of it. But she's not really in a position to give it up, even if she wanted to – which she probably doesn't. You know what she's like.'

'And you don't think it'd be easier just to ask Sam?'

'No point. Trust me. Not with the little we've got at the moment.'

Maybe after the weekend, she thought. Maybe then she might have filled enough gaps to feel better about confronting him, but for now there were just too many of them for him to slip through. If he decided not to come clean, she didn't have enough to twist his arm.

'Ellie … you absolutely sure about this?'

'Kate, you know what he's like –'

'I don't mean Sam – I mean … all of it. This whole business. Are you sure you want to keep digging like this?'

Ellen recognised the unusually serious note in her friend's voice. She paused as she lifted a second crumpet to her mouth.

'Of course. Why wouldn't I?'

'Well … gift horses spring to mind, for one thing.'

'Meaning?'

'Meaning you don't have to go up there tomorrow. You could just put it all back into the solicitor's hands, ask him to sell the cottage and walk away with the money, no questions asked.'

'But why would I do that? What's wrong with trying to get some sort of explanation?' She licked more goo from her fingers and put the plate on the coffee table for a while. 'Are you telling me, if you were in my place, you wouldn't be curious about who this woman was and how you were connected to her?'

'I'm sure I would be. But I'd have you there pointing out the obvious to me, wouldn't I?'

'Which is?'

'That there's something very iffy about all this.'

'Iffy?'

'What would you call it? I mean, you hear out of the blue that you've inherited this cottage from a total stranger. You go up to have a look around and you haven't been there five minutes before some journalist's on your doorstep, lying his head off about who he is and why he's there. You've got a private detective agency traipsing around the country, looking for someone, presumably you, in places you've never even been in your life. Then, just a few hours after you've left the cottage, you've got someone breaking into it and –'

'Not someone. O'Halloran.'

'You don't know that. Not for sure.'

'Oh come on, Kate – who else is it going to be?'

'I don't know, Ellie, and neither do you, which is pretty much the point I'm trying to make here. You've got all these things going on around you and I get that you don't like being the only one in the dark but if you're right and people close to you are keeping things from you, isn't the most likely explanation that they think it's for the best? What if you're better off not knowing?'

'Now I *know* you're not serious,' Ellen laughed. 'Is this by any chance the same Kate Goodwin who spent the best part of two years telling me that running away from my problems with Jack and burying my head in the sand wasn't going to solve anything?'

'Different, and you know it. With Jack you just had a straight choice to make – pull out or settle for a life of second best. You knew exactly what you were dealing with. Here you don't. Look, I'm not trying to put you off going up there tomorrow or anything like that. You tell me you still want to go ahead and I'll be there with you, asking as many questions as you like.'

'Good, 'cos I'm going. I'll see you tomorrow, OK? Bright and early.'

Kate sighed. 'One or the other,' she said. 'Can't do both.'

Ellen smiled and hung up.

March 1974: Josef

A couple emerge from the Prince's Arms and start making their way up the hill towards him. The man is dressed in a three-quarter length coat, fastened at the throat with the collar turned up to protect him from the wind. The woman is wearing an inadequate-looking waist-length jacket, a short skirt and high-heeled shoes which are patently ill-suited to conditions underfoot. Their body language suggests there's been a disagreement between them. He's pointedly walking a few yards ahead of her as she tiptoes her way up the slope. She stops for a moment, leaning against the door of the telephone kiosk while she removes one shoe and tips it upside down. She calls out to him and he waits for her to catch up before offering an arm by way of grudging support. His impatience is unmistakable.

They're heading straight for his car and he thinks for a moment it's him they've come to see. Then, at the last moment, they pause at the yellow Citroën immediately in front, exchanging a few words which he's unable to decipher. The man unlocks his door first and rummages around inside for a good ten seconds before reaching across and letting her in. Through their rear window, he watches as she switches on the interior light and studies herself in a compact mirror which she's taken from her bag. The man reaches over immediately and turns it off, and they're still arguing as he pulls away, a touch more abruptly than the conditions will allow. The rear of the car slews round and it fishtails its way down the hill for a few yards before he manages to straighten it out. Josef can only imagine the conversation between them as the rear lights disappear into the distance.

With nothing to distract him, he realises that his hands are still shaking. The unexpected encounter in the pub, almost literally bumping into the boy like that, has thrown him. It was so much more difficult than he'd expected. In the flesh. Close enough to touch. Everything seemed so straightforward in the abstract. Walk in, confront him, say what he has to say and leave. Simple as that. No discussion. No recriminations. In and out. He's not interested in anything the boy might have to say – doesn't see what possible purpose an apology would serve anyway. All he wants is to see the shock of recognition in his eyes and to have his say. It's a long way to come just for the sake of a few words, but it'll be worth it. He knows he'll never have another opportunity.

He stretches his arms out and grips the steering wheel in the ten to two position, locking his arms straight in front of him in an attempt to exercise a modicum of control over the trembling. It works for as long as he maintains his grip. He's obviously miscalculated, underestimated the effect all this would have on him. In his present state, he's not sure he'll even be able to face the boy, let alone string together a few coherent sentences. He hopes it's just the shock and that he'll be OK in a few minutes.

It could have been worse, he supposes. At least the boy didn't recognise him and take off like a startled rabbit. Mr O'Halloran doesn't deserve that, not after all the work he's done to set this up. The fact that the boy went on into the pub without even a backward glance and still hasn't come out again suggests no damage has been done. He doesn't suspect anything – not yet, at any rate. It's still on. He just needs to compose himself. Taking a few deep breaths, he looks at his watch: another ten minutes or so before he's due to go in. If he can just stop his hands from shaking...

He puts one hand in his coat pocket and fingers the folded sheet of paper. Eyes closed, he tries to visualise the words on the page.

I need a few seconds of your time, he begins. *You've taken so much from me – it's not so much for me to ask of you. Two minutes, that's all – two minutes to tell you about my wife. You owe her at least that much.*

My wife is a loving, decent Christian woman who deserves far better from life than what she has received. It is … it is…

He curses and takes out the sheet, which he unfolds on the dashboard. Peering closely at it, trying to decipher the pencil markings in the poor light, he finds the place where he's stumbled.

It is your great misfortune, and ultimately ours, that you have not had anything approaching her influence in your life. For that, if no other reason, you have my sympathy. If she had played any role at all in your upbringing, you could not have failed to be a better person for it.

Despite the evil you have inflicted on us, despite the fact that you've ruined her life and taken from her the only person who has ever really mattered to her, she would forgive you in an instant if she had the opportunity. If she were standing here right now, her faith is such that she would seek to convince you it's not too late for you to do something decent with your life. She cannot bring herself to believe that God has abandoned you and that what you did is no more than a random act of cruelty.

I do not have the consolation afforded by her faith. My belief in God was never strong and any possible connection was severed the moment you took our daughter from us. You should know that I do not forgive you. I never will. At my time of life I should be seeking ways of building bridges and tying up loose ends, but I do not have it in me. I am not a saint. I can assure you that my dying breath will be spent cursing the day you were brought into this world.

So I do not ask anything of you for myself but for my wife. And for my daughter. You took her life. Ever since that moment, it has become your responsibility to live it for her. My wife believes in the power of redemption. She is convinced it is not too late for you to learn from what has happened and turn the ultimate in evil into something worthwhile. For her sake, I ask you to do something positive with your life to make sure that our daughter's death is not the meaningless sacrifice it has been until now. You owe us both at least that much.

He looks up briefly from the sheet, his subconscious alerted to signs of activity further down the hill. Two couples have emerged from the Prince's Arms. In the pool of light just outside the entrance, they're exchanging embraces and handshakes before going their separate ways. He watches as one couple turns right, walking away from him in the direction of the car park. The other two huddle in the entrance for a few moments, casting anxious eyes towards the darkened skies from which the snow is still descending in flurries. Then they wrap their arms around each other and start to climb the hill towards him.

Even as he allows his attention to drift back to the sheet in front of him, he's aware of something at the periphery of his vision, something his mind hasn't quite processed – a flash of yellow that causes his heart to beat a little more quickly. He sits bolt upright, rubbing furiously at the windscreen with a gloved hand while the other fiddles with the ignition key to activate the wipers. He leans forward, pressing his nose against the glass as he tries to get a better look.

The couple are looming ever larger in his vision, effectively blotting out all but occasional glimpses of the main focus of his attention. They draw level with the phone box and his heart skips a beat as a hooded figure in a yellow kagoul steps out from behind them, pulls the door open and steps inside. Even with his back turned while he lifts the receiver and dials, there is no disguising who it is. The logo on the back, with its printed face locked in an inane grin, is all he needs to see.

And now the blood is really starting to pound in his head. The questions come flying in thick and fast. Who's he phoning? Why's he out here? Has there been an argument or something? In his agitated state, all he can think is that the boy is planning to leave. He's calling for a taxi – either that or he's ringing someone else for a lift. And he knows he can't allow that to happen – not until he's spoken with him. Not after he's lied to Dorrie about where he was going and spent the best part of a day just getting here. Inside, in a crowded bar, Mr O'Halloran can control things, remind the boy that the last thing he can afford to do is draw attention to himself. Then it will be time for his own entrance and Mr O'Halloran will have the photograph and the story he so badly wants and he can go back home and get on with what's left of his life. But out here there's nothing to stop the boy making a run for it and it will all have been for nothing. No, he decides. That can't happen.

He wonders what's happened, while he's been sitting out here, to make the boy want to leave so early. They can't have had more than twenty minutes together. If there's been an argument of some sort, Mr O'Halloran wouldn't leave him literally in the dark, would he? He wouldn't just stay inside, sitting on his thumbs while the boy wanders off. He'd have to do something.

Surely he'd want to get a message to him to let him know they needed to bring it all forward. He'd be at the entrance somewhere, trying to attract his attention. He leans forward again and peers through the windscreen for any sign of him. There *is* someone at the entrance but it's a much older man who seems to have come outside for a cigarette and a bit of fresh air. There's no sign of Mr O'Halloran.

He forces himself to calm down. Wait. Unless he's left with no choice, he doesn't want to mess things up by jumping in prematurely. Far better to sit it out, at least for as long as it takes the boy to finish his phone call. If he *is* phoning for a taxi or a lift, it's not as if it's going to arrive immediately, is it? He can afford to wait and see what happens next. If he's not leaving this minute, he'll probably go back into the Prince's Arms anyway. That would be the logical thing to do. The boy will be better off waiting in there than out here. Whatever it is that's gone wrong, it doesn't mean the chance has gone. If there's a change of plan now, Mr O'Halloran will still have time to let him know.

He snaps to attention as the door to the kiosk opens and the hooded figure steps out into the open again. Arms wrapped around his chest to ward off the cold, the boy skips easily down the hill, making light of the conditions. He appears to slip at one point but manages to turn it into a controlled slide as he draws nearer to the pub. He nods at the man who has come outside for a smoke and the pair appear to exchange a joke about something. Then the boy reaches the entrance but instead of turning he keeps going and Josef gives a silent scream.

His fingers feel as if they belong to someone else as he wrestles with the ignition key and fires the engine into life. This isn't how it was meant to be. The boy is now ten yards the other side of the entrance, heading away from the pub. The only thing out there is the car park and another line of cars parked on the verge. He's not waiting – it looks as if he's leaving now. He forces the car into gear and, in his anxiety, hits the accelerator too firmly for the conditions. The back of the car comes round in an uncontrolled slide and swipes the wing mirror of the nearest vehicle but he doesn't stop. No time now. No time. The boy's still on the move.

And the silent scream is no longer silent. *I need a few seconds of your time*, he's yelling through the closed side window. *You've taken so much from me – it's not so much for me to ask of you. Two minutes, that's all – two minutes to tell you about my wife.* And Dorrie is there in front of him all of a sudden, not the gentle, smiling woman who's done everything to hold things together but a younger version, a dim, distant figure at the end of a corridor, a long, antiseptic corridor busy with people in uniforms and bustling metal trolleys. And he can see her there, talking with a man in a white coat and he's about to call out to her when he sees her throw her head back in what looks, even from this distance, like despair, and she's slipping to the floor as the man reaches out to grab hold of her, only he can't keep her from falling, all he can do is prevent her head from hitting the lime-green tiled floor, and now he's running, running towards her and it takes him an eternity to get there, which is probably no more than five seconds but long enough – long enough for him to know he's never going to see his daughter again.

She would forgive you in an instant, he's screaming, as the car skids past the pub entrance and careers on in pursuit. And now it's Julie there before him, not the fourteen-year-old teenager who was taken from him but the miracle who came into their lives when they had long since given up hope and the toddler who used to sit on his lap and pull his cheeks around with such an earnest, thoughtful expression on her face and the little girl who was always there at the door, waiting to greet him when he came home from work and *You should know that I do not forgive you*, he's screaming as the boy looms large in front of him. *I never will.*

And he's on his way back up the hill, heading for the village and the freedom of the open roads beyond it by the time he reaches the crucial line, the most honest thing he has to say to the boy. *My dying breath will be spent cursing the day you were brought into this world*, he says, his voice trailing away into the darkness.

Somehow he doesn't feel the need to say any more.

February 2008: Ellen

Having assured Kate that she'd be in bed within the next ten minutes or so, Ellen remembered there was just one thing she still wanted to do. She'd been thinking of asking Kate what she thought but it had slipped her mind as the conversation drifted into more sensitive waters. Now she decided to go ahead with it anyway.

She picked up the card from the kitchen shelf where she'd left it the previous evening and carried it through into the lounge. Then she picked up the phone and started dialling. It rang several times and she was on the point of hanging up when a weary voice came onto the line.

'Hello?'

'This is Ellen Sutherland,' she said, her manner brisk and business-like. 'We met yesterday afternoon at the cottage.'

'Ah yes, Mrs Sutherland. Of course. Well, what a pleasant surprise. You know, I was saying to my dear wife only this morning...'

'I think we can do away with the pretence now, don't you? I know who you are, Mr O'Halloran.'

There was a pause. She could almost hear him gathering his thoughts and deciding how best to play this.

'Ah, I see. Well, well ... we have been busy then, haven't we? Or has our young friend Liam been less than discreet?'

'I didn't need any help from him,' she said, happy to take any opportunity to puncture his irritating self-assurance. 'Your act needs a little polish. He did his best with the hand you dealt him.'

'I'm sure he did. I must remember to thank him next time I see him.'

'That won't be happening.'

'It won't?'

'No, it won't. I don't think you'll be having any further contact with Liam Sharp.'

'And why would that be?' he asked, with more than a touch of amusement in his voice.

'Have you heard about the break-in at the cottage, by any chance?'

'Break-in, you say? At Primrose Cottage? Dear me, I'm sorry to hear it. Was anything taken?'

The disingenuous tone grated on her nerves. She decided she was going to enjoy bringing him down a peg or two over the next few days.

'I've no idea yet. That's one of the reasons I'll be going there tomorrow. I'm told the police don't have much to go on at present, other than the fact that some local resident mentioned seeing a dark blue Escort parked opposite the church at the relevant time. If Mr Sharp were to let slip that you drive one yourself, I rather think they might be interested to talk to you, don't you? And you know how *indiscreet* he can be.'

'Ah, so that's it,' he laughed. 'I suppose I've only myself to blame for bringing all these suspicions on myself, what with my little charade at the cottage yesterday. I can see where you're coming from but I can assure you, dear lady, that if you think I've got something to worry about, you're sadly mistaken. I don't know anything about any break-in.'

'Really? Now how did I know you were going to say that?'

'Your sarcasm is understandable, I suppose, but you're welcome to run any check you like on my whereabouts yesterday. I can account for my every movement after I left you. I went straight from the cottage to my place, worked there the whole afternoon, then spent the entire evening at a pub in Withington. The Mill, if you want to ask around. Lovely chicken in the basket they do there. Plenty of people around. I'm sure someone will be able to vouch for me.'

'Well, if you go anywhere near Liam Sharp, if he's suddenly dismissed on the basis of information received from some anonymous source, I'm sure the police will be happy to look into it. They might also be interested in your reasons for turning up here yesterday and misrepresenting yourself the way you did. Unless, that is, you decide pursuing him for no better reason than petty revenge is really not worth the time and trouble it's going to cause you.'

'Oh, don't be too quick to dismiss petty revenge,' he said, with an edge to his voice that had been absent until then. 'Personally I've always found it very satisfying. Even so, let's suppose I grant you that much – not that I have anything to hide as such, but generally it's not a good idea to encourage the police to go poking their noses into your business, however innocent and law-abiding it may be. But if I agree with you that I've no real interest in making life difficult for our young friend, especially since he's of no further use or interest to me – where does that leave us exactly?'

'That's something we can discuss when you come to the cottage tomorrow. Shall we say four o'clock? I'm sure we'll find plenty to talk about.'

'You don't think you're being just a tad presumptuous here? I mean, what if I decide I've better things to do with my afternoon?'

'Oh, you'll be there, Mr O'Halloran. I'll give you until five past and then it'll be the police asking you the questions instead. And by the way, while I think of it, you should know that I'll have someone here with me and will also be making sure several people know you're meeting us at the cottage. You'll excuse the paranoia but I'd rather we understood exactly where we stand.'

The laughter from the other end of the line was instinctive and genuine.

'My God, I can't believe you just said that. Are you serious? You don't think maybe you've been watching too many films?'

'Tomorrow at four,' she repeated, calmly. 'Oh … and one more thing, Mr O'Halloran.'

'And what would that be?'

'I never said, not at any stage, that it was *yesterday* the cottage was broken into. You might like to think about that, next time you're tempted to see yourself as infallible. Do sleep well.' She dropped the handset back onto its base and clenched her fist.

Yes, that felt better.

March 1974: Peter Vaughan

A quarter of an hour into his meeting with John Michael, he knows he can't do this. He's had nearly a fortnight to come to this decision, has in fact reached it several times in the past few days, only to turn round mentally each time and trudge reluctantly back to where he started. Even in the van during the journey up from Ashbury, he's found himself embracing both extremes of the same argument with equal conviction within the space of twenty miles or so.

One minute his conscience is telling him that John Michael has to come first. Not *David*. This is John Michael and his safety's all that matters. Any kind of deal with O'Halloran is a risk and he was a fool to let him come within a hundred miles of Inverness. Trouble is, he knows that tipping off his son wouldn't have worked either. O'Halloran has found them this time – who's to say he couldn't do it again? He's like one of those sticky burrs you pick up on your clothes when you walk through woods. And he's obviously getting help from someone on the inside. Refusing him now just means that next time he shows up, he won't be giving any warnings at all. No, says another voice – he needs to keep O'Halloran on board somehow, not go out of his way to annoy him. Once he has what he wants, maybe he'll find something else to obsess about and leave them alone.

And there's Ashbury too, and the new life he's managed to carve out there. If he crosses O'Halloran, that's over – no question. Done with. Overnight. O'Halloran will make sure of that. There'll be no time to explain it all – not in a way she'll be able to understand. He can't even imagine how he'd start such a conversation anyway. *Oh, by the way – I have a son. Never guess who he is...*

So he's reluctantly stuck with the idea of going along with O'Halloran. Let him have his precious interview for that damned book he's planning to write – the definitive inside story on JMA (those god-awful initials!) ... Every Parent's Nightmare. Maybe it'll buy him precious time. A lot can happen in a year or two. By then he'll have a clearer idea of whether or not he has a future in Ashbury ... with her. He may even have found a way to break the news to her, let her decide whether he's worth it with all the cards on the table in front of her.

But now, at the crucial moment, reality's hit home and the other voice is gaining ascendancy. This is his boy sitting here in front of him, and in all of his internal to-ing and fro-ing he suspects he's lost sight of that fact. It's no longer an abstract debate. This is flesh and blood – *his* flesh and blood. This is his son, Jennifer's damaged little boy, older yes but still just as vulnerable and more than ever in need of his protection. His voice may be at least an octave deeper, but it feels like it's still the twelve-year-old John Michael sitting opposite him, as if the previous seven years have never taken place, and that's when he knows for sure that there's no debate to be had here. He has to talk O'Halloran round. Somehow.

So at an appropriate pause in the conversation he invents an excuse, a phone call he needs to make to Ian, the friend whose van he's borrowed. He reaches across the table and pats his son's hand as he gets to his feet. He won't be long – there's a phone box just outside. He hands over his wallet and suggests John Michael might like to get some more drinks in while he's waiting.

The boy asks him where his coat is and he explains he left it in the car earlier. John Michael says he'll need something out there – *it's chucking it down* – and throws over his kagoul. He catches it and gives a reassuring smile before pulling it over his head. Then he heads for the door, followed at a discreet distance by O'Halloran, who has folded his newspaper and is on the move the moment he sees him get to his feet.

They meet in the foyer, talking in muted voices to avoid attracting the attention of others as they enter and leave. He explains what he's decided, calmly but firmly. O'Halloran is asking too much of him, he says – he can't go through with it. The smile that gradually spreads across O'Halloran's face is far from reassuring.

'So you're saying … what exactly?' he says, taking a quick look at his watch. 'We've come all this way, I've gone to all this trouble and expense, and now I'm just going to turn round and walk away with nothing, just because your conscience is playing up – is that it?'

It's the disbelief in his voice as much as what he has to say that strikes home. O'Halloran has no need to compromise on anything. Appeals to his finer feelings will be just so much hot air. If he's getting cold feet at the last moment, that's his problem. It's not going to cut much ice with O'Halloran. He does his best to bluff him, to meet fire with fire. He tells O'Halloran it's over. He can do his worst, publish whatever he likes. He's drawing a chalk mark right here. He's leaving now and taking his boy with him.

O'Halloran isn't fazed in the slightest. He peers round the edge of the door to the public bar, as if to make sure this is not some diversionary tactic designed to enable John Michael to sneak out through a side door. Then he turns back to face him and tells him it's a bit late in the day to find a little backbone. As it happens, he's parked his car in such a way that the van is blocked in so no one will be going anywhere until he says so. And besides, the moment John Michael shows the slightest sign of setting foot outside the bar, he'll be yelling at the top of his voice to let everyone in there know who he is.

'You think the two of you can make it out of here before they catch up with you, feel free to give it a try,' he says. 'You think maybe they won't give a shit?' He laughs, checking his watch again. 'Hell, this far north they'd probably give him a good kicking just for being English. But John Michael Adams...?'

He lowers his voice as the door to the saloon bar opens and a man barges his way through, carrying on a conversation over his shoulder with a woman in a blouse and short skirt. She pauses in the doorway to zip up a waist-length jacket and her husband, if that's who he is, takes the opportunity to let her know exactly what he thinks of her decision to invite her sister to stay. Neither seems remotely concerned that others are able to listen in to their argument. A blast of cold air rushes along the corridor as they pull open the front door and disappear into the night.

'Listen, what are you doing out here?' O'Halloran asks.

'What –?'

'Your boy – what did you tell him? What's your excuse for being out here with me?'

He frowns. 'He doesn't know I'm with you. He thinks I'm phoning someone.'

'Then go and do it. I'm going back to my table. You need to give it a while before you follow me in.'

He clutches at O'Halloran's arm. 'No. I don't want you talking to John Michael without me there.'

'You haven't been gone long enough. You go back in now, especially with that cape bone dry, and he's going to know something's up. Is that what you want?'

'No, but –'

'Then do as you're told. I'm not going near him till you're back and you've had a chance to talk some more, OK? Now go and make that call.'

They both look up quickly as two more couples emerge from the saloon bar and linger in the entrance to say their respective goodbyes. O'Halloran looks pointedly at the hand which is still holding on to his arm.

'I'll see you in a few minutes,' he says, shaking it off and opening the door to the public bar.

'O'Halloran?' he calls out, the plea in his voice making any further explanation redundant. O'Halloran turns to look at him, makes a phone gesture then disappears inside.

The couples in the doorway have separated now and the door starts to swing closed behind them. He reaches out to hold it open, then steps through into the chill night air, pulling the hood over his head and fastening it with the toggle at the throat. The snow is so much heavier now than when he arrived. O'Halloran's right about that at least. If he'd gone straight back inside, the dry kagoul would have been a total giveaway.

He starts to climb the hill, his thoughts following O'Halloran into the bar. It's only as he draws level with the phone box that he realises he does want to make a call after all. He's already rung once from the same kiosk, when he first arrived here. Now, even though no more than an hour and a half has elapsed, he wants to hear her voice again. He needs her to breathe a semblance of normality into a world that's threatening to spiral out of control. He knows she'll be on Reception for another half-hour at least unless there's been a run on the bar. It'll be easier for her to talk now than later, with so many people within eavesdropping range.

He empties his pocket of coins and spreads them out on the metal shelf in front of him. Then, having rejected the ones that will be of no use to him, he dials the number and tries to picture her all those miles away.

She answers in her business voice, the vowels more clipped, consonants with a sharper edge. She's surprised, amused even to hear from him again so soon but not displeased, it seems to him. She asks him if he's met up with his training partners yet and he's quick to steer the conversation towards another topic, one that doesn't make him feel quite so bad for having lied about the reason for his visit. He tells himself, as he has done several times already today, that this is the last time he'll ever do it. Ever. Once he gets back, he'll sit her down and tell her everything. If they're to have a future together, it has to start now.

She asks what time the race is tomorrow and he's not sure what he's told her before but plucks 10.30 out of the air. He says he'll need to shower, eat and maybe rest a while afterwards but promises he'll set off as soon as he can, late afternoon with a bit of luck. He'll ring some time tomorrow once he's got a better idea of when she can expect him. It's going to be the wrong side of midnight, he warns her. She probably shouldn't wait up.

She asks him to hold for a minute and he can hear her through the muffled receiver, dealing with a customer who's asking for his key. Then the pips start and he just has time to call out that he misses her before the line goes dead. He's not even sure she's heard him.

The temperature outside has reached arctic proportions now, made worse by a driving wind which is pushing it lower by the minute. He wraps his arms tightly around his chest and tries to break into a jog, which proves beyond him in these conditions. He slips and manages to turn it into a graceful slide, much to the amusement of a man who's watching from the entrance, a cigarette dangling from his fingers.

'Fecking cold, eh?' he says, coughing up a mouthful of phlegm and spitting into a plant pot just outside the entrance. 'Freeze the tits off Sonja fecking Henie.' He laughs and shapes as if to squeeze past him. Then, on the spur of the moment, he decides that he may as well retrieve his coat from the van since he's out here. He's going to be grateful for it later. While he's there he can check on whether or not O'Halloran was bluffing about having blocked him in.

He's aware of the car's engine almost immediately. It registers as a high-pitched scream and he imagines it must be an inexperienced driver, trying to ensure that the engine, having caught, won't stall. Then the revs settle down and he's almost blocked it out when there's a squeal of tyres and a grating sound as the car, an old Austin Cambridge by the look of it, scrapes along the side of another vehicle parked by the roadside. The idiot must have been drinking, he tells himself. Instead of slowing, he's tearing down the hill at a speed which no one in his right mind would countenance in conditions such as these. One bad patch of ice and he'll be flying off the road before he knows what's happened. Some people should never be allowed behind the wheel of a car.

Instinctively he hurries towards the stretch of pavement which borders the car park, some ten yards or so ahead of him. It's not alarm he feels as such, just the desire to get out of potential harm's way as quickly as possible. As he reaches the relative sanctuary of the pavement, he hears an angry yell from the man in the entrance and turns to get a clearer view of what's happening.

When the car mounts the kerb and keeps coming towards him, he has maybe a second and a half to react. In theory this might be enough. If his instincts are up to the task, a second and a half might just give him enough time to throw himself at the stone wall that separates him from the car park. He's fit enough to clear it. It's not that high – say, four foot, four foot six at the outside. He can do that – he's still in good shape. It wouldn't be a problem if the thought had occurred to him in time.

But it doesn't. Instead he backs away, hands raised as if he might somehow have it in him to ward the car off with a strong shove. There are no thoughts of John Michael or the future he has planned at Ashbury. No flashes of Jennifer and those golden early days, especially when she was expecting their son and the rest of their lives seemed to stretch out in front of them like a glorious summer's day. No time for anything but the present, which is bearing down on him like the past, with an inevitability he can't hope to outrun.

There's a flash of blue as the car scrapes along the wall. Then it lifts him, high into the air, turning him head over heels. If his eyes were open, he'd see the world spinning wildly out of control, telegraph poles flipping with him, the wind whipping at his hair and the snow beating an insistent tattoo against his eyelids. He's cleared the wall now alright. Four feet six is no problem at all as he soars and falls and bounces off the spare wheel on the front of a VW minibus, which has gathered an impressive layer of snow since he left it there earlier. Had his eyes registered anything in those final few seconds, he might even have smiled at the realisation that there was nothing blocking its exit.

8

February 2008: Ellen

The journey to Cheltenham seemed a lot quicker second time around. Having Kate for company was a help, as was the fact that the route was now more familiar. The most significant factor however was Kate's driving, which would have earned a few nods of approval from Liam Sharp. Where Ellen tended to be more conservative, conditioned by several years of having two small children in the back of the car, Kate had never suffered from any such inhibitions. Her version of conservative in built-up areas was 45mph. On motorways the needle frequently strayed the wrong side of 90. Ellen had long since given up commenting on it. At least it meant that even though they were much later getting away than planned, they'd already clawed back half an hour by the time they reached the offices of AWL.

Wilmot was waiting for them, looking as dapper as ever in the same light grey suit. His one concession to the fact that this was a Saturday morning was a Cambridge blue scarf, draped casually round his neck in place of the more formal tie. He ushered them both in, apologising for the temperature in the office. He shook hands with Kate and then went on to ignore her for the time it took him to go through the formalities. He produced more papers for Ellen to sign. She did her best to listen to him while shutting out Kate, who was pulling faces whenever he looked away. Eventually he was ready to hand over the keys. He took great pains to explain the purpose of each, despite her assurances that she'd be happy to find out for herself by trial and error.

He reminded her that the house was now secure, the broken window having been replaced the night before. Waving away her thanks, he assured her she would be billed for any expense incurred. Then he told her he'd contacted the police again after their conversation on the phone. Personally he suspected they had more pressing things to deal with than a ten-a-penny break-in but he'd taken the opportunity to inform them that the laptop was not in fact missing after all and need no longer be considered part of their investigation. His body language made it clear she was not forgiven.

When Ellen and Kate left AWL, they stopped at a small grocery store and bought a few items to see them through the weekend – tea, milk, sugar, biscuits (Rich Tea for Ellen, Hobnobs for Kate), rolls and fruit for lunch, and for the evening two large thick-based pizzas, a number of salad ingredients, a tub of Ben and Jerry's Caramel Chew Chew and two bottles of Cabernet Sauvignon. Then Ellen typed *Oakham* into the sat nav and they followed the same route she'd taken two days earlier on her white-knuckle ride with Sharp – Prestbury, Cleeve Hill, Winchcombe, Toddington. She warned Kate to watch out for the hidden turn to the village and they were grateful even so for the warnings from sat nav, so suddenly was it upon them. Finally they pulled up outside Primrose Cottage just before 11 a.m. and Ellen opened the gate, standing back to let Kate go first. She wanted to enjoy her friend's initial reaction.

She was not disappointed. Kate was every bit as enchanted as she herself had been two days earlier. She too wanted to do a complete tour of the outside first, sighing over the pergola with its rockery and natural spring, cooing over the view out across the fields from the rear garden, chuckling delightedly to herself as she sat on the swing hammock and rocked herself back and forth, for all the world as if the crisp, wintry air had given way to the height of summer.

'Jesus, Ellie', she said, swinging her legs high in front of her. 'Talk about falling on your feet.'

She was just as fascinated by the inside, trailing her fingers across every surface, examining one object after another as she passed. In the front room, she paused to pick up the photos for a closer look.

'Is this is her then?' she asked, pointing to the young woman at the lychgate in the wedding picture. 'The mysterious Eudora?'

'I guess so.'

Kate pointed to the man in uniform next to her. 'In which case this must be Mr Nash.'

'I don't think his name was Nash.'

'No?'

Ellen shook her head.

'It occurred to me last night after you'd left. Wilmot said Eudora had a sister who died a few years ago. Her name was Nash too so unless they both married brothers or somehow managed to pick out husbands with the same surname...'

Kate picked up the photo and studied it more closely.

'So, you're saying ... what exactly? Eudora was divorced?'

'Or went back to her maiden name after he died, maybe.'

'But why would she do that?'

'Aha,' said Ellen, waving her finger mysteriously in front of her face. 'Why indeed?'

Their conversation was interrupted by three sharp raps as the front door knocker sounded loudly throughout the building. Kate almost dropped the photo, managing to clasp it against her chest at the last moment. Ellen glanced at the clock, which still maintained it was ten past four. She promised herself she'd have a look at it later – maybe it just needed winding. Her own watch made it five hours earlier.

'I'll get it – you put the kettle on,' she said. 'Kitchen's through there.' She stepped into the cloakroom area, half-expecting to see O'Halloran as she opened the door. It wouldn't have surprised her at all if he'd tried to catch her off guard by arriving early.

Instead she found herself confronted by a short, squat woman with a cheery smile and bright eyes which twinkled from deep within the folds of her face. She was almost circular in shape, reminding Ellen instinctively of a Weeble doll Sam and Mary had given her when she was small. *Weebles wobble but they don't fall down.* She'd loved it, and wondered briefly what had happened to it.

The man standing behind her offered as vivid a contrast in body shape as was likely to be found anywhere, a walking definition of an ectomorph. He was wearing a brown overcoat and a hat, which he raised in acknowledgement the moment Ellen appeared before them.

'We saw your car out front and guessed it must be you,' the woman said, her voice burbling like water trickling over stones.

'Rose and Bob,' she offered, as Ellen inclined her head. 'The Woodwards – from next door.'

'Oh right,' said Ellen, smiling and extending her hand for each of them to shake in turn. 'I recognise the name. You're the ones who disturbed the intruder, right?' She smiled at the husband who smiled back with an uncertain glance towards his wife.

'Awful business,' Rose tutted. 'And you not even moved in yet. Honestly, the things that go on nowadays. I was only saying the other night, wasn't I, Bob? Time was, we used to leave our front and back doors unlocked and neighbours just walked in without knocking. Now you can't trust anyone. I tell you, there's no shame in people any more, Julie.'

'Ellen.'

'Sorry?'

'Would you like to come in for a while?' she asked, stepping back to open the door a little wider. 'We're just making tea or coffee, if you're interested.'

'Not for us, thanks,' said Rose, stepping forward none the less and manoeuvring herself through the doorway. 'We had a cup at ten. Next one's at twelve. We like our routine, don't we, Bob?'

Her husband removed the hat once more and stepped through after her, dutifully wiping his shoes on the mat. He followed his wife as she turned left and headed through the kitchen en route to the conservatory. Unlike O'Halloran two days earlier, they clearly knew their way around. Ellen offered to take their coats – *no thank you, dear. Can't stay long* – and introduced them to Kate as they passed her on their way through.

'Ah, brought a friend with you. That's nice,' said Rose as she dropped into the welcoming folds of the sofa with a contented sigh. Bob stood awkwardly in the middle of the room for a moment until Ellen invited him to join his wife. She went into the kitchen and brought a wooden straight-backed chair into the room for herself, leaving the rocking chair for Kate. The shortage of seats suggested Eudora hadn't been used to many visitors.

'Actually, I wouldn't mind a glass of water, if it's no trouble', said Rose. 'Straight from the tap'll be fine. Much better for you than that stuff they put in bottles nowadays. Bob'll have one too, won't you, dear?'

Ellen smiled and called through to Kate in the kitchen before turning her attention back to the Woodwards. She'd been hoping for something like this, the chance to talk to Eudora's friends and neighbours. Rose certainly didn't seem the sort to hold anything back.

'Well, as I understand it, I've got you to thank for frightening the intruder off,' she said, smiling at Bob to encourage him to join in. 'I'm told you came along just in the nick of time.'

'You don't know the half of it,' continued Rose, leaning forward and putting behind her a cushion she'd spent the past few seconds plumping up. 'Pure luck we came back when we did. Been to Tewkesbury, hadn't we? Our daughter, Tracy – she lives there. She's just had our second grandchild – Isabella, lovely little thing. That's why we weren't here to say hello when you arrived, otherwise we'd have offered you lunch or something.'

She wriggled in her seat to enable her to pull at the hem of her dress, which was caught up beneath her.

'Anyway,' she continued, 'Tracy wanted us to stay for dinner, only I don't like Bob driving at night – his eyesight's not what it was, is it, dear? – so we left earlier than we might have. We were just going past Eudora's gate and I saw this light, sort of flicking backwards and forwards like a torch or something. Bob thought I was imagining things till we walked back and then he saw it for himself. Told me to go home and phone the police while he had a closer look.'

'That was very brave of you under the circumstances,' said Ellen, addressing Bob.

'It's what you do, isn't it?' Rose continued, undaunted. 'Neighbours an' all that. I was a bit worried, if truth be told. He's not getting any younger, bless him, but off he goes down that path and, well, whoever it was must have seen him com-ing 'cos he took off out the back like a skinned rabbit before Bob could get there. Still, I gather nothing much's been taken, is that right?'

'So I'm told,' said Ellen, getting to her feet and walking over to help Kate with the tray she'd just brought in. 'They didn't get the laptop, that's for sure – I'd taken that back home with me. As for the rest, I'm probably not the best person to judge. I only had the briefest look around the other day and there's so much packed away in boxes. I really wouldn't know if something was taken from there.'

'I could have a look for you, if you like,' offered Rose, rock-ing forward twice as a necessary prelude to escaping from the confines of the deep sofa. 'I might notice if there's something obvious missing.'

Ellen held out her glass of water and assured her that wouldn't be necessary. The police seemed fairly certain that the conserva-tory was the only part of the house that had been touched. Rose took the glass and nestled back into her seat.

'Well, if you're sure,' she said, taking a couple of sips. She held the glass up to the light, as if checking for impurities. 'You know, you can't beat the water in this area. Same source as the spring in Eudora's garden – well, *your* garden, I suppose I ought to call it now. You should try it. Much better for you than all that caffeine. What's the water like where you are?'

'The water?' Ellen frowned. 'Well … it's not bad, I suppose.'

'Well, you look good on it, I must say. You look like you've recovered OK.'

'Recovered?'

'From the journey – such a long way to have to come.'

'Oh, it's not so bad,' said Ellen, taking a spoon from the tray and stirring her tea. 'And in any case, Kate drove, not me.'

Rose shook her head.

'No – not today, dear. I mean before. I suppose that's why you weren't able to make it to the funeral, having to come all that way and everything.'

'No. Not really. I'd have been here if I'd known about it. Unfortunately, by the time Mr Wilmot – that's Eudora's solicitor – by the time he got in touch, it was too late.'

'Oh, I'm sure everyone understood, dear. And Reverend Williams gave her such a lovely send-off. The whole village was there too, just about. Such a shame you didn't get to see it for yourself. Which reminds me, we've got a message for you, haven't we?'

'A message?'

'From Reverend Williams. He rang this morning and said he'll be over this way for most of this evening. I know he's going to visit Josie Killick after Evensong. She's not been well, bless her. Anyway, he said he'd welcome the chance to drop in for a while, if it's OK with you. Just for a couple of minutes. I said we'd ring and let him know if we happened to see you.'

Ellen looked at Kate, whose expression suggested that spending even a portion of Saturday night with a member of the clergy was not what she'd had in mind when signing up for this weekend but Reverend Williams was one person Ellen most definitely wanted to see while she was here. She asked Rose to tell him they'd be in all evening and he was welcome to drop by any time.

'He'll be pleased to hear that,' said Rose, clearly gratified by her role in having brokered the deal. 'He seems so keen to meet you. You'll like him – everyone does. I expect he'll want to talk to you about Perth, what with him having spent time out there himself … although he was in Brisbane himself. Is that anywhere near?'

Ellen exchanged a puzzled glance with Kate, who mouthed the word *Perth?*

'Seems to be all the rage nowadays,' Rose continued, barely drawing breath. 'When I was your age, people hardly ever left the village. Trip to the seaside once a year maybe, and that was it. Now it's like you haven't had a holiday worth mentioning if you haven't flown halfway round the world. Tell someone you had a week in Weston an' they look at you like there's been a death in the family or something.'

She paused to take another sip from the glass.

'Don't see the attraction personally. They say it plays havoc with your body clock. And Bob doesn't much fancy the thought of flying, do you, dear? Thinks it's unnatural. Still, you seem to be thriving on it, I must say. How are the children?'

'The children?'

'Did you bring them with you?'

Ellen frowned as she struggled to keep pace with the sudden shifts in Rose's conversation. 'No – they're ... they're with their father.'

'Ah, bless them. I don't suppose you've got a photo, have you? They must have grown quite a bit. Don't suppose we'd recognise them now.'

'Recognise them?' said Ellen, putting her cup and saucer on the floor next to her and leaning forward. 'I'm sorry, I don't understand. Why *would* you expect to recognise my children? This is the first time we've met, isn't it?'

'Well, of course it is but ... you know ... we've seen the photos so often –'

'What photos?'

'Well, Eudora's photos, of course – of you and the children.'

'She has photos of *us*?'

Now Rose was frowning too, as Ellen's confusion began to register.

'Well, yes. The ones on the dresser. In the front room.'

Ellen shook her head. 'The only photos in there are two old prints from, what, sixty years ago?' She looked to Kate for confirmation and received a nod in return. 'We assumed they were of Eudora and her husband.'

'Well, yes, dear,' said Rose, with the air of someone accustomed to having to explain the self-evident to everyone around her. 'Obviously I don't mean those. I'm talking about the other three.'

'There are no others – at least not in the front room.'

'Are you sure?'

'Absolutely certain.'

Rose put a hand to her mouth.

'Well, that's strange, I must say. They were always there every time we came round to see her, weren't they?' She turned to her husband for support and he nodded.

'You don't suppose the intruder took them, do you?' asked Kate.

'No way,' said Ellen. 'There were no photos there Thursday – not of us. I'd have seen them. If someone's taken them, it must have been before the break-in. When did you last see them?'

'Oh ... I couldn't say for certain. We used to pop in most days to see Eudora, just for a quick chat and to make sure she was alright. We didn't always go into the other room though, did we? It's so much nicer in here. So I suppose we wouldn't necessarily have known if the photos weren't there. Mind you, I'm sure Eudora would have said something if they'd gone missing. It's all very strange.'

'Well, they're probably upstairs somewhere. Maybe they've been packed away in one of those boxes.'

'I don't see why she'd have done that,' said Rose thoughtfully. 'She loved those photos.' Bob nodded silently alongside her.

Questions, thought Ellen. Everywhere she turned, more questions. More mysteries.

'These photos,' said Kate, pausing as she lifted a Hobnob to her mouth. 'You're sure they were of Ellen?'

'Ellen?'

'Of me. Me and my children.'

'Oh, no question. There was an old black-and-white one from long ago. You were a lot younger – in your teens, I'd have said. Still at school, at any rate. She was wearing her uniform, wasn't she?' she asked, turning to check with her husband.

'Then there was a more recent one. Your hair was a bit longer maybe, but it was definitely you. Very smart, you looked, as if you were dressed for work or something. Eudora said you had a really important job, a manager or something, so you always had to look your best. I remember you were wearing a white blouse and there was this necklace with a silver barrel on it, wasn't there?'

Ellen stared at her in astonishment, then reached slowly inside the neck of her jumper and lifted a silver chain into view. 'You mean, like this one?'

Rose's eyes lit up.

'Oh, you've still got it, then. Yes, that's the one. Very pretty, isn't it? And then, in the other photo, you were on a park bench near a playground with swings and there was a little girl helping you get a baby out of a pushchair. I think that was the most recent.'

The playground on the sea front. She'd taken the children there almost every day when she was on maternity leave for Harry. Had she ever posed for a photograph? If she had, she couldn't remember it.

'Mind you, Eudora said even that one was out of date,' Rose chirped up again. 'I suppose the children must be a lot bigger now.'

'They're ten and eight,' Ellen replied distractedly. Her thoughts were racing as question after question flooded her mind. She was having difficulty in marshalling them into some sort of order.

'Ten and eight,' cooed Rose. 'Is that all? Well, you take my advice and enjoy it dear, 'cos before you know it they'll be out the door and leading lives of their own and you'll wonder where –'

'Why did Eudora have photos of me and my family?' asked Ellen.

'I'm sorry?'

'Did she say who sent them to her?'

Rose looked blankly at Bob for a second, then turned back to face her. 'Well ... we always assumed you did, dear.'

'Me? No. Why would I?'

'Why would you?' Rose frowned, then broke into a throaty chuckle. Clearly she was as puzzled as Ellen by the way this conversation seemed to be taking two steps back for every forward move. 'Are you sure you're alright, dear?' she asked, concern etched into her features. 'Maybe the journey...'

'No, I'm fine, thank you. Just a little confused. I don't understand why she had these photos or where they came from.'

Rose looked to her husband for help.

'Well, we always assumed it was you as sent them,' he said, his voice surprising Ellen with its deep, broad, West Country burr. 'That's what Eudora told us. *Look what my little primrose has sent me*, she said.'

'Her what?'

Rose laughed.

'We thought it was so sweet, didn't we? She always called you that. *My little primrose*. It must feel funny having a cottage named after you. Don't remember what it was called when that actor fellow owned it...'

'Gable End,' said Bob, in full flow now.

'That was it. Gable End. Heaven only knows why. It hasn't even got one. A gable, that is. Unless he named it after Clark – before your time, dear. Anyway Eudora changed it to Primrose Cottage as soon as she moved in. We all thought she was expecting primroses everywhere in the garden, she said, amused by the memory. 'She could have called it Julie's Cottage, I suppose. Might have saved some confusion.'

'Julie?' queried Kate.

'I know – doesn't have quite the same ring to it, does it?'

Ellen held out a hand to ward off the inevitable follow-up from Kate. There were so many things she herself wanted to have cleared up, but for now there were limits to the price she was prepared to pay. She suspected discretion was an alien concept as far as Rose Woodward was concerned. If every clause and sub-clause of this exchange was going to be common knowledge throughout the village and picked over by everyone after Evensong, she'd prefer to keep a few things to herself for now.

She replayed their conversation in her head, looking for a way in.

'So, you and Bob,' she said, reaching down for her cup and taking another sip. 'You say you were here before Eudora?'

'Oh goodness, yes. Been here for ever, we have. Nineteen sixty-six we left Moreton. You ever been there, dear? Moreton-in-Marsh? Well, it's easy enough to remember 'cos it's the year England won the World Cup and they were playing one of their matches the day we moved in. Bob was in a grumpy mood, 'cos he couldn't watch it. Had the wireless on all afternoon, didn't you dear?'

'Portugal,' said Bob. 'Semi-final.'

'So that means we've been here for ... what ... over forty years now. Almost long enough to be accepted as "old village". And Eudora, bless her, when was it she came? Early Eighties? Not long after your father died, at any rate.'

Ellen nodded vaguely, remembering Eudora's password – *Primrose82*.

'And you saw quite a lot of her, I guess. You were close?'

Rose smiled, although there was a touch of uncertainty about it.

'Well now, close ... I'm not sure I'd go *that* far, would you?' She looked at Bob who backed her up as usual. 'I mean, we got on fine and all that. We like to think we're good neighbours so we kept an eye on her, like you do – you know, calling round for a cup of tea and a chat, checking to see if there was anything she wanted from the village store, that sort of thing. Especially when she started to get a bit shaky on her pins, poor thing. We're only talking about the last few years, mind you – she was amazing till then. You'd never have guessed she was as old as she was.

'So like I said, we got on well enough but I wouldn't go so far as to say we were *close* exactly. Your mother ... she wasn't what I'd call congregarious as such. Is that the word? She liked her privacy. I mean, what we've been talking about earlier, we didn't get all that from her overnight – just little things dripping through over the years, that's all. And then, she thought such a lot of your two little ones, didn't she? I think she was glad to have someone she could share it all with.'

Ellen put one hand to her forehead, trying to assemble her thoughts, a gesture Rose was quick to misinterpret.

'Oh, don't you go fretting about all that, now. It's not your fault. You had your own life and she never once complained about it. She understood how difficult it was for you. I'm sure she'd have liked to see more of you out there in Australia but you were so good with those emails of yours. They meant a lot to her.'

'My emails?'

'She used to print them off and let us read them. It sounds like you've got such a healthy life out there. I think she felt bad about not taking you up on your offer to let her have your back room. She knew how much you wanted her to move out there with you but, like she said, at her age you can't just up sticks like that and start somewhere else. I think she was afraid she'd be a burden.'

'Do you happen to know if she spoke to anyone else about all this?' asked Ellen, more intrigued than ever. 'Someone she talked to a lot?'

Rose shook her head.

'No dear, not really. Apart from Reverend Williams, of course. If there's anything you want to know about Eudora, he'd be the one to tell you. You never know – maybe *he'll* know what happened to those photos. I *do* hope they turn up somewhere. They meant such a lot to her.'

Rose glanced across at her husband, who was checking his watch, and nodded to herself. 'Lunch doesn't make itself,' she told them. 'I expect I'm keeping you from yours too. Unless you want to come round and eat with us? You're more than welcome to.' She rocked herself back and forth two or three times before struggling to her feet with the help of Bob's proffered hand.

Ellen thanked her for the offer and assured her they'd be fine.

'Well, what about tomorrow?' asked Rose. 'If you're here for the weekend, we'd be happy to have you round for Sunday lunch. Roast pork?' she said, dangling the offer in front of her like a bunch of keys.

Ellen thanked her again, explaining that they weren't sure just yet what their plans were. A lot depended on how much they managed to get done that afternoon and evening. Rose insisted that the offer be left open rather than turned down flat and Ellen escorted them both to the front gate. She waved as they walked off down the road, then went back in and closed the door, leaning against it for a few seconds, as if to gather her thoughts. After a few moments she went back into the conservatory where Kate was on one knee, flicking her way through the LP collection. She straightened up to face Ellen as she came back in and the two of them looked at each other for a few moments without saying a word. Then, almost on cue, both burst out laughing at the same time.

'They think Eudora's my *mother*?' said Ellen, spreading her hands in disbelief.

'Jesus, I was so afraid you were going to take her up on her offer of Sunday lunch. Can you imagine what *that* would be like?'

'How old was Eudora? Ninety-one? Haven't they done the maths? I mean, if she had me when she was ... forty, for God's sake, that would make me fifty-one!'

'Yeah, well, they did say you looked good. Must be all that sun and surf.'

'Please – do I really look that old?'

'Well, I've been saying for some time you could make more of what you've got...'

Ellen picked up a cushion from the settee and threw it at her, then dropped back into the sofa. As she did so, she realised her drink was still on the floor, beyond her reach, so she did a pantomime of Rose, struggling to get up.

'If I ever get like that, promise you'll shoot me,' she said with a sigh.

'You'll have to find someone else,' said Kate. 'You get anything like that, I'll be long gone.'

Ellen reached across for her cup and took another sip. It was a little on the lukewarm side now but still drinkable.

'Jesus,' she said, thinking back over the conversation with the Woodwards. 'Just how weird was all that? You think Eudora was having a bit of fun at their expense?'

'Depends on what she told everyone else, I guess. We'll probably have a better idea when we've spoken with this vicar.'

'You don't suppose Eudora said granddaughter and they just got their wires all crossed, do you?'

'Why? Would that make any more sense?'

'Well ... I'd feel a bit better about it for starters.'

Kate sat down in the rocking chair, resting her feet on the rockers and swaying vigorously back and forth. Ellen was dismayed to note that it didn't seem to make the same protesting noises for Kate as it had for her two days earlier.

'Well, you can rule out Barbara's side anyway,' said Kate. 'Her parents died before you were born, didn't they?'

'Her mum did. Her dad died when I was about twelve months. So she says, at any rate.'

Kate fixed her with the look she reserved for whenever signs of paranoia about her mother came to the fore. It was a well-rehearsed routine.

'And even if that still leaves your father's side of the family, this is still a load of crap. *Nanny Eudora?* Do me a favour. If she actually told them you were her *grand*daughter and they got the wrong end of the stick, there might have been some sort of misunderstanding for maybe a week or two but come on – they've been sitting here, having the same conversations for *years*. No way.'

'I suppose so.'

'And if you're her granddaughter, why just you and the kids in the photos? Where's her son? How come they didn't spend the past twenty years pumping her on that one? If there was something funny going on, you think Rose would have been slow to let you know just now? I don't think so. By the way, you've got –'

Kate waved a finger, pointing vaguely in the direction of Ellen's face. Ellen lifted a finger to her mouth and came away with a smear of blood, where she had managed to make her lip bleed. She had no idea she'd been concentrating that hard.

'There's still such a lot we don't know,' she said, reaching into her pocket for a tissue, which she used to dab gently at her lip. 'I mean, what's all this about emails I'm meant to have sent? And from Australia, for Christ's sake! And what's with all this Julie business?'

'I know – good stuff, all this. Any time you want to go away for a weekend, you make sure you call me first, OK? I wouldn't miss this for the world.'

'Well, there's got to be a connection of some sort. That much is obvious. You don't just leave everything to a total stranger, do you?'

'Unless this is just some sort of fantasy of hers.'

'So she what … just picked me out at random? How does that work? And the photos – if the Woodwards are right and she's got them going back to when I was at school, where did she get those? Who's been sending them to her?'

'You know what?' said Kate, springing to her feet so quickly that the chair continued to rock unoccupied for several seconds. 'We're not going to solve anything sitting here. I vote we start with those boxes upstairs. I feel a working lunch coming on. You up for it?'

Ellen smiled and held out her hand. Getting out of the sofa wasn't as easy as it looked.

March 1974: O'Halloran

O'Halloran shoulders his way through the crowd in the doorway and resumes his place at the table. He watches as the boy comes back from the bar, carrying a pint of lager and a glass of that awful concoction his father insists on pouring down his throat. Sad bastard. Must have shit for brains if he really believes he can back out now, after everything's been put in place. O'Halloran shakes his head and dismisses their brief exchange from his thoughts. Not worth spoiling the mood.

Some moments, it seems to him, should remain frozen in time. If there's such a thing as a benevolent supreme being, a concept with which he personally has never quite managed to come to terms, then surely something like this ought to be preserved in amber. Or even better, it should be permanently on tap, a memory you can sip and savour at your leisure rather than a dry museum piece you can only look at behind protective glass. Everyone should be able to pull a pint of fresh nostalgia now and then.

Because no more than fifteen feet from where he's sitting right now is John Michael Adams. That's *John Michael Adams*, for fuck's sake! This is not just any young lad – this is a world exclusive right here, and yet there's nothing to highlight the significance of the moment. No cameras, no crowds pressing closer to pick up every word, every nuance of the conversation.

There must be – he takes a quick look around – a hundred or so people in the bar. Once the story breaks, he has no doubt that in every office, every workplace within a plausible radius, there'll be ten times as many willing to swear on their mother's life that they were at the Prince's Arms the night John Michael Adams walked in with his father. They'll recall seeing the pair of them, sitting there at the table, oblivious to the music and apparently lost in each other's company. Some will remember queuing at the bar with one or the other and exchanging a few pleasantries while they waited. The more creative will claim they knew instinctively there was something funny about them – they'll remember saying so at the time. It was obvious from the strange way the boy seemed to be glaring at anyone who came too near. *You could tell, just looking at him – those eyes! He's a nutter.*

Losers. The reality is those who are actually here right now haven't got a clue. *Not a sodding clue!* They're far more interested in listening to the group performing onstage or chatting up the woman next to them. He's the only person who knows what's going on here and he's managed to put it together with no help whatsoever from the big boys in London or even journalistic minnows like the *CDG*.

Even now it hurts that they saw fit to toss him aside the way they did. He was the only person to get close to all the major participants in the story. This was his exclusive, a chance to make a name for himself and launch himself on to bigger and better things. He was very much flavour of the month when he engineered that interview with Martin Adams. Back then it was all *gosh, Frank – how on earth did you manage that?* But once the boy was shut away they all seemed to lose interest. The story could still have had legs if only they'd shown a little faith and support. Instead they'd done nothing but gripe about other stories he was supposedly neglecting and harp on about his reluctance to let go. *Obsessed*, they'd called him, as if a true professional could be anything other than driven. They're the reason he's never been able to get the recognition his efforts deserve. To them he's still the number one fuck-up who gets the call whenever there's a staff shortage or something as mind-bogglingly stultifying as a town council meeting to cover. But that's going to change very soon – *oh yes,* is that going to change!

He's pleased to note that this half-hour the boy has had with his father seems to have had a positive effect on him. He looked jittery when he came in, eyes skittering everywhere, and that wasn't in anyone's best interests. Far better to give a little, he thinks. Sometimes, when you've got someone on the floor and your foot is pressing on his throat, it's not a bad move to ease off and let him have that quick gasp of air. Never take away the hope – always leave them something to cling to. Personally he feels he owes them nothing. The boy is damaged goods as far as he's concerned, a little shitbag who should have been strangled at birth. As for the father, he deserves whatever he gets, but if letting them have a few moments to themselves oils the wheels a little, then who's he to complain? It's not as if it'll cost him anything – he still has his hands on the reins and can jerk them back any time he wants.

The first inkling he has that things might not be going strictly according to plan is when someone comes running in from outside and tries to push his way through the crowds gathered at the bar. He's shouting to be heard above the din and gesticulating urgently. A handful of people immediately disappear through the door and there's talk of calling for an ambulance, which makes him think there's probably been a fight outside ... not that unusual on a Saturday night.

Then two lads return to a table near by with reports of an accident – *some mad bastard* has lost control of his car, mown down a pedestrian, then panicked and driven off without stopping. O'Halloran hears this and he's out of his seat like a shot because he's been wondering why old man Kasprowicz hasn't shown yet and even though there are any number of other possibilities on offer here, he just knows somehow that something's gone wrong.

Even as he moves towards the door, he's sifting quickly through his options. What he really needs to do is get out there and assess the situation for himself but he doesn't much fancy the idea of leaving the boy behind with no one to keep an eye on him and he can't be in two places at once. From the doorway he can see that a crowd has spilt out from both bars and gathered in the entrance, where they can follow the drama outside without having to brave the worst of the elements. He looks back over his shoulder at the boy who seems oblivious to everything. He's tapping his feet to the music and doodling on the table with his finger dipped in a pool of ale that has slopped over the rim of his glass. If he's at all concerned by the fact that his father hasn't yet returned, he gives no sign of it.

O'Halloran curses, checks his watch again and decides he can't afford to leave it any longer. He takes one last look at the boy, then pushes forward, pressing his way through the crowd. Two minutes maximum, he promises himself. Two minutes.

The snow, he discovers as he steps outside, has eased off a little. The wind however has not. It's bitterly cold, slapping his cheeks and squeezing tears from the corners of his eyes. Even in a heavy greatcoat, which he's rapidly fastening to the chin, he feels the contrast between these raw arctic conditions and the warmth of the bar he's just left. He hunches his shoulders and tries to burrow down inside the coat, using the upturned collar to protect his ears from the icy blast.

The main activity appears to be centred on the car park away to his right, where a dozen or so hardy souls, including one complete idiot wearing nothing more than an open-necked shirt and jeans, have gathered just inside the entrance. Adams and Kasprowicz, he notices instantly, do not feature among them. He looks left towards the phone box and his heart leaps in anticipation as he sees the door swing open, only to sink once more as a young girl steps out and starts to pick her way carefully down the slope. Where the hell is Adams?

He starts to head over towards the group in the car park, aware for the first time of a sinking feeling in the pit of his stomach, an uneasiness whose origins he might possibly be able to articulate if given time to think things through. As it is, he's three-quarters of the way there before he catches his first glimpse of the crumpled figure lying on the ground, shrouded in a yellow kagoul. His mind instantly flashes back to his conversation with Adams just a few minutes earlier – *you go back in now, especially with that cape bone dry, and he's going to know something's up.* His heart begins to race a little faster. He hurries forward to get a better view, even though he knows by now exactly what he's going to find. There's no blood, at least none he can see. He can tell though, from just a cursory glance at the grotesque angle formed by head, neck and body, that Martin Adams is out of the picture now. And a thousand voices are screaming at him, each one telling him that this just isn't fair – it's all gone wrong, so horribly wrong. *It's all fucked up.*

His facial expression must betray the sense of shock because a woman on the fringe of the onlookers puts a tentative hand on his shoulder and asks if he's feeling OK – *was it someone he knew?* He doesn't answer. He's confused and alarmed at the speed with which control over events has been wrested from his grasp. Already it seems like a lifetime ago that he was sitting at his table, congratulating himself on how things had worked out.

Now the only thing he knows for sure, an urgent siren drowning out all other thoughts, is that the three of them, he, Kasprowicz and the boy, can't be here when the police arrive. They can't afford to be linked in any way with the body lying in the car park. There are going to be far too many questions for which he doesn't yet have answers. But if he can just earn a little breathing space, maybe this doesn't have to be a disaster. Might it even be possible to salvage something positive from the wreckage? At the back of his mind, an idea is already germinating – *tragic reunion for JMA and his father. Heroic reporter succeeds where all others have failed in tracking them down.* Something along those lines. But he'll need to think it through carefully from every possible angle and for that he'll need time. And first things first, he has to get the boy and the old man away from here. The further away the better.

He retraces his steps towards the pub, desperate now to get back inside. He breaks into a jog, not something which comes naturally to him, and within five paces he slips and goes down heavily, earning cheers and a round of sarcastic applause from some of those clutching pint glasses in the doorway. He hauls himself upright and brushes his coat, smearing a trickle of blood from a nasty-looking cut at the base of his thumb, but he has no time just now to worry about whether or not that might need a stitch. And as he looks up, he sees that the boy's already outside, hovering near the entrance. Something has clearly unsettled him. Maybe he's just curious like everyone else – or maybe a few whispers have drifted inside, a few more details about the accident, like the yellow kagoul perhaps. Whatever the reason, he's decided to come out and investigate for himself. He's peering about him, bewilderment and the need for reassurance at war with each other in his expression, as he steps out into the cold.

He heads towards the car park, seemingly unaware of O'Halloran until he steps across his path to block him with an outstretched arm.

'You don't want to go there, son,' he says.

O'Halloran knows the boy must be able to see the flash of yellow from here but there's nothing to suggest he knows it's his father lying there. He may be in shock, of course, but seems more like a distracted neutral observer as he turns to face this stranger who's standing in his way. Then he looks pointedly at the restraining arm, as if inviting O'Halloran to release his grip. Instead he tightens it.

'Listen to me, *John Michael*,' he says, whispering into his ear. And this gets his attention alright – this breaks through the mask in a way the sight of the kagoul apparently could not. The boy whips his head round as if fearing others might be about to descend on him and pushes at O'Halloran's chest, trying to free his trapped arm.

'My name's David,' he says.

'Yeah, sure. David Vaughan, right? And him over there, that'd be Peter and I'm guessing his name's Vaughan too. And I'll bet he loves fell-running and works at a pub in a little village called Ashbury on the east coast of England, which rather begs the question what's he doing all the way up here, right? How'm I doing so far?'

The boy looks up at him. He's so much slighter, a good six inches shorter than O'Halloran and appears more vulnerable at close range, as if several years younger than he actually is. It's hard to imagine how such an unimposing figure could have done what he did to those girls.

'Now, we can carry on playing silly buggers till the police turn up, if you like,' says O'Halloran, taking a handkerchief from his pocket and pressing it against the cut on his hand, 'only you might want to bear in mind that the media aren't going to be far behind and they're going to have a lot of questions of their own – and I promise you're not going to like them. And at some stage you're going to realise how much easier this would have been if you'd just done what I said right from the outset instead of wasting valuable time. So, you want to stop pissing me about and listen to what I have to say?'

The boy stops struggling and stares at him. He feels he can afford to loosen his grip.

'Who are you?'

'I'm a friend of your father's. He brought me here with him.'

'Unh unh.' The boy shakes his head disbelievingly.

O'Halloran sighs and raises his eyebrows, his patience sorely tested. 'OK – how about this? He was going to come up by train but changed his mind at the last minute because he managed to borrow a mate's minibus. He's only got this evening 'cos he couldn't get any longer off work. As far as they're concerned back at the pub, he's away on a training weekend for one of his fell races. Am I getting through yet?'

'Why did he bring you with him?'

'No time for that now. You can ask all the questions you want the moment we've got you out of here and somewhere safe.'

The boy shakes his head.

'I'm not going anywhere with you – I don't know you.'

O'Halloran gives him his best condescending smile.

'Listen,' he says, putting a huge paw on the boy's shoulder and stooping slightly to look him in the eye. 'There's no time to piss about here, OK? You think you're better off waiting to be picked up by your security people, then fine – you go ahead. But just ask yourself one question before you make a very big mistake.' He pauses for maximum effect, then leans forward to whisper in his ear again. 'How d'you think they knew where to find you?'

'What do you …? I don't understand.'

O'Halloran waves a hand in the general direction of the car park.

'You think this was an accident? How many people are here at the moment, d'you reckon? Couple of hundred maybe? And out of all these people, it's your father who's been run down. You think that's a coincidence?'

The boy's eyes seem clouded with uncertainty.

'I don't know…'

'And whoever was driving is in such a panic he decides not to stop, which is nice and convenient because – surprise, surprise – that means there's no one here to explain what happened and why. That's a coincidence too, right? Well, let me give you another one to chew on. When he left the pub, your old man was wearing a cape which you brought in yourself, right? Think about it – thick snow, lousy visibility, he's probably got the hood up. Who d'you reckon they thought was wearing the cape? Eh?' He looks around quickly to reinforce the idea that someone may be watching them. 'Look,' he continues, recognising the need to embroider things into a more convincing weave. 'I told you your father brought me here for a reason, right? Well, I'm a private investigator, OK? He contacted me a couple of weeks ago and asked for my help.'

The boy studies him closely as if trying to decide just how likely this might be.

'Your help with what?'

'He was worried. He didn't trust the authorities, thought there might be a leak somewhere. He said he was being followed and was worried about meeting up with you in case it put you in danger. He asked me to drive up a few car lengths behind him just to make sure. And now, first time you two get together ...' He spreads his hands to invite the boy to work it out for himself. 'Look, I don't blame you for being suspicious but right now the only thing that should matter is getting you out of here before anyone realises who you really are. You either come with me or stay here and try to sort it out on your own, in which case good luck to you, 'cos I reckon you're going to need it by the bucket load. Like I say, son – up to you, only I've got myself to think about too and no way am I hanging around here for ever...'

He waits for what must be three or four seconds, although it seems much longer. Then he turns on his heel and starts to walk away, counting the steps. He reaches *eight* before he hears the boy say 'Wait.' He turns to face him.

'How do I know I can trust you?' the boy asks, still making no move to close the gap. O'Halloran shrugs his shoulders.

'Honestly?' he says, taking his wallet from his coat pocket and removing a card, which he holds out in front of him. 'You don't. But I'd say you sure as hell need help from *someone*.'

There's a moment's indecision when O'Halloran feels that everything is in the balance. Then the boy steps forward and takes the card from his fingers. *Trevor Bassey*, he reads: *Private Investigator*. An address in Skegness. He hands it back.

'So where are we going?' he asks.

O'Halloran does his best to disguise the surge of relief. 'My car's up here,' he says.

He bundles the boy into the back of the car, covering him with a blanket, then tells him to wait there.

One down, he thinks to himself. *Now for old man Kasprowicz.*

February 2008: Ellen

The photos turned up almost immediately. They were lying near the top of the first box they opened, the frames wrapped in tea towels for protection. Ellen uncovered them carefully and studied each in turn, sitting on the floor in the spare room with Kate alongside her.

The first one was the most recent. Ellen instantly recognised the playground on the sea front, which had been like a home from home during her two brief spells on maternity leave. It was pretty much the highlight of the day, a chance to get away for an hour or so from the never-ending merry-go-round of domestic chores and baby paraphernalia that threatened to drown her. It was like a reminder that somewhere out there was a life, waiting for her to reclaim it.

She examined the photo more closely to get a sense of when it might have been taken. Harry was strapped into Megan's old pushchair, which meant he couldn't have been more than six to nine months maximum because she'd bought a brand-new one not long afterwards. The wretched thing was more trouble than it was worth – one of the wheels had a habit of locking without warning, causing it to pull suddenly to the right. And Harry had hated it, created hell for as long as he was trapped in it. He developed this less than endearing habit of arching his back every time she tried to fasten the straps, then went stiff as a board, his features screwed into a furious scowl. If she managed to get one arm in, he'd yank it free the moment she turned her attention to the other one. It was easier with Jack there but he rarely came to the playground. *Writing time,* he always used to say, the moment she reached for their coats. *Only chance I get. You have a nice time, you hear?*

And Megan certainly hadn't reached her third birthday yet, she decided. She was still wearing the Barney jacket which they somehow contrived to leave behind at the Adventure Warehouse after her party and never saw again. That must make it early 2000 then.

So who was it, no more than twenty feet away, taking the photo without her even realising? Ellen knew instinctively that she hadn't posed for it. She wasn't keen on that sort of thing at the best of times, but in this photo her hair had been blown into oblivion and her mouth was wide open, probably just calling innocently to the children but looking for all the world as if she was screaming abuse at them. She might not be photogenic but she could do a whole lot better than that with a bit of warning.

Maybe it was Jack after all, she conceded. He might have taken it on one of his rare forays into concerned parenting but if that was the case, why had she never seen it till now? And how had it ended up here, wrapped in a tea towel in a packing chest in Eudora's spare room?

She turned her attention to the second photo and recognised it straightaway. She knew exactly when this one was taken. When she came back from Sussex with a first-class degree in June 1995 to start full-time at Langmere, Sam was determined to make a big thing of it. The local press, usually happy to oblige whenever he came to call, were quick to respond – full-page spread, a head-and-shoulders photo taking up at least a quarter of it. *The new generation at Langmere.*

She'd hated the attention at the time and squirmed her way through the photo shoot, but had to admit that the end result was unusually respectable. Flattering even. She looked professional, quietly confident that the future held nothing but blue skies. Twelve months down the road, she and Jack would be married. Within three years they'd already have two children and the long, irreversible slide in their relationship, which in truth was probably already well under way, would be gathering pace. She felt a moment of tenderness for this wide-eyed innocent and wished there were some way she could protect her from what was to come. She looked closely again at the unassuming smile, as if searching for any hint of doubt, but if there was anything there, she found no trace of it.

She was sure she must have a copy of this photo at home somewhere although she couldn't remember seeing it for some time. Again, she had no explanation for the fact that Eudora had a copy of her own.

The real surprise though was the third photo.

'Pretty girl,' said Kate.

'Mmm.'

'Who is she?'

'No idea.'

She was surprised the Woodwards could ever have imagined it might be her. There were very few points of comparison with the other two photos, if any. This girl was far too pretty and her cheekbones lent a definition to her face that Ellen could only appreciate with a sigh. At that age she had been gawky and plain. She was in her mid-teens before she'd come under the modernising influence of Kate, who was responsible for introducing her to the basic principles of make-up, fashion sense and street cred, as if determined to drag her single-handedly out of the 1950s. The girl in this photo, by way of contrast, carried about her a self-awareness that Ellen had lacked at that age and for some time afterwards.

Apart from the fact that the girl didn't look much like her, the photo anyway appeared far too dated. Ellen had one somewhere at home of herself when she was about this age – a glossy colour print of herself on the beach with Bess, the retriever she often used to walk for Sam and Mary. There was nothing on this third photo to say when it was taken but the faded quality of the print suggested the 1950s or '60s, a good twenty or thirty years before Ellen herself would have been that age. Quite how the Woodwards never managed to spot the anomaly for themselves, she couldn't imagine.

'Is this the mysterious Julie then?' asked Kate.

Ellen nodded. *My little primrose.*

There were other photos, lower down in the same box, but none of these had been framed. Two large albums with brown covers held some of them, the rest were loose in an A4 envelope. They tackled the albums first. One contained a set of wedding photos, all of them variations on the two pictures on the shelf in the front room. Eudora and her husband had been snapped individually, together and with several combinations of family and friends. The photographer clearly preferred the lych-gate as a backdrop but some had been taken in the porch of the church and also a few indoors at the reception. Ellen turned the pages carefully, hoping with each new photo for some clue as to where she herself fitted into this mystery. Against all logic, she found herself checking each close-up of Eudora for any vague resemblance to her own features but found none that stood up to scrutiny.

The second album was devoted totally to the girl – Julie. There were something in the region of thirty photos, most of them in black and white. The earliest ones had been taken in the hospital, and then at a family gathering which Ellen took to be the christening. Then they followed her from infancy through the toddler stage and into childhood, where her features already hinted at the devastating prettiness that would eventually radiate from the framed photo. Eudora, or someone at least, had taken to writing labels under each photo after a while. First day at primary school. Seventh birthday. Boscombe cliffs July '61. Josef and Julie '61. Nativity play '62. First day at secondary school.

The final photo was not that dissimilar to the framed one. Julie had been caught in the act of raising a spoon to her mouth and turned, mouth open, towards the camera. Underneath it

Eudora had written *Birthday girl,* '66. After that, there was nothing, just several blank pages. Ellen and Kate exchanged glances but said nothing.

Having gone through all the loose photos as well, Ellen and Kate spent the next two hours emptying and repacking crate after crate of books, clothing and miscellaneous papers, working their way through their packed lunch as they did so. Their task was made considerably easier by Eudora's apparent love of order, with every scrap of paper tucked away in a relevant manila folder. The problem was the sheer volume of it – Eudora had clearly been a squirrel, hoarding everything that came her way rather than risk binning something she might need later. There were bank statements and utility bills dating back over twenty years to the time she'd first moved into Primrose Cottage. It took only a few folders before they lost patience.

The business correspondence files seemed a more likely source of information but although they made a modest contribution to their understanding of Eudora's day-to-day life in Oakham, they provided nothing that went any way towards explaining her decision to leave the cottage to Ellen. In fact, what was more significant was what they did *not* find. For instance, there were several letters from AWL, usually from Derek Wilmot himself, but not one of these made any reference to an investigation carried out on her behalf by the SJM Agency. Nor, indeed, was there a single sheet of paper from the latter which, given the relative triviality of much that *had* been retained and filed away, surely had to mean something.

The private correspondence file was disappointingly thin – either it had been similarly pruned or Eudora's letter writing had tailed off in recent years. The only letters she'd kept were family ones, divided into three separate packs, each secured with an elastic band. One pack contained around twenty letters, all dated between June 1982 and March 2001 and each one signed *your loving sister, Emily*. They were perfunctory affairs, little more than updates, brief sketches of a spinster's life in Northampton and of no great interest to anyone – including, Ellen imagined, Eudora herself. It was routine correspondence, seemingly born of a sense of obligation rather than any genuine desire to communicate. Sisters they may have been, but there was little to suggest they'd been particularly close.

The second stack consisted of just three letters from Eudora's mother. The first was written in 1961 and appeared to be an attempt at some sort of reconciliation, following the death of Eudora's father. The next contained further entreaties, urging Eudora to reconsider and the final one was a terse acceptance of their irreconcilable differences. It was couched in language that vividly highlighted the rift between the two women. Ellen had no way of knowing for sure but she would have been prepared to wager a tidy sum that Eudora's mother never got to see her granddaughter.

By mid-afternoon they'd cleared most of the crates and were beginning to doubt that there was anything left which would shed more light on things. Despite the three-bar heater which Kate had brought through from Eudora's bedroom, it was uncomfortably cold upstairs and any excitement which had carried them through the early stages of the work was rapidly draining away. When the sound of the door knocker clattered through the house once more, they were more than ready for a break.

Ellen pointed to her watch as they made their way carefully down the twisting staircase. O'Halloran was early – as predicted.

March 1974: O'Halloran

The old man's not here ... and with that simple statement of fact comes the grudging acknowledgement that he's known all along. Since that first flash of yellow, to be precise.

He's been averting his gaze from a reality he doesn't feel equipped to deal with just now, scuttling from group to group, hoping against hope that Kasprowicz will be there among the onlookers. He's checked every car, been through both bars twice, including the men's toilets, and checked outside again, calling the old man by name with an increasingly anxious edge to his voice. And it's only now, having run out of alternative explanations, that he's ready to face facts. *If it looks like shit and smells like shit...*

He's obviously misjudged Kasprowicz. Never thought for one moment he'd be capable of something like this. Phil Bingham, maybe – he's a loose cannon, which is why he's had nothing to do with him. But Kasprowicz? No way.

Now's not the time though for self-recrimination. All that matters at this precise minute is getting back to the boy and getting the hell away from here, the sooner the better. He has no idea what bullshit story he's going to feed him, but he can worry about that in the car, make it up as he goes along. That's what he's always been good at, thinking on his feet.

Next priority will be to establish exactly what happened here. His initial optimism about saving the story has quickly evaporated and he needs to know just how much trouble he might be in. Under different circumstances he might appreciate the irony of it all. If this gets out, there won't be a person this side of Timbuktu who won't have heard of Frank O'Halloran, which was pretty much the idea going in. But he knows how these things work – the focus now is not going to be on the unbelievable job he did in tracking down John Michael Adams. Instead his actions are going to be put under the microscope by less talented hacks who would give their right arm for such a story and who resent like hell the fact that he's beaten them to it. There are going to be questions about his role in all of this – after all, he's the one who put the whole thing together and made it possible for Kasprowicz to take his revenge on an innocent man. He's going to come across as some sort of shameless opportunist, prepared to endanger the lives of others for the sake of a few moments of fame for himself. At best he'll emerge as naive and irresponsible, a stumbling buffoon, out of his depth. *No way that's going to happen.*

One step at a time, he thinks. First get the boy back to the hotel. Then, if he can get to Kasprowicz before he's picked up by the authorities or turns himself in, there are still ways he can salvage something out of this. He just needs the chance to talk with him and make sure they get their stories straight … that and maybe a bit of luck thrown in too.

And he's no more than twenty yards from the car when it dawns on him that the rear door is hanging wide open.

February 2008: Ellen

Apparently O'Halloran didn't do shamefaced. If Ellen had expected any degree of contrition or imagined that his demeanour might suggest embarrassment over his previous visit, she'd have been disappointed. From the moment she opened the door to him, she was struck by the self-assurance he exuded and the condescending tone of voice he used to address both her and Kate.

This, he seemed determined to establish, was no meek penitent come to seek forgiveness. If she wanted to exchange information in a spirit of co-operation between equals that was fine by him, but she needn't think she was going to get anywhere with threats or intimidation. He was a professional and wasn't about to play second fiddle to a couple of amateurs. Kate took an immediate and obvious dislike to him but Ellen herself was mildly reassured to detect this touch of complacency in his attitude. She knew from their previous meeting just how careless he could be when sure of himself.

From the outset he made it clear that any questions about the break-in were strictly off-limits. He knew nothing about it and if strange cars had been seen parked at the end of the road, that was nothing to do with him. Yes, he'd been less than honest with her on Thursday. Yes, he had his reasons for wanting to have a good look through any documents that might be hidden away. But he hadn't yet given up on the idea of persuading Ellen to let him look for himself – he certainly didn't need to resort to criminal activity. That was the way things were and they could take it or leave it as far as he was concerned.

Ellen recognised a dead end and let it drop for now. Instead she switched her attention to Eudora. Clearly he seemed to feel there was a story worth pursuing here. What exactly was he looking for? O'Halloran paused for a moment, steepling his fingers in thought, as if deciding where best to begin.

'Not sure how far back you want me to go,' he said. 'What do you know about her already?'

'Eudora? Not a lot, to be perfectly honest.'

'What about her daughter?'

'Assume we know even less.'

O'Halloran was clearly unimpressed. 'Bit more specific, maybe?'

'Well ... we know her name was Julie.'

'Is that it?'

'And we're assuming she either died or Eudora lost contact with her in some way.'

'You're assuming?' Clearly this was not what O'Halloran had been expecting to hear. Ellen was thrown for a moment, wondering if she and Kate had missed something obvious. She glanced quickly at her in case there was anything she wanted to add.

'Well, we've looked through everything upstairs,' she continued, 'and we haven't come across a single photo of her from her teenage years onwards. There's no mementoes, no letters ... nothing.'

O'Halloran gave a deep sigh.

'I get the feeling this is going to be *some* pooling of knowledge. Is that really all you know?'

'Yeah, well – we're not all globetrotting investigative reporters,' Kate chipped in, clearly unimpressed by his tone. 'Some of us have real jobs. How are the garden fetes, by the way?'

'This has only just landed in our laps, don't forget,' Ellen continued. 'Wednesday was the first time I ever heard the name Eudora Nash.'

'So what about Eudora Kasprowicz?'

'Who?'

'Josef and Dorrie Kasprowicz – ring any bells?'

Ellen's thoughts turned immediately to the photo she and Kate had found earlier. *Josef and Julie '61.*

'That was her married name?'

'Yeeess,' said O'Halloran, drawing out the syllable to make his point. 'Still no bells?'

Again Ellen checked with Kate before shaking her head.

'Tell me you've at least heard of John Michael Adams.'

'Of course,' frowned Ellen. Even though the events dated back to before she was born, everyone knew about the playground killings. 'Every Parent's Nightmare', they called him. It was that sort of news story, one that somehow stuck with you, never went away. All it needed was another sickening act of violence somewhere, another Thompson and Venables to burst onto the scene, and the photo of the pale, sickly boy, glowering at the camera, would be trotted out again. There would be further speculation about the identity under which he was now living his secret life, always assuming he *was* still alive. False sightings were still commonplace. He was everywhere – a butcher in a village in Andalucia, a realtor in St Louis, a civil servant in Ottawa. Only last year there were convincing reports that a family on an Alaskan cruise had seen him, working at a trading post during a stopover in Ketchikan. Like everyone else, Ellen found herself absorbed by the whole affair, albeit against her better judgement. What she didn't understand was what any of this had to do with Eudora.

It was Kate who made the connection.

'Wait a minute,' she said, intrigued. 'One of the girls ... wasn't she a Julie?'

'Eureka,' said O'Halloran, shaking his head in apparent disbelief.

'She had a foreign-sounding name, didn't she?'

'Houston, we have lift-off.'

'Eudora's daughter was one of the victims?' asked Ellen. The first few tingles of alarm were beginning to make themselves known, undefined as yet but palpable none the less. The implications of Eudora's identity and, more specifically, the unknown history that presumably linked the two of them in some way, were risks for which she thought she'd come prepared. This however ... this was a long way beyond anything she'd been expecting. It was almost surreal.

O'Halloran seemed pleased at having been able to wrong-foot her so easily. He launched into a detailed account of the interview with the boy's father which he'd managed to arrange when he was still no more than a junior reporter. For her part, Ellen was barely listening. There were other matters buzzing around her head, far more pressing than his past successes.

'So are you telling me this is the reason for your interest in Eudora?' she asked. 'I mean, all this business with John Michael Adams was ... what, forty years ago? It's ancient history now.

I don't understand why you're still pursuing her after all this time. It doesn't make sense.'

'I'm not *pursuing* her,' sighed O'Halloran. He sat back, tugging at the neckline of his sweatshirt which looked as if it hadn't seen an iron in some time.

'Look,' he continued, 'when Eudora moved here she more or less cut herself off from everyone else. That's why she changed back to her maiden name. Kasprowicz was a bit too obvious, you know? Tended to stick in the mind too easily. She wanted to get away from it all, start afresh. I doubt if anyone here had a clue who she was and that suited her just fine. But she was always happy to see me 'cos I was the only one who'd shown any interest in her as a person, not just as the mother of Julie Kasprowicz. I was there when she buried her daughter, there when she did the same for her husband and she never forgot that. Didn't matter what I was doing, I always found time to come over and visit her. If she was here right now, she'd tell you – I was a good friend to her.'

Ellen suspected a lot of revisionism was at play here. Rose Woodward had made no mention of these supposedly frequent visits, besides which she hadn't forgotten his lack of familiarity with the layout of the house. She did her best to keep the scepticism from showing on her face.

'But what is it about these papers?' she asked. 'What is it you're hoping to find in them?'

O'Halloran sat forward, as if doing so might add more emphasis to what he had to say.

'Anything, basically … anything that will help me with the book.'

'What book?'

'On John Michael Adams.'

Ellen laughed. 'Another one? After all these years? You don't think the carcass has been picked clean by now?'

'Oh, I think people will want to read this one,' he said with a smile.

'Why? What makes yours so different?'

'I'm the only one who was on the inside from the very start,' he said, ticking off the points one by one. 'How many of the other writers managed to get an interview with Martin Adams? Not one. How many of them can produce transcripts of the tapes from that interview? How many actually bothered to spend time getting to know the families of the victims? The moment the fuss died down, they forgot all about them. How many of them do you suppose took the trouble to come out here and visit Eudora? Or even knew this was where she lived now?'

'Maybe they had the decency to leave her in peace,' said Kate. 'Ever think of that?'

O'Halloran shrugged her off. 'They didn't follow up on the story because they didn't really care about it. Not deep down. They don't carry it around with them the way I do. And trust me, there are things I can tell that no one else knows the first thing about. *No one.*' He paused, as if reining himself back in, calculating exactly how much more he wanted to reveal just now.

'I think you need to get a life,' said Kate, yawning ostentatiously.

'Let's go back a bit,' said Ellen, who was picking her way mentally through the threads of the earlier exchanges. 'You say you and Eudora were so close, right? If that's the case, where does Liam Sharp fit into this? What's all that about?'

O'Halloran looked a little sheepish for the first time but there was something about it which struck Ellen as slightly artificial.

'Yeah, well ... I suppose I've brought that one on myself. Not my finest hour, to be honest with you. But it's not how it looks, I assure you. Just a bit of impatience on my part.'

'Impatience?'

'Being devious and taking shortcuts is a bit of a reflex in this line of work. You see, Eudora knew all about the book. She was one hundred per cent behind it, wanted me to tell the real, human story behind the lurid headlines. I think she saw it as some sort of memorial for her daughter, you know? Only problem was, she didn't want to have to deal with any of the publicity that would flare up, so her only condition was that I couldn't have access to any of her papers until after her death. Problem was, I wanted it earlier than that ... couldn't wait to get started on it, to be honest with you. I didn't want to sit around, twiddling my thumbs, when I could have been doing all the prep work on it. I tried everything to persuade her, gave her my word nothing would come out until after she was gone but she wasn't having any of it. So I took a bit of a shortcut, that's all. Our friend Liam was meant to give me a bit of a heads-up if he came across anything that looked like it might be useful.'

Ellen shook her head. 'That doesn't explain the report and why it's such a big deal.'

'Report?'

'The letter from the agency Wilmot hired on Eudora's behalf.'

'I'm not sure –'

'I know you've seen the letter, OK? I also know you were in a complete panic over it. Why were you so desperate to find out whether you were mentioned anywhere in it by name?'

O'Halloran raised an eyebrow and tried a less than convincing smile.

'I'm afraid you've got the wrong end of the stick. One thing you should know about our friend Liam – he can be very creative and has a strong sense of what the person holding the purse strings might be wanting to hear. I wouldn't set much store by anything he has to say, if I were you.'

'So the report, if we come across it, doesn't hold any interest for you?'

'Oh, I wouldn't go that far. I'll admit I was surprised when I was first told about it. I knew Eudora was having a good sort out – you do when you get to that age. But she hadn't said a word to me about hiring any private investigator. You can't blame me for wondering what it was all about and whether it was tied in to John Michael Adams in some way. I mean, who else is she going to be looking for? Even if it was no more than an outside chance, you could understand me jumping at it.'

'But the letter makes it quite clear she was looking for a female,' said Ellen.

'Yes, but I hadn't seen the letter then, had I? That was later.'

This much, at least, Ellen recognised to be true.

'So when you realised it was me she was trying to trace,' she continued, 'did you know anything at all about me at that stage?'

O'Halloran paused before answering.

'You think it was you she was trying to find?'

'Well … who else?'

'I've no idea. I admit, I thought that too for a while, but the time frame's a bit of a problem, don't you think?'

'In what way?'

'Well, these agency people were looking for her, when, eight years ago? This Stuart Mahon character sold up and buggered off to New Zealand in 2006 and the people who bought him out have no records at all of any investigation for Wilmot or Eudora, which suggests it was all over and done with some time ago. She must have known for years where to find you, in which case why's it only now that she chooses to get in touch, eh?'

Ellen thought about it and decided O'Halloran might have a point. She hadn't thought to ask the Woodwards just how long ago the photos of her and the children had first appeared on her mantelpiece but somehow she'd gained the impression this was no recent development.

'But who else could it be? I'm the one she's picked out as her beneficiary – why would she do that?'

'You really don't know?' He seemed surprised at this.

'I really don't know.'

'Then the answer has to be among her papers somewhere.'

Ellen shook her head. 'We've been through more or less everything. If there's something that links me to her, I can't for the life of me work out what it is.'

'Then maybe you should let me help,' said O'Halloran, sliding a well-used notepad and a chewed biro from his pocket. 'Perhaps if you answered a few questions instead of asking them, we might get somewhere. You've probably seen what you're looking for and not made the connection. Maybe you just need a fresh pair of eyes. Take Ashbury, for instance.'

'Ashbury? What about it?'

'Well, seems to me there must be something that ties you to it. These investigators didn't just pluck it out of the air for no reason. What do you know about it?'

'Nothing.'

'Ever been there?'

'No.'

'Know anyone from the area?'

'No.'

'What about the New Inn?'

'What about it?'

'Ever heard of it?'

'No. Never.'

O'Halloran paused, as if weighing the merits of his next question.

'How about the name Peter Vaughan? Mean anything to you?'

'Peter...?'

'Vaughan. Ever heard his name mentioned?'

'No. At least, I don't think so. Why? Who's he?'

'And you're sure you've never been there?'

'Of course I'm sure. Look, what's this all about? What's so significant about this *New Inn*? And what makes you think I might know this Peter Vaughan character?'

'Bear with me. I need more background. Tell me about your family.'

It was the word *family* that jolted Ellen back into the moment, suddenly uncomfortable with the way in which the balance of power had shifted. Somehow she'd allowed herself to be manouevred into a situation in which she was the one filling in the gaps.

'My family and friends are none of your business,' she said emphatically. 'And I didn't ask you here so that you could ask *me* questions.'

O'Halloran shrugged his shoulders.

'So just how far d'you think you're going to get if I don't?' he asked, turning to Kate to see if she was any more receptive than her friend to the logic of his argument. 'Tell me you don't know more now after five minutes of conversation with me than you'd managed to find out for yourself. If you're not going to work with me on this…'

A troublesome thought had been nagging away at Ellen for the past few moments. Now it clawed its way to the surface at last.

'Maybe if you asked the right questions, I might trust you a little more,' she said.

O'Halloran frowned. 'I'm not with you.'

'Well, it just seems odd to me that here you are, an experienced reporter, anxious to get to the heart of a story, and you haven't even asked me the one question that would have been top of my list, if I'd been in your shoes.'

'Which is?'

'You've asked me about Ashbury and what links I might have to the place, yet you haven't said a word about Inverness, and I find that very odd.'

O'Halloran removed a handkerchief from his pocket and blew his nose.

'Nothing odd about it,' he mumbled nasally, rearranging the cloth and blowing again. 'The investigators wrote it off and started looking somewhere else – you've seen the letter.'

'But there has to be a reason why they were looking there in the first place, surely? You said yourself, something must have sent them there. I mean, we're talking about the other end of the country here. If they thought it was worth their while to trek halfway up Scotland and snoop around, you'd think they must have had pretty solid reasons, wouldn't you?'

'Like I said,' sniffed O'Halloran, 'it's a long way to go to come up empty-handed. If there'd been anything in that letter that was worth following up, I'd have gone there like a shot but I've got better things to do with my time than drive all that way on a wild goose chase.'

Ellen watched him closely as he fiddled with his handkerchief for a while before stuffing it back into his pocket. There was a touch of colour to his cheeks that wasn't there earlier.

'You see, I don't believe you,' she said at length. 'Maybe if you'd gone to Ashbury and found all the answers there … or then again, if you'd gone to the agency and found someone who could tell you everything you needed to know, then OK – maybe then I could understand it. But you clearly haven't managed to make sense of this whole business or you wouldn't be grubbing around here for answers. You say on the one hand that you get your success from attention to detail and going the extra mile, yet we're supposed to believe that you couldn't be bothered to follow up a genuine lead in Inverness when all the others went cold? Not only that, you don't even bother to ask me if I'm linked in any way – I mean, I could have family there. It could have opened up all sorts of new avenues of enquiry for you. And the fact that you don't seem interested makes me think maybe you're not asking because you already know whatever you need to about Inverness.'

O'Halloran laughed. 'Think what you like, young lady,' he said, the colour in his cheeks deepening.

'For the record, the answer to the question you haven't asked is no – I've never been to Inverness in my life and don't know a soul there. But I think you probably know that already too.'

'I can assure you that's not the case.'

'Well, I'm afraid I don't believe you.'

O'Halloran reached for his hat.

'In that case,' he said, hauling himself to his feet, 'I'm not sure there's much point in continuing. I've driven over here and given up the best part of the afternoon in all good faith because I thought we might be able to help each other. Seems like I misjudged the situation.'

Ellen walked across to the front door and lifted the latch.

'Yes,' she said, as O'Halloran stepped through the opening and into the cold late afternoon air. 'I'm sure you did.'

March 1974: John Michael

God only knows what's going on but one thing's for sure – he's not hanging around here to find out. Later, maybe … a bit of time and space to think things through and maybe then he'll be able to make sense of it all, but that's for some other time. Right now all that matters is putting as much distance between himself and this godforsaken place as he possibly can. And if Perry Mason over there thinks for one minute he's going anywhere with him, he can think again.

He's furious with himself for getting sucked in like that, even if it was only for a minute or two. The shock may have knocked him off balance but he knows he can't use that as an excuse. If he's going to stay ahead of everyone out there who's coming after him, he can't let anything distract him … *anything*. How many times has he been told that? Wandering around in a trance like he did just now is not an option. He's lucky the adrenaline kicked in eventually, even if it *was* a bit late in the day.

At least he had enough about him to search the car first chance he got. The fake ID cards in the front pocket are one thing – anyone claiming to be a PI is going to have a selection of those. But the folder wedged down the side of the passenger seat is something else altogether.

He says he drove up today but the petrol receipts show he filled the car somewhere near here early yesterday evening and there's a hand-written receipt from the Belle View Hotel for a two-night stay, starting last night. That's more than enough to justify his suspicions. Add to that the fact that the receipts have been made out not to a Trevor Bassey but someone named Frank O'Halloran, and *that's* enough to scare the hell out of him. It's not a name he's likely to forget easily.

He still remembers the article like it was yesterday – the shock he experienced when he read it and the sight of his father, pleading with him for some sort of understanding, insisting it wasn't his fault, that he'd had too much to drink and his words had been twisted. All those lies in the article, lies deliberately put there to make people think badly of her. Vile, bitter lies. No – there's no way he'll ever forget the name Frank O'Halloran.

But this is no time to be thinking about him. He needs to get well away from here while there's still time. So he slides out of the back seat and opens the boot, hoping there'll be a thick winter coat inside, maybe a hat and woollen gloves, something that will offer some sort of protection against the wind which is biting into his skin. The only thing he can find that will be of any use is what looks like the twin of the blanket O'Halloran's already given him. Not ideal but it'll have to do. He snatches it out of the boot and wraps it tightly around his upper body. Then he sets off and he's thirty yards up the road before it dawns on him that the roadside's not his friend. When O'Halloran gets back and sees he's gone, first thing he'll do is drive back that way to look for him. *Think*, dummy.

So what are the options? One side of the road is lined with open fields which stretch as far as the eye can see. The other's protected by a ditch and a hedge, beyond which there are more fields – but in the distance he can see a wood which will at least offer some sort of shelter from the wind, even if he can't stay there for long. No time to think things through. He slides down into the ditch, scrambles up the other side and squeezes through the hedge. The blankets catch on it and he wrestles angrily with them until they come away, and then he's off, stumbling across the field towards the first port in the storm.

He knows he's leaving footprints in the snow and that if they come after him, even without tracker dogs, he's got no chance. But there's no real alternative – he can't just stay here and wait to be picked up. If O'Halloran was telling the truth about anything, it's that he can't trust anyone right now, not even the authorities. This new identity of his was supposed to be safe as houses and yet his life as David Vaughan is over before it's even started. This new beginning that's been planned so meticulously and whose every detail has been rehearsed till he's sick to death of it is gone, history. He's going to have to start again. Only this time he'll have to do it on his own. There's no one out there he can turn to.

And it's as he reaches the edge of the wood and finds some temporary relief from the elements that it dawns on him this isn't strictly true. There *is* someone he can rely on, at least some-one who's always been there for him whenever he's needed sup-port or a friendly arm around the shoulder. And all of a sudden that race across the fields no longer seems like running away. It's starting to look like the first steps on a long journey that's been mapped out for some time now, even if it's taken him this long to recognise it.

He has no more than the vaguest idea where to go. South, obviously ... but after that is anybody's guess. Their conversa-tions over the years rarely strayed into the personal and those occasional forays have left him ill-equipped to track him down. But the professor's a famous man – how hard can it be to find out where he lives? He'll find him somehow.

And when he does, he'll know what to d-d-d-d-do.

February 2008: Ellen

Reverend Williams arrived the moment they sat down to eat.

Once O'Halloran had left, Ellen and Kate had spent the rest of the afternoon, working their way methodically through the remaining upstairs rooms. They'd emptied every cupboard, every drawer, sifting through the contents in the hope that their efforts might unearth that crucial detail which would slot neatly into place and make sense of everything. They found nothing.

The internet seemed a far more attractive proposition. Kate had brought her own laptop with her so they were able to work simultaneously, Googling the names Eudora Kasprowicz and John Michael Adams and trawling through the virtual mountain of information on offer. Ellen was taken aback by the sheer volume of it all. It seemed amazing that an event, which had taken place several years before the internet even existed, could have generated so much material. The story, for whatever reason, had transcended its moment in time. Horrific as they were, the actions of John Michael Adams had surely been rivalled and even outstripped several times since then, but for some reason the waif-like figure, glaring out at her from the same grainy photograph in more or less every document she opened, seemed to have hit a particular nerve, ensuring his place for eternity in the public consciousness. If ever a life was defined by a single act, surely this was it.

The more Ellen read, the more acutely she was aware of a certain lack of proportion in all of this. It was easy enough to understand how this might have come about – the act itself had been shocking and public opinion rarely needed much in the way of encouragement to turn against any individual who stepped so obviously beyond the bounds of acceptable behaviour. But there was something about the unrelenting tide of moral outrage levelled against the boy and the violence of the language in which it was expressed that simply didn't sit well with her. She had no difficulty in sympathising with the families of the victims. She was, after all, the mother of two young children herself and this was every parent's nightmare, wasn't it? You kiss your daughter goodbye one morning, there's no reason to suppose it's the last time you'll see her alive. Too awful for words.

And yet this same maternal instinct kept bringing her back to the photo of John Michael Adams. When all was said and done, this was an eleven-year-old boy. She'd seen the photo so often that her instincts, like those of everyone else, had become dulled by it, anaesthetised to the reality that lay behind it. There was a life here, she told herself. This was a real person, a boy barely older than her own children. She thought of Megan, the would-be sophisticate who longed for the time when she'd be allowed to go to Friday night discos in town and still took to bed with her the same Tigger blanket she'd hugged in her cot. And Harry, who would die rather than hold his mother's hand anywhere in town, yet couldn't get to sleep at night without the glow from his bedside lamp. They were babies still and her instinctive sympathy for the underdog made it impossible for her to accept that it could be right to heap that level of accountability on shoulders so unprepared for it. The idea that this boy's whole life should turn on one moment of madness seemed obscene somehow. There was a hysteria and a theatricality inherent in the response of the general public that made her think of small-town America. She fancied she knew a witch hunt when she saw one.

And Professor Carl Holmbach, whoever he was, clearly felt the same way. His name seemed to crop up at regular intervals, a letter here, an article there. His writing was restrained and dignified without sacrificing one iota of conviction that this was an injustice which needed to be put right. He was an articulate, determined champion of the underdog and for Ellen the logic of his reasoning and the power of his writing stood out like a beacon of common sense in a raging torrent of hysteria. She wondered whether she herself, if put to the test, would have the moral courage to swim against the tide of public opinion in the way he'd chosen to do. She doubted it.

It occurred to her that this man might be someone worth contacting, in the hope that his clearly obsessive interest in the Adams case might have unearthed some reference linking her to Eudora. These hopes however were soon dashed by the discovery of a *Times* obituary – Carl Holmbach had died in May 2001 from an aneurism. Another door closed, like so many others, long before it had been located.

At getting on for seven o'clock, they decided it was time to get something to eat. Through the conservatory windows, they could see that the heavy snow, confidently forecast for later in the day, had arrived more or less on cue, making Ellen very glad they'd decided to eat in. Being driven around by Kate during daylight hours was one thing. She didn't much fancy it at night, in sub-zero temperatures, on unlit country roads that presumably wouldn't have been gritted.

She decided now was as good a time as any to give the children a ring but couldn't seem to get any network coverage for her mobile. She wandered from room to room, holding the phone up at different angles, but just about everywhere inside the cottage seemed to be a dead spot. She went to the front door and lifted the latch, peering outside for a closer look at the weather. The darkened skies were full of it, not isolated flurries but a thick swathe of fat flakes which settled in clusters on her outstretched sleeve. The thin dusting on the lawn and the path leading up to the front door was clearly no more than underlay for the thick carpet to come.

Ducking back inside, she went upstairs and rummaged around for a blanket which might suit her purposes. Then, leaving Kate to make a start on the meal, she slipped outside and tiptoed her way down the garden path and through the gate, which was swinging to and fro in the stiff breeze. She fastened it behind her, then slithered her way over to Kate's car and draped the blanket across the windscreen and bonnet, securing it beneath the wipers. Then she let herself into the Toyota, which was so cold and damp as to be almost sepulchral by now. Here she was able to get two bars on her mobile and spent ten minutes talking to Megan and Harry about their day. Harry burbled enthusiastically about some zombie film he'd been allowed to watch, which would probably give him nightmares for the next few weeks. At least he remembered to say he was missing her, unlike Megan, who clearly couldn't wait to get back to her make-up session with Shannon which the phone call had interrupted. Ellen told her she loved her and managed to extract a perfunctory *you too* before letting her go. It felt like meagre reward for freezing her backside off for the past ten minutes. She wished like mad that she'd thought to keep the blanket with her until *after* the call.

As she ended it, she noticed that the signal had brought with it a number of messages and several missed calls. She toyed with the idea of listening to them but for one thing it was too cold to think about staying out there any longer than she needed to. More significantly, she could see that they were from Sam and she didn't feel too inclined to jump just because he'd whistled, especially if all he was doing was trying to keep tabs on her and steer her away from Eudora. She turned her phone off and slipped it inside the pocket of her jeans. He could damn well wait.

Back in the kitchen, Kate had put the pizzas in the oven and was well under way with the salad. Ellen put her freezing cold hands on her friend's cheeks and asked what she could do to help, only to be told to keep out of it. If she wanted to make herself useful, she could see to the drinks. She rooted around in the cupboards until she found two rather cloudy wine glasses and opened the second bottle of Sauvignon. Kate asked her to check whether the TV set in the dank and decidedly uninviting front room could be moved into the conservatory, where they'd decided to eat, as there was some variety show she wanted to watch. Ellen had a look but, in the absence of either an indoor aerial or an external socket in the conservatory, the reception was so appalling they decided to give it a miss. Ellen for one wasn't too disappointed. There was plenty for her and Kate to discuss over dinner.

But they barely had time to raise their glasses and take a first bite out of the pizzas before the sharp rat-a-tat-tat of the front-door knocker resounded once more. Kate groaned and shook her head. 'Don't answer it,' she said. 'Ten quid says it's Rose.'

Ellen smiled and got to her feet. She was pretty sure who it would be.

The most surprising thing about Reverend Williams (*please, call me Rowan*) was his appearance. Her only experience of the clergy had come from primary school, where the local vicar would turn up every year, just before the Christmas break, make a few waspish comments about how few of the children seated in front of him had crossed the threshold of his church in the preceding twelve months, and then mumble his way through the same passage from the Bible, starting with the decree from Caesar Augustus and culminating in the visiting shepherds. He'd been a frail, elderly man with a wispy grey beard, so unsteady on his feet that he surely could not have been long for this world.

Reverend Williams, by way of contrast, was young – or not much older than she was, at any rate. He was also tall and broad-shouldered, more likely to be mistaken for a rugby player than a member of the clergy. He smiled as he introduced himself and held on to Ellen's hand long enough to wrap his other one around it as well. She invited him in, insisting he wasn't interrupting anything, and took his hooded jacket before ushering him into the conservatory, where he shook hands with Kate, switching his canvas bag to his left hand.

He was mortified when he realised he'd disturbed their meal and had to be almost manhandled into a seat. He told them he wasn't planning to stay, he'd only popped in to make sure they were alright.

'I don't know if Rose explained, but I've arranged to call in and see one of my parishioners this evening,' he said. 'She's not been well, bless her, and her family seem to think a visit from me might help cheer her up a little. But then I was aware you didn't know when to expect me, so rather than interfere with any plans you might have for the evening, I thought I'd just pop in beforehand and make sure you've got everything you need.'

Ellen thanked him and offered a share of the pizza and a glass of wine, both of which he politely declined. He checked his watch and said he had ten minutes at most.

'It's really just to show my face,' he said. 'I'm sure we'll get a chance to talk for longer some other time.'

His glance fell on the desk with the broken drawers, which had been removed and stacked in a corner of the room.

'I heard about the break-in, of course,' he said, with a sorrowful shake of the head. 'Such an awful start for you. If it's any consolation, it's really not that sort of village. I don't think anything like that's happened in all the time I've been in the area.' He smiled as the irony of his words dawned on him. 'I don't suppose that *is* much of a consolation, is it?'

Ellen returned the smile.

'Still,' he continued, 'I understand from Rose you had the laptop with you the whole time, so that's a bonus. It's a good thing you thought to take it with you.'

'I'm not sure Mr Wilmot sees it that way,' said Ellen.

'No,' he said, 'I can imagine he wouldn't.' The discreet smile playing at the corner of his mouth suggested he'd seen enough of Eudora's solicitor to understand the point she was making.

'Mind you,' he continued, 'what really matters is that whoever broke in didn't get his hands on it. I'm sure, in his way, Mr Wilmot's as relieved about that as I am. You must be desperate to have a look through it. I suppose you want to know the password?'

'Primrose82?' said Ellen, enjoying the look of surprise that flashed across his face.

'I'm impressed,' he said, after a brief pause. 'You know a thing or two about computers, I take it?'

'No, but I know a man who does.'

'Handy. So ... you'll have already read the documents, then? Only when I was talking with Rose just a while ago, she was under the impression you were still very confused about a number of things.'

'I am ... we both are. Which documents are you referring to exactly?'

He frowned at this. 'Well, there are two Word documents in particular. I know they're there – I've seen them a few times when they were still a work in progress. You can't miss them, they're named after you. *Ellen 1* and *Ellen 2.*'

Ellen looked at Kate, who shrugged her shoulders. Then she turned her attention back to her visitor.

'No,' she said, shaking her head. 'There's nothing there with my name on it. It's all church business and day-to-day things. We've been through it several times – trust me, if it was there, we'd have found it.'

There was a lengthy pause while he took this in. Then he looked again at the broken drawers in the corner of the room and sighed.

'Well, if that's the case, it looks as if I owe Eudora an apology. I'm afraid I thought she was being a little paranoid but it looks as if she was right after all.'

'She was expecting a break-in?'

'I'm not sure expecting's the right word,' he said, pursing his lips, 'but she was definitely a bit anxious about losing everything she'd typed. It was such an effort for her, you see. It took her several days, so she really didn't like the idea that it could all disappear if anything happened to the laptop, which is why she ran off a hard copy. I imagine that's what our friend was looking for, don't you?' He nodded again at the drawers.

'She kept it in the desk?' asked Ellen, her heart sinking yet again.

'Oh no,' he said, a broad smile spreading across his features, as he reached into the canvas bag. 'She left it with me.' He was now holding two envelopes in his hand. The smaller one looked as if it might contain a letter, the larger one was much thicker. From where she was sitting Ellen could see the labels *Ellen 1* and *Ellen 2,* inscribed in a precise, elegant script.

'I only brought it with me as an afterthought, to be honest,' he continued. 'I was going to tell you the password then let you get on with reading the documents. It's only as I was coming out of the house I thought it might be easier for you to read it all from the hard copy instead. Lucky I thought of it.'

He reached across and handed the two envelopes to Ellen, who handled them oh so carefully as if fearing that, even now, they might suddenly crumble away to nothing. The possibility that all of a sudden, as if out of nowhere, the answers she'd been pursuing for the past few days might actually be within her grasp was almost too much for her to take in.

'You need to read the smaller one first: *Ellen 1*,' he continued. 'Eudora was absolutely adamant about that. It seemed to matter greatly to her.'

'*Ellen 1* first,' she repeated automatically, turning it over as if looking for clues.

'And I'd better let you have my phone number,' he said, reaching into the bag once more and retrieving a ballpoint pen. 'Just in case there are things you want to ask me later – when you've read it all. I've no idea how long I'll be with Josie but this is for my mobile and you're welcome to ring any time, OK?' He took the larger envelope back from her for a moment and scribbled the number on the reverse side. Then he looked at his watch and decided his time was up. If it was OK with them, he'd leave his car outside the cottage and walk up to Josie's place – it wasn't far and it might be easier to walk up to the farm than drive there in these conditions.

Ellen thanked him for everything and walked him to the door. As she opened it, a sharp gust of wind sent a flurry of snow into the hallway. The sudden change in temperature seemed to wake her out of the trance she'd been in since learning about the envelopes.

'Do you mind me asking,' she said, clutching his sleeve as he made to leave, 'have you read this?'

'No.' He sketched a brief, self-deprecating smile. ' Not the finished version, at any rate. I'd like to be able to claim some sort of credit for that but the honest truth is, Eudora and I have talked so often over the past few years, I'm fairly sure I know most of what's in there, so the temptation was never really that great. And anything she didn't tell me ... well, maybe it's because she didn't want me to know.'

'But you do know why she left me this place?'

'Yes.'

'Are we related in some way to each other?'

'Related? No.'

Ellen paused before continuing.

'Was she related to my mother?' she asked eventually.

This time he was the one who seemed hesitant. He reached behind his head and flipped up the hood of his coat. Then he wrapped his scarf firmly around the lower part of his face before he answered.

'I really think you should read the documents,' he said, his voice muffled. 'You have my number. You're more than welcome to call if there are other things I can help you with later, but Eudora went to a lot of trouble to get these documents to you. I'm not sure she'd have been happy to have me feeding you pieces at random.'

He reached out and grasped her shoulder, giving it a reassuring squeeze before stepping out into the cold night air. The snow was already several inches thick by now and his feet left clear prints that seemed unlikely to be there in an hour or so. She watched him trudge his way up the hill until the cold drove her back indoors, where Kate was reheating the pizzas in the microwave. When she'd finished she brought them back through to the conservatory and sat down next to Ellen.

'How d'you want to play this?' she asked. 'You want to read these on your own first?'

Ellen looked at the envelopes on the sofa next to her. She took the plate that Kate was holding out to her and rested it on a cushion on her lap.

'I can go and freeze my backside off upstairs if you want a bit of privacy,' Kate continued. 'Of course, I may never talk to you again but...'

Ellen looked across at the drawers and frowned.

'O'Halloran was the one who broke in here, right?' she asked.

'Right.'

'So do we assume this was what he was looking for?'

'Makes sense to me. '

'So how did he know about it?'

'I'm not with you.'

'What made him think there was a hard copy? In fact, how did he know Eudora had typed these documents in the first place?'

Kate shrugged her shoulders. 'I dunno. Maybe she let something slip. Who knows? He's a reporter.'

'And who got rid of the file on the laptop?'

'He did.'

'When?'

'When he broke in and ...' Kate's voice faltered.

'Exactly. The laptop wasn't here. So what are we saying? He wiped it some other time?'

'He must have.'

'But when? I mean, if it was after Eudora died, he'd have had to break in, wouldn't he? But no one's said anything about a previous burglary. And anyway, if he'd already broken in once, why would he need to come back last week and do it again? And why wouldn't he just take the laptop with him the first time instead of deleting the documents? Come to that, how the hell did he know the password to get into it in the first place?'

Kate took a sip from her wine glass and waved a slice of pizza at the envelopes.

'Well, maybe it'll make a bit more sense once you've opened those,' she said.

Ellen picked them up and put the larger one on the arm of the sofa. She held the one labelled *Ellen 1* in the palm of her hand as if weighing it, then patted the space next to her.

'OK,' she said. 'You ready for this?'

PART THREE

THE DISCOVERY

9

August 2007: Ellen 1

Dearest Ellen,

I hope you don't think I'm being too presumptuous in addressing you in such a familiar way. I'm sure it must seem odd coming from someone you've never met but, in truth, you've been anything but a stranger to me for some time now. I could hardly blame you if you found it unsettling to learn that someone has gone to such lengths to track you down but, for what it's worth, I promise I have only your best interests at heart. If the choice lay solely with me, we wouldn't be strangers at all. Far from it.

It's so difficult to write this letter in the dark, so to speak. I'd feel much more comfortable speaking to you in person but if you're reading this you will know by now that's no longer an option. I have no way of knowing how much you've already managed to work out for yourself. I'm hoping against hope that the answer is not very much because, a touch selfishly perhaps, I'd like you to hear things from my point of view, before you make up your mind about everything that's happened. I wouldn't want you to pick up just a few fragments that might colour your view of things.

You'll see that I've called this document Ellen 1. If everything has gone to plan, that should mean you have its sequel in your possession. Whether you choose to open it is up to you. If you're still completely in the dark as to who I am and why I've decided to leave Primrose Cottage to you, Ellen 2 should answer any questions you have. It's as comprehensive an account of events as my memory will allow me to compile. If it seems a little long, forgive me. I've erred on the side of inclusion, in the hope that you'll find it easier to make sense of everything. There is however a but … and a very large one at that.

I mentioned earlier that it's for you to decide whether or not you want to read it. It's only fair to mention here that there are those very close to you who don't think you should. It was never my intention for you to learn about me this way but when I first spoke with your mother, she was absolutely clear about the fact that she didn't want me to have any contact with you whatsoever. I did my best to change her mind. I even travelled by coach to see her a few years ago but she wouldn't be persuaded. I didn't agree with her stance on this but felt obliged to respect it. I gave her my word I'd keep my distance and I've done so.

I'm aware that her illness has worsened in recent months, which puts me in a difficult position. I don't want to feel that I've somehow taken advantage of her situation. Nevertheless I'm sure you've always suspected that there are whole areas of your past of which you know very little. Your mother has done a wonderful job of shielding you until now and believes that the less you know, the safer you'll be. I cannot agree. If this life has taught me anything at all, it is that innocence offers very little protection against the harsh realities of this world. I know I shan't be part of it for very much longer and when I leave I want to be able to say that I did the best I could.

Ellen, I have committed the unpardonable sin of living for far too long. I've outlived everyone who really mattered to me and until that happens to you (and heaven forbid that it should!) you won't really be in a position to understand how desperately I've sought some reason to carry on. You've provided me with that reason.

I confess that the interest I've taken in you might be viewed by some as unhealthy. There's no better illustration of this than that some poor souls in this village are under the misapprehension you're my daughter, a mistake I confess I've done nothing to discourage. I can only apologise for this simple act of deception but it has helped me to deflect awkward and painful questions. As a result you've become very dear to me and I want to do everything in my power to make sure you're safe and happy. It's my genuine belief that the chances of this happening are significantly improved if you are allowed to hear what I have to say. It's always so much easier to deal with a situation if you know what it is.

Whatever you decide, Primrose Cottage is yours. I hope you'll accept it and learn to love it as much as I have. It's been a daily reminder to me that not everything I've touched in this life has turned to sand. And whether you choose to read on or leave the second envelope unopened, I pray that when you reach my age, you'll look back on life with fewer regrets than those I've had to carry around with me for far too long.

Love those closest to you and hold on to them for dear life.

Yours with affection,

Eudora

February 2008: Ellen

Ellen's response, on reaching the end of the letter, was to go straight back to the beginning. The second time she read slowly, searching for any significant detail that might have escaped her. Kate was content to wait, reaching for the wine bottle and refilling both glasses. She watched as Ellen took a couple of sips and put the glass back on the table without once taking her eyes from the sheets in front of her. She could have been drinking bleach for all she knew.

Kate sat down next to her, turning sideways on and lifting her feet onto the sofa. She hugged her knees and chewed on another slice of pizza as she nestled into the corner, studying Ellen's face for some hint as to how she was taking this. There was nothing to be gleaned from her expression, nothing to suggest she was reading anything more significant than a TV magazine, but that was Ellen. Kate knew her well enough to be sure there was plenty going on underneath. She couldn't possibly be unaffected by all this.

Eventually Ellen looked up from the letter and gave a deep sigh, tucking behind her ear a strand of hair that had fallen across her face.

'You OK?' Kate asked.

'Fine … just a bit … I dunno … *weird*, I suppose.' She fanned herself with the sheets, staring vacantly into the middle distance.

'You OK about Barbara?'

Ellen gave a rueful smile. 'Yeah … sure. It's not like it's some big surprise, is it?'

'No, but even so…'

'You were there, Kate. You know what she was like. At least she was consistent. She never made any bones about the fact that she was keeping things from me.' She arched her back, easing the stiffness from her joints. 'Wish I could say the same about Sam,' she added.

'Sam?' Kate sounded surprised. 'Am I missing something?'

Ellen speared a couple of slices of carrot and put the fork to one side. 'Here,' she said, skimming back through the letter. 'She said *those* … plural. Where is it?' She ran her finger down the lines of text until she found the sentence she was after. '*There are those very close to you who don't think you should.* See? Not *someone* or *your mother*. *Those*.'

Kate looked over her shoulder.

'Bit tenuous, isn't it? You sure you're not reading too much into it?'

Ellen shook her head emphatically. 'That's no throwaway comment. Remember what Reverend Williams said … about how Eudora took ages over this? If she said *those*, that's what she meant.'

'So?'

'So who else could it be? I mean, assuming we can rule out Megan and Harry, if it's someone close to me, it's got to be Sam and Mary, hasn't it?'

'Cheers, El,' said Kate, raising her glass in mock tribute to their friendship.

'Yeah, well, you don't count. If I can't trust you, I might as well just pack it all in.'

'And you don't trust Sam?'

'Of course I do. Well ... I *did*. But he's been really off lately – ever since I first mentioned Eudora's name. *And* now it turns out he's been ringing me all day.'

'Since when?'

Ellen explained about the missed calls she'd discovered earlier in the car. If he was so desperate to get hold of her, it could only mean one thing – *somehow*, although God only knew how, he'd managed to find out what she was up to and was determined to reel her back in. The more she thought about it, the more she felt *hounded* by him – that wasn't too strong a word.

'Have you rung him?'

Ellen shook her head. 'Why? I know what he's going to say. I don't want to hear any more evasions and half-truths, Kate. And anyway I don't trust myself just yet. I'm fed up with being ... *manipulated* like that. He can sit and stew for a bit. It'll do him good.'

Kate flicked at a piece of fluff from the cushion that had attached itself to her tights. She watched Ellen work her way through the momentary flash of temper, managing it just as she'd always done, right from their time at school through to the darkest days of her relationship with Jack. Ellen was a slow burner who had never felt comfortable with public shows of anger, preferring instead to store up resentment until it sizzled at the edges. All she ever needed was a few moments to compose herself, open the valve and let the pressure subside.

After a while, Ellen put her plate on the table alongside her wine glass and leant back so that her head was against Kate's legs. She folded the letter carefully, reinforcing the creases, and slipped it back into the envelope. Then she picked up the larger one and studied it closely. This one was much, much thicker and, unlike the letter she'd just read, it was sealed with several strips of Sellotape. As if she hadn't even trusted Reverend Williams to keep his word, Eudora had signed her name across the flap.

Ellen twisted slightly so that she could look up into Kate's face.

'What would you do?' she asked.

'Me?'

'If you were me – would you read it?'

Kate picked up another slice of pizza and took a bite out of it.

'Doesn't matter what I'd do,' she said. 'I'm not you. I can lift the lid and have a good look inside and just walk away if I don't like what I see. It's not going to hurt anyone but me.'

'Whereas I've got Megan and Harry to think about.'

'Whereas you've got Megan and Harry.'

'And once you know something, you can't unknow it, right?'

'Right.'

'And ignorance is bliss.'

'So they say.'

Ellen nodded. 'You know I'm going to read it, don't you?' she said.

'Never doubted it for a minute,' said Kate.

August 2007: Ellen 2

I feel I have to start with my husband, Josef. Someone ought to speak on his behalf and I'm sure he deserves a more eloquent testimony than mine. Unfortunately I am all he has, poor soul.

You need to understand that Josef was a good man. A kind man. A *gentle* man in all senses of the word. He was never less than considerate to me, and to Julie he was a devoted, loving father for those few years God saw fit to grant him that role. One moment of madness should not be seen as typical of him. The Josef I knew was a man of moderation who never acted impulsively. Violence was simply not in his nature.

I first met him in the spring of 1941. In those days I was working as a seamstress, making alterations to beautiful dresses I could never imagine wearing myself, until the war started and we were put to the monotonous task of making uniforms. I was the elder of two daughters in what my father described as a middle-class family. If my mother had any thoughts on that or any other matter, I never discovered what they were. There was room in that household for one opinion only.

I was a considerable disappointment to him in two specific respects, neither of which seemed entirely fair to me. My greatest sin, it seems, lay in having been born the wrong gender altogether. My mother was expected to produce a son who might look after the family business some day. Instead she gave birth to two daughters, giving him an excuse to withdraw almost completely from family life, emerging from his self-imposed exile only when he felt there was a need to reassert his authority and make life as difficult and unpleasant as possible for my younger sister and me.

My other major failing, as far as he was concerned, was that I was still living at home. Throughout my teenage years, his one consolation had been that before long I would surely be whisked away by an unsuspecting suitor, and become someone else's problem. Unfortunately, with so many young men being called away to fight for their country, potential husbands were thinner on the ground than they might otherwise have been. To add to this, the crippling shyness which had blighted my adolescence showed no signs of releasing its hold as I moved into adulthood, leaving me ill-equipped to fight my own corner in such a competitive environment.

My prospects of finding a suitable partner might have been better, were it not for the restrictions placed on my social life. My father had his own ideas about how respectable young ladies were expected to behave. They did *not* go out in the evenings during the week, for instance. *Tarts* did. *Trollops* did. Decent girls did not. I was allowed out on a Saturday night to go to the cinema with Jane, a work colleague who was already married with a baby girl even though she was three years younger than I was. She was deemed acceptable, partly because she was living with her parents while her husband was away on active service but principally, I suspect, because there was always the hope that if I spent enough time in her company, some of her magic might rub off onto me.

If the cinema was considered acceptable, public houses most certainly were not. As for dance halls, they were generally regarded as suspect, although for some reason he seemed to view the Saturday night dance at Cheltenham Town Hall with a less critical eye. Perhaps he felt that anything taking place in such august surroundings must have an element of respectability about it. Whatever the reason, Jane and I started going there whenever a big band was in town, and it was at one such evening that I first met Josef Kasprowicz.

He was twenty-eight years old and had come over from Lodz in Poland as a fighter pilot. I was three years his junior but the gulf in experience made the real difference between us so much greater than that. You'd be hard pressed to imagine just how young and naive I was, even allowing for the fact that those were far more innocent times. It's no exaggeration to say I probably knew less then about the ways of the world than the most sheltered teenager does now.

Suffice to say, I was dazzled by him. I thought he was the most handsome man I'd ever met. He was polite, considerate and I was immediately drawn to him, not least because of the slightly exotic air conferred upon him by his lack of facility with the language.

From the outset, he presented my father with something of a dilemma. In almost every respect, Josef was the answer to his prayers. Here at long last was someone who was not only prepared but even anxious to take me off his hands. Even better than that, he was a hero, a decorated fighter pilot, one of our brave and gallant boys. Unfortunately his prospects as a future son-in-law were marred by the fact that he wasn't actually one of our boys ... not *really*. Josef was a Pole, wasn't he? *A Polack*. My father, as he was to prove so graphically in the coming years, had little interest in me as a person but the thought that the Nash bloodline might in any way be tainted was anathema to him. No grandson of his was going to be fathered by someone who could barely speak the King's English.

Josef finally proposed shortly after the end of the war. I don't know to this day exactly what was said behind the closed door of my father's study or what reasons he gave for denying Josef his blessing. All I do know is that when Josef left our house that evening, he asked me to go with him and I did. Without even thinking. It took me no more than five minutes to throw clothes and a few essentials into a case while my mother stood by the door, telling me I was making a dreadful mistake. Then I was gone and I never saw them again ... not once. Josef and I were married in June the following year.

The first few years of marriage were hard. Once he was back in civvy street, Josef tried to find work as a draughtsman, the career for which he'd qualified in Poland before the war. Employment possibilities however were scarce and he soon discovered that any currency his medals and citations might have earned him counted for very little in the reality of post-war Britain. Now he was just another returning serviceman looking for work and a *Johnny Foreigner* to boot. He managed eventually to find a job on a dairy farm near Andoversford, gruelling work which entailed not only anti-social hours but also a nine-mile cycle ride each way. As ever he saw nothing in this to complain about, volunteering for any extra hours on offer. Sometimes I didn't see him between the hours of six in the morning and nine at night.

We were renting a flat in Hewlett Road and money was tight enough for me to have to do a couple of afternoons a week in the local newsagents but we were happy enough, inasmuch as I ever really thought about it. That, I suppose, is the point. I hadn't ever given it any thought at all. In that first year, everything was new, exciting. I had escaped the tyranny of Havelock Road and that was all that mattered. But once the initial onslaught was over and we began to settle into some sort of rhythm, we gradually became aware of just how different we were.

It was nothing too dramatic to begin with. I loved the cinema and would happily have gone every weekend if our finances had stretched that far. Josef came with me at first, holding my hand in the dark and doing his best to be enthralled by what was happening on the screen. He was restless though, happier doing something than being passively entertained. Before long we decided it was pointless paying good money for him to sit there and be bored. Instead I started going with Jane or, more often than not, on my own.

For his part, Josef loved going for long walks across the hills on a Sunday afternoon, seven-mile hikes in all kinds of weather. The *idea* of sharing this with him was appealing enough but the reality was very different. The honest truth is that the great outdoors did nothing for me. Ten minutes into the walk I would already be pining for the flat. I would have been so much happier curled up in a blanket, reading one of the classics. The library in town was like a second home to me and these hours spent trekking across the countryside began to feel like a waste of valuable reading time.

Even socially we were struggling to find the right balance. Josef's friends from his days at RAF Duxford were very important to him. It was a part of his life I'd never been in a position to share but at least I could appreciate the importance of the bond forged by their wartime experiences. I wanted to support him whenever they all got together for reunions but somehow always ended up feeling like an outsider, even among the wives. My inadequate social skills were probably at the root of it but, for whatever reason, I never felt totally accepted by them and sensed after the first few attempts that, far from supporting Josef, I was making it difficult for him to relax and be himself.

I don't recall discussing these problems with him – not once. He was probably trying to protect my feelings. For my part, I was acutely aware I'd made this particular bed, as my father would have been pleased to put it, and over a period of time these differences simply became part of the daily routine. We made room for them by gradually drifting further and further apart. If anyone had asked me at any stage whether or not I loved Josef, I wouldn't have hesitated to say *yes – of course I do. He's my husband*. But it would have been no more than a reflex. I never dared to ask myself the question.

What we lacked was a shared interest, the focal point Julie would eventually provide. Perhaps that's why we agreed we'd start a family the moment our finances would stretch to it. Maybe we both hoped that bringing an extra factor into the equation would distract us from focusing too closely on what was missing. For my part, I know I was more than ready. I was almost thirty when Josef and I got married, thirty-three by the time we agreed the time was right. My body clock was not so much ticking as screaming.

So when Josef finally landed a job in the drawing office of a local architect, it felt like a new beginning in more ways than one. With our finances on a sounder footing, there was no reason why we shouldn't start a family. For me, this was more than just the logical next step in our relationship. I'd come to view it as a chance for me to redeem myself. I'd been a failure as a daughter and was now failing as a wife, but if I could make a success of raising a family, there was hope for me yet. I could hardly wait to get started.

Except, of course, it wasn't that simple. Now we were no longer obliged to take precautions, I naively assumed it wouldn't be long before I would be expecting. I'd imagined so often the moment when I would know for sure, rehearsed the way I would break the news to Josef, almost tasted the surge of joy which would miraculously sweep away the awkwardness between us. We'd never been as comfortable in our intimacy as we might have been but I could see this all changing overnight, now that we had a common goal to pursue.

But three months slipped by, then six, then nine, each one bringing its own little disappointment. Josef was so solicitous the first few times. I suspect he knew how important this was to me and understood that each month that passed was like a little death. From time to time I would find on my pillow a posy of wild flowers he'd picked on the way home from work. Alternatively he might suggest a small consolation prize – *forget the money, we'll go out for a meal.* But not even someone as considerate as he could hope to keep this up indefinitely. And after eighteen months, it gradually ceased to be a topic of conversation between us.

It was my fault. I knew I was to blame. I was doing something wrong. I never felt comfortable talking about such matters so it's an indication of how desperate I was that I went to see Jane, who by now had five children of her own and clearly knew how to carry out her responsibilities in a proper and adult manner. Her immediate response was to laugh until she saw how close I was to tears. Then she sat me down, put her arm around me and did her best to reassure me. There was nothing wrong with me or with how I was conducting myself. I was too anxious, that was all. I needed to relax, stop fretting so much. I couldn't hurry these things – they had a timing all of their own. *You'll be fine, you'll see.* And as it turned out she was right … although not in the way I'd imagined.

I was in my mid-thirties when Josef announced he'd booked a week's holiday for the two of us at a B&B in Torquay. We'd never had a holiday before, apart from a week in Blackpool for our honeymoon. For the first couple of years we'd been unable to put aside more than the bare minimum. Things were much improved once Josef started work at the architect's, but we still felt holidays were a luxury we could ill afford. We preferred instead to save for a house of our own and the family we both wanted so much. His decision, out of the blue, that we would have a week away felt portentous somehow, as if this was his way of telling me he'd given up on that particular golden future.

I hadn't. I still wanted to keep the dream alive. My body clock by now may have been reduced to the occasional plaintive whimper but I couldn't bring myself to give up just yet. I still felt as if I had a child in me, so to speak. Enthusiastic as I was about the prospect of a week by the sea, I couldn't help feeling dispirited at what it might actually represent. It felt as if we were letting go in some way.

I realise this might be interpreted as a plea for some sort of understanding, given what happened next. I can assure you that's not the case. Infidelity seems to be so lightly regarded nowadays but I am a product of my age. I was appalled then by my actions and am no less harsh a self-critic now. I didn't seek forgiveness from Josef, even with his dying breath, so I'm not about to ask it of anyone else. I don't deserve it.

I would prefer not to dwell for any longer than necessary on what happened next. It's a source of great embarrassment to me. Suffice it to say that Josef had surprised me with tickets for a show in Torquay one evening and we were having afternoon tea when he was taken violently ill. We called a doctor who decided it was mild food poisoning – presumably the seafood he'd bought on the promenade at lunchtime. Josef decided to stay in bed and try to sleep it off but urged me not to waste my ticket at least. He knew I'd been looking forward to the show and didn't want me to be disappointed.

And I so nearly didn't go ... oh, the irony of it. I offered to stay and look after him and would have done so if he'd just asked me to. But as usual he was thinking of me and insisted I go without him, which somehow makes the whole thing seem even more of a betrayal. Because at the show I found myself sitting next to an American boy, whose father was over here as a visiting naval attaché. He must have been ten years younger and he was lively and entertaining and his eyes hadn't yet lost the freshness I believed I'd bleached out of Josef. And he was obviously oh so interested in me and I felt flattered. Wanted.

And nine weeks later I found out I was expecting.

July 2001: John Michael

Guy sitting across the aisle, the one with the sharp blue suit and enough gel on his head to grease an axle. Business man. That's three times now in the last five minutes he's looked up from the paper he's reading and stared in his direction. Not just looked – *stared*. It's the sort of thing he notices, even now. Nothing like that to get the blood pumping.

First time it happened, John Michael turned away, casual like, and gazed out of the window. Nothing too obvious. Country-side's fascinating all of a sudden. After a while, when it's safe to risk a quick look, the guy's gone back to his paper, so no prob-lem. Only two minutes later, damned if he doesn't do it again, which means this time he has to turn away and get his face out of the firing line. He wonders what it must be like to be able to return the look, stare someone out and not worry about being recognised. Not something he's ever had the chance to do. Num-ber one on the professor's list of no-nos. But he often thinks it'd be nice, just once, to say *sod it* and give it a go … *really* give someone the eye.

Then, the third time, he wonders whether maybe he's got it wrong. Looks like maybe the guy's just day-dreaming rather than actually staring. Probably thinking about something he's just read or some deal he completed this morning. And now he's calmed down a bit and started to think straight, he can see the guy's way too young anyway. Twenty-five tops. He'd have been in nappies back then. It's the older ones he needs to worry about. They're the ones who'll never let go.

So he goes back to the book he's been reading and takes a few deep breaths. Worrying about nothing. Even so, he tells himself … if it happens again, he'll get up and change com-partments. No point in asking for trouble.

It's like that woman on the ferry this morning, out on top deck. The moment he sits down opposite, she's pulling the lit-tle girl closer to her, taking a sudden interest in the shells she's been playing with. Lifts her up and holds her on her lap, rather than let her wander too close, like he's some sort of paedophile or something. And the little girl's struggling to get down while the mother clings on for dear life, jiggling her up and down on her knee to keep her happy – and he hasn't even done anything. Hardly even looked in her direction. Once upon a time he knows he'd have read too much into that. Now he has to remind himself she didn't mean anything by it. People are just wary of strangers, that's all. It's nothing personal.

He gives it ten minutes or so, then realises he's been going over the same paragraph three or four times and hasn't got much idea what's happened in the last few pages. It's a cheap thriller he picked up at the station, thinking it might take his mind off things for a while. Some chance of that. He snaps it shut and stuffs it in his jacket pocket. Then he turns up his collar, rests his head against the window and hunkers down for a while. Chance to switch off.

Funny to think this is England flashing past. It's been over twenty years now and in all that time he's hardly ever thought about coming back, let alone done something about it. Last month was probably the closest he's come in all that time ... and some stroke of genius that would have been. Embarrassing to think he got as far as the outer office, was just minutes away from asking the man himself for compassionate leave, before he finally came to his senses. God only knows what he was thinking.

OK – it *was* right out of the blue. Granted, the professor was no spring chicken, but there was nothing to suggest he'd suddenly go like that. John Michael had seen him only two months earlier and he looked as fit as a butcher's dog. He had something permanent about him, did the professor – something indestructible. To read just those few small paragraphs in the paper like that was a real hammer blow. After all, he owed him just about everything, not least the fact that he actually belongs somewhere now. After all this time, he feels he can say that much. Even if it hasn't been without the occasional scare, he's been able to lead what his neighbours and colleagues at work probably think is a pretty ordinary, uneventful life. They've no idea who he is ... *was*. And that's all down to one man.

So yes, he owes him – of course he does. Big time. If it wasn't for the professor's money and contacts which made all the documentation possible, there's no way he'd have made it over there in the first place. It's the professor's summer cottage he's been 'renting' all this time. It's his references and reputation that helped him get his first job in the area. And he's been the one constant in his life, the closest thing to family he's had for a long time now, so the temptation to come over to England for the funeral was always going to be hard to resist.

But the professor wouldn't have thanked him for it – not for one moment. Goes against everything he's ever taught him. Seems like all his life he's been having the same message drilled into him – *keep your head down, never stand out in a crowd, p-p-p-play the p-p-percentages*. Then, the moment the professor's not around any more, first time he has to do some real, joined-up thinking for himself, what does he do? He dives straight in – no risk assessment, no exit strategy, no *plan* even, of any description. Enough to make you cringe. Such an amateur.

Part of the problem is that, having been out of the headlines for a while, he's tempted to think he's yesterday's news, even though he should know deep down that's never going to happen. All it takes is some new 'sighting' and everything flares up again. Out come all the old photos, the old hysteria. He can have a quiet laugh over the places he's supposed to have turned up. And as for these age-enhancement pictures they come out with every so often, they're just a joke – nothing like him now. He always makes sure of that. But it's not really that funny – the search has never died away. He has to believe there's always someone out there, looking for him. There'll always be an O'Halloran or another just like him. And if someone like the professor dies, this is a big opportunity as far as they're concerned. It breathes a bit of life into the corpse. They'll have been staking out the funeral, just waiting for him to show his face, and he'd be mad to think otherwise. They'll have been there, alright. Count on it.

So would the professor have been any happier about this little trip then? Probably not. He'd still say it's way too danger-ous, that it's crazy to even think about going. But at least he'd understand *why*. And if John Michael insisted on going anyway, against his advice, the professor would have sat down with him and worked out exactly what the risks were and the best way of getting around them.

The journey wouldn't have worried him. Passport con-trol maybe, but that's only a problem if you lose your head. London should be OK too – always safety in numbers. It's when he gets to Ashbury and starts asking questions ... that's when he's really sticking his head up in the air. He's going to need a good story then, that's for sure. That's the bit that would've had the professor biting his nails and asking if he's sure about this. *Really* sure?

But when it came down to it, the professor would have backed him because he understood – he knew how he felt about gaps. How helpless they make him feel. For those first few years, she was always there with him, all day, every day. He fell over, she picked him up. He sneezed, she was there with a hanky. It was like he was all she ever thought about. Then she went away and he was left with nothing, just a gaping hole. And just when it looked as if there was a chance his father might be the one to fill it after all, he too was snatched away. Since then it's the professor who's been there whenever he's needed someone.

The moment it really hit home that he was gone, that he was back on his own again, he found his thoughts drifting back to those years when they shut him away while his father ran off to start a new life somewhere else without him. And for the first time he's really curious about what sort of life that might have been. He doesn't know many of the details; his father always seemed to shy away from talking too much about what he was doing, as if he felt it would be tactless to say too much. And there was no way he was going to ask because he was so busy trying to make him feel bad about that newspaper article. He resented the fact that his father could just up sticks and start all over again without him as if nothing had ever happened, while he was left behind to fend for himself.

But now he's older, settled ... and curious. He does wonder about that part of his father's life. Nearly seven years he spent in this Ashbury place. You don't just sit and do nothing in all that time. You move on. He must have met people, done things, formed relationships. He can't remember most of the little details that came up in conversation – they would have gone in one ear and out the other. He knows he was working at an inn, that he tried to keep his running going. Names are a complete blank but he *suspects*, from one or two things that emerged the last few times they were together, that there might even have been someone he was close to. But it's the lack of detail that's the problem. He's at that stage in life where he doesn't want mysteries any more – what he wants is answers. And he's more aware than ever, after the recent health scare, that he might not have as long as he's always assumed. The clock's ticking.

So if this trip means taking a few risks, stuff it. With any luck, if things start to get a bit hairy, he's still got his old life to run back to. It's just that lately, especially since the professor died, he's had the feeling that if that life is going to mean anything to him, he's going to have to fill in all those gaps first.

And he knows he needs to start with Ashbury.

August 2007: Ellen 2

I was thinking just now about the sermon Reverend Williams gave last Sunday. He was talking about a film he'd seen on television about a woman whose future is determined by whether or not she steps through the doors of a London underground train. The film depicts two parallel universes, showing what would have happened to her in each and the point he wanted to make is that our lives are governed by what seems like a random collection of moments. We like to talk about luck, chance, coincidence, how things could have been different if fortune had smiled on us. We're less keen to look closely at ourselves and accept our own share of responsibility for what's happened. Fate is a more convenient handle on which to hook our disappointment.

Reverend Williams knows nothing of my guilty secret. I know I should tell him but am also sure I never will. I have a great deal of respect for him and don't think I could bear to see the disappointment in his face. If I were to tell him though, I'm sure he'd be quick to point out that fate had little to do with the way things have turned out for me.

I could, if I were so inclined, point to my own series of sliding doors that might have led to a very different future. Josef, for instance, was tired that morning in Torquay and not really in the mood for a stroll along the sea front before lunch. He only came along to keep me company, otherwise he'd never have seen the seafood stall in the first place. Having done so, he might easily have decided not to buy the tray of cockles and whelks that struck him down later that afternoon. And if he'd been able to go to the show, I would have made no more than nodding acquaintance with the person next to me, who in turn could just as easily have been one of the many pensioners who made up the bulk of the audience, rather than a lonely boy far from home. So yes, there were any number of moments which might have worked out differently, but that's life, I suppose … a series of choices. What matters is that when you have the chance to take the reins yourself, you accept responsibility for your actions. It's too easy to look back years later and blame it on the vagaries of fate.

When I first discovered I was expecting, there was a moment when I might have confessed all to Josef. I knew his capacity for selflessness. It's not inconceivable that if I'd managed to summon up the moral courage to seek his forgiveness, there might still have been a different outcome. If anyone was likely to be willing to bring up another man's child, it was Josef.

But the stakes were so high. Divorce in those days was much more of a taboo than it is now. In telling him what I'd done, especially in view of what I'd just discovered, I would have been running the risk of social disgrace. I'd already been abandoned by my family – if Josef were to walk out as well, where on earth would that have left me? And quite apart from my own selfish concerns, how could I possibly do that to him? After all those years of desperately wanting a son or daughter of his own, how was he supposed to cope with the knowledge that I was expecting the child of a total stranger?

But, as fate would have it (that word again), our last night together in Torquay provided me with the chance to take the coward's way out. You'll probably have gathered by now that, as a rule, Josef and I were not as intimate with each other as we might have been. He was laid low for twenty-four hours by his bout of food poisoning but once he'd recovered he was full of the joys of spring and determined to make the most of the holiday time we had left. Without wishing to be indelicate, our last night in Torquay was the first time we had shown that level of interest in each other for several months. It did little to ease my conscience but it did at least prove fortunate in providing me with an escape route.

You'll probably wonder how I could have been so sure back then that the baby was not Josef's. I can't explain it to you. It was no more than a feeling, yet it burnt in me so strongly. Perhaps, despite everything I said just now, I'm a fatalist after all. But I can assure you, there's no element of hindsight at play here. From the moment my pregnancy was confirmed, I was convinced that Josef was not the father. I'm sure a psychologist would be quick to identify feelings of guilt and the need to punish myself but for my part, I can only tell you how it seemed to me at the time.

I offer no excuses for the choice I made. I considered the alternatives and went for what seemed the least painful of the options available to me. I had no desire to reap the whirlwind so

I said nothing to Josef about my fears and chose to live with a lie in the hope that everything would be for the best.

If I needed any encouragement, any persuading that I'd done the right thing, his reaction to the news was all I could have hoped for. His kindness had never been in short supply but to it he now added an element of tenderness I was unaware of until then. And nothing was too much trouble for him. During the first few weeks, which he constantly referred to as *the danger period*, I was barely allowed to get up from the settee while he was around. Cups of tea, hot-water bottles, a plentiful supply of books from the library ... all were brought to me the moment I threatened to move a muscle. I'm not sure he'd ever cooked a meal – a *proper* meal – in his life but he was happy to stand there in the kitchen and respond to instructions as I called them out to him. In time he built up a small repertoire of presentable dishes.

Once we were safely past the first three months, he became less fearful and things gradually reverted to normal but he was still solicitous in the extreme, always looking for ways to help or thinking of little treats he could arrange for me. His draughtsmanship skills had earned him a couple of promotions in the last few years and the extra money, even allowing for the amount we felt we needed to put to one side, enabled him to buy a second-hand Morris Minor, which he took great delight in showing off on weekend trips to a succession of Cotswold villages; Bourton-on-the-Water one week, Ledbury or Stow-on-the-Wold the next. I think, looking back, that we were probably more of a couple during those few months than at any other time.

Then, when I reached eight months, everything changed. One evening he came home from work and was sullen and unresponsive. I put it down to a bad day at the office and did my best to coax him out of it but the mood, if that was the word for it, persisted. It would be easy to exaggerate here – he wasn't angry; there were no sharp exchanges between us. He certainly wasn't disrespectful or unkind in anything he said or did. It's just that he ceased to be the person he'd been for the previous few months – overnight, it seemed. The weekend trips, shopping expeditions to buy things for the baby, the little bar of chocolate I would occasionally find on my pillow or the flowers he'd bring home in the evening ... all of these came to a shuddering halt. The change in his attitude towards me made itself more apparent in absences than anything else. No real interest over the dinner table in what I'd been doing that day. No inclination to join with me in drawing up lists of names. No sharing of light-hearted moments at work. I would have had to be totally insensate not to notice.

I tried on several occasions to draw him out and was rebuffed each time – never unkindly but always decisively. He said he was just tired but deep down I was worried that this cloud that had settled over him suggested a change of heart. Maybe he was having second thoughts about raising a family and didn't know how to broach the subject with me.

It was only when I woke him in the early hours one morning and asked him to drive me to the hospital that he seemed to snap out of it. And I'll never forget the moment when he came in to see Julie for the first time. His face was a picture as he held out his arms and took her from the nurse. Of course I can never be sure that what I saw in his expression was actually there and not just the product of my overactive imagination. But it seemed to me as if he was summoning up every paternal instinct in his body and somehow fashioning from it a protective shawl in which he was wrapping her, even as he trembled with fear that his hands might be too rough or his movements too clumsy. He was drawing a line in the sand, marking her out as someone to be protected at all costs, and the smile he turned in my direction made me so grateful for the decision I'd taken all those months ago. Whatever doubts I might have had back then, there were none now. Whoever the real father might be, this was destined to be Josef's baby. I wouldn't have it any other way.

I don't intend to write about Julie's life in these pages. I have no idea how I would go about decanting the essence of her into so small a vessel. She lived for five thousand one hundred and twenty-two days and I could probably summon up an anecdote for every single one of them. Equally I'm sure you'll understand if I give a wide berth to the circumstances of her death. I assume you already know more than enough on that subject – everyone else seems to.

When Julie died, something reached inside, ripped out a part of me and tore it to shreds. I imagine it must have been the same for Josef, although I can't be more specific because we never really talked about it. Even in grief, we preferred to shut ourselves away and find our own way of coping. Initially, particularly during the days leading up to the funeral, things were so hectic we barely had time to think. There were the usual arrangements to be made and so many people who wanted to express their condolences – friends, work colleagues, even total strangers who wrote in their hundreds to offer their sympathy, thus making my own family's silence seem even more reprehensible in my own eyes. Meanwhile Josef had taken it upon himself to keep the intrusion from the media to a minimum. He threw up a protective shield for which I was more than grateful, uncomfortable as I was in the spotlight. So for that brief period we tended to see ourselves as the rest of the world did. We were defined by our loss, the grieving couple, turned back in on ourselves, each clinging on to the other for dear life.

But once it was all over, and the period of intense exposure had died away, we suddenly found ourselves with the rest of our lives stretching out ahead of us and no real idea as to how we were going to fill such a vast expanse of time. It was only then that we understood how important Julie had been in providing a bridge between the two of us. Now that she'd been taken away, we seemed to be on opposite banks of some fast-flowing river and by the time we realised what was happening, our two futures had drifted a long way apart.

Josef threw himself into his work, staying later and later at the office and accepting invitations to occasional weekend conferences and seminars. When he wasn't working, he was playing golf or tennis, two sports to which friends at work had introduced him and for which, to his great surprise, he had a certain aptitude. And when he was not playing either, he was going for walks of increasing distance, setting out early on Sunday mornings and staying away for the best part of the day. He always made a point of inviting me to come along with him but must surely have known what my answer would be. I don't imagine he was too disappointed.

As for me, I set out to put right one of the many injustices I felt I'd suffered during adolescence. I'd always shown promise at school and was encouraged by my English teacher to stay on and give serious consideration to applying for university. I'd have liked nothing better but knew my father well enough to understand there was little point in even raising the matter at home. He'd made it clear from the word go that universities were a waste of time and money. He was out there in the real world at fourteen, earning a decent wage – *never did him any harm.*

Now though I had time on my hands so I opted for a correspondence course in English Literature, eventually committing myself to an A level in one year. Having successfully negotiated that, I signed up for a course in freelance journalism, which turned out to be money well spent. Within three years, I was contributing book and film reviews to a monthly magazine, a lucrative little sideline which I was able to continue until relatively recently.

I also had my faith which, perhaps surprisingly, had been strengthened rather than shattered since Julie died. Until then it had been more of a superstitious hangover from my childhood days, when I'd gone along unquestioningly with whatever I was told at Sunday school. Now though I found myself asking more pertinent questions and, to my surprise, found answers that made a huge difference to my life. Josef, bless him, probably asked himself the same questions and came up with answers that were diametrically opposed to mine. Any tenuous faith that might have outlived his experiences during the war had melted away to mere contempt after his daughter was taken from him.

So there we were, to all intents and purposes leading separate lives under the same roof. We still had a social life of sorts. From time to time we would be invited out for dinner at the home of one of Josef's work colleagues and we would of course feel obliged to reciprocate. There was also his company's annual Dinner/Dance, a glamorous affair which provided us with the chance to dress up and enjoy an evening in the company of others. And on Valentine's Day, without fail, Josef would book a table at a restaurant in town and make sure I had a red rose to take home with me. Somehow though that was symptomatic of the problem between us. It was all symbols – smoke and mirrors. It served its purpose in keeping the illusion alive and I'm sure those who knew us had very little idea of just how far apart we actually were, but the reality was that if you stripped away the affection, the politeness and the sheer habit of it all, there was precious little else.

The gulf between us widened with every passing year. Even so, I would have had to be blind not to notice how ill he was becoming. Josef wasn't a tall man but he was broad-shouldered and the years of working on the farm had endowed him with a strong, healthy physique. Even in times when food was harder to come by, he was always the sturdy boy of country stock. Towards the end of 1973 though, the change in his physical appearance was so noticeable even I felt the need to say something. His clothes seemed to hang off him and he started walking with something of a stoop, as if hunched over to protect himself. I'd often envied him his youthful appearance in the past but those days were long gone.

His appetite had always been hearty – he loved a cooked breakfast and still, even after thirty years in this country, regarded a traditional fish-and-chip supper as a real treat. Now, as often as not, he'd come home and ask for something simple, just a couple of pieces of toast maybe. I would end up cooking for myself, then watch him chew thoughtfully at the bread which he washed down more and more frequently now with a glass of ale. When we did eat together, he would pick at whatever I served up and leave half of it on the plate before disappearing off to the shed. And at some stage in the early hours of the morning, I would be woken by the sound of his bedroom door opening, as he tiptoed into the bathroom where, despite the precautions he took in shutting the door and running the taps, I could hear him bringing back up the meagre amount he'd succeeded in swallowing.

I asked him about it – of course I did. Several times. He brushed my concerns aside. Nothing was wrong. He'd been overworking maybe. I needn't concern myself. If I pushed too hard, he became defensive and I knew it was time to back off. There were distinct echoes here of the way he'd been in those last two months before Julie was born: the same evasiveness, the same touchy response whenever I asked what was wrong. And it was impossible for me to go back to that time without thinking of the doubts that had assailed me then, the worry that he might have changed his mind about wanting a child after all, which naturally led on to thoughts of Julie and what she'd meant to both of us. It has never been very far below the surface.

I made one last attempt to get him to tell me exactly what was wrong with him or, failing that, to promise that he would at least go to see our doctor. Again he tried to shrug it off but this time I was determined to turn it into a confrontation. Eventually he frowned and asked me why I was making so much of it. When I told him that I was worried, that I cared about him, he snapped at me, something about how it was a bit too late in the day for that. I was hurt by the sharpness of his tone. We didn't have arguments. I suppose there has to be some passion, some emotional connection there for rows to develop. But this time there was an edge to his voice that made me back off, wary. And if I never raised the subject again after that evening, it was less out of respect for his wishes than my fear of raking over coals that were long since dead. I knew from years of experience that if Josef didn't want to talk, he wouldn't.

Towards the end of February 1974, Josef reminded me casually over lunch that the annual reunion dinner at RAF Duxford was scheduled for the following weekend. I say *reminded*, although the truth is I had no real recollection of it having come up in any previous conversation. Certainly, when I checked, there was no reference to it on the wall calendar in our kitchen. I assumed it was an oversight on my part or maybe one of those occasions when I was guilty of 'tuning out' of a conversation, which often happened if I had a book in my hands. Josef explained it would be a weekend affair, involving a coach tour to a couple of RAF air bases with an overnight stay at a hotel in Manchester. The plan was for him to drive up early on Saturday morning and get back late Sunday afternoon ... always assuming I didn't mind.

The last part was purely a matter of form. It would have been interesting to know what his reaction would have been, had I come up with some objection, but I'm sure he knew he was on safe ground. I'd spent occasional weekends on my own while he was away on business and actually quite enjoyed the freedom to do whatever I wanted, with no need to take anyone else into consideration. If I was at all anxious, it was only because I didn't like the idea of him driving all the way to Manchester. Josef was as safe as houses behind the wheel as a rule but the weather forecast for the weekend was not at all good, with heavy snowfall expected. In addition I still had concerns about his health and felt such a trip would be doing him no favours at all. I asked if there was no one else who might be able to give him a lift, but he brushed aside my concerns and that was the last we spoke of it.

On the morning in question I got up early and prepared a cooked breakfast for him. I knew he wouldn't be able to cope with anything too filling but I wanted to make sure he set off with something warm inside him at least. He made a point of clearing his plate, then gave me the usual perfunctory kiss on the cheek, said he hoped I would enjoy the film that evening and picked up his coat. He got as far as the door before pausing for what must have been no more than a second or two – just long enough for me to wonder what it was he'd forgotten. Then he turned round, walked back over to me and, to my great surprise, rested both elbows on my shoulders. He cupped my cheeks in his hands and tilted my head forward before planting a gentle kiss on the top of my head. I started to pull back but he held me there for a moment, his head resting in my hair. He mumbled my name, then said something about taking good care of myself before he wheeled away and walked out of the door without another word.

At the time, I was completely taken aback. I had no idea what had just happened. It was as if he'd forgotten his lines for a moment, stepped out of his role and allowed a glimpse of the real person underneath. Even now I can't know for certain what was going through his mind, but what I was to learn in the coming weeks helped to put it into some sort of context. It's difficult to shake the feeling that he was trying out a sliding door of his own.

I remember very little of the rest of that day. I assume I went to the cinema in the evening, as that's what I generally did on a Saturday, but other than that nothing comes to mind. I *do* remember having great difficulty in getting off to sleep and I don't suppose I'd dozed for more than an hour or two before I was disturbed by the sound of a car drawing to a halt. I rolled over and pressed the illumination button on the alarm clock to check the time. It was 5.30.

My first impression was that the car had pulled into our driveway. I did think of getting out of bed to peer through the window but knew that would almost certainly wake me completely and I was still in desperate need of sleep. Instead I reasoned it must be our young neighbours who were accustomed to keeping bizarre hours. Telling myself they'd probably just returned from some all-night party, I rolled back over and must have gone off again in seconds.

The next thing I remember is the alarm dragging me out of my slumber. I'd set it for 7.30 because I planned to go to nine o'clock communion but it took every ounce of commitment for me to throw back the sheets and drag myself out of bed. I slid my feet into my slippers, pulled on my dressing gown and drew back the curtains to a blur of white falling from the darkened skies. But for that, I would almost certainly have turned away immediately and not noticed the car in the driveway until much later. As I rubbed at the frosted window though and peered through it to check on how deep the snowfall had been overnight, I could just about make out a dark shape below me, parked at an awkward angle to the fence. The car was definitely Josef's.

A number of thoughts raced through my mind. I remember thinking first of all that he must have been very quiet coming up the stairs because I hadn't heard a sound. Then my scrambled mind managed to fasten on to the more obvious question of what exactly he was doing here. What had made him leave Manchester and return a day early? Not only that, what had possessed him to leave in the early hours of the morning and drive home in the dark? The only answer that came to mind was that he must have felt too unwell during the day to stay there any longer. Maybe the coach journey and the excitement of visiting an air base with his old friends had taken its toll and he'd decided he wouldn't be able to continue with the rest of the tour. Even so, surely he would have been better off spending the night there and travelling back in the morning.

I checked the alarm clock again and realised he couldn't have had more than two hours sleep at the outside. Deciding it would be better to give him a while longer to recover, I collected my things as quietly as possible from the bathroom and, tiptoeing past his room, I took them downstairs with me in order not to disturb him.

While I was filling the kettle from the kitchen tap, I glanced out of the window and noticed again the strange angle at which the car was parked. That in itself suggested Josef must have been in a hurry to get inside. Normally his sense of order would never have allowed him to leave the car with one wheel resting in the flower border. No matter how late the hour, he would have reversed and straightened the car rather than invite puzzled stares from neighbours taking their dogs for an early-morning walk.

I'm not sure why I went to the front door. It certainly wasn't because I intended to go out and park the car for him, because I was still in my dressing gown and slippers. But something made me unlock the door and peer out into the drifting snowfall – again, call it fate, if you will. Because if I hadn't done so,

I wouldn't have seen the shadow just beyond the frozen windscreen.

I hurried out to the car, forgetting that the path was iced up. I caught hold of the door to stop myself from falling and yanked it open to find Josef slumped over the steering wheel, his head resting on the dashboard. He looked for all the world as if he was gone but as the door flew open, he slowly raised his head and turned to face me, his eyes vacant. In my panic, I'm sure I shouted at him, asked him what on earth he thought he was doing but the moment my hands came into contact with his, I knew I was wasting valuable time. They were icy to the touch, seemingly frozen to the steering wheel, and I had to prise his fingers loose one by one. He still hadn't said a word. The fact that he'd raised his head was the only indication that he was still alive.

I kept talking to him as I tried to get him out of the car, which was every bit as cold as the air outside. I knew there was no way I'd be able to carry him but fortunately he seemed to respond a little as I rubbed vigorously at his hands to try to get some semblance of warmth back into them. He mumbled my name, just as he'd done immediately before leaving, only this time with an upward tilt to his voice as if seeking reassurance it was really me. Then he shifted his weight slightly to help me manoeuvre his legs through the open car door.

I've no idea how I managed to get him inside the house and upstairs into his room. They say that in times of stress the human body is capable of the most remarkable feats of strength and I suppose I'll have to put it down to that. All he could manage was the most faltering of steps and with his arm draped across my shoulders I had to take most of his weight. He was probably a couple of stones lighter than he'd been before the illness but I was still exhausted by the time I'd helped him to undress and get into bed. There was no time to rest even then. I went back downstairs and put the kettle on to make two hot-water bottles for him, before picking up the phone to call for a doctor.

I'd already dialled the surgery before I remembered it was only eight o'clock and a Sunday into the bargain – no one would be there. I thought about calling 999 but wondered if that might be a little premature. I'd only just managed to get him into bed. How stupid would I look if the ambulance arrived, only for me to discover that he'd warmed up considerably and was feeling much better? Josef would be cross that I'd sent for a doctor, without the added embarrassment of an unnecessary call to the emergency services.

I put the phone down for a few moments while I gathered my thoughts, then remembered Jim Burnside, who worked at a local surgery and had been Josef's doubles partner at the tennis club for years. There must have been something he picked up in my voice when I called him because he was on our front door-step within fifteen minutes.

He took one look at Josef and asked if he could use my phone to call for an ambulance. I showed him where it was, then waited by the bedside, rubbing Josef's hands and arms and talking to him as the clock ticked slowly by. I've no idea what I was saying. I know I was crying from frustration, tinged with more than a little fear, because there was nothing at all in his expression to suggest he could understand a word I was say-ing. I thought about the possibility of phoning the hotel in Manchester to speak with one of his friends there to find out what had happened, but realised I had no idea which one that would be. I had no recollection of Josef giving me either a name or number.

When the ambulance arrived, Dr Burnside asked me for the car keys and suggested I go with Josef – he would drive our car there so that I'd be able to get home again afterwards. I thanked him profusely and climbed into the back of the ambulance, holding on to Josef's hand for dear life and cursing myself for not having got out of bed earlier, when he first arrived home. I couldn't dismiss from my mind the thought that those couple of hours might have been crucial. How many more ways would I find to let him down?

As the ambulance drew up outside the hospital, my sense of foreboding wasn't helped by the realisation that the last time I'd been here was when Julie was brought in. I was ushered into what may well have been the very same waiting room as that awful day and forced once more to sit and wait for news. Dr Burnside arrived some time afterwards and handed me the car keys. He was rubbing his hands, complaining about how cold it was in the car – did I know that the heater wasn't working? He asked me how long Josef had been in the car before I found him and I didn't need to see his face to know how concerned he was when I told him that, allowing for the journey from Manchester as well, we were talking about four hours at the absolute minimum.

He was also curious about some external damage to the driver's side. One of the headlights was smashed and there was a sizeable dent in the front bumper. Did I know anything about these? I explained that when I found Josef earlier it was dark, and getting him inside the house had been all that was on my mind. But I wouldn't have noticed whether anything was amiss with the car, even if it had been broad daylight. As far as I was aware, it had been fine when Josef left on Saturday morning. If there'd been a collision of some sort, maybe that was why he'd decided to come home early. Dr Burnside nodded and went off to share this new information with the staff seeing to Josef.

We'd been there for some time before we were seen by a specialist who explained they were going to have to keep Josef in for observation and further tests. I told them about his weight loss over the past year or so and the difficulty he had in keeping food down, and about how his desire for privacy made him all the more reluctant to come in and allow himself to be examined. The specialist exchanged a couple of meaningful glances with Dr Burnside, then thanked me. He suggested I might as well go home for now, as there was nothing I could do there. He promised to call me the moment the situation changed.

I dug my heels in. I was going nowhere. The moment Josef was up to seeing anyone, I wanted to be there. As a compromise, I took an hour out to give Dr Burnside a lift home and to call in at our house to collect a few things to help pass the time before returning to the same waiting room.

They finally let me in to see Josef for about an hour or so later that afternoon. I sat there, holding his hand and talking to him. He was still more or less unresponsive, verbally, at any rate, but every so often I was aware of a slight pressure as he squeezed my hand. By the time they suggested, more forcefully this time, that I really did need to go home and get a good night's sleep myself, I was feeling a little more optimistic about things.

That evening I decided I needed to investigate. I knew I would find phone numbers for some of his friends in our address book and forced myself to wait until eight o'clock, by which time

I was sure they ought to be back from Manchester. Then I phoned Esther Ciemniak who like me had found herself a Polish airman and persuaded him to stay on after the war.

When she answered the phone, she actually sounded pleased to hear from me until I started asking about the weekend in Manchester. It was clear she hadn't a clue what I was talking about. There was an awkward pause before she passed me on to her husband, Jacek. He was upset to hear that Josef was in hospital and asked a lot of questions before admitting that he knew nothing of any reunion that weekend. Was I sure I had the details right? Maybe I'd misunderstood? I agreed that must be the case, thanked him and put the phone down.

I had no idea what to make of this. There was no way I'd mis-understood Josef. I knew almost every detail of his plans for the weekend, and it was only then that I realised how unusual this was in itself. Normally he barely took the time to explain anything beyond the absolute essentials, confident that I wasn't really interested. This time there was so much detail, I felt I should have been suspicious far earlier. Josef was not a very accomplished liar, principally because he had so little need for it. He might not have been averse to the occasional white lie for the sake of convenience but even then, as often as not, he would colour up and give himself away. But it was absolutely clear that whatever he'd been doing the previous day, he hadn't been to any reunion. How had I missed it? And, more to the point, where had he been?

My thoughts were interrupted by the doorbell. As a general rule, I don't like to speak ill of someone. I prefer to let others make their own judgement and decide for themselves. In the case of Francis O'Halloran however, I'll make an exception.

I think you need to be told about him because he's very plausible and utterly unscrupulous, which makes for a dangerous combination. It's possible that you won't come into contact with him, but somehow I doubt it. He's been obsessed for so long now with the Adams boy and the mythology that has grown up around him that I don't imagine he'll ever be able to walk away from it, so I'll tell you about him now. That way at least you'll know where you stand with him.

To begin with, he was no more than a name which seemed to crop up with increasing regularity. Cards would be put through our door, messages would be left for us. He sent a lovely bouquet of flowers once, I remember. Many other people did the same but they didn't feel this somehow entitled them to pursue us from pillar to post in search of an interview we had no wish to give. The other unfortunate couple, Mr and Mrs Bingham, seemed to court publicity with a vengeance and I imply no criticism in saying that. We learnt for ourselves that people have to find their own ways of coming to terms with their loss and if that worked for them, then all well and good. It wasn't for us though.

O'Halloran didn't seem to understand this – or at any rate, if he did, he ignored it. At one point I remember suggesting to Josef that we might be better advised to let him have his wretched interview. Maybe then he'd leave us alone. Josef stuck to his guns though. He said that some people don't know when to let go and, once they have a foot inside the door, they think they're entitled to a bed for the night. I wasn't sure then that he was right. I am now.

My first reaction, on seeing him on the front doorstep, was to wonder how on earth he knew that Josef was in hospital. It soon emerged though that this was a complete surprise to him. I gave him only the briefest outline of the events of the past few hours and tried to close the door but he held it open and asked me if I knew where Josef had been the previous day, which might have struck me as an odd question if I'd been thinking straight. I stood by the Manchester story which I had at least *believed* to be the truth until a few moments earlier and told him I had no time to talk any more, as I wanted to get an early night. To my surprise he seemed happy to leave it at that and went on his way.

The following day one of the nurses told me that a journalist had been sniffing around, asking questions. He'd wanted to talk with Josef but had been told it was out of the question. I needed no physical description to know this must be O'Halloran but couldn't for the life of me understand how he thought he might get a story out of this. Why on earth would anyone be interested? However such questions were dislodged from my thoughts by the fact that I was able to spend most of the day with Josef, who seemed a little less groggy than last time. He wasn't up to much in the way of conversation as yet and it was obvious from the way he gasped and held his stomach at times that he was in quite a bit of pain. Even so it was such a relief to see him respond to simple questions and even make requests of his own that I felt mildly encouraged.

I spent most of the day reading while he dozed. Every now and then he would wake and ask for a drink of water or get me to rearrange his pillows for him. Then he would take hold of my hand once more and drift back off to sleep. I was dying to clear up the mystery of where he'd spent Saturday evening and, more importantly, why he'd lied about the reunion but understood that these were questions for another time when he was fully recovered.

Then, just as I was packing away my things for the night, he woke again, this time grabbing my hand with more urgency than before, as if emerging from a bad dream. I was startled because I'd almost drifted off to sleep myself in the muggy atmosphere. I asked him what was wrong. He reached across with the other hand as well, trapping mine in both of his, and started rambling, his voice shaky and uncertain, about his shed of all things. He wanted me to know where he kept all the important documents: insurance, mortgage, savings accounts. They were in a filing cabinet towards the back, behind the garden chairs which he kept stored in there during the winter. The key to the filing cabinet was hanging on a nail just above the lintel of the shed door. He made me repeat it back to him several times to make sure I'd understood.

I was confused at first, thinking he wanted me to find a particular document and bring it in but he shook his head and I realised he was trying to make sure I knew where everything was in case he didn't make it out of the hospital. This threw me into such a heightened state of anxiety that I scolded him, told him I didn't want to hear such nonsense but I could tell my words were having no effect whatsoever. All day I'd been thinking things were a little brighter than before and here he was, dead set on assuming the worst. While I was planning for full recovery, for him it was only a question of which got him first, the hypothermia or the cancer.

To my eternal shame, I felt at the time that he was being melodramatic, making a play for my sympathies. I bridled at what I interpreted as a touch of selfishness on his part. He wasn't the only one who'd been suffering. Who had been there at his bedside every time he opened his eyes? Who had been worrying herself sick ever since she found him slumped over the steering wheel? Was anyone showing any great concern about me and what I was going through? And if having a husband at death's door wasn't bad enough, why did I have to be saddled with any number of unanswered questions about where he'd been and what he'd been up to? If anyone had a right to feel sorry for herself . . .

So as I stood up to leave and leant over to kiss him good-night, I paused briefly, then went back on the promise I'd made to myself. I told him I knew there was no reunion that weekend. Don't ask me why – I have no idea. Maybe I was hurt that he seemed to be giving up so easily while I clung on by my bleeding fingernails. Perhaps I felt that if he was up to serious conversations of that order, the least he could do was answer the question that had kept me awake half the previous night. Either way, I wish I hadn't done it.

He looked at me with a frown of incomprehension at first, as if wondering how he'd given himself away. Then he turned away from me and faced the wall. I waited for him to say something and, when he didn't respond, I pushed it further, asked him where he'd been. What had he been up to? Why had he deemed it necessary to lie to me? Again he said nothing but, as I leant closer, I watched a solitary tear drip from one eye. I was amazed. In all the time I had known him, through the death of his daughter, news of the deaths of his parents in Poland, I'd never once seen Josef shed a tear. He grieved as much as the next man, I was sure of that, but he internalised everything. If he'd ever cried in his life, it was well away from me.

He was still facing the wall so I had to lean in to hear what he was mumbling. I could make out just two words, repeated over and over again. *I'm sorry*, he said. *I'm sorry*. And those were the last words I ever heard from his lips because the following morning, while I was on my way back to the hospital to see him, having spent another restless night wondering how best to take the subject further, Josef died. Alone.

Two days later, as I was sorting through the filing cabinet, looking to make sense of our financial situation, I found a file labelled *Medical* and withdrew a sheet of paper from the hospital – one I'd never seen before. It was a straightforward, matter-of-fact letter, informing Josef that his recent tests had revealed that he was sterile and would never be able to produce children of his own.

It was dated one month before Julie was born.

July 2001: John Michael

Another train. Compartment all to himself for the past half-hour or so, which suits him just fine. St Pancras coming up, then bus to Victoria, heading further south. North means home and safety. South means he's really serious about all this.

He was right about Ashbury. No way of knowing what he was walking into but the few people there who remembered Peter Vaughan were more than happy to talk about the old days. If that was worth the risk, he knows he's got to go with his gut instinct and assume the same goes for the next step. No choice – he can't back off now, not having come this far.

Ashbury's pleasant enough. A bit quiet but not that different from where he's been living for the past twenty years or so. It's easy to see why his father picked it, why it would have appealed to him. It's funny – if anyone had suggested to John Michael when he was younger that he'd turn out like his old man, he'd have thrown a fit. Now here he is, more or less the same age his father had been that night in Inverness. Doesn't seem like such a stretch to imagine the two of them might have got on, given the chance.

It's a good thing there's no real physical resemblance though. He can remember his nan once, long time ago, saying he was a right chip off the old block – *spitting image of your dad*. Just trying to let her son know how proud she was. But everyone else knew who John Michael took after. Same high cheekbones, same little kink on the bridge of the nose – even the same blonde eyelashes. Mummy's boy, right enough. Just as well in a way 'cos it wouldn't have done to turn up in Ashbury, asking questions about Peter Vaughan and looking like he'd come back from the grave, would it?

That old girl – Jenny Moore, was it? *Go ask Old Jenny Moore*, they said. *If she can't help you, nobody can.* There'd been a moment when they were sitting there in her kitchen. The way she kept staring at him, he wondered if maybe she'd put it all together. Made him feel a bit uncomfortable for a while but it was probably just nerves getting the better of him. You get to her age, your eyesight's probably not that hot. And anyway, even if she did suspect something, it's no big deal having Peter Vaughan as his father. Not like being the son of Martin Adams.

She says Peter Vaughan wasn't the easiest person to get to know. Kept himself to himself for the most part. She liked that about him. *The ones who take longest to get to know are usually the ones worth knowing*. Not that she got to know him as well as some though...

And he knew all along the woman at the inn – the one his father kept slipping into the conversation the last few times they spoke together – he just knew she was going to be the key to it all. But if Old Jenny Moore's guess is correct and it's not just a case of an old woman filling her empty days with a bit of gossip ... well, that'd be something else, wouldn't it?

And he's supposed to walk away from this and forget everything he's heard? Yeah, right.

August 2007: Ellen 2

I flatter myself that I can write. After a lifetime of reading and having spent years putting together book and film reviews, I like to think I have a way with words. Even so, I'm at a loss to describe how I felt when I discovered the letter from the hospital.

I'm not exactly a shrinking violet. I've managed to get by without the support of my family since I walked out all those years ago with Josef. I've learnt to cope with the loss of a husband I never truly appreciated until he was no longer there. I may never come to terms with the loss of my daughter but at least I've managed over the years to compartmentalise my feelings and think of her only when it's safe to do so.

But thoughts of that letter and its implications still produce a physical reaction in me even now, a catch in my throat, a prickling at the back of my eyes. And it comes out of nowhere. I can be doing nothing, thinking nothing, and all of a sudden I find myself, for the umpteenth time, wondering just how I failed to realise what a remarkable man I'd married until it was too late. If ever I feel the need to bring my ego down a peg or two, I go back to those two months before Julie was born, when Josef was struggling to get his head around the fact that the baby he'd always wanted couldn't possibly be his while I, sensitivity personified, accused him of sulking. Or I remind myself that even though he knew I'd been unfaithful to him, he never once used it against me, however great the temptation must have been over the years. My reward to him for such loyalty was to poison our final few moments together with petty recriminations and, to my eternal shame, to make him weep. That's some legacy I've had to carry around with me all these years.

In the days and weeks immediately after Josef's death, I threw myself into as many practical tasks as I could think of. There were a number of jobs around the house and garden that I'd been putting off for a while. These provided me with a much-needed focus. I wrote a list and worked my way steadily through it, barely pausing to tick off each completed job before moving on to the next one. Any task, however menial or mundane, was welcomed as long as it kept me occupied.

One of these tasks was to arrange for someone to repair the heater in the car and to have the dent in the bodywork seen to. I took it to my local garage – Josef had always been impressed with them, pleased in this day and age to find people he could trust to do a good job for a fair price. The manager brought it back two days later and along with the keys he rather sheepishly handed me a sheet of paper, which I at first assumed to be the bill.

He explained that one of his men had found it, wedged down the side of the front passenger seat. I thanked him and asked how much the repairs had come to but he insisted there would be no charge. It was for Josef, he told me, and he was sorry for my loss. I thanked him and took the sheet of paper inside.

I opened it and was surprised to recognise Josef's handwriting. It looked like a letter, obviously only a draft because it was on a scrap piece of paper with jagged edges where it had been torn from a notepad. What really took the wind from my sails was the fact that although there was no name at the top, it could only have been written for one person, and that was the Adams boy.

He was writing to the boy, or young man as he must have been by then, to express the hope that he might make something useful of his own life to atone for the one he'd taken from us. In doing so Josef seemed determined to attribute to me qualities I'm quite sure I've never had and I think that letter stands as a more eloquent expression of his love for me than ever I received from him in person.

Once the initial shock had passed, I sat there for some time, wondering about this. Had he at some stage completed a neat copy and sent it? And if so, where had he sent it? Around that time there was a great deal of speculation about the Adams boy and whether or not he had been released. Josef and I obviously talked about it and he tried as best he could to prepare me for the likelihood that John Michael Adams had already been granted his freedom with a new identity. But even if he had reasons for supposing this had already happened, how on earth had he come by an address?

That question was still exercising my thoughts that same evening when the phone rang. The caller, an elderly lady with a strong Scottish accent, asked if she might speak with a Mr Josef *Kasprovik* – the name was so often mispronounced that I rarely took the trouble to correct anyone. I asked who was calling and she went into something of a dither. She said she was probably panicking about nothing but could I just reassure her that the gentleman was alright and had arrived home safely from his trip to Scotland a few weeks ago. She and her husband ran a small B&B on the outskirts of Inverness and Josef had booked in there on the very night he had told me he was in a hotel in Manchester. He'd stayed only briefly to pay and to complete the necessary forms (which was how she knew our home phone number), then had gone out again. She and her husband had urged him not to because the conditions were so awful and they were sure he had to be tired after such a long journey. He insisted he was fine – he was meeting someone and would be back later.

They gave him a key and had no idea he hadn't returned until her husband took the breakfast to the annexe the following morning. His car wasn't in the drive and the bed clearly hadn't been slept in. Her immediate fear was that something had happened to him but he *had* told them he was meeting someone. They assumed he'd taken one look at the road conditions and spent the night at his friend's place instead, rather than risk driving back to the B&B.

Just recently though there was an awful story in the news about an elderly gentleman who had tripped in the snow in his own back yard and died of exposure. It had brought it all back and she felt she needed to phone just to set her mind at rest.

I assured her Josef had returned safe and sound, thanked her for her concern and put the phone down the moment it was possible to do so without seeming impolite. Now I had even more mysteries to consider. Inverness? What on earth was he doing up there? More to the point, how long must it have taken him to drive there? I calculated that the trip must have taken him something between eight and ten hours ... one way. And he had done it twice. In twenty-four hours! What's more he'd done it in awful driving conditions in a car that was like a freezer compartment! What on earth had possessed him? And who was this person he was supposedly meeting? Whoever it was, Josef most certainly had not spent the night anywhere other than in his car, which was absolute madness. If he'd already paid for the B&B, why hadn't he stayed there for the night and travelled back in daylight?

I went back to the note Josef had drafted, sensing I was missing something and this time it leapt off the page. There were two phrases that sounded slightly off-kilter to me. I don't recall the exact wording but in the first he was saying something along the lines of: *I need two minutes to tell you about my wife, and then I'll leave.* Then somewhere else he was talking about me, saying that *if it was me standing there and not him* ... something like that anyway. The point was, in both cases it didn't sound like a letter. It was more like a speech, as if he was planning to deliver these lines in person. I read the whole thing again to make sure and was even more convinced I was right. If this sheet of paper was found in the car, the chances were that Josef had taken it with him to Inverness. Why would he do so unless he was hoping to confront John Michael Adams there? But for that to be possible, he would have to know exactly where to find him, and how on earth he could have known that was beyond me. It was too fantastic for words.

I almost convinced myself I was imagining things until I remembered Frank O'Halloran, and his surprise visit the evening after Josef had returned. I tried to recall that conversation in detail. I remembered the shock that registered on his face when he learnt that Josef was in hospital and in particular that strange non sequitur of a question about where Josef had been the previous day. If it hadn't seemed suspicious at the time, it certainly did now.

I wanted nothing more than to ring him straightaway but didn't have his number, which was ironic really. Over the past few years there must have been at least twenty occasions when he'd pressed his card into our hands or posted it through the door, and each time we'd torn it up and thrown it away. When I did eventually manage to track him down, he was at my front door within minutes, bright-eyed and out of breath. He offered belated condolences and his notebook and pen were out of his pocket before I'd even closed the door. Clearly he was anticipating another significant addition to his John Michael Adams portfolio. He seemed surprised when I told him to put it away.

While sitting around waiting for him to arrive, I'd been pondering over the best way to approach this meeting. To say I knew him well would be something of an exaggeration. Even so, I'd had enough contact to form the strong impression that simply asking him to tell me everything he knew about the weekend in Inverness was not the way to go. He didn't strike me as a man to be persuaded by appeals to his better nature. It seemed to me my best chance of finding out what I wanted to know would be to mislead him into thinking I already knew it.

So the moment he sat down in Josef's armchair I first made it clear that this conversation was *off the record*, as they say. Once that was established, I asked him if his interview with John Michael Adams had been worth it, which at least had the effect of removing the smile from his face. I led him to believe that, just before he died, Josef had told me everything about his trip to Inverness and that I was holding him personally responsible for my husband's death.

He reddened and was quick to protest that Josef had left and returned in his own car – no one was twisting his arm. In fact, he would have much preferred it if Josef had kept well away from Inverness, rather than barging in like that and destroying months of hard work. This threw me a little and I'm not sure what I said next but whatever it was, I must have overreached myself and given the game away because, after a brief pause, the smile returned. He relaxed visibly and complimented me on a nice try, but if I wanted to know what happened in Inverness, why didn't I just ask him outright instead of playing games?

According to him – and I understand I would have to be a simpleton of the first order not to view this as a highly slanted account – the rumours about the Adams boy being released with a new identity were true and every reporter in the country was out there trying to hunt him down. O'Halloran wanted me to believe that he had actually managed to do it – and not only that but he'd also talked his way into a place at the table for the first meeting between the Adams boy and his father in exchange for keeping his silence as to the boy's new identity.

He claimed Josef's arrival was a complete surprise. He had no idea how he knew about the meeting. He couldn't even say for sure what happened. All he knew was that one minute Josef was there, the next the boy's father had been mown down by a hit-and-run driver and Josef was nowhere to be found. He himself had put two and two together and got out of there as quickly as possible because he wanted to get Josef's side of the story first. Now of course it was irrelevant. He would never know for sure what got into Josef that night. Of course, much of this I recognised immediately as self-serving nonsense. For one thing, there was only one way Josef could have known about the meeting in Inverness. The idea that he'd somehow managed to find out for himself was simply ridiculous. *Someone* had told him and that could only have been O'Halloran. Equally preposterous was the idea that Josef had driven all that way with the intention of harming anyone. I had a sheet of paper which suggested Josef had gone to Inverness to talk with the boy, to urge him to do something with his life, not to seek revenge.

I had to admit though that I had no explanation for what *did* happen that evening. No matter how strong my conviction that Josef could never have done such an awful thing, there was the damage to the car to consider. Josef had certainly hit something. And then there was the fact that he hadn't returned to the B&B for which he'd already paid, but had chosen instead to drive all the way back home in freezing conditions in a car with no heating. What's more, having arrived, he'd stayed in the car rather than come into the house to get warm. These were not the acts of a rational man and I knew, even without O'Halloran's testimony, that whatever happened in Inverness, the balance of Josef's mind must have been seriously disturbed.

O'Halloran assured me he had no intention of adding to my grief by telling anyone what he knew. I had nothing to worry about. You have to know him to understand just how worrying that was in itself. I suspected he had his own reasons for not wanting to go to the police with what he suspected but I was less sanguine about the prospect of being in collusion with him. He wanted me to believe that he was doing the noble thing in protecting Josef's memory and clearly saw me as being in his debt. I suspected this would not be the last I would see of him.

Time would prove me right, although I have to admit it could have been worse. He has become an irritant more than anything. Like the proverbial bad penny, he has a tendency to pop up out of nowhere every so often. There might be a year or so between visits and I'd reach the point where I'd more or less forgotten about him, only for him to arrive on the doorstep and invite himself in for *a cup of tea and a chat*. I'm not sure what he thought these visits were achieving. If, as I suspect, I was being pumped for information each time in case, as mother of one of the victims, I might have been told something by the authorities which could help him in his search for the boy, he must have been sorely disappointed over the years. I always hoped he might eventually lose interest but he's nothing if not persistent.

In early 1982 I decided to move here to Oakham. Josef's life-insurance policies and my reclusive existence since his death had left me in the enviable position of having more than enough money and not a great deal on which I wished to spend it. My freelance work was the catalyst which dragged me out of my cocoon and encouraged me to feel maybe the time was right to make a fresh start. Primrose Cottage was one of the first properties I looked at and I knew the search was over the moment I first saw it – this was where I could start to rebuild. I would no longer be Dorrie Kasprowicz, grieving widow, tragic mother. Step forward Eudora Nash, freelance journalist and

lady of independent means. I was ready to shake off the past –
including Frank O'Halloran.

I told him nothing about Primrose Cottage. I was hoping,
perhaps naively, that once he discovered I was no longer living in town, he might decide it wasn't worth the time and effort
required to track me down again. His obsession with John
Michael Adams must surely have its limits. I suppose I must
have been in Oakham for three days at most when the envelope
came through the door. Inside was a card with a picture of a
Cotswold cottage which bore an uncanny resemblance to mine
and a brief message, wishing me all the best on my recent move
and expressing the hope that we would have the chance to speak
soon. As I said, he is not easily deterred.

From the moment I moved to Oakham I went out of my way
to involve myself in every aspect of village life. You'll appreciate this was something of a departure for me but I confess my
motives were not entirely selfless. I didn't want my past to intrude
in any way on the present and if being a little more sociable
and outgoing helped to keep the curiosity and speculation of
others at bay, it was well worth the effort. So overnight I became
someone who stops in the street to exchange a few words with
passers-by and pat pampered dogs on the head. I learnt to linger
for a while to chat with Joyce or Rose in the village store, confident that any version of reality I chose to give them would be
common knowledge in no time. I invited neighbours in for mid-
morning coffee and afternoon tea and cakes and earned a bit of
a reputation for being a good listener, even a source of sound
advice when it was needed.

And, somewhat to my surprise, I took to it like a duck to
water. In no time at all, it seemed, I'd managed to establish

myself in the village. My work, which I still regarded as little more than a rewarding hobby, came to define me. I was Eudora the writer, alongside Angela the show jumper, Lois the daytime TV presenter and Maurice the ac-*tor*, who popped up on the TV screen every now and then in a bewildering series of minor roles, most of them indistinguishable from each other. I somehow acquired a local network – I knew to whom I should turn if the drains were blocked, if the car wouldn't start, if a window needed replacing. There was a genuine sense of community and for once I was a part of it, not outside and seeking to be left alone. Apart from the all too brief time I was allowed with Julie, I can honestly say those were the happiest, certainly the most serene years of my life.

Then came a major health scare, which landed me in hospital for quite a while. I shan't bore you with the details but suffice to say that, given my age, I would have been foolish in the extreme not to have *intimations of mortality*, as they say. That period of three to four weeks, when my chances of pulling through were very much in the balance, taught me something about myself that I'd never acknowledged until then – I wasn't ready to go just yet. I was assailed by an overwhelming sense of futility. Surely this couldn't be it – there were things I still needed to do. I couldn't have told you what a single one of these things might be but I knew I wasn't about to bow out with anything like equanimity. There had to be more to life than this. *Had* to. And when it eventually became clear that the illness was no more than a warning shot across the bows and that I was going to be around for a while longer, it felt as if I'd been granted a second chance – one I was determined not to waste.

I'm not sure how Martin Adams came into the equation. For years he'd existed only as a vague figure somewhere in the outermost reaches of my thoughts. If ever I had occasion to refer to him, I rarely did so by name. He was 'the boy's father', as if that said all that needed to be said about him. But he was more than that, of course – and if anyone was in a position to know that, surely it was the mother of Julie Kasprowicz. I had allowed myself to buy into the lazy caricature created by the media. It was too easy to forget that this was not some cardboard cut-out but a real human being. I was not alone in having endured more than my fair share of suffering. He'd lost his wife in tragic circumstances, as I'd lost Josef. At more or less the same time as I was dropping Julie off at school that morning, he was saying goodbye to his boy with absolutely no understanding that their time together was over. And as if he hadn't suffered enough, just as it looked as if he was about to be granted *his* second chance, it had been ripped from his grasp by a man he personally had never wronged. Wife. Son. Self. Gone, just like that.

Except, of course, it wasn't quite like that. I came to realise over the next few days that in much the same way that I'd never really thought of Martin Adams as a person, I'd been equally remiss in glossing over the details of his life. Now that I was imbued with this new determination to start again and look at my life afresh, it occurred to me for the first time that there were problems with the chronology of my version of events. I'd been guilty of grouping all the disasters together as if they were one and the same thing whereas in fact there had been significant intervals between them. His boy had been taken from him in November 1966, his wife sometime before that. But it wasn't until March 1974 that he and Josef had made their separate ways to Inverness. That was an eight-year gap. And eight years is a long time. What had he been doing during that period?

I knew from O'Halloran that he'd moved away and started a new life under a different identity. So where had he been living during those missing years? It was safe to assume his new identity had held up, or it would have been headline news otherwise. How hard had he found it? I wondered. What was it like, living in constant fear that, at any moment, someone might recognise him and bring all he'd been building crashing down around his ears? Again, I was struck by the similarities with the way my own life had unfolded. Had he found an Oakham of his own, a Primrose Cottage where he could put down roots and dare to dream of a future which didn't involve looking over his shoulder every few seconds? Had he made new friends? More than that, perhaps?

I gave this some thought, tried to picture him in the courtroom day after day, a sad, lonely figure, head bowed as if seeking to avoid the glares of others. He would have been in his midthirties. That was no age at all and eight years would easily be long enough for him to meet a lot of people and form all manner of attachments. For a while I tormented myself with mental pictures of a devoted wife and children, saying goodbye to their father for the weekend, unaware that they would never see him again. My own life seemed like a patchwork quilt of stories just like this, families snatched from cosy domesticity and plunged into a nightmare for which nothing had prepared them and from which there was no escape. I wouldn't allow myself to imagine he could disappear without leaving an indelible mark on *someone*.

The more I tried to dismiss these notions, the more they came back like small brush fires in a forest. Eventually I came to the conclusion there was only one way I was going to be able to put them out. I had to find out as much as possible about what he'd been doing in those missing years.

Arriving at this decision was one thing, knowing how to go about it was another matter entirely. I had a date – March 5th, 1974. I had a location of sorts; it might not have been in Inverness itself but it seemed reasonable to suppose it wouldn't have been far from the B&B that Josef had booked. But when it came to a name, I had nothing. I was fairly sure O'Halloran would know, but I was not about to ask him.

I turned instead to Derek Wilmot. His father, Hugh, was our family solicitor for years and had shepherded me through the legal minefield when Josef died. Derek joined the firm many more years ago than I care to remember and took over when his father retired. You will have met him by now, of course, and will know he can be a little particular, prissy even, but he is level-headed and resourceful and if integrity is not his middle name, it should be. If anyone was likely to be able to help, it was he.

He was a little dubious about the cloak-and-dagger nature of it all but otherwise offered no opinion on the matter, other than to say he knew of someone who might be able to help. He gave me the name of a local agency, one with something of a reputation for dealing with sensitive investigations. He knew the owner personally and had made occasional use of his services in the past. I emphasised strongly that this had to be handled with the greatest discretion. No one must know about my involvement. I wanted everything to be done through AWL and did not wish to meet in person with any of the investigators. I might have aged considerably in thirty years and certainly no one in the village had recognised me, but I didn't want to take any unnecessary risks. There must be no chance of my identity being revealed. Derek assured me he understood what was at stake here and asked me to leave it with him.

He rang the following day to say that everything was in place, if I was happy to proceed. The owner of the agency, Stuart Mahon, had been apprised of the sensitive nature of the investigation and was happy to report to me only via the offices of AWL. In order to keep this on a *need-to-know* basis he would conduct the investigation himself and keep all paperwork, other than the final report, as non-specific as possible. He would be free to start the following week.

Derek warned me, as a matter of course, that this might be expensive and that I should prepare myself for the possibility that, with so little information to work with, the investigation might come to nothing. I was unconcerned about the money but spent an anxious few weeks, worrying about what I could possibly do next if this proved to be a dead end.

I have to say though that Mr Mahon more than lived up to his reputation. If you ever wish to read the final report in its entirety, you will need to visit AWL. The only copy is locked away in the safe and I have left instructions that it should stay there unless you arrive in person to take possession of it. When you have read it, you'll find it easier to understand my caution. For now you'll have to make do with my own summary of its contents. If nothing else, it should make clear the reasons for my decision.

Mr Mahon, it seems, realised from a very early stage that he would need to visit Inverness in person. He had been hoping that his preliminary checks might do much of the leg work for him but was puzzled to discover that his usual sources were unable to confirm any record of a hit-and-run in the Inverness area for the given date, even when he extended the period to one week either side. Several accidents were reported in the local newspapers due to unusually hazardous road conditions but he was unable to find a single instance of a fatality or of a driver leaving the scene of an accident.

In Inverness he gained the strong impression that he was being given what he described as 'the runaround'. The local police seemed unimpressed that he was wasting their time with questions about an incident of which there appeared to be no official record. Far from wanting to help him, they seemed suspicious about his reasons for showing an interest in the first place. He had more or less resigned himself to the need to look elsewhere when a sympathetic officer suggested in private that he might like to speak with a former colleague named George Appleby, who had retired from the force some time ago. He was now working as a security consultant for a company in Dingwall and a visit to his home proved to be the turning point.

Appleby showed none of the reticence of his former colleagues and wasn't remotely surprised when March 5th, 1974 was specified. He knew exactly which incident was being referred to and was surprised it had taken so long for someone to ask him about it. In these days of freedom of information, he'd been expecting something to surface long before now.

He claimed he and his partner had been first on the scene that evening, responding to a hit-and-run report. He remembered the weather and road conditions were atrocious and by the time they arrived at the village, most potential witnesses had already drifted away. The only person claiming to have seen what happened was able to offer no more than a vague description of the car that had driven off and had not managed to get the vehicle registration. As for the victim, it was obvious at first glance that his neck had been broken by the impact.

There was no wallet or documentation to establish his identity but they found keys in his pocket, attached to a fob with the initials IB, and eventually matched them to an old VW van in the car park. Appleby radioed the details through and as far as he was concerned, the whole business was over and done with.

The following day he was told there had been some confusion over the identity of the victim. Although the van was registered to an Ian Blair of Skegness in Lincolnshire, it had been loaned to a friend, a Peter Vaughan, who lived in a village a few miles away. Appleby couldn't recall the name but was sure he would recognise it if he heard it.

Then, two days later, Appleby and his partner were called in to speak with what he referred to as a 'suit', who was brief and to the point. The incident to which he and his partner had responded was not in fact a hit-and-run but a simple accident. No criticism would go on their record – Appleby and his partner had done a professional job and come to the only conclusion possible, given the evidence they had before them. Since then however, new evidence had come to light and the case was now closed. He and his partner were asked to get together their official reports and any other documents relating to the incident and hand them to the DCS in person. He was reminded that the entire interview was classified and was then dismissed.

Appleby was far from comfortable about what had just happened but his partner, who had been around a fair while longer and understood how these things worked, told him to forget it. He had no time for the 'suits' but wasn't about to hand anyone a stick with which they might beat him. If they wanted him to believe black was white, that was fine by him.

Appleby might have been able to live with this, were it not for the fact that a few days later he was called in yet again. A close acquaintance of the deceased was asking to visit the scene of the accident and leave a bouquet of flowers there. Appleby was charged with driving her out to Lachlie and then making sure she was on the next train home. He picked her up on his way through Reception and drove her out to where the incident had occurred. She placed the flowers near the entrance to the car park, then bowed her head in prayer while he stood around awkwardly, wondering whether or not he should join in. Then she thanked him quietly and they returned to the car.

She said nothing during the drive back to the station until they drew up in the forecourt. As she got out of the car, she paused and asked him if he would clarify something for her. When she was first notified, the police were talking about a hit-and-run. Now it seemed the incident was being treated as nothing more sinister than a straightforward accident, and whenever she pressed for an explanation as to why, she found it difficult to get a straight answer. She asked him to swear, hand on heart, that there was nothing untoward about all this. He looked her straight in the eye and lied, and she burst into tears, thanking him for his kindness. As he drove off, he tried not to think of her on her long, lonely journey back home. She had travelled all that way to pay her respects and ask a simple question and he hadn't been able to summon up the decency to answer it honestly. He claimed his disenchantment with the job started right there – he'd never felt so bad about himself in all his life.

When Mr Mahon asked again about the name of the village near Skegness, Appleby fetched a road atlas and came across what he thought might be the name. He couldn't be one hundred per cent sure but Ashbury sounded familiar. The woman's name though ... he was quite clear about that. The surname might be lost in the mists of time but her Christian name, he said, was definitely the same as his wife's. It was Barbara.

February 2008: Ellen

Kate was a gist reader – always had been. She supposed she was no different in this respect from any other small-business owner. Years of dealing with legal documents did that to you. You learnt to skim the surface, scanning for those few key words which might persuade otherwise interminable sentences and sprawling paragraphs to give up their meaning. It was that or go under – death by a thousand sub-clauses.

With Eudora's documents she was paying much more attention to detail, fascinated by where the narrative might take her, and yet she still found herself finishing each sheet a good twenty seconds ahead of Ellen, who seemed to want to turn every shirt collar of a sentence inside out, looking for labels. Usually Kate was happy to wait patiently while her friend made her laborious way towards the foot of the page but this time, when she reached Barbara's name, she sat back and made great show of rubbing her aching neck muscles. She wanted to be in a position to gauge Ellen's reaction when she saw the name.

She'd expected Barbara to figure in this somewhere. Her life-long obsession with keeping her past from Ellen suggested a guilty secret or two and Kate had started reading in the firm expectation that these papers would fill in a few blanks. But she hadn't expected anything like this. Even after all this time, just the mention of John Michael Adams automatically cata-pulted things into another realm altogether. She was aware of all manner of implications, buzzing away in her subconscious, demanding to be heard, but there was no time to listen to them just yet. Taking stock could come later. For now she wanted to press on.

She watched closely as Ellen ran her finger along the bottom line of the sheet. There was a pause when she reached the name. A brief pause. There might even have been a slight shake of the head as she licked her finger and transferred the sheet to the bottom of the pile. Otherwise there was nothing to suggest her life had just changed for ever.

Not a thing.

August 2007: Ellen 2

When he reached Ashbury, Mr Mahon spoke with a number of people who still remembered Peter Vaughan. He'd appeared one day out of nowhere and was taken on at the New Inn, initially for a trial period, to look after the grounds and general main-tenance. Before long he'd made himself indispensable to the Sutherlands and earned the respect and trust of the village as a whole. If he was a little on the quiet side and not at all inclined to talk about his life before he arrived in Ashbury, then good luck to him. A man's private life was his own business. Deeds counted far more than words anyway and he was clearly of the old school, a man who appreciated the value of a job of work and wasn't afraid to roll up his shirtsleeves. Old man Sutherland, who didn't offer praise lightly, thought highly of him ... and more than one villager suspected his daughter Barbara felt the same way.

His death certainly hit her harder than most. She had never been the most outgoing of people, but in those first few weeks after Vaughan's accident the barriers went up with a vengeance. She shut herself away, rarely venturing out of the inn and keeping well clear of the bar during the evenings, as if determined to avoid all expressions of sympathy. Then, two or three months later, she left the village without a word to anyone. There was talk of a disagreement with her father, a lot of silly rumours such as you always get in such cases, but nothing was ever substantiated. Bob Sutherland stubbornly refused to talk about it, other than to say that she'd taken a job in London and wouldn't be back. It was a private matter and respected as such.

She did in fact return just once ... for his funeral eighteen months later. She accepted condolences and exchanged pleasantries as if she'd merely been away for a short holiday rather than cutting herself adrift but she was quick to slip back into her shell the moment any conversation edged its way towards the life she was now leading. She spent the afternoon on the arm of her uncle, who was remembered in the village as a scrawny young thing with holes in his socks before he went off and made a name for himself. He'd brought her there in his expensive-looking car in which, according to one of the villagers, a child's rattle happened to be lying on the floor, just in front of the rear seat. Everyone knew young Sam and his wife had no children of their own so it made a few tongues wag.

Different villagers commented on different things. Some had picked up on the occasional glance between Barbara and Peter when they worked together behind the bar – nothing significant but just enough to put the sensors on alert. Others commented on her response to the news of his death, so much more extreme than anyone expected, and her insistence on setting off for Scotland to bring his body home. Everyone was intrigued by the unexplained disagreement with her father and her sudden disappearance. But above all else, there was the mysterious bouquet of lilies that was delivered to Peter Vaughan's grave every year on the anniversary of his death, an anonymous tribute from someone who, if nothing else, clearly did not want him to be forgotten. For many in the village, it told a story.

Mr Mahon followed up the bouquet lead and traced the direct debit back to an Interflora account in Chichester. His search for Barbara's uncle, Sam Balfour, led to the same area. From there it was relatively easy for him to discover that Barbara had been working at the holiday park which Sam and his wife had set up on the outskirts of a village called Ryhill.

And that she had a daughter named Ellen, who was born on the 22nd of September 1974, some four or five months after Barbara disappeared from Ashbury.

When Derek forwarded the report to me, I knew immediately what I wanted to do. I'd failed Josef in so many ways as a wife – now I was being given one final chance to do the right thing as his widow. This woman – your mother – had lost the only man she really loved, not just lost him but had him ripped from her in the cruellest way imaginable. Then she'd travelled all the way to Scotland in search of answers, only to be denied them. She must have feared, when Appleby lied to her, that the truth was never going to come out and that she'd never know what really happened in Inverness that evening. Now I understood why God had seen fit to spare me for a short while longer. I would see her, explain everything and in so doing go some way towards wiping out the only debt that Josef ran up in his time on this earth. It all seemed so clear.

I decided to phone your mother, using the contact details Mr Mahon had provided. I might have realised, had I just taken the time to think it through properly, what a shock it would be for her. She certainly sounded very apprehensive, especially when I explained it was to do with Peter Vaughan. Heaven only knows what thoughts must have been going through her mind at that instant. Under the circumstances, it's not surprising she hung up on me.

The following day I phoned the local coach company and booked a weekend return to Chichester, telling myself that if nothing else were to come of it, at least I could have a few days by the sea. When I pulled into the bus station, I took a taxi first of all to the address I'd been given for her. There was no reply but a neighbour suggested I try Langmere Grove. Apparently, although she'd supposedly retired the previous year, she still worked part-time plus occasional weekends if they needed extra staff. When I finally tracked her down there, she seemed alarmed at first but agreed to talk with me. I don't know which was the more significant factor in her decision – the fact that I had travelled all that way or her fears that there might be some sort of scene. Whatever the case, we had a cup of tea and a slice of cake in the cafeteria next to the swimming pool and I spent the next half-hour explaining everything I knew about the death of Peter Vaughan, including both his real identity and the tragedy that bound us together.

And she cried, of course. You'll think me remarkably stupid but I don't think it had dawned on me at any stage that this might be something she wouldn't want to hear. I was so bound up in the lies and the secrecy and the overwhelming need for the truth to come out that I never once asked myself whether she might be better off not knowing, especially after all this time. If I'd been blessed with a little more imagination and, dare I say it, empathy, I might have realised she'd managed to find a way to come to terms with what had happened and was happy with the distorted version of the truth that had been fed to her. It was only when the tears began to flow and she started shaking her head that I became aware of my questionable motives for making this journey. It might have been cutting the cancer from my own heart but it certainly wasn't doing much for her.

But there was another aspect to this which didn't strike me immediately. Instead it crept up on me, starting as a vague suspicion and eventually developing into full-blown conviction. It seemed to me her tears were reserved for Peter's death and the mind-numbing futility of it all – Josef's illness, the mistaken identity, O'Halloran's quixotic crusade. But there was no real sense of shock over his true identity. I'm not sure what I was expecting exactly – anger, disbelief, outrage maybe? But there were none of these – indeed, she seemed more taken aback by my own connection to the whole history of John Michael Adams than that of Peter Vaughan and it was difficult to escape the conclusion that at some stage he must have confided in her – and

I can only marvel at the courage required for such a conversation, given what would have been at stake. I was so convinced that she knew that I asked her outright but she simply shook her head and cried once more. Somehow it felt intrusive to pursue it any further.

We took a walk around the grounds to avoid being conspicuous and when she'd had a chance to compose herself, she asked exactly what it was I wanted. When I told her I hoped to leave the cottage to her, she said she didn't need it. She was perfectly civil about it but quite adamant. She didn't want it. When I said I wanted to do it for Josef, to go some way towards making up for what had happened all those years ago and that maybe I might leave it to you instead, she became angry for the first time. She was absolutely determined that this was not going to happen. I did my best to talk her round but it was obvious I was wasting my time.

I tried ringing her again the following week but had to leave a message. In the end, it wasn't Barbara who rang back but her uncle, Mr Balfour. He was very pleasant, charming even, but equally firm in his stance. He explained that your mother didn't want to be reminded of things that had been buried for so long. She had no interest in inheriting any cottage from me and was equally insistent that her daughter be kept out of it altogether.

When I asked him if you had a right to know the truth and decide such things for yourself, he took me to task for imagining that your mother had not been through these selfsame arguments a thousand times over the past thirty years. She'd decided on what she believed to be in the best interests of her daughter. Did I really think I knew better? And to round things off, he asked me if knowing the truth was always the best way forward. Did I, for instance, feel my life had changed for the better the moment I discovered what Josef had done? And was there nothing in my past that I had kept secret rather than share with those closest to me? You can just imagine how that particular point struck home.

So I did as I was asked. I kept my silence and stayed away, leaving you with the version of reality they've chosen for you. It's only now, as I sense my life is drawing to a close, that I feel the need to backtrack slightly. And it *is* only slightly – I left plenty of checks in place to ensure that you would only learn what you decided to know. If you've reached this stage, you'll appreciate that I left it very much up to you. You've had plenty of opportunities to walk away. But I felt the need to do this, Ellen. The truth *does* matter. My life is a testimony to what can happen if you try to suppress it. Once I'm gone, the truth disappears with me unless I leave a trail for you to follow. I can only hope that, for once, I've done the right thing.

Just one more thing before I leave. I didn't tell you everything about my trip to Langmere Grove. When I first arrived there, I was asked to wait in Reception while someone went to fetch your mother. While I was sitting there, the main doors opened and a woman came through, manoeuvring a pushchair with one hand and clinging on to a little girl with the other. She went up to the main desk and lifted the girl onto the counter, exchanging a few jokes with the women on Reception. At one point she turned and smiled briefly as if to acknowledge my presence, before returning to the conversation she was having. Then, after a few minutes, she picked the girl up and disappeared into one of the offices at the rear of the building.

You won't even remember it, Ellen, but I do. I've never forgotten. And I suspect that even if I hadn't received the photos from Mr Mahon, I would have known you.

Anywhere.

Yours with affection,

Eudora

February 2008: Ellen

Ellen finished the final page, acutely aware of Kate's eyes boring a hole in the side of her face. When she reached Eudora's signature, she lingered over it for a few seconds, pretending to reread the entire sheet. She traced the final few lines with her forefinger and only when she was absolutely sure she'd be able to pull it off did she turn to her friend and offer a reassuring smile.

She isolated the final page and slipped it onto the back of the pack before reaching for the envelope on the table. As she did so, a handful of sheets slid from her lap and onto the floor as she grabbed frantically to secure them. With a muttered curse, she reassembled the pack, making sure the pages were in the correct order. Then she tapped all four sides on the surface of the table to even out the edges before thrusting the sheets back into the envelope. It was a tight fit and in her impatience she pushed too soon, causing the envelope to tear down one side. With a sigh, she threw it onto the table and closed her eyes, allowing her unsupported head to loll uncomfortably over the back of the sofa.

'You OK?' she heard Kate ask.

'Fine.'

A floorboard creaked upstairs – even though she knew it was just the cottage adjusting itself, her heart thumped wildly for an instant. How did anyone ever get used to this degree of isolation? She could only assume that something in Eudora's nature had put her in tune with the place so that these noises became part of the furniture for her.

'You want to talk about it?'

'Sure. Not now though, eh?'

'OK.'

'Maybe later.'

'Whenever you like.'

Kate sounded so solemn Ellen almost wanted to laugh, however inappropriate that might be. It was so not Kate. Somehow it just added to the air of unreality that had crept over her during the past hour or so … as if none of this had actually happened, nothing had really changed. At any time she could get to her feet and walk back into the life she'd always known. As if…

'Is it me or is it hot in here?' she asked, getting to her feet and heading for the hallway.

'Hot?'

'Stuffy.'

She plucked her hat and coat from a peg and walked back into the conservatory, grabbing a scarf as an afterthought. Kate looked up in surprise.

'Where are you going?' she asked, unable to keep the concern out of her voice.

'Out. Just for a bit.'

'You can't go out in this. It's Ice Station Zebra out there.'

'I'm not going far. Just fancy a bit of fresh air.'

'I'll come,' said Kate. She started to rise from the sofa but Ellen waved her back down.

'Ten minutes, Kate. OK?'

Kate started to protest, then looked closely at her before nodding.

'OK,' she said. 'Ten minutes ... and then I call for the huskies.'

Ellen smiled and finished buttoning her coat. She pulled the hat down low over her forehead and wrapped the scarf around the lower half of her face. Then she gave Kate a hug.

'Stick what's left of the pizza in the microwave,' she said. 'We'll finish it when I get back.'

Kate picked up one of the remaining slices and deliberately took a bite out of it. Ellen smiled again, then walked back into the hallway. As she opened the front door, the wind howled and threw it against her, causing her to fall back against the boot racks in the hallway. It was enough to make her pause at least before she finally stepped out into the cold night air.

'Ten minutes, mind,' she heard Kate call out as she pulled the door to behind her. Then she bowed her head and tried to follow the outlines of the footpath beneath the snow which had now risen above ankle height. At the gate, she turned left for the first time. She knew the bottom half of the village by now but had never followed the winding road up the hill towards the pub whose virtues Liam Sharp had been extolling. She had no idea how far it was – it certainly wasn't visible from the cottage, even in clear daylight. Even so, she reasoned, there was no harm in setting off in that direction. It wasn't as if there was much to look at, whichever way she went. The snow was falling less densely now but the road was unlit and the strong wind watered her eyes, making it difficult to see too far in front of her face.

After no more than a few yards the road came to a fork. She had to step right up to the signpost to read what it had to say. It seemed to be guiding hikers to footpaths in all directions but the one she wanted read: 'WAYFARER'S INN – 150M'. She bore left and carried on climbing, following the winding road until she could make out the hazy glow up ahead. By the time she reached the empty car park, it felt as if she'd walked miles.

She nudged open a gate and hurried the final few yards to the entrance. Once out of the wind, she unravelled the scarf and shook the snow from it, as the pub sign creaked and groaned above her head. She waited until she was through the doors before she did the same with her hat and opted to keep the coat on until she knew for sure how warm the Lounge Bar would be.

She was pleasantly surprised when she stepped through into a brightly lit room with a low oak-beam ceiling and old stone walls. A roaring log fire in a large open hearth dominated the far corner of the room and she headed straight for it, unbuttoning her coat as she went and draping it over the arm of a sofa which had seen better days. Then she went to the bar, nodding briefly at the three men standing there who seemed to be the only customers willing to brave it out on such an awful night. They made a half-hearted attempt at conversation about the weather, then left her to order her drink from a saturnine barman, whose hangdog expression evinced barely a flicker of curiosity as to what she was doing here on a night like this.

She opted for a glass of red wine before changing her mind at the last minute. Instead she asked for a brandy, then made it a double, causing one of the men to raise an eyebrow. *In your dreams*, she thought. Where the double brandy had come from, she had no idea. She hadn't had a glass in years, not since Jack had gone through his connoisseur phase and tried to win her over to Armagnac. She'd never really taken to it but remembered it as something that burned her insides on the way down and brought tears to her eyes, which was just fine by her. If ever she needed cauterising, it was now.

She took her drink over to the table and settled into the sofa, which was considerably more comfortable than its well-worn condition had suggested. The fire was close enough for the heat to wrap her in a warm fug, which the brandy only enhanced. Somewhere far away, at the back of her mind, was an awareness that she'd come here to think, to absorb what she'd learnt and assess exactly what it would mean for her and her family. For Megan and Harry. She tried to focus but it was all too much of an effort right now. Everything was just too far out of reach. Every so often random thoughts broke through – Josef sitting in a car in the snow in Inverness; her mother placing flowers by the roadside in a village in Scotland; Eudora dragging Josef from a freezing car and struggling to get him up the stairs and into bed ... and JMA.

John Michael Adams.

She pushed the thoughts away. She wasn't ready for this. Not yet. Maybe after a good night's sleep, she might be able to get a handle on things but right now, with several glasses of wine and most of the double brandy inside her, she just wanted to let it all go. It felt as if she'd been holding on for far too long.

She got to her feet and stood directly in front of the fire for a few minutes, allowing the heat to wash over her and flinching every time a spark flew off the logs and disappeared up the chimney. The men at the bar had looked her way once or twice but no one had made a move in her direction and she didn't know whether to be relieved or distressed at further evidence of her gradual decline. *Not so gradual these days*, she told herself. She tried to imagine what she must look like right now. No wonder no one was interested.

The ringtone on her mobile took her by surprise. She whipped it out of her coat pocket, confident it would be Kate. Ten minutes, she'd said. She'd been gone at least half an hour and hadn't once thought about her friend, who must be worried sick. To make matters worse, she'd been so self-absorbed, she hadn't even considered the possibility that staying in a strange, creaking cottage, especially after the events of the past few days, might be unsettling at best for her. Feeling guilty, she flipped the phone open.

'Kate, I'm so sorry –' she began.

'Where are you?' The urgency in Kate's voice drew Ellen up short.

'I'm just up the road. Is everything OK?' she asked anxiously.

'Ell … you need to get back right away.' A pause, then Kate continued. 'Isaac's here.'

'Isaac?' Ellen noticed the curious looks she was getting and instinctively lowered her voice. 'Isaac Ross?'

'Yes. How long will it take you to get back?'

Ellen shook her head as if that might bring things into sharper focus. She tried to think of a good reason why Sam's solicitor might have driven all this way in these conditions at this time of night. She couldn't think of one that didn't spell bad news.

'I don't know,' she said. 'Five, ten minutes? I don't understand –'

'Where are you exactly? He says we'll pick you up.'

Ellen laughed. 'You can't – he'd never get the car up here in this. I'll be back down before he's made it halfway up the hill. What's going on, Kate? Why's he here?'

There was a silence for long enough for Ellen to wonder if the line had gone dead. Then, after what seemed like an eternity, Kate came back on the line.

'I'm really sorry, Ell,' she said, her voice almost unrecognisably subdued. 'It's Barbara.'

February 2008: John Michael

OK, he tells himself ... *enough*. Enough of the fretting, all this pacing up and down in your room. It's not helping one bit. If that got you anywhere, you'd have been there ages ago. Forget it – forget all the what-ifs, the maybes, the will-she-won't-shes. Focus on what's in front of you.

So ... *does she know?* No. Probably not. Not yet, at any rate.

Is she getting closer? Looks like it.

Does that matter? Yes! If she's going to find out, he wants to be the one to tell her.

So why not tell her? 'Cos it's not that easy. What if she freaks out, turns to the media?

Why not just go then? It's not like you're part of her life as it is – not in any meaningful way. Maybe not ... but at least he's there. He's around. He can watch from a distance. And anyway, he doesn't want to run any more. He's had enough of it. Would rather take his chances and hope she doesn't put it all together.

So what would the professor say? He'd say the tide's turning, you're not in control any more, if you ever were. He'd say that when your emotions get the better of your judgement, it's time to cut and run.

So is that what you're going to do?

Is that what you're going to do?

10

February 2008: Ellen

By the time they reached the M4 at Swindon, the snow had dwindled into isolated flurries. There was nothing either overhead or on the gritted road surface to justify the relatively sedate speed that Isaac was maintaining and Ellen's anxiety grew with each passing minute. She had to remind herself that it would be churlish to complain, given how far he'd travelled to collect her.

Isaac had insisted on driving her back to Chichester. He felt refreshed, having been chauffeured all the way to Oakham by one of his nephews. The latter was now at the wheel of Kate's Celica, much to her disgust. She'd protested long and hard, insisting she was perfectly capable of driving until Ellen held up the two bottles of wine they'd consumed between them. Reluctantly agreeing to hand over the keys, Kate insisted on sitting in the front passenger seat where she could keep an eye on the lad. He looked a little too keen for her liking.

Once she and Isaac were under way in the Bentley, Ellen listened as he put flesh on the bones he'd already served up. He'd never been one for soft-soaping and he didn't pull any punches now. The word *if* was no longer on the agenda, he told her. It was now just a question of *when*. Barbara was in a coma and was not coming out of it.

She'd been rushed to hospital just before 1 p.m., having suffered another stroke, this one much more serious. The staff at Calder Vale had tried repeatedly to contact Ellen without success. In desperation they rang Langmere Grove and someone there had the presence of mind to ring Isaac, who was a family friend as well as the firm's solicitor. He'd immediately called Sam in Barbados and between them they'd spent the best part of the afternoon pinpointing Ellen's precise whereabouts. It wasn't until he managed to track down Jack at his parents' house that their suspicions were confirmed. She and Kate were in Cheltenham, he told them. *Sorting out a will or something.*

'And of course, Sam didn't need to ask where Eudora lived, right?' asked Ellen. 'He'd been in contact with her before.'

She took his silence as confirmation.

'So how long have you known about this?'

He reached down to turn the heating on to *screen*.

'Long enough,' he said eventually.

'And you didn't think to say anything to me?'

Isaac sniffed and continued to peer intently at the road ahead. Ellen knew how to interpret the lack of response.

'So how much do you know?'

'As much as I need to, I suspect.'

'You know who Eudora was?'

He nodded.

'You know about her daughter?'

'I know what happened to her, yes.' A little more cautious this time.

'And my father?'

No reply. The wipers began to make a grating sound as they scraped their way across the windscreen. Isaac turned them off.

'You know I have a half-brother?'

He removed his glasses with one hand, keeping the other firmly on the steering wheel as he breathed on the lenses and polished them on the lapel of his coat. 'If you want my advice, I think you'd be a lot better off trying to get some sleep – even if it's just a couple of hours. You may feel like you've been put through it today but I suspect there's much worse to come.'

Ellen thought about prolonging the argument but turned away instead, staring out into the darkness. On one level she knew Isaac was right. She was almost beyond tired and if she didn't grab some sleep now, it might be a while before the opportunity would next present itself. Far better to make use of a couple of dead hours in the car than doze off later when she was going to need all her wits about her.

At the same time though, she suspected that sleep wasn't going to come as easily as that. She was too wound up, her head buzzing not from unanswered questions for once but from the uncertainty engendered by the *answers* she'd received – answers, she reminded herself, that she'd been pursuing with a vengeance. The irony was not lost on her. She was the one who had wanted to know, had *insisted* on it and the answers that were supposed to bring some sense of tranquility were instead threatening to turn her world upside down. What was it she'd said to Kate just a few hours ago before opening the envelope? *Once you know something, you can't unknow it, right?*

'You say you contacted Sam,' she said. 'How did he take it?'

'Oh … you know Sam,' said Isaac. 'The ultimate coper. Busy organising the moment he heard.'

'So they'll be coming over, I imagine?'

'They'll be here tomorrow lunchtime … make that today,' said Isaac, checking his watch.

'Already? But that's … how did he manage to get a flight that quickly?'

'He booked the seats on Thursday morning – after you rang Wednesday night, asking about Eudora Nash. He knew things were about to escalate and wanted to get over here as quickly as possible.'

'But we talked just yesterday,' said Ellen, hesitating for a moment – was it really possible that the video-conference call was as recent as that? It felt like worlds away, another lifetime. 'Why didn't he say he was coming over?'

'Because he knew that once you heard about Eudora, you wouldn't be able to let it go. He was sure you'd be off to Oakham before he had the chance to talk face to face if you knew he was on his way. Unfortunately Saturday was the earliest flight he could get.'

Ellen thought about this and acknowledged to herself that Sam was right. She'd have gone immediately – not to spite him, but because it was easier that way.

'So when's the flight?'

'They should be in the air any time now,' said Isaac, signalling left as the Newbury exit loomed up ahead. 'It was scheduled for late afternoon their time but there was a four-hour delay. You can imagine how that went down.' He chuckled and despite everything Ellen found herself smiling too. Sam had always stormed through life as if nothing lay beyond his control. Having to wait around at an airport, when his thoughts were already winging their way across the Atlantic, might provide a salutary lesson in humility but it certainly wouldn't do anything to improve his mood. She suspected some airline executive was going to get it in the neck.

They took the exit and dropped down to the series of traffic lights at the foot of the slip road. She watched as the lights of Chieveley Services slipped past on her left. She recognised this as more or less the halfway point of the journey. Another hour and a half or so to go.

Without knowing what she was doing, she found herself trawling through the missed calls on her mobile. She scrolled down to the first in the list and there it was: 12.57 – Calder Vale. Just before one o'clock – what had she and Kate been doing right then? She cast her mind back to earlier in the day and realised they'd have been working their way through the boxes in the bedroom upstairs. Rummaging through the life of a woman she'd never met, in search of clues which might unlock a mystery. Snacking on rolls and fruit and sipping wine and laughing while her mother...

She cursed herself for failing to spot the missed call when she went out to the car to phone Megan and Harry. She'd seen the sheer volume of calls from Sam and assumed any others would also be from him. If only she'd checked, she berated herself. If she'd picked up the message back then, she and Kate would have driven straight to the hospital and she'd have been there for hours now instead of sitting here, ticking off the miles one by one and wondering if she was already too late.

She rested her head against the window, looking up beyond the lights and into the inky darkness beyond. She thought of how Eudora had turned up at the hospital one morning, expecting everything to be as she'd left it the night before, only to discover that Josef had gone in the night, taking with him her only chance to say the things she'd always left unsaid. It had struck Ellen when she'd read this as particularly sad that there was no opportunity for any reconciliation and it had never occurred to her for one moment that a matter of hours later she might find herself in exactly the same situation.

So she prayed ... to the darkness, to the elements, to the God in whom she barely believed and to anything or anyone who might be listening. She prayed she might be granted just a few minutes with her mother. Just an hour, she told herself – surely that wasn't too much to ask.

February 2008: Barbara

That hour becomes two days. As if somehow aware that her daughter is on her way – as if she has picked up her desperate prayer on some ethereal wavelength – Barbara will dig in for a further forty-eight hours.

Sightless, unhearing, unresponsive ... she'll lie there on a hospital bed, surrounded on three sides by drips and banks of monitors which emit a ghostly glow and a series of metronomic beeps guaranteed to lull her back to sleep, should she ever wake. Which she won't.

Every so often a nurse will slip silently into the room and take readings from the screens. She'll dutifully record them on the clipboard which she's unhooked from the end of the bed before turning her attention briefly to Barbara. She'll make sure the patient looks comfortable, that the bed cover is straight and the hospital corners still tucked in, even though there's no way they're likely to have been disturbed. Then she'll take her leave, padding just as silently from the room as if anxious to maintain the illusion that all is well here, that a step out of place might somehow disturb the slumbering patient, even though the closed window blinds tell the real story – that the world beyond them is no longer any of Barbara's concern.

Sightless, unhearing, unresponsive ... she'll be there when Ellen bursts in, wild-eyed and dishevelled, still disoriented from the all-too-brief slumber which she's managed to grab during the latter stages of the journey and from which she has been brutally snatched.

Sightless she'll watch as her daughter lifts one of her motionless hands from the bed and presses it between her own, pumping it like a blood pressure gauge as if seeking to squeeze some semblance of life into it.

Unhearing she'll listen as the words pour out like tears – bitter, angry words at first, which gradually lose their force and dissolve into self-recrimination as the storm disappears over the horizon. And somewhere in here, if she could only hear it, is the germ of a conversation she's been meaning to have for so long now. It's always been there between them, never a question of *whether* she should explain everything to Ellen, merely *when*. When exactly? During her time at primary school maybe, when little girls have best friends who expect to be told everything and the temptation to come up with something truly spectacular for *show and tell* might prove irresistible? Or during those rebellious teenage years when she had to watch Ellen like a hawk, knowing her daughter needed no second invitation to use any available weapon against her? Or how about when Ellen came back from university with a hapless drifter in tow and dived headlong into a marriage that was so obviously a mistake ... maybe then? It was one thing to identify this as a conversation that had to take place, quite another to decide when that should be. The only thing she can say for certain is that if there ever was such a thing as the right time, she's missed it.

And now she's reduced to this. All she can do is lie there, *sightless, unhearing, unresponsive,* as her daughter strokes her hand, slowly, gently, a gesture more eloquent by far than all the tears and unfamiliar words which precede it. And if she could ... if only she could, she would find some way to let Ellen know that it's OK. *Shhhhh, it's alright.* Nothing more needs to be said. The time for words is over and besides, she's never doubted, not for one minute, that the fierce, tigerish devotion she feels for her daughter is a two-way street.

So she'll hold on for another forty-eight hours. She'll lie there while different faces come and go in shifts, while visitors come to pay their last respects and offer Ellen their support, while machines beep and drips drip and trays rattle, while doctors pore over charts and trolleys come and go and one of the porters offers up the same tuneless whistle and Ellen dozes fitfully at her bedside between bouts of remorse and despair. She'll tough it out until she feels maybe Ellen herself is ready to let go and face the first day of the rest of her life.

And when that moment comes, she'll look down at her hand, still enclosed in those of her sleeping daughter, and see her own six-year-old hand, the one that needed four stitches when she sliced through it while learning how to chop onions at her mother's side in the kitchen at Ashbury; her nineteen-year-old hand from which she stripped a thin gold band which it had worn so ill-advisedly for no more than a year; an older hand but one still bright with hope which once drew intimate circles on Peter's chest while she curled up alongside him; a mother's hand which had reached out to take her daughter from the nurses and cradled her ever since, cradled and protected. She'll look down at it as it lies cocooned in Ellen's tender grip and she'll squeeze, *squeeze* with all her might as if the laws of nature mean nothing when stacked up against a mother's love for her daughter.

And then, when she's sure the time is right, she'll steal gently away into the night.

Ellen woke with a start as a nurse brought in a vase of flowers and made room for it on the bedside cabinet. She'd been dozing in the visitor's chair, leaning forward at a ninety-degree angle with her head resting on the edge of the bed. Sitting bolt upright, she winced and arched her shoulders to ease the stiffness in her back. Then, suddenly remembering where she was, she leant forward and seized Barbara's hand, angry with herself for having let go, even for a moment.

'You back with us?' asked the nurse, taking a few of the flowers out of the vase and rearranging them. Ellen ran her tongue across her teeth and pulled a face. Her mouth tasted stale from the wine of the previous evening and her hair felt as if it hadn't been washed or brushed in months.

'There's a bathroom just next door by the way … in case you want to freshen up a bit.' Ellen smiled ruefully, taking the offer as confirmation that she looked every bit as rough as she felt. She glanced at her watch: nearly 9.30. She'd arrived just before three, remembered being awake at five but nothing after that. So, four hours then. Nowhere near enough, if the dull ache in her head was anything to go by.

'Where did those come from?' she asked, nodding at the flowers.

'You've had your first visitor.' The nurse's lapel badge was difficult to read from where Ellen was sitting. Looked like Reiha – not a name with which she was familiar, at any rate.

'Male or female?'

'Male. He didn't stay – said he didn't want to disturb you. Left a card though,' she said, taking a yellow envelope from her pocket. Ellen opened it, expecting to find a traditional get-well-soon card inside. Instead she pulled out a photo of the staff at Calder Vale, assembled on the steps in front of the main entrance. Turning it over she found a brief message, printed in the same block capitals as those on the envelope:

MISS YOU. HURRY BACK TO SEE US
BEST WISHES
JACOB.

She turned back to the photo and picked him out in the front row, a dapper little man with his hands folded on his lap and his knees pressed together. Everyone else appeared to be shouting and waving at the camera while he seemed satisfied with a shy smile. She remembered how kind he'd always been to

Barbara, all the extra little treats he saved for her and the lengths he went to just to make her feel a little more special. And now, here he was, first to arrive and check on how things were. She was touched even more than usual by his kindness and was sorry she'd missed him.

'How long ago did he leave?' she asked.

'Ooh, an hour or so. Maybe longer. He was here very early. Said he might pop back in after work. People are kind, aren't they?' she added, taking a step back to admire her handiwork with the flowers. She flashed a smile at Ellen as if inviting her opinion.

'Yes,' she responded, wondering if this was something Jacob routinely did for all the residents he worked with. 'Yes, they are.'

Kate arrived just after ten, bright-eyed and brimming with energy: teeth gleaming, make-up immaculate, hair just so. As was always the case, Ellen felt a wreck alongside her.

'In case you haven't had breakfast,' Kate explained, holding up sandwiches, apples and a bottle of Evian and looking around for the best place to put them. She couldn't stay long, she said. Adam was due back from Madrid around midday and, for all her brave words a few days ago, it was more than her life was worth to be out when he arrived. It sounded plausible but Ellen knew her well enough to be sure this was just an excuse. Kate didn't do hospitals any more than she did sitting around and this particular errand of mercy would entail plenty of both.

Sure enough, she seized upon Isaac's arrival an hour later as a suitable opportunity to leave. He came in with news that Sam and Mary had just phoned from Gatwick. They were still waiting to reclaim their luggage but a taxi was waiting for them and they were expecting to arrive at the hospital somewhere around 12.40.

Ellen smiled at this, confident that the words 'somewhere' and 'around' could be safely disregarded. She thanked Isaac for everything he'd done. He waved it away and asked if she'd like to take a bit of a break while he sat with Barbara for a while. It wasn't until then that she realised she'd spent the past seven hours sitting in the same position and holding on to her mother's hand as if letting go might somehow snap the flimsy thread connecting the two of them. It would be good to grab some fresh air and stretch her legs, she thought – even if only for a few minutes. She thanked him for the offer and promised she wouldn't be long.

The first thing she did once she was outside was call Jack to discuss how best to break the news to Megan and Harry. He agreed to bring them to the hospital later that afternoon so that she might come out to meet them in the car park. Then she rang Langmere Grove and explained to Colin, her deputy, that he would need to look after things for the foreseeable future. He told her not to worry about a thing and offered his condolences but she had great difficulty in dismissing the mental picture of him rubbing his hands the moment he replaced the receiver.

Only as an afterthought did it occur to her to ring Calder Vale. She didn't know for sure that Jacob would be there but she felt bad about the fact that he hadn't been able to see Barbara and didn't want him to think his efforts weren't appreciated. She was put on hold for a few minutes and then, just as she was having second thoughts about interrupting him at work, he came to the phone.

'The flowers were lovely,' she told him. 'I'm so sorry you didn't get to see her. You really should have woken me.'

Jacob said it was nice of her to call but really not necessary. 'I just popped in on my way to work,' he said, in that curious accent she'd never been able to place. 'No trouble at all.' Something Gaelic about it – she'd never been very good with accents, either identifying or mimicking them. She'd meant to ask but somehow never got around to it.

He asked if there was any improvement and she could tell from the tone of his voice that he wasn't expecting any. She passed on what she herself had been told – barring a miracle, Barbara wasn't coming out of this. Jacob pointed out that specialists had been made to look silly in the past but she sensed it was more the cheerleader in him than any genuine conviction.

'I never had the chance to tell you before,' she said, getting to the real reason for her call. 'I wanted to make sure you know how much I appreciate what you've done for her. I know you'll tell me that's what you're paid for but I couldn't help but notice the way you were with her ... all those extra little touches to make her feel special. I'm sure it meant a lot.'

'Ah well, she's a lovely lady, isn't she?' he said, obstinately sticking to the present tense. 'She has her ups and downs like the rest of us but she's very philosophical about things, very good at accepting what she can and can't do. I should cope half as well as she does when my time comes.'

'That's nice to hear,' said Ellen. 'It's always so hard for me to know how she feels about things. I mean, Sundays aren't so bad but weekdays she's always so tired by the time I get to see her. A lot of the time I'm not even sure she knows it's me anyway.'

'Oh, she knows alright, don't you worry about that. I know it must be difficult for you, the way she keeps drifting in and out – you never get to see her at her best. But during the day, till recently, at any rate, she's had spells when she's been sharp as a tack. And she can talk up a storm when she has a mind to.'

Ellen experienced a momentary pang of something … jealousy, was it? It seemed Barbara was capable of normal conversation with just about anyone but her. She wondered what they'd found to talk about – had she been tempted to tell him things she'd kept from her own daughter? She wanted more details but didn't like to ask directly.

She realised Jacob was still talking and tuned back in at the mention of goody bags.

'… always thought that was a lovely idea,' he was saying. 'Not so much what's in them, more the thought behind them. They mean a lot to her. Always telling the other residents, she is – how her daughter spoils her.'

'I'm sorry,' said Ellen, groping her way back into the conversation. 'Goody bags?'

'Your little parcels.'

'*My* parcels?'

'From Webster's … the grocer's in the village.'

'Someone's been sending her parcels?'

There was a momentary pause at the other end of the line.

'Biscuits, lime juice, Jaffa Cakes, couple of magazines each time … you mean, they're not from you?'

'No. I don't know anything about it. I thought the Jaffa Cakes were all your doing.'

'Mine? Oh dear, there seems to have been some confusion.'

He sounded genuinely distressed over the mix-up.

'So how long have these parcels been arriving?'

'Oh, I couldn't say for sure. Quite a while though. Can't have been long after she first came here.'

'And who brings them?'

'The boy from the village store, I imagine. I'm never actually here when they arrive but he cycles out here every morning with the newspapers and a few other odds and ends.'

'And he said they were from me?'

'I don't know. Like I said, I've never actually spoken to him myself. I could check with the other staff if you like. I'm sorry, we just assumed they were from you, I suppose, because you're the only person who comes to see her.'

'In which case, I'd have brought them with me, wouldn't I?' she asked. 'I wouldn't need to have them delivered.'

'No, I suppose not. We just thought you'd set it up as a little surprise for her to look forward to. But – if it's not you who's been sending them all this time, who is it d'you suppose? Bit of a mystery, isn't it?'

Not really, she thought to herself. *Not if you know Sam Balfour.* It was just the sort of flourish he'd think of, a thoughtful gesture from four thousand miles away and one she herself would never have come up with in a million years. Why was she so incapable of taking the broader view? Was it really, as she tried to convince herself, because she was head down in the swamp all the time with hardly a second to look up and draw breath? Or was it, as seemed more likely, a lot simpler than that? Did it just come down to who she was – dogged but unimaginative, uninspired? How was it Sam could see these things and she couldn't?

It crippled her to have to admit it but she knew immediately what it was about these goody bags that hurt her the most. It was the thought of Barbara sharing out the little treats with her fellow residents and burbling cheerfully about her daughter's thoughtfulness when in reality she'd had nothing to do with it. It seemed to encapsulate their relationship just perfectly – crossed wires, missed turnings, lost connections.

And it hurt.

February 2008: John Michael

He's been thinking about that afternoon again – the afternoon in the park. Third time in as many days. Must be years since he found himself going down that road. He naively imagined it was all behind him, he'd outgrown it somehow but the last few nights the memories have come flooding in the moment his head hits the pillow. Not a nightmare exactly – he's wide awake the whole time. Sleep's the only thing that drives it away and it won't come quickly enough.

It's just the uncertainty – he knows that. If he could only see a few weeks down the road and know for sure how things are going to pan out, he's sure he'd be fine. And he knows that, whatever happens, he can deal with it once it's there in front of him. He likes the life he's made for himself here and would rather stay but if it comes to it and he's left with no choice but to run, he can do that – it's not like he's never done it before. But he needs to know where he stands if he's going to make the right decision. And it's the waiting that's doing his head in. He doesn't like not being in control. He has to get a grip, stay on top of this or someone's going to notice before long. And drawing attention to himself is the last thing he wants.

He's tried thinking of other ways to take his mind off it – some problem at work, a TV programme he's watched recently, that article he was reading the other evening. Waste of time. If he lets his guard slip for just a moment, he's back there again in the park with Carol Bingham and the others and it's all so fresh in his mind it could be yesterday, not forty-odd years ago. The sense of humiliation is as strong as ever.

And what makes it worse is he seems to be remembering details he thought had gone for good, like the black V-neck sweater with the red zig-zag pattern around the waist which he wore over his school uniform. And the area of scorched earth where the grass hadn't yet recovered from the bonfire the local scouts group had built, still fenced off even though Guy Fawkes Night was a fortnight earlier. And the little old man who spent most of the day sitting on a park bench, taking abuse from the local kids because he walked with a permanent stoop and talked to himself and who his father insisted was a war hero and ought to be treated with a bit of respect. Details like these should have been wiped from his memory a long time ago and yet here they are, dancing in front of his eyes, clear as anything.

You'd think the shock of what came next would have wiped them out for good.

February 2008: Ellen

Sam and Mary arrived at 12.57. The traffic may well have been a mitigating factor but Ellen suspected those extra seventeen minutes had probably cost the taxi driver a sizable tip. Sam was a firm believer in results. One of his favourite mantras – *excuses don't pay the bills, Ellen.*

Mary was first to enter. She gave Ellen a hug which went on for long enough to convey her emotional frailty. Then, eyes shining, she stepped back and dropped her hands to her side, taking in Ellen's overall appearance. She tilted her head, first one way then the other, before coming up with the adjective *healthy.* Ellen knew exactly what that meant.

Sam made his entrance two minutes later with two suitcases, a couple of nurses and one specialist in tow. He broke off to give Ellen a hug and a perfunctory kiss on the cheek before resuming his interrogation of the staff. Only when he was satisfied with the answers did he drape his overcoat across the back of a chair and give her his full attention. Ellen was familiar with this sort of bravura performance, Sam Balfour in full flow, but she couldn't help feeling this one was a little overcooked. Maybe it was her imagination, but he seemed determined to establish the ground rules from the outset. Apologies were not going to be on the agenda.

Mary suggested Ellen and Sam might like to grab a bite to eat while she stayed with Barbara. She said she wasn't hungry herself and besides, she'd welcome the chance to have a few moments to catch her breath. It came across as just a little staged, probably pre-rehearsed in the taxi, but Ellen went along with it. She wasn't particularly hungry either, and she was a little apprehensive about leaving Barbara, but she was more than ready to clear the air with Sam.

She took his proffered arm and agreed to his suggestion that they should try the pub across the road from the hospital – he wanted a good old-fashioned pint and a proper meal, *not some pre-packed synthetic rubbish.* And as they took the lift, walked endless corridors to the main entrance, crossed the road and chose their drinks and meals, they talked about everything and nothing – the flight, the traffic on the M23, the miserable English weather, even his eyesight which had deteriorated enough for him to struggle with the Specials board. The real conversation hung there between them all this time – she apologised for jogging his elbow as they reached for the bar menus, he fidgeted with his watch strap and seemed excessively interested in banalities that wouldn't have made a blip on his radar under different circumstances.

They chose a table which looked out onto a car park rather than the road, the only two options available. Ever the gentleman, Sam pulled Ellen's chair out for her and took his seat opposite. He pulled a face at the music which sounded like a compilation of hits from the '60s. She wasn't sure if he was objecting to the choice or the volume, and she told herself that if he started reminiscing about what he was doing when the Swinging Blue Jeans were in the charts, she'd scream.

Eventually, as if responding to some inner signal that the time was right, Sam reached across the table and patted her hand.

'So how are things?' he asked. 'You bearing up?'

She nodded.

'Sure?'

'Sure. You know.' *My mother's dying as we sit here. I've got to explain it all to my kids this afternoon. Oh, and I've just discovered that the boy who set two girls on fire and is one of the most hated figures in the history of tabloid journalism also happens to be my half-brother but apart from that...*

'Bearing up,' she said.

She reached into her bag for a tissue, using it as a pretext for pulling her hand away. He left his own resting there on the table for a few moments before withdrawing it.

'I gather I'm not very high on your Christmas-card list at the moment.'

Ellen smiled ruefully. 'Is there anything Isaac doesn't pass on to you?'

'I didn't need Isaac to tell me you'd be pissed with me. You think I don't know you after all these years?'

'Yeah, well ...' she said, lifting her glass of orange juice from the table and pausing to take a sip. 'We don't always know people as well as we imagine, do we?'

Sam took a much longer draught from his own glass, then wiped his lips, his eyes locking on to hers.

'OK,' he said. 'Message received. Let's get it all out though, shall we? You got things you want to ask, then fine – go ahead. I'll sit here and answer as many questions as you want to throw at me, 'cos I figure you're entitled to at least that much. But bear in mind I've had a shitty flight, hardly got any sleep in the past twenty-four hours and my back's killing me, so if you're just here to throw some hissy fit, you'll have to excuse me – I've got better things to do with my time. Up to you.'

In the space of a few words, he'd swept her back to when she was eight years old and he'd caught her smoking behind one of the store buildings at Langmere Grove. Then again, she could have been fourteen, sitting through a lecture on how ungrateful she was after she'd presumed to criticise Barbara in front of him. Her instinct now was to carry the fight to him, to let him know she couldn't be so easily subdued any more, but there were still so many questions. The last thing she wanted was for him to get up and walk out on her.

'Why didn't she want me to know?' she asked, working hard to control her voice.

'That I'm her uncle?'

'Let's start there.'

'OK.' Sam sat back in his chair, apparently satisfied that his point had been made. 'For one thing, she knew the time would come when you'd want to track down your father and she was determined to shut down as many leads as possible.'

'And you're a lead?'

'You'd have traced my history back to Ashbury and she didn't want you anywhere near there, digging around for answers. If we're not related, you're not going to be looking there, was how she saw it.'

'Why would it matter if I did? I find out my father *might* have been someone called Peter Vaughan. So what?'

'Yeah, well... it wasn't just what *you* might find. She was afraid anyone looking for her might think to check out her wealthy uncle at Langmere Grove.'

'But that doesn't make sense. Who did she think would be looking for her? She didn't even know Peter Vaughan's real identity at that stage.'

She caught Sam's expression and realised she was missing something.

'She knew two weeks after his death,' he explained. 'You don't think she left home and hid herself away at Langmere Grove just because she was pregnant, do you?' Ellen thought about it and knew instinctively he was right. Barbara was a tough woman, far too thick-skinned to worry about what others in the village might be saying behind her back. If she felt the need to leave Ashbury altogether, it would have to be something more significant than that. She wondered how the obvious hadn't occurred to her before now.

'But ... how did she know?' she said, struggling to slot the pieces into place. 'I assumed the first she knew about all this was when Eudora got in touch.'

Sam broke off for a moment, leaning back to make room for the waitress, who had arrived with their meals. He waited until they were alone again before resuming.

'She was clearing out his room,' he said, giving the salt cellar a few violent shakes followed by a couple of taps on the base before giving up and removing the lid. 'Not long after the funeral. He had this diary and a couple of photos taped to the underside of one of the drawers – she said they were so well hidden she'd have missed them if she hadn't been having a complete clear-out. Anyway, you can imagine what that did to her when she read through it. She'd only just found out she was expecting his baby. Hadn't even told her father she was pregnant.'

She wouldn't have, was Ellen's immediate reaction. *Not her.* She wondered how that frail woman whose bedside she'd just left would react if she knew that all these secrets, which she'd fought so hard to keep, were seeping out right now. Had she really intended to take them with her to the grave or would she be quietly relieved to have such a burden removed from her shoulders at last?

'So,' Sam continued, 'she sat on it all for a couple of days, trying to decide what to do. The only thing she knew for sure was that she wanted to have the baby and she was worried sick that if she hung around in Ashbury, someone would show up asking questions before long. She wanted to be out of there by the time that happened.'

Ellen's scepticism kicked in at this.

'You don't think she was being a bit paranoid maybe?'

'Maybe. But she already knew about this one guy who'd called in to see Peter a couple of times just before he went off up to Scotland – supposed to be an old friend but Barbara said he didn't look that friendly and one of the last entries in the diary made it sound like maybe he was a reporter –'

'O'Halloran,' said Ellen.

'You know him?'

She waved him on and he looked closely at her before continuing.

'Anyway, once she'd decided she needed to get away from Ashbury, she called me to ask for help.'

'Why you?'

'You what?'

'Why you and not her father?' *My grandfather!*

Sam put down his knife and fork for a moment, reaching down to pat a golden Labrador that had sidled up to the table. He picked up a chip from the bowl and dangled it tantalisingly out of the dog's reach before dropping it into its mouth.

'Bit of hero worship, I suppose,' he said eventually. 'She and I were really close when we were younger. I was a bit of an afterthought, so although I'm her uncle there's not that much of an age difference between us. We've always been more like brother and sister really. And besides, I was the big success story, the one who got away from the village and made a name for himself, whereas the only time she'd been away was the year or so she spent married to that worthless piece of shit from the local garage, 'scuse my French. As far as she was concerned, I was right up there. If I couldn't sort it all out, nobody could.'

'So it was your idea for her to come to Langmere Grove?'

Sam shook his head. 'Hers. I was just there for moral support. She thought her old man might be more receptive to the idea if he thought it had come from me. He wasn't happy about it but by that stage he knew he was seriously ill and, with my sister having already gone early, he wanted to make sure his daughter was safe and settled with someone he could trust.'

'And what about you and Mary? Were you happy about it?'

'I wasn't unhappy. I thought it was a bit of an overreaction, to be honest. Seemed to me they were jumping at shadows a bit. But Mary was all for it – she and your mother had always got on so well together and Barbara had been there for her when we finally had to give up on the idea of having kids of our own. Seemed like the perfect solution as far as she was concerned. She'd be able to look after you while Barbara was working at Langmere. It worked out well for just about everyone.'

That much was true, Ellen acknowledged. Bringing up a child alone and trying to hold down a job would have been hard enough for Barbara, without the added pressure of constantly looking over her shoulder to see if anyone had picked up her trail. At least this way she'd had all the support she could ask for and at the same time Mary and Sam had the chance to become surrogate parents. Better for everyone, she agreed – herself included.

'So all the time she and I were at each other's throats because I couldn't get her to tell me anything about my father she thought she was protecting me?'

'Convinced of it. She'd built this brick wall around you and wasn't about to let anything breach it.'

'I always thought it was because she was ashamed.'

'Ashamed?' Sam almost choked on his steak and kidney pie.

'Like it was some grubby encounter in a back alley with a total stranger or something and she couldn't tell me without losing face.'

Sam put down his knife and fork and leant forward as if to lend emphasis to what he was about to say.

'I'll tell you how ashamed she was,' he said. 'Apart from you, Peter Vaughan was the single most important thing that ever happened in her entire life. If it hadn't been for her *paranoia*, as you call it, she'd have liked nothing better than to sit down and talk all evening to you about him. God knows she did it often enough with Mary and me once you were off to sleep. She became a different person when she talked about him. Twenty years younger – you wouldn't have recognised her.'

'But what about after the diary?'

'What do you mean?'

'Once she'd read the diary and knew who he was. She must have felt differently then.'

'Why?'

'Because he'd lied to her. He wasn't who he was pretending to be.'

Sam smiled. 'As far as she was concerned, he was Peter Vaughan, someone who came wandering in out of the blue one day. His life before he arrived in Ashbury was nothing to do with her. Besides, she read enough in his diary to know how he felt, both about her and having to keep things from her. She was sure he was building himself up to tell her before long.'

'Like she was going to tell me, I suppose.'

'She was always going to tell you, Ellen.'

'But somehow she never quite got round to it, did she?'

Sam tipped the rest of the chips from the bowl onto his plate, spearing several of them with his fork. He paused in the act of raising it to his mouth, pointing it at her.

'How about I ask you a question for once?' he asked, thrusting them into his mouth.

'OK.'

'Are you going to tell Megan and Harry?'

'About my father? Of course.'

'You going to tell them who he was?'

'I'm not going to hide the truth from them.'

'And which truth is that, girl? You going to stick with a few shadowy details about their grandfather or tell them they've got a new half-uncle they're not allowed to talk about?'

'Where are you going with this, Sam? I told you, I'll sit down with Jack and we'll decide together exactly what we'll tell them and how.'

'And when?'

'And when.' She made herself sound a little more convinced than she actually felt.

'Well, good luck with that,' said Sam, holding up his glass to toast her. 'And good luck with Jack too. A story that huge? *I was married to the secret sister of John Michael Adams?* Hope he never feels the need to boost that glittering writing career of his and cash in. But hey, you know Jack. I'm sure you can trust him.'

Ellen put her fork down and thrust her salad away from her. She'd had enough for now.

It wasn't until they were waiting to cross the road in front of the hospital that she brought the subject back to the diary Peter Vaughan had been keeping. It hadn't occurred to her before to ask what had happened to it.

'Oh, she's still got it. It'll be tucked away somewhere with all the other papers.'

'She didn't destroy it?'

'Destroy Peter's diary? Are you kidding? She kept this shirt of his in her bottom drawer for twenty years until it pretty much fell apart. Now the diary's all she's got. She'd give up several vital organs before she'd let that go.'

'Have you ever read it?' she asked, holding up one hand to thank a considerate driver who'd allowed them to cross.

'Just the once. Flicked through it more than read it, to be honest. Felt a bit like prying, if you know what I mean.'

'So how far back did it go?'

'Not that far.' He paused for a moment to fuss with one of his laces although Ellen suspected it was really to catch his breath. She wondered if maybe she'd been walking a little too quickly for him. He was such a force of nature it was easy to forget he was in his mid-seventies. 'He must have started it soon after he got to Ashbury, I guess. It didn't go back as far as all that business with his boy, if that's what you mean.'

He held the door open and stepped to one side to allow a woman on crutches to enter the hospital before him. She smiled and thanked him. *Such a nice man.* Ellen could almost hear her thinking it.

'You mentioned other papers – what are they?'

'Oh, just things she's collected over the years. Articles she cut out of newspapers, that sort of thing. And the books she bought … you know.'

'What books?' Ellen tried hard but couldn't remember ever having seen her mother with a book in her hands. The Barbara she knew existed on a diet of soaps and reality TV.

'Oh, anything about the boy, really. Biographies. Welfare reports. Psychological studies. Right little library she's got tucked away somewhere – probably in the attic at home.'

'But why was she so fascinated by him?'

'Peter's boy,' said Sam, stepping into the lift and leaving Ellen to press the button for the correct floor. 'There's no one she can talk to about his father. I think she sees him as some way of connecting with the Peter she never got to know, if that makes sense.'

'But that's ridiculous,' said Ellen. She caught him by the arm as they stepped out into the corridor – she didn't want to get back to Mary until she'd milked the conversation for every last drop of information. 'You're talking as if she seriously expected to find him. How was she going to do that when just about every reporter worthy of the name had failed?'

'I don't think logic came into it,' said Sam. 'She just got swept along by it.'

'And did she talk to you about what she'd learnt?'

'All the time. Although you'd be better off asking Mary for details. A lot of it just bounced off me, if I'm honest.'

'Why's that? You didn't approve?'

'Not really. I mean, losing someone the way she did is tough, OK. It's not going to be easy to get over something like that. But ... I don't know. It just seemed a bit obsessive to me. There was no balance in her. She used to get so worked up every time there was a new rumour about where the boy might be and she hated the way he was portrayed in the media – hated it. She felt only one side of the argument was being put forward. It was like she couldn't bring herself to accept that he could possibly be as bad as they were making out. Not Peter's boy.'

Less than twenty-four hours previously Ellen had been sitting in Eudora's conservatory and thinking the exact same thing. She remembered now the maternal instincts that had kicked in when she looked at the photo of John Michael Adams and the doubts she'd experienced surrounding the way he'd been labelled for life for one moment of madness. How strange was it to learn that her mother had beaten her to the very same conclusion?

'I'll be honest with you, I thought she'd been brainwashed by all these do-gooders she'd been listening to,' Sam continued.

'There was this one guy, a professor. Pretty famous he was at the time – did some big series on TV.'

'Carl Holmbach.'

'Yeah, that was him. How the …? Anyway, back in the sixties and seventies he was always on TV or in the newspapers, claiming the boy never received fair treatment at the hands of the media. Produced this book too, laying out the reasons why he felt society had been too quick to label the boy. Barbara bought it and read it from cover to cover in just about one sitting. She was so impressed she wrote to him – said she wanted to meet him. He wasn't remotely interested so she wrote again and said she wanted to talk to him about Peter Vaughan and you can imagine how quick he was to get back to her after that. Only a handful of people had ever known about that name, apparently.'

'But why did she want to meet him?' asked Ellen. 'I thought she spent her whole life trying to keep me safe. Surely that was putting everything at risk?'

'Exactly what I said at the time but she was convinced she could trust him. He was on her side, one of the good guys. She just wanted to talk to someone who'd known Peter, I guess. Chance to swap notes.'

'So did she tell this professor anything about me?'

Sam shook his head. 'She might have been obsessed but she wasn't stupid. She wouldn't go that far. I suppose she might have done if they'd met more than just the once but it never became an issue, as it turned out. He died soon after – probably for the best, when you think about it. She was already getting sucked in too far for my liking. But I know it hit her hard when she heard about it. It was like the last link had been severed somehow.'

'And since then? Has she been trying anything else?'

'She did for a while. Then the illness kicked in and...'

Sam let his voice trail away. He turned to face Ellen and gave her shoulder a quick squeeze. Then he pushed open the door and walked in to rejoin Mary.

Only later did Ellen manage to pin down the thought that had been eluding her.

'I suppose it's you I ought to thank,' she said. 'The goody bags?'

Sam and Mary looked blankly at her.

'The little box of presents every two or three weeks. It was your idea, right?'

'What box of presents?' asked Sam.

November 1966: John Michael

He's squatting down near the duck pond when he sees the three distant shadows enter the park. It's only a couple of hours since Mr Dukakis was asking him to draw the blinds so that everyone could see the blackboard but the light's fading fast now and it's hard to make out their faces from this far away. Even so, he suspects he knows who they are ... two of them, at any rate.

Most days he'd be home by now but this morning his dad handed him a couple of large shopping bags and a list of groceries for him to pick up from Macey's, which meant the moment school finished he had to set off in the opposite direction from usual. He could have stuck to the roads on the way back but the short cut through the park saves at least ten minutes and when you're carrying that much shopping and you've already got a duffel bag on your back, you pick the shortest route possible, so the park it was.

Stopping near the duck pond wasn't part of the plan but he needs a break. His arms ache and the handles of the bags are digging into his fingers, especially on his bad hand. He remembers when they took the damaged little finger away along with the tip of the one next to it. The doctor came and saw him after the operation, patted him on the head and said he'd be fine, wouldn't even notice it was gone. He hadn't believed it then and he certainly didn't now. She was right when she told him to be careful with the doctors. She knew they'd be useless. *Don't say a word, Johnny ... our little secret.*

And he hadn't. Not a word, unless you count his dad, and even then it was only because he wouldn't let it drop. He didn't believe it was an accident. Somehow he seemed to know what she'd done so there wasn't much point in denying it after a while. Even so he wishes he hadn't told him. All he can remember of the last few days before she went is the two of them arguing about it and it seems unfair somehow. His dad wasn't even there when it happened. If he wants to blame someone, it shouldn't be her. She wasn't the one taking money from someone else's purse. He had to be taught a lesson – it was for his own good. If he can accept this, he doesn't understand why his dad can't. And anyway, it's fine now. Doesn't even hurt any more. Unless he has to carry heavy bags.

The figures are still on the path at the top of the mound so he doesn't think they've noticed him yet. He wonders whether it might be better if he stays where he is now, crouched down below their eye level. Any movement might attract their attention, but they'll be coming up to a fork in the path in a moment and if they turn right they'll come down nearer to the pond, in which case they're bound to see him. He'll look silly, squatting down like that – they'll know he was trying to avoid them and that'll be worse for him in the long run. He decides he'll be better off picking up the bags and walking away from them, even if it does mean adding a lot more on to the journey. With any luck it'll be a while before they spot him and once he gets to the other side of the pond, there's the copse with the waste ground beyond it. If he gets that far without being seen, he'll be fine.

He knows it's Carol Bingham and Julie. The third person is much taller and he's not sure who that is but it's the two girls he's anxious to avoid. He's still embarrassed about yesterday and they've made it worse by telling everyone at school, which he was desperately hoping they wouldn't do. So now everyone in his class knows he asked Julie Kasprowicz if she'd like to go to the pictures with him, which means they've spent the whole day teasing him about it. It wouldn't be so bad but he still can't see what he's done that's so wrong. He knows she's older than he is but there's no law says third years can't go out with first years if they like. And he asked properly, just the way she'd brought him up to. *A girl likes to be wooed, Johnny. Likes to feel special.* He'd told her he'd pay for her ticket, even picked her some flowers on the way to school and asked her if she'd do him the honour and all they did was laugh. He really doesn't understand.

He picks up the bags and scuttles around the far side of the pond, heading for the copse. He looks back over his shoulder and sees that he's made the right decision because the three figures have turned right as he thought they would – they'd have been bound to see him if he'd stayed squatting where he was. The bags are hurting him already. His damaged hand is practically begging him to stop again and let it have a rest but he can't stay here, not out in the open. Maybe once he's made it to the copse, he can put the bags down for a minute or two.

Then he hears a voice ring out and he knows Carol's seen him. She's calling out 'Romeo' and yelling at him to stop and he wonders if he'd be better off doing as she says because he doesn't want to make her angry and give her an excuse to pick on him but the copse is hardly any distance away now and they're still a long way behind him. Maybe if he can get that far, they won't bother to chase 'cos they'll know there are plenty of places he can hide. Surely they'll have better things to do than waste their time searching for him in there, especially now it's starting to get dark. It's enough to make him forget the pain in his hand for a minute as he picks up the pace and heads for the trees.

If he can get to the footpath leading from the wasteland beyond the copse back to the housing estate, he'll be safe. He has no idea what they're planning to do but whatever it is he's fairly sure they won't try anything there – too many grown-ups around. Only problem is, the pain in his hand is back and he knows he'll never make it that far without stopping at least once and letting the bags rest on the floor. No way.

He risks a quick glance over his shoulder and although he can hear their shouts and laughter getting closer they're not in sight just yet. Trusting his instincts, he turns left off the path and wades through waist-high weeds and nettles which clutch at his clothes and sting his unprotected legs. Once he's through the worst of it, swinging the bags to help clear the way, he finds a piece of level ground behind a cluster of trees that offers the right sort of protection. Then he squats down again on his haunches, confident no one will be able to see him. He lowers the bags to the ground and waits, concentrating hard to control his breathing.

He knows he's made the right decision when Carol comes haring past seconds later, closely followed by a much older boy. This must be her boyfriend. He's never seen him before but he's heard about him. Everyone at school is talking about the fact that Carol's going out with a boy who's seventeen and got a Vespa. They say he's a Mod, although he's not sure what that is exactly and doesn't like to ask in case it makes him look stupid. By pretending he does know, he's at least managed to work out that when you grow up you have to choose which you're going to be, a Mod or a Rocker. Stuart Biggs told him that Rockers have to wear leather clothes all the time, even when it's hot, and that if you want to join their club you have to let all the other members pee all over your jacket and then you have to wear it for a month without washing it. He thinks he'll be a Mod when he's older.

They race past him and deeper into the woods and he's expecting Julie to come past too but there's no sign of her. He wonders if she's given up on the idea of chasing him or maybe didn't want to do it in the first place. It was probably all Carol's idea, knowing her. He gives it another minute or two, long enough to be sure that she and her boyfriend have reached the housing estate, then decides it's time to make a move. If they double back of course, he'll have to hope he sees them first and has somewhere decent to hide but he doesn't think they will. Surely they've got other plans for the evening that don't include making his life a misery.

Peering cautiously out from behind one of the trees, he decides the coast is clear and starts to battle his way back through the weeds and nettles. It's only as he reaches the path that a quiet voice says 'Hello', almost in his right ear, so close it scares the life out of him. Julie has been sitting there on the path all along, hidden from view by the weeds, and is clambering to her feet. It's as if she knew where he was and has been waiting for him.

He probably looks startled because she tells him it's OK – the other two have gone on ahead. He says he knows and rubs furiously at his legs. She tells him he needs to rub dock leaves on them to make the stinging go away and looks around to see if she can find any. He says it's fine – it doesn't hurt that much.

It feels funny talking to her like this. It's just like he thought – she's very different when Carol's not around. It's like she has to pretend to be someone she isn't when others are there but deep down she's quite a nice girl really. He's pleased he made such a good choice, even if she did say no.

She asks him where he got the flowers he offered her and he says he picked them himself. She asks why he wants to take her to the pictures, although she calls them *the flicks* which he thinks sounds a bit common. He's embarrassed by the question because he doesn't know how to frame the answer, to tell her he thinks she's the prettiest girl in the school. So he looks at the ground and says he needs to get home – his dad will be back from work soon. She asks him again and he's just about to summon up the courage to tell her when there's a triumphant shout from further down the path and Carol and her boyfriend come running into view. And all of a sudden Julie's grabbing him by the arm and jumping up and down, giggling about how she managed to catch him all on her own, and it's as if some alien has invaded her body and driven the real Julie Kasprowicz out. He thinks he could probably get his arm free if he really tried but there doesn't seem much point. It's not as if he can outrun them when they're this close, especially with the bags to carry.

Carol's out of breath by the time she reaches him. She stands in front of him, doubled over for a few seconds. Then she straightens up and there's this smile on her face which he doesn't like at all. It just doesn't look right on someone like her. He thinks he prefers her when she's angry.

February 2008: Ellen

Jack arrived with the children as agreed at 4.30. Ellen met them in the car park and clambered into the back with Megan and Harry, who knew they were here because Nanny B was ill but had no idea how serious things were. She took each of them by the hand and explained the situation in as much detail as she thought they could digest in one go. She told them this was their chance to see Nanny B for one last time and say goodbye. It was entirely up to them – it didn't matter if they preferred not to. Sometimes it was better to remember a person the way she used to be. She herself was going to stay with Nanny B until it was all over, which would probably be some time this evening. They would spend the night with their father just in case and could go there now if that was what they wanted but they were being given the choice because they were old enough to make up their own minds. She flashed a glance at Jack who smiled complicitly. Go, Team Harrison.

She sat back and waited to see how they would react. Before they arrived she'd prepared a mental checklist of things they might ask. Although not religious herself, she didn't want to deny her children the consolation of some form of afterlife, however simplistic and formulaic it might be. She'd worked out in her mind some notion of Nanny B always being there with them, looking out for them, maybe pointing out a star in some distant galaxy and identifying it as Nanny B's. It was something she wouldn't mind believing for herself.

As it turned out, they said nothing. Harry ducked his head, burying it in her chest while Megan turned to face the window, dry-eyed and inscrutable. Ellen gave them a few moments, then squeezed their hands, tugging them into her own lap.

'So ... what's it to be then?' she asked. 'You want to come in or not?'

Harry said he didn't want Nanny B to be upset if he didn't. Ellen explained she wouldn't even know whether or not they were there, which was obviously what he'd been waiting to hear. He shook his head – he'd rather not see her.

'How about you, Megan?' she asked, giving her hand another tug as if trying to drag her back into the car. Megan started doodling on the window which had begun to mist up.

'What about my fish project?' she asked.

'Your –?'

'It's in my bedroom at home. I need it for school tomorrow.'

'OK,' said Ellen cautiously. 'Well, you'll be calling in at home to pick up clothes and things for tomorrow so you'll be able to collect it then, won't you?'

'You said you were going to have a look at it this weekend before I take it into school.'

'Yes, I did, didn't I? Well, I'm sure Daddy will go through it with you. And maybe Miss Shelby will let you bring it home again for me to look at. If not, you've got an Open Evening coming up soon. I'll get to see it then, won't I? I'm sorry, love,' she added lamely, wishing she'd taken the time to check her daughter's work earlier. Surely she could have done it some time during the week instead of leaving it till the last minute. She wondered how it was life managed to sneak up and mug her – how did she manage to disappoint her daughter so often ... and so easily?

'What about Nanny B?' she prompted once more. 'Do you want to see her?'

'No.' The doodle spelt out *Megan* in a series of swoops and curls with a couple of kisses underneath. When she'd finished, she wiped it clear with one sweep of the hand, her focus still settled on something far beyond Ellen's reach. She decided to leave her daughter to it for now.

She gave both children a goodbye hug and kiss and patted Jack's shoulder to thank him for his support. It occurred to her that he hadn't asked anything about her weekend and the mysterious Eudora. She'd have to have something ready to tell him before long. And then there were the children – she'd have to explain everything to them too. And she would, she told herself. Not now, obviously. They had enough to deal with for the time being – more than enough. But some time soon she'd sit them down and tell them what she'd discovered in the past few days, because they had a right to know. She definitely would.

Some day.

Soon.

November 1966: John Michael

He's not frightened of her. Not really. She's bigger than he is, stronger too probably, even though she's only a girl. And he knows that if she decides she wants to punish him for running off, for ignoring her, for anything at all really, there's not a lot he can do about it. But it's not like there's anything new about this – he's been here before and been hit by bigger people than her. The Ward twins punch him so hard sometimes his arm goes numb. Stuart Biggs once hit him in the face with one of his plimsolls and his nose bled so much he had to spend the afternoon wearing someone else's shirt from lost property and sit in the classroom with a wedge of cotton wool sticking out of his nostril. And he can remember when she was still alive, how she used to sit there next to him while he had his bath, stroking his hair and telling him he should never fear anything. Not in this life. *Walk in the path of righteousness, Johnny,* she used to say, *and be sure He will always walk with you.*

So no, he knows better than to be scared of the likes of Carol Bingham. But he *is* anxious because he's known from the moment they entered the park that if they saw him they'd have to give chase. And now they've managed to catch him they'll have to think of something to do with him and if he knew in advance what it was they had in mind, he could grit his teeth and get ready for it, because he knows from past experience that it won't last long. If he just stands there and lets them get on with it, they'll soon get bored. Half an hour from now, he tells himself, he'll be lighting the fire in his front room and warming up the house for when his father gets home and that'll be it for another day. Half an hour is nothing – he can do thirty minutes. It's the uncertainty that's making him anxious.

He's not sure even Carol knows what to do with him. She's standing in front of him and her boyfriend has moved round behind so he can't see them both at the same time. He wonders if they're going to play the old trick where one of them kneels down while the one in front pushes. If they do, he'll go along with it and allow himself to fall. Get it over with. Pretend they've fooled him. Let them have their fun and move on.

She's calling him *Romeo* again, asking why he ran away from them. *Doesn't he like them any more?* She's talking in a silly voice as if she's a little girl and she's stroking his face with this strange, far-away look in her eyes. He flinches but knows better than to raise his hand to stop her.

He tells her he wasn't running away. He's in a hurry to get home – has to get the shopping back to his dad, who's there waiting for him. He's not, of course. He won't be back from work till six, but they don't know that and there's no harm in planting the idea that someone might come looking for him if he doesn't return home soon.

Carol seems unimpressed and wants to know how come, if he wasn't running away, he was hiding in the bushes. *What was he doing in there – having a piss? Or was he having a wank?* And she's really pleased with this, especially when Julie and her boyfriend start giggling as if it's the funniest thing anyone's said all week. He doesn't know what a wank is and thinks he probably doesn't want to, because *piss* is bad enough. It's a word common people use and he can feel himself blushing, even though he tries not to.

She tells him he's a dirty little boy – he'll get warts. She grabs one of his hands as if to check for early signs of them, then shrieks and lets go when she realises it's the damaged one. She gives a shudder which is so obviously fake, then grabs his sleeve and waves his hand in the air for the others to see. He doesn't like this. He hates it when anyone draws attention to it but there's not a lot he can do about it right now. The stage belongs to Carol.

She tells her boyfriend about *poor Romeo's loony mother* and how she chopped his fingers off with a kitchen knife because she'd had too much to drink. It's a lie – one of a thousand different versions whispered in every corner of the playground, each group trying to come up with something more sensational than the previous one. He wants to shout her down, tell her that's not what happened. She wasn't like that. She loved him and would never have done anything that would hurt him unless she'd had to. They weren't there – they didn't see the tears in her eyes as she held his wrist and slammed the car door, nor the way she hugged him afterwards and told him how proud she was of her little man, how he was saved now. But he says nothing.

Carol's noticed the bags now and is nudging them with her foot. Peering inside, she takes the items out one by one, holding each one up in the air for the others to see and saying how nice of him it was to go all that way just to buy these things for her. He tries to explain that they're for his father, as if that might in some way scare her off but she takes no notice.

She seems disappointed with most of what he's bought. *PG Tips? Nescafé? What sort of present is that? Doesn't he know a girl likes to be spoilt? Where's the chocolates? Where's the Milk Tray?* She's happier when she reaches the chocolate biscuits, which she immediately opens, taking several for herself and offering the rest to the others. She even asks if he'd like one and he decides he might as well, now that he won't be able to take the packet home with him. She seems amused by this, chuckling to herself as she delves deeper into the bag.

She's so careful as she takes out the box of eggs that he's pretty sure he can write these off as well. He knows it's all part of the act. Sure enough, as she takes one of them from the box and holds it up between thumb and forefinger for her audience to admire, she pretends to juggle with it and, as she lunges after it with both hands, she lets the box containing the other five eggs fall to the floor. Then, as if in horror at what she's done, she puts both hands to her cheeks and drops the remaining egg, which also smashes on impact. He makes a point of looking shocked because he knows this is what's expected of him and besides, the bag's nearly empty now. He figures they must be getting towards the end of the game. A few more hurtful comments for him to ignore, maybe a couple of punches on the arm and a quick tumble over the back of the stooping boyfriend and perhaps they'll let him go.

First of all though, Carol wants to know how he's going to explain all this to his dad. She hopes he's not going to dob in his friends. *Maybe it's best if he says he lost the money,* she suggests. *How much did he spend on all that rubbish anyway?* When he tells her, she snorts and says he'd have been better off taking Julie out somewhere. *Oh, forgot . . . Julie said no, didn't she?* She laughs again and tells her boyfriend that this is the first-year kid who asked Julie to go to the flicks with him. *Dirty little sod. Bet he only wants to shag her.* He's horrified at this because shagging's something he definitely knows a bit about. The others talk about it all the time in the playground and he finds himself listening in out of curiosity, even though he suspects he shouldn't. He's seen dogs doing it before now and Stuart Biggs claims he once sneaked up on his older brother and watched him and his girlfriend in the bushes down the rec. The idea that he might want to do that to anyone, let alone someone as pretty as Julie, is just too much for him. He risks a look at her and is pleased to see she looks shocked as well, although he's less impressed when she announces in a sniffy voice that she'd rather shag a tramp than him. Again, the word doesn't sound right coming from her lips.

It's a shame they've stumbled onto this topic because just as he was hoping Carol might be running out of steam, this seems to give her a new burst of energy. She steps back and looks him up and down, then announces that maybe Julie's missing something here. *He may be just a first year but maybe Romeo's very advanced for his age. How does Julie know he's not hung like a donkey?* He doesn't have time to dwell on this strange image because he's concentrating so hard on her every movement, wondering exactly when she's going to plant both hands in his chest and push. She looks around to make sure no one else is entering the woods, then grins over his shoulder at her boyfriend and he's sure this must be it. She's standing very close now, so close he can smell the bubble gum she's been chewing and popping every so often. *How about it, Romeo?* she asks, leaning in and whispering in his ear. *You got something in there that would interest our Julie?*

And before he's had time to make sense of what's happening, he can feel her hand sliding down the front of his trousers and it dawns on him for the first time that she's trying to touch his JT, which is so disgusting he can't help himself. He tries to jump back and get away from her but the boyfriend has got hold of his arms now and he can't move. He has nowhere to go.

What you got then? she's whispering, and she brings her face directly in front of his so that they're nose to nose. He's not sure what terrifies him more, her roving hand which is now struggling with his belt or the idea which has seized him that she's going to kiss him on the mouth any minute. It's disgusting either way and he squirms away from her, struggling to break free, even though he knows that's the worst thing he can do, but he can't just stand there and let her do this. He opens his mouth to yell and is cut off in mid-scream by a huge hand which is clamped across his mouth. It smells of petrol and it's pressing so hard against his nose he's finding it difficult to catch his breath. Carol's boyfriend is using his other hand to lock both his arms behind his back, making it impossible for him to break free.

And next thing he knows there's a rush of cold air and Carol's tugging frantically at his trousers and underpants, trying to drag them over his shoes which are caught inside the material. She staggers backwards as one of the trouser legs comes free, then suddenly she's waving them above her head like a captured flag and pointing at him, laughing so much the words come out in fits and starts between gasps. *Oh my God,* she's yelling. *Anyone got a magnifying glass?* And he's crimson now because this is just the worst thing ... absolutely the worst. Carol Bingham will burn in hell for this. He knows this for sure. She will burn in hell.

And she leans in close again and whispers *Is that the best you can do, Romeo? You think Julie's gonna be impressed by that?* She takes it in her thumb and finger and pulls, as if trying to stretch it. Then she lets go and starts wiggling her little finger in his face, chanting 'half inch, half inch' in a high, squeaky voice, which is the cue for Julie and the boyfriend to do the same, and he thinks that of all the things they've said and done this afternoon, this must be the unkindest and most hurtful of them all. It's not his fault he doesn't have all his fingers.

The boyfriend is so busy laughing that he loosens his grip for a moment and he's able to break free. He tries to grab his clothes but Carol's too quick for him and she's off down the path before he can get near her. He wants to run after her but feels ridiculous standing there with his lower half open for everyone to stare at, so instinctively he charges back through the weeds and nettles, taking no notice of the countless stings he picks up on the way, until he's regained the relative safety of his earlier hiding place. He knows they won't follow him in here.

Carol stands there on the path, holding up his trousers and underpants and asking if he's forgotten something. *Don't you want them then, Romeo?* She waits for some sort of response, then seems to decide she's had enough of that particular game. She drops the clothes to the ground and starts to walk away, stamping on the egg carton as if to sign off on the afternoon's entertainment. Then, just as he's daring to hope that it's all over, she stoops at the last moment and picks up the trousers again before launching them into the trees, high above her head. She tries the same with his underpants which for some reason refuse to catch on the branches until she's finally successful at the third attempt. Then she calls out something he doesn't quite hear and sets off down the path, heading back towards the park, having apparently forgotten all about him already.

He waits till he's sure they've gone. Then he gives it another ten minutes just to be absolutely certain no one else is coming before he emerges from his hiding place and beats his way back to the path. This time he uses a large stick to carve a way through but his bare legs are already hurting so much it hardly seems worth the effort. He decides he'll have to find some dock leaves the moment he's rescued his clothes.

But getting them down from the tree turns out to be easier said than done. The branch is far too high for him to reach, and even with the stick to help him he's still a few tantalising inches short every time he jumps. Then, while he's looking desperately around for a longer one, the sound of a dog barking just beyond the entrance to the wood sends him darting back through the undergrowth to his hiding place, from where he watches as two women come into view. And for the first time he's starting to realise just how cold it is now the sun's gone.

February 2008: Kate's voicemail

Hi! You're through to Kate. Sorry I'm not here at the moment. You know what to do.

Hi Kate. I was hoping I'd maybe catch you before you set off for work ... never mind. Just wanted to let you know ... she's gone, love. Last night. While I was sleeping, would you believe? Isn't that just ...? Ah ... Jesus! Anyway, I'm OK. Promise. And everything's under control here. You know Sam. He's probably got the funeral and memorial services for the next ten years all booked and sorted. Not a lot here for me to do really. Anyway ... give me a ring if you like or come round once you get off work ... whatever. Speak to you soon. Bye.

November 1966: John Michael

He lies to his father. Tells him he lost the money on the way to school – he was running and thinks it must have fallen out of his pocket. He's crying as he explains what happened and he's not sure why. He went over this version of events so often in his head while crouching in the bushes that he's almost persuaded himself this is what actually happened. He's not sobbing because he thinks it'll add weight to his story and he's certainly not looking for sympathy. He doesn't deserve it – he's a liar. A liar and a coward. He knows what she would have expected of him in just that sort of situation and he's fallen so far short it's embarrassing. Even so, he can't seem to hold back the tears once they've started to flow and his heart's still racing as if he'd just run to the shops and back.

His father isn't angry. He's disappointed, frustrated probably. He's always saying they're not made of money. They have to watch their pennies so something like this is the last thing they need. But he doesn't shout the way she would have done. She'd have seen through his lies the moment he opened his mouth because she could always tell when he wasn't being honest. And she'd have found a way of punishing him to put things right, to wipe out the wrong he'd done, even though it always hurt her so much afterwards to see him in such pain. She would have known.

But his father's too easily swayed by the tears. All he does is ruffle his hair and tell him not to worry. No point crying over spilt milk. They can always go and buy what they need in the morning. *But maybe he'll do it himself, eh? Bit cheaper that way.* Then he goes through to the bathroom to clean up from work so he can make a start on dinner. And it's just like any other evening, as if nothing's changed. Nothing's happened.

He goes to bed early and lies there in the dark, hugging the blankets because he still hasn't quite managed to shake off the cold from earlier. He wonders if he's caught a chill. He has no idea how long he stayed there in the bushes, trying to decide what to do. He'd pulled his sweater over his head and tied it round his waist so that even if he looked ridiculous he'd at least be half-decent if anyone walked past. And twice he peered out from his hiding place and watched as strangers passed through, totally unaware that he was there. Both times he almost plucked up the courage to call out and ask for help, but the words died in his throat the moment he opened his mouth and he ducked back down at the last moment, staying out of sight.

In the end it was the cold that forced his hand. On a warmer evening he might still be there now, agonising over how to get his clothes back, but even sheltered as he was from the worst of the wind, he was defenceless against the frozen fingers creeping up from the earth beneath his feet, which clutched at his legs and hands until he could hardly feel them any more. In desperation he'd taken a chance on a man in a suit who looked respectable, even if he *was* walking an Alsatian. He wasn't tall enough to reach the clothes either, but he was strong enough to break off a longer branch and managed after several attempts to shake them free. He turned out to be a very kind man. He didn't ask lots of questions about how the clothes had ended up there. He just offered to walk home with him and make sure he got there safely, an offer which might have been tempting if not for the fact that his father was due home any minute. As it was, he barely made it through the front door in time.

He gives the blankets another tug and buries himself inside, doing his best to ignore the stinging sensation in his legs. He knows the worst thing he can do is scratch them. Once he starts that, they won't give him a moment's peace all night. He's rubbed some vinegar on them when his father wasn't looking but it doesn't seem to have done a lot of good. Again he can feel the tears prickling at the corners of his eyes and has to work hard to keep them under control.

He tries not to think about it but can't stop his mind from straying to tomorrow and what he can expect in the playground. Everyone will know by break time. Carol will make sure of that. They'll all be trying to find him, whichever little hiding place he picks out for himself, and he'll be the target all day for their stupid jokes about how he was stripped naked by Carol Bingham and how she's not only seen his JT ... she's played with it. It's going to be the worst day of his life. He knows all about sticks and stones and is usually pretty good at ignoring others when they start to tease him but this feels different somehow. Very different.

He wonders about pretending to be ill. He's never done this before but if it means he doesn't have to be there and listen to the chorus of laughter and jeers it might be worth it just this once. But he knows, even as the idea is forming inside his head, that it won't solve anything in the long run. He can only put it off for so long – eventually he's going to have to face up to this, whether he likes it or not.

He buries his head in the pillow and tries to imagine what she would have advised him to do in a situation like this. She was a fighter – he can remember that much. She was never one for sitting back and keeping her thoughts to herself if she knew someone was in the wrong. He could remember her running out into the street on more than one occasion and giving a piece of her mind to neighbours she thought were gossiping behind her back. If she was here now, she'd be telling him to stand up to

Carol and Julie, he was sure of that. *Never let evil have its way, Johnny,* she'd be whispering to him. *Let the wicked prosper and some of their evil becomes a part of you.* She'd expect him to fight fire with fire.

But how? he wondered. *How do you do that?*

February 2008: Ellen

There was no logical reason why she should have chosen her mother's bedroom as the first room to clear. If she had been looking for the diary and books, it would have been far more logical to start with the attic, which was where Sam thought they might be. And not only were they in the bedroom, they were under the bed, the first place she looked. It was, she reflected, as if it was meant to be, as if she was being guided to them. As if they were actually looking for *her*.

The moment she slipped the catches on the suitcase and lifted the lid, all thoughts of clearing out the house went out of the window. She plunged her hands into the treasure trove, lifting out the books and checking the titles: *A Matter of Convenience; The People versus John Michael Adams; A Question of Intent; Every Parent's Nightmare; A Miscarriage of Justice.* Then there were the papers, some of them letters, most of them articles cut from newspapers or photocopied from psychiatric journals – hundreds of individual sheets, few of them stapled and none collated into coherent bundles, a chaotic sprawl of evidence reflecting the disorderly workings of an obsessive mind. When exactly had Barbara found time to gather all this, let alone read it? And more to the point, how had she herself failed to notice any of it? How had she managed to know so little about her own mother?

After a few minutes of indiscriminate rummaging, she realised she couldn't work like this. She needed to impose some sort of order before she could hope to make sense of these papers, let alone follow the labyrinthine workings of her mother's mind and understand exactly what it was she was looking for. Putting the books to one side for the moment, she concentrated on sorting the documents into piles, grouping them chronologically or by subject matter or by author ... anything that would make it more accessible.

It was getting on for eleven before she was finally ready to start reading. First up was Peter Vaughan's diary, a simple black notebook, untitled even inside. There was just a starting date – June 2nd, 1970 – written in scratchy blue ink in an untidy sprawl which suggested that this sort of thing didn't come easily to the writer. That impression was further reinforced by the lengthy gaps between entries. They covered a period of nearly four years in total but were often several months apart and clearly prompted by specific events: visits to spend time with his son, fell-race competitions, birthdays. There was little in the way of introspection or soul-searching – even on paper it was easy to recognise the intensely private person the villagers in Ashbury had come to know and respect. He might hint here and there at problems in his relationship with John Michael or reflect wistfully on his diminishing levels of fitness but he was clearly not one to agonise over life's imponderables and bare his soul on a nightly basis.

Most of it would have made fairly turgid reading, were it not for the fact that anything – anything at all – that opened up her father to her was automatically rendered more exotic than would otherwise have been the case. She was particularly intrigued by the later pages when the name of Barbara gradually began to feature more prominently. At last she had something she could get her teeth into. Even here the writing was spare and unemotional but at least it afforded occasional glimpses of the mind guiding the pen and the strength of his feelings for both his son and this soul mate, who had come so late into his life. Reading it a second time, Ellen was forced to agree with her mother's assessment – there was little room for doubt that Peter Vaughan would have opened up and told her everything at some stage, if circumstances had only permitted it.

After the diary, she turned her attention to the papers, starting with the earliest articles dating from immediately after the trial. By mid-afternoon, when it was time to pick up the children, she still felt as if she'd barely scratched the surface. She quickly gathered all the papers together, now safely secured with paper clips and elastic bands she'd found in a drawer, and placed them with almost reverent care in the suitcase before dashing off to school. Only once the children were tucked up in bed several hours later was she was able to take them all out again and pick up where she'd left off.

She finally fell into bed around one. As she lay there she reflected on what she'd read so far. Apart from the diary, she hadn't had a chance to open any of the books but suspected she knew what they would contain if the articles were anything to go by. Impartial they were not. Taken individually, she supposed, they might have seemed objective enough but several hours of reading the same arguments from a number of different perspectives was a little like being hit repeatedly with a mallet. For these were the conclusions ... more than that ... the *convictions* of like-minded people who knew enough about the subject to declare unequivocally that the treatment John Michael Adams had received, from the courts initially and subsequently from the general public, amounted to a gross miscarriage of justice and an abuse of his human rights. There were no dissenting voices. Ellen knew well enough that another side to the argument existed, a powerful one which had been trotted out ad nauseam in the media and which would have informed the thinking of the vast majority of people. But Barbara had found no place for any such articles here. Her criteria for inclusion were selective to the point of censorship.

It occurred to Ellen that as a general rule she would have reacted against such a lack of balance and gone out of her way to find reasons for embracing the other side of the argument. As she lay there in bed though, she found herself if not totally convinced by what she'd been reading then at least sympathetic to the point the articles were trying to make. Perhaps it was that same gut reaction she'd experienced in Oakham, when she'd realised that the boy in the photo was barely any older than her own children. And maybe, on a much simpler and altogether more human level, it was simply a case of wanting desperately to find common ground with someone she'd lost and wasn't yet ready to release. Whatever the reason she felt engaged, committed to something as if somehow a relay baton had been passed to her. And she knew already how she would be spending the following day.

She woke at twenty to six and tiptoed to the bathroom to avoid waking the children so early. Then, unable to get back to sleep, she switched on the bedside lamp and reached for the first of the books, which she'd brought to bed with her. She'd chosen it because she had heard so much now about Carl Holmbach and was curious as to whether she would find him as convincing and inspirational as Barbara had. The front cover carried the obligatory scowling photo with the title *Every Parent's Nightmare* emblazoned across it in lurid red capitals. Somehow the boy looked even younger than she remembered.

A number of pages were dog-eared and, when she turned to each of them, she found sentences and even whole paragraphs marked with vertical double lines in red biro. Instantly she was back in the university library, late-night sessions in pursuit of her Business degree, marking interesting paragraphs for future reference. She wondered what had prompted Barbara to choose these particular passages and decided to read them first.

In some sections Holmbach was intent on highlighting the failings of Mr Justice Lawson, whose errors of judgement, not least his failure to step back from the proceedings, had made it impossible for the boy to receive a fair trial. In others the focus was on the behaviour of the media who immediately seized on this as a story which would grab the public's interest and were determined to sensationalise it at every opportunity, at the expense of the truth if need be, in order to keep it alive.

But Ellen's attention was drawn in particular to the third category, the relationship between John Michael Adams and his mother. Here the professor was able to draw upon hours and hours of exclusive interviews with the boy over a period of years and shade in the background that everyone else had been content to leave empty, because it interfered with the stereotype they were hell-bent on perpetuating. His privileged access had enabled him to establish a rapport which no one else had enjoyed. As a result the boy had opened up, giving him an insight into his early life which Ellen found fascinating. She wasn't remotely surprised that this section contained more marked passages than any other.

And one incident in particular made her pulse quicken just a fraction. She actually read on for two or three sentences before the possible significance of what she'd just read sent her backtracking for the relevant quote. It was enough to cause her to put the book to one side and sit bolt upright in bed as she thought things through. It stayed with her while she washed, dressed and woke the children, while she made breakfast and bundled them into the car for the start of another school day. A day like any other.

And it wouldn't go away, even though she knew it was all so unlikely and that she was probably letting her imagination run away with itself. But she couldn't help thinking back to the break-in at Primrose Cottage and the fact that neither she nor Kate had managed to come up with a convincing explanation as to when or even how O'Halloran had managed to wipe Eudora's documents off the laptop, even though both were convinced he'd been responsible.

Probably nothing, she told herself. A few hours from now she could be sitting down with Kate and having a good laugh about how easily she'd allowed herself to get carried away. *You watch too many films, Missy.* But she also knew the thought wasn't going to go away. Not until she'd at least checked it out.

And she knew exactly how to go about it.

*　*　*　*

Webster's Grocery Store was no more than a mile from Calder Vale, an easy cycle ride for the return journey but more than demanding on the way out because of a couple of steady inclines which would have more than tested the delivery boy's legs. Mr Webster himself was a cheerful man with a florid complexion and enough surplus pounds around his waist and thighs to suggest that he might have benefitted from doing the deliveries himself.

Ellen had tried phoning several times from home but either there was a fault on the line or no one at the store had time to answer. In the end she'd given up in exasperation and made the half-hour journey herself rather than wait. She hoped the speed cameras she passed on the way weren't in operation.

Long way to come for a two-minute conversation, she told herself. *Especially one which might easily amount to nothing at all.* She did her best, as she waited for Mr Webster to serve a queue of customers, to keep it all in perspective. This was probably a wild goose chase, another dead end. Every chance she'd end up feeling very silly. About time she got a grip on herself and her overactive imagination.

In the event, she left feeling more pumped up than ever.

Forty minutes later she swung in through the gates at Langmere Grove, tapping her feet impatiently as she waited for Des on Security to raise the barrier. Most mornings she'd wind the window down and exchange a few words of greeting before driving through but this time she made do with a wave and a forced smile. She suspected he'd find it difficult to come up with the right words of sympathy and she wasn't ready to receive them anyway. More importantly though, she didn't want any further delays.

She gave a grim smile as she realised that Colin, not content with taking over her duties for a few days, had also made use of her parking space. Pulling into the one for the deputy manager, which he'd left vacant, she leapt from the car without bothering to lock it and headed for the Reception area. Angela looked up in surprise and started to get up from her seat but Ellen waved her back down and marched off to her office, which she was pleased to find empty. A half-drunk cup of coffee, which had been left on the desk, suggested Colin had moved in here too but at least she didn't need to deal with him just yet.

Putting her coat next to his on the stand in the corner, she sat down at her desk and logged on to her computer. Angela buzzed to ask if everything was OK and she took the opportunity to check with her on the easiest way to access the employment records. Angela walked her through it and, bless her heart, offered nothing in the way of condolences, other than to ask if she wanted a drink. Ellen said yes to a coffee and clicked her way through the various options until she found what she wanted.

Even now she expected one side of the equation to collapse. Something wouldn't add up somewhere – after all the morning's speculation and frantic chasing, she'd be left grabbing at thin air and looking foolish. For every number that was falling into place, and there were now quite a few, she couldn't quite bring herself to accept the sum of the parts. This sort of thing didn't happen in real life ... not to someone like her.

But the moment she called the relevant page up onto the screen, read through the details and did a few rapid calculations, the fantastic bubble her imagination had blown that morning was still hovering there in front of her and she was running out of explanations that might burst it. She knew that at some stage she'd need to decide whether this was something to be welcomed or dreaded but not now. Her thoughts were in such turmoil, she felt her instincts were all she could rely on.

When Angela brought the coffee in, there was just one more thing to check.

'He's not in today,' was the reply. 'Called in sick this morning. Not like him at all.'

Ellen held her breath for a moment, then checked the screen in front of her. Tearing a sheet from the pad on the desk, she scribbled down an address, then grabbed her coat, almost pulling the stand over in the process. The cup of coffee stayed where Angela had left it, untouched.

February 2008: John Michael

He read this book once. *The Dice Man* by Luke someone or other. About this psychiatrist who relies on the roll of the dice for every decision he makes. To spice things up he makes sure he always throws in a couple of options that are way out there – things he'd never dream of doing normally. And whatever the dice tell him, he forces himself to go through with it. Backing out would defeat the object.

Reading it was the professor's idea – all part of the ongoing training, preparation for the real world outside. *This is what happens if you don't accept responsibility. Don't let yourself be influenced by outside factors you can't control.* He thinks dice would be overkill the way things are right now. Feels like a coin would be more appropriate – heads you leave, tails you stay. End of.

Last night he was all but out of there. No dice or coin, just a fit of blind panic. When he heard the knock on the door, his first thought was *that's it*. That late at night, it's never good news. His hand was actually shaking as he opened up and when he saw it was just old Mrs Anderson from down the hall, asking everyone in the block if they'd seen her cat lately, the relief…

He took it as some sort of message from the gods, like he'd been granted a second chance or something. No time at all he had everything packed and waiting there for him on the bed. Quarter of an hour was all it took. All those years crammed into just fifteen minutes, two suitcases and a holdall. Can't get much sadder than that.

Maybe that's what made him take a step back in the end. No one wants to look in the mirror each morning and see the word *loser* stamped across his forehead and his first thought, when he saw the cases was, *Is that it? Is that all there is?* They're the same ones he'd brought with him. He remembers the professor picking them up at a car boot sale nearly twenty years ago. So the only difference between now and when he first moved in is one scruffy black holdall instead of two Sainsbury's bags, otherwise it's the same depressing snapshot. If that's what he's got to show for it all…

So he decided to sleep on it and first thing he saw when he opened his eyes this morning was the sun, streaming in through the window and lighting up the room like it was the middle of June not February. That seemed at least as significant an omen as the old lady last night. And all through breakfast he's been gradually talking himself back down from the window ledge. The cases are still there by the front door, packed, ready to go at a moment's notice, but he doesn't see it happening just yet. Not now the initial panic's over.

He needs to put all that training into practice now: sit down, write it all out and make an informed decision, while he's holding things pretty much together. So he's called in sick at work, which is a first, and he's grabbed a sheet of paper and is ready to go as soon as he manages to track down a biro. Pros and cons of baling out and starting again somewhere else. The professor's boy after all.

Twenty minutes in and it's all down on paper but he's still none the wiser. He knows now he can express it any way he chooses, two plus two is always going to make four and there's not a thing he can do about it. He doesn't want to go but he's afraid to stay.

If he could be one hundred per cent sure it was safe, there's more than enough to keep him here ... things you can't cram into a couple of battered old cases. But he knows how bad it could get if things go against him. Ellen knows about Eudora Nash. Two days later she disappears off to the Cotswolds of all places for the weekend and that's a coincidence? Right. And then there's Barbara – he remembers when the professor died there were all sorts of things that came out of the woodwork. Death's like that. Doors that have been slammed shut for years spring open and suddenly everything's up in the air. If he could just be sure, one hundred per cent certain, about how much Barbara knew and what she's passed on to Ellen, there wouldn't be the same sense of urgency. But he can't and at almost any other time in his life, that would have been more than enough to make him go. He'd have left skid marks.

But this is not any other time in his life. It's now. Two days ago he celebrated his fifty-third birthday and, just like the others since the professor died, he spent it on his own. No one knew a thing about it. And if he gets on his bike now and runs away like he's done so many times before, then fifteen, twenty, thirty years from now he'll still be doing the same. The professor used to say something about people who don't learn from their mistakes being doomed to repeat them. Something like that anyway. Isn't that what will happen if he gives up on any chance of settling here?

And he's still batting the same thoughts back and forth in his head when old Mrs Anderson knocks at the door again and he's trying not to show his irritation as he lifts the latch because he understands the cat's all she's got in her life and, God, doesn't that sound depressingly familiar? How about that for an omen? But when he pulls the door back, it's not Mrs Anderson standing there and all of a sudden he knows it's neither heads nor tails because this time someone's snatched the coin away before he even had time to toss it.

PART FOUR

THE DECISION

11

February 2008: Ellen

In the six and a half years she'd known Alan Wharton, Ellen had rarely given any thought to his life away from Langmere. He was her go-to man for anything involving landscaping and increasingly her saviour whenever the network crashed. Beyond that she barely gave him a moment's thought.

She'd known many of the staff at Langmere since she was a child, especially those who used to work with Barbara in the supermarket or, in later years, on Reception, and although she'd never shown any great interest in their private lives, somehow the odd detail had seeped into her consciousness, as if through some form of social osmosis. Even though Alan was still a relative newcomer, she'd have expected to pick up the occasional anecdote or snippet of information about him. That had never happened though. And now she understood why.

If there'd ever been any mention of close friends or a romantic attachment of any kind, she was sure it would have registered, if only because it would have struck her as incongruous. She'd have been prepared to wager a tidy sum that he lived alone, had very little in the way of a social life and compensated by snapping up the latest iPod, iPad, iPed and iPud the moment it came onto the market. And no, she wasn't blind to the irony – she was well aware that if children were substituted for gadgets, this was a more than passable description of her own day-to-day existence.

But at least one preconceived notion was dispelled the moment she stepped into the flat. She'd been expecting some sort of homage to geekdom, a dismal breaker's yard of discarded keyboards and disused monitors with half-dismantled computers competing for limited space with a tangled undergrowth of cables and wires, all groping their way towards the corners of the room like tree roots in search of water. What she found instead was a light, airy room with gleaming windows, polished shelves and not a speck of dust to be seen anywhere. The furniture, faded to the point of drabness, looked as if it had come with the flat but even here an effort had been made with brightly coloured cushions and throws designed to catch the eye. It looked cared for and lived in, with more than a nod to the 1950s maybe but none the worse for that.

She took the seat she was offered, straightening the armrest cover as she did so – the flaw in the diamond, apparently. She accepted his offer of coffee, not so much because she wanted it but because she thought it might buy her a little time. Having been in such a rush to get here from Langmere, she'd barely had a chance to think things through and wasn't really sure how she felt about everything just yet.

He said nothing while they waited for the kettle to boil, merely stood there in the tiny raised kitchen area, tapping the fingers of his ungloved hand on the work surface. She'd come prepared for prolonged bouts of silence. Most of her previous conversations with him had been pretty much one-way traffic. She assumed the fact she was his employer accounted for some of it but even here, on home territory, he seemed almost crippled by shyness, doling out every sentence like marked currency.

She took another look around the room and her gaze fell on the suitcases by the door, with the holdall propped up against them. 'Thinking of going somewhere?' she asked, one eyebrow raised in surprise. He didn't answer, simply shrugged his shoulders and turned back to the kettle. Without actually looking at her, he held up the milk and sugar and she asked for white without. Then, when the kettle had boiled, he brought her drink over to her and sat on the far edge of the sofa. He'd made nothing for himself.

'I'm sorry about your mother,' he said eventually, so quietly she could easily have missed it.

'Thank you.'

'She was always very kind to me.'

'Is that why you arranged for those parcels to be sent to Calder Vale?' she asked. 'The little treats?' Mr Webster's description had been very detailed. The hoodie, jeans and trainers might not have been conclusive on their own but the moment he mentioned a baseball cap worn back to front, she was pretty sure who it was. And the black glove on one hand was the clincher. A work accident back in Ballymena was what he'd told everyone at Langmere but she knew better now.

She was having difficulty in putting together the boy she'd been reading about in bed just a few hours earlier and the diffident man almost twenty years her senior who was sitting just feet away from her. How on earth was she supposed to get her head around the idea that this was John Michael Adams?

It dawned on her that she was staring at his gloved hand – she looked away quickly, hoping he hadn't noticed.

'I'm not going anywhere,' he said, nodding at the cases. 'I mean, I was ... sort of. Not now.'

A calypso tune started up inside Ellen's bag – she reached inside for her mobile and switched it off without checking it.

'You were thinking of leaving. Just like that?' she asked.

'It doesn't matter now.'

'Is that your answer to everything ... running away?'

Even as the words left her mouth it occurred to her how unfair and pointless it was to judge him by normal standards. Of course his response when threatened would be to disappear. What other options were open to someone in his situation? Why did she have to sound so judgemental all the time?

'You're worried I'm going to tell everyone who you really are? Is that it?'

Again the shrug of the shoulders, which seemed to be his fall-back position for any question he found remotely challenging.

'Jesus,' she said, getting up from her seat and carrying the cup over to the window. 'You're my own brother and I don't even know what to call you, you realise that? Is it Alan or John Michael?'

'Alan,' he said quietly.

'So think about it, Alan. How am I going to tell anyone? The moment I say anything there's not a camera or microphone in the world that won't be pointing at my family. You think I want my kids to be at the centre of a freak show for the rest of their lives?'

He offered no response and she cursed herself for not being a little more tactful. The situation was difficult enough as it was – insensitive comments weren't likely to help things along at all.

'How did you know?' he asked eventually. 'I suppose she told you?'

'She?'

'Your mother.'

'Barbara?' This was something she hadn't anticipated. 'Are you telling me she knew who you were?'

'I think so.'

'What do you mean, you think so?'

'Maybe. I don't know for sure. She never said. Not in so many words.'

'So what makes you think she might have?'

He shook his head, as if disclaiming any responsibility for the plausibility or otherwise of what he was about to say. 'It was just … she used to sit and talk with me. In the canteen. She was part-time when I knew her, so she wasn't in all that often but when she was she always seemed to pick me out.' There was a lengthy pause and Ellen wondered for a moment if that was it. She had to resist the urge to hurry him along.

'She'd ask me what sort of a morning I'd had, whether I enjoyed my work – things like that. Then she'd tell me about her day so far. It was nice, you know? She didn't have to do that.'

'That doesn't mean she knew who you were,' objected Ellen. 'She was probably just being sociable.'

'Maybe. But this one time she'd been telling me what a good job I'd done on that area of waste ground – you know, the one the other side of the pool that we landscaped a few years ago? Said she used to have this friend, back when she was a lot younger, who did that sort of thing. Worked for her father. Good with his hands. She said he'd have been really proud to produce something like that … and she looked at me like she was testing me or something.'

'So what did you say to her?'

'I didn't say anything. I just sat there until she smiled and said something about having to get back to work, couldn't sit there all day, and I thought it was all over. But as she got to her feet she said she often found herself thinking about this friend of hers, even all these years later. Thing was, he had a son, only he hardly ever got to see him for some reason. Very sad about it, he was. And she put her hand on mine and said *That boy meant such a lot to Peter*. Then she smiled and walked away.'

'Dammit,' said Ellen, rolling her eyes and flopping back into the confines of the chair. 'She knew.'

'I wasn't sure.'

'She knew. Of course she knew. God …' She bit her lip and worked hard to fight back the tears she could feel gathering.

'It was only that one time. She never mentioned any of it again.'

'She didn't need to. She was sounding you out. You'd already given her the confirmation she needed.'

'But I didn't say anything.'

'You didn't need to.'

He got up from the sofa and walked over to the chest of drawers. Taking a handful of tissues from a box which was resting on it, he handed them to her and returned to his seat.

'She didn't say anything to you, then?' he asked at length.

'No,' she laughed, dabbing at the corner of one eye. 'No, she didn't.' *Maybe that's what ought to go on her gravestone*, she thought grimly. The ultimate epitaph – *she never said a sodding word.*

'So if it wasn't from her, how did you find out who I was?'

Ellen blew her nose and tucked the tissue into the cuff of her sweater before answering.

'Where to begin,' she said, puffing out her cheeks. 'Did you know she went to see Carl Holmbach just before he died?'

He didn't. And if appearances were anything to go by, he was stunned to hear it.

'He didn't say anything to me about it.'

'I think he was worried you might get ideas – from what I can gather, he wanted you to concentrate on the here and now rather than chasing the past.'

'But she knew my father. He knew I'd want to meet her.'

'That's what I meant.'

He said nothing in response to this but she could see him turning it over in his mind, recalibrating his relationship with the professor. *Welcome to the club*, she thought.

And as the morning drew on she took him through it, retracing her own journey step by step. It seemed surreal to be sitting there discussing something so momentous – she could still hardly believe how far her efforts had brought her.

She started with Eudora's document that should have been on the laptop and wasn't, how she and Kate had been so obsessed with O'Halloran, they'd missed the obvious. The idea that it had been erased *after* the break-in hadn't even occurred to them because the only person who'd had the laptop then had been Ellen herself ... apart from when she gave it to Alan.

As for the rest of it, it was like sitting down on a Saturday evening and watching the lottery balls fall into place. There was the passage from Carl Holmbach's book, describing the accident which had resulted in the loss of the boy's little finger and the top of the one next to it, a deformity about which he was so self-conscious that he always wore a black leather glove. It was the kind of thing she could easily have skipped, a tiny detail that might never have registered if she hadn't already been in a heightened state of alert. Then there was the mystery of the parcels being sent to Calder Vale. If it wasn't Jacob or Sam, who was it? And why? She told him how she had sat there, expecting to see her barely formed theory blasted out of the water with the drop of each new ball, only to discover that yet another of her numbers had come up. By the time she'd checked the employment records and discovered that Alan Wharton had arrived at Langmere barely three months after the death of Carl Holmbach, she knew she wasn't going to need any bonus ball.

Then it was her turn to ask questions and he told her about his visit to Ashbury in search of a detailed picture of his father's life there and in particular the woman who had obviously come to mean a lot to him. Ellen had no problem at all understanding his need to fill in the gaps – it felt as if she'd only just embarked on a similar kind of odyssey herself. He told her about the conversation with Old Jenny Moore which changed everything – the one in which she told him about Barbara's sudden disappearance from the village and the rumours that the reason she'd left was because she was pregnant. If they were true, there was only one possible father, which meant that if he could track Barbara down, maybe he'd find another branch of his family he'd known nothing about. Maybe he wasn't alone after all.

And as the sun inched its way across the living-room floor and the almost untouched cup of coffee grew cold to the touch, Ellen went with him as he followed in almost the exact same footsteps that Stuart Mahon, at Eudora's bidding, had taken in the latter stages of his own journey just a few months earlier.

She shared the sense of triumph John Michael – Alan? – must have felt when he finally tracked Barbara down at Langmere, was able to read in his expression the joy and sense of wonder when he discovered that he not only had a sister but was an uncle as well ... twice over. It didn't escape her attention that the longer they spent in each other's company, the more he relaxed, to the point where he was actually initiating conversation. He even smiled at one point, apologising for having deleted Eudora's file. He told her he'd kept a back-up copy if she wanted it, at which point she smiled too and it felt as if a bridge had been crossed.

Eventually, during a momentary lull in the conversation, Ellen looked at her watch and said she ought to be thinking about getting back. He offered to make lunch, then admitted ruefully that it would have to be jam sandwiches as he hadn't been to the shop yet. She thanked him anyway. The Balfours were coming round later to see her and go over the arrangements for the funeral which was just three days away and there were still things she wanted to do before she picked up the children.

The door was only a few paces away but she suddenly felt unaccountably awkward, as if unsure how to cross that space. They'd talked, which was important. They'd made a start of sorts, and she'd even managed to relax a little in his company, but she was aware that the person she felt comfortable with was Alan Wharton. John Michael Adams was a different matter. He cast a long shadow and she wondered if she would ever be able to shake it off. She was aware of the uneasiness which had quickened her pulse and rattled her coffee cup whenever the subject of her children was raised, especially when he referred to himself as their uncle. It was one thing to appreciate how much it meant to him that he still had family after all but there seemed to be an assumption somewhere in all this with which she felt far from comfortable – an assumption of inclusivity. She didn't want to leave him with any misapprehensions.

He seemed equally preoccupied as he got to his feet.

'So,' he said, looking at the cases. 'What do I do about them?'

Ellen shrugged her shoulders.

'Do you want me to leave?'

'I told you, I'm not going to tell anyone.'

'That's not what I asked,' he said, and for the first time ever, as far as she could recall, he actually looked her in the eye, unflinchingly. Clearly the answer mattered a great deal to him. She was the one who looked away first.

'No, I don't want you to leave,' she said. 'Not on my account. But I don't want ...' She fished her car keys out of her jeans pocket and took a deep breath before continuing. 'I don't want you to get any wrong ideas, OK?'

He frowned. 'What wrong ideas?'

'About my family.'

'I don't –'

'It's just – you work at Langmere, right? I'm your employer. That's how it's been till now and anything different is going to get people talking. That's all I'm trying to say.'

He looked at the floor, nudging one of the cases with his foot and looking as if he was picking his words carefully.

'It doesn't feel like that's all you're trying to say,' he mumbled, as if to himself.

'Look, I'm sorry,' said Ellen, reaching for the door and pulling it open. 'I can't do this now.' She stepped past him into the hallway before forcing herself to turn and face him.

'I'll see you tomorrow at work, OK?'

'I've still got a job then?' he asked.

'Of course you've still got a job.'

'I'm sorry about today ... you know...'

There was something so childlike, so pathetic about him that she reached out and patted his arm, before turning away.

She was sitting in the car, trying to get the key into the ignition before she realised just how much her hand was shaking.

12

Ellen: three days later

'Thank God it's stopped raining,' said Kate. 'I always think rain at a funeral's such a cliché.'

Ellen smiled, picking up instantly on the reference. Kate had stayed over last night and they'd watched a dreadful film which was so predictable they found themselves guessing not only what would happen next but even what the characters were about to say. They'd given up on it halfway through and watched repeats of *Friends* instead, working their way steadily through the one bottle of wine they'd agreed would be the limit.

'What's a cliché?' asked Megan.

Kate draped an arm around her shoulder and pulled her in close, exaggerating the embrace. 'You see,' she said, 'that's such an intelligent question. When I was your age the only questions I ever asked were about Adam Ant and Wham, which is why I've ended up cutting people's hair for a living and you, young lady, are going to go to university and become my solicitor.'

Megan beamed, as she always did whenever she was complimented on either her intelligence or her maturity. Ellen thought again what a blessing it was that Jack had cried off that morning with *a raging temperature of 102*, almost certainly Jack-speak for a heavy cold. She didn't doubt he was unwell – he'd never have missed the funeral if he could help it because he took this kind of thing very seriously – but the atmosphere inside the car would have been so different with him there, asking Megan and Harry every five seconds if they were sure they were OK. They'd have been distraught by the time they arrived. With Kate the mood was so much lighter and it was easy to take their minds off what lay ahead.

The driver pulled up outside St Matthew's church and helped each of them out onto the cobbled pathway. Ellen warned Megan and Harry to avoid the puddles as they stepped out. She called them over in turn and fussed over their appearance for a few seconds, as much to compose herself as anything. Sam and Mary joined them from the car behind, Mary looking drawn and pale, Sam watching the pall-bearers closely as if ready to offer advice at any moment. The vicar stepped forward to greet them, glasses perched halfway down his nose and hands clutching a large black bible as he beamed down at the children.

Before Ellen knew what was happening the coffin had been hoisted onto six pairs of shoulders and she was falling into line behind it, holding Harry's hand with Megan and Kate alongside as they made their way along the path. Long before they reached the entrance, she could make out organ music drifting through the vast wooden doors. The vicar began to intone in a strong, clear voice, his words ringing out from speakers in every corner of the building.

I am the resurrection and the life, sayeth the Lord.

There was a sudden rustling, a susurration of clothing and order of service sheets as the congregation rose in sequence like a Mexican wave, heads resolutely facing the front, as if turning to look at the coffin might be considered disrespectful. Ellen took a deep breath, then moved slowly forward. Harry tugged his hand from her grasp and she wondered if maybe she'd been holding on too tightly. She draped an arm over his shoulder instead.

He that believeth in me, though he were dead, yet shall he live, and whosoever liveth and believeth in me shall never die.

Even out of the corner of her eye, she couldn't help but notice how many people from Langmere were here. She wondered exactly who was manning the fort back at the Grove, especially when she saw Colin at the end of a row, sitting slightly apart from his co-workers, which she thought was a fairly appropriate metaphor for his management style. Two rows in front of him Jacob from Calder Vale turned and actually smiled at her and she wanted to hug him for that gesture alone. She smiled back, then faced the front again, her eyes fixed now on the coffin, which the bearers were lifting from their shoulders before resting it on a trestle table in full view of the congregation.

We brought nothing into this world and it is certain we can carry nothing out. The Lord gave, and the Lord hath taken away.

Even as she took her seat in the front pew, she found herself wondering if he was here somewhere. She'd phoned Angela two days ago to check that he'd returned to work as promised so she knew he hadn't run off. He'd spoken so fondly of Barbara that she couldn't imagine him missing her funeral but she hadn't actually spoken to him since that visit to his flat and had no idea what his plans might be. She'd thought of ringing him, even going so far as to pick up the phone on one occasion but what was she supposed to say to him that she hadn't already said?

We have come here today to remember before God our sister, Barbara.

Several times during the past few days she'd wondered how she would feel if he *did* decide to leave. She still didn't know for sure. Until very recently it would have been a no-brainer. He might be family, the only link with her past, but he was a ticking time-bomb, wasn't he? And if there was any chance he would go off some day, she didn't want her children to be anywhere near him. The Ellen of little more than a fortnight ago would have slammed the door shut. Everything in her world was safe, risk-assessed, predictable.

Then suddenly, in the space of a few days, black was white and all points of reference were way off-centre. The past two weeks had washed over her like a tsunami, uprooting certainties and destabilising the bedrock of her oh-so-safe existence. Even if she was still having problems in adjusting, at least no one could accuse her of having been *safe* and *predictable*. She'd never felt so exhilarated, so ... *alive* in her entire life.

If she could be sure he'd be happy to stay on and watch from the outside as he'd been doing for so long, she might be able to live with that. It would be nice to meet discreetly from time to time and talk about their father – he was her only remaining link after all and there was so much she wanted to know. But would he be satisfied with such a minor role in their lives?

Safe ... but predictable

Alive ... but ticking.

At some stage she was going to have to decide which way to turn.

When everyone began to sing the first hymn, it occurred to her how much Barbara would have liked this. She had a lovely voice when she was younger. Ellen recalled breakfasts from her own childhood, her mother singing some show tune she'd heard on the radio while she waited for the kettle to boil. It seemed wrong somehow that she wasn't able to join in now. Ellen herself was having trouble getting the notes out and could have done with her support.

And all of a sudden a memory springs up out of nowhere and for a moment she's back at university, at the graduation reception on the lawns, talking to one of her lecturers, who's spent the past six months trying to persuade her to stay on and do her Master's. And she's feeling really good about herself, sipping champagne and enjoying the attention when, out of the corner of her eye, she sees her mother heading towards her from the building she'd sought out a while earlier so that she might 'powder her nose'. Ellen can see she's hesitating, wandering from group to group, trying to locate her daughter somewhere on the crowded lawn, seemingly oblivious to the stares she's attracting with that ridiculous hat she's borrowed from Mary, which looks like something better suited to Ladies Day at Ascot or maybe a Carmen Miranda tribute show. When Ellen, watching from the wings, sees the patronising smiles aimed her mother's way the moment her back is turned, she's desperate to find a way to get out of this conversation right this minute and move off somewhere with her dignity intact before anyone manages to bracket her with this strange woman. And as she makes her excuses and heads off in the opposite direction before Barbara has seen her, what she feels is relief – the relief of a selfish little madam with her head buried so deep in her own preoccupations she can't even smell the rosebushes that have bordered every path she's ever taken in life, bushes planted and nurtured by the woman she's not even prepared to accept as her own mother. How had it taken so long for her to acknowledge this?

She was brought back to the present by a tug at her sleeve. The final notes of the organ were dying away and the congregation had taken their seats, leaving her as the only one standing. She looked down at Harry and ruffled his hair, wondering why he looked so concerned until she felt the first tear dripping from her chin.

The rest of the service passed in a blur. Afterwards she would recall that Sam read a tribute in a strong, resolute voice although none of the detail stayed with her. The order of service confirmed that there must have been another hymn but she couldn't remember it. As for the sermon, that was unusually brief and to the point by all accounts and much appreciated by everyone as a result but none of it registered. Her thoughts were exclusively with Barbara who had faced the same decision all those years ago. Face up or run. She'd put her unborn daughter first and left the village and the life she knew rather than invite the potential chaos of the past into their lives. And yet ... and yet. Later in life she appeared to have changed her mind. When the opportunity presented itself, instead of staying away she'd decided to get involved, contacting Carl Holmbach and eventually managing to track down Peter's son. Ellen, who had never once sought her mother's advice while she was alive, would have given anything to be able to ask her why. And whether she ever regretted it. The irony was almost painful.

She looked up from the photo of Barbara on the back of the order of service – things were drawing to a close. The pall-bearers were discreetly making their way to the front, positioning themselves either side of the coffin. Then the funeral director leant over and had a quiet word with her, letting her know it was time for the funeral party to follow the coffin outside. She nodded and caught hold of Harry's hand as she got to her feet.

As the procession prepared to move off down the aisle once more, she looked up and prepared herself mentally for the ordeal ahead of her – this was going to be so much tougher than when they'd entered. Now she was actually facing the congregation and everyone was looking at her, each individual trying to convey in that one moment some sort of solidarity with her, a wave of affection and sympathy for what she must be going through. The feeling that she didn't deserve it – had *never* deserved it – was overwhelming.

And now, as she looks away to her left, she catches sight for the first time of the slight figure, sitting on his own, partially obscured by a huge marble pillar some seven or eight rows back. He hasn't seen her – he's looking down at his order of service sheet. He looks different, smarter for one thing. His hair, usually hidden beneath the seemingly inevitable baseball cap, has been brushed back from his forehead and the dark blue suit surprisingly makes him look younger than the more youthful clothes he normally wears to work. She watches as he absent-mindedly slips a finger inside the collar of his shirt and tries to work the top button free. Then, as he looks up from the sheet, she quickly turns away, hoping he hasn't noticed.

The procession starts to move back down the aisle. Kate glances across at her and offers an encouraging smile. Ellen returns it and takes a deep breath. She finds an excuse to straighten Harry's collar, to stroke Megan's cheek with the back of a finger and tell her how lovely she looks ... anything that will spare her the need to look people in the eye as the cortege makes its way oh so slowly back towards the entrance. She isn't aware she's been counting the rows but she must be, because she knows she's drawn level with him without even looking up.

Safe . . . and predictable.

Alive . . . and ticking.

She stops suddenly, a move which causes an element of confusion behind as there was no warning. Not that she could have given any because there are no rational thought processes underpinning this, just instinct.

She turns to her left to face him, as the pall-bearers draw further away, and he looks alarmed for a moment, as if convinced she's about to raise her finger and denounce him here and now. And now that she's closer she can see that even though he's tried to sweep it back his hair's sticking up, years of being fed through the clasp of a back-to-front baseball cap dictating how it should lie. His tie is slightly askew, now that he's undone the top button of his shirt, there's a mark on the shoulder of his suit jacket where he's been leaning against a wall or something and all in all he looks a bit of a mess but . . . but . . .

He's here. The risks are even greater for him but he's here.

When she nods at him, he looks as confused as everyone else. Kate looks across at her, then follows her gaze to see who it is she's nodding at. Sam taps her on the shoulder and asks if something's wrong. But she ignores everyone else and when she nods again, this time holding out her hand, he gets slowly, uncertainly to his feet, casting an anxious glance around him at the sea of faces now peering in his direction, their curiosity undisguised.

He can't reach the aisle without squeezing past several others so he exits the pew on the far side and walks round the back, joining her as she reaches the start of the aisle. He falls into line next to her and they leave the church together, eyes fixed firmly on the coffin in front of them. Once they're outside, he whispers to her.

'What are we doing?'

'I'm not sure,' she whispers back out of the corner of her mouth.

'How are we going to explain this?' he asks, as if he expects her to have this all thought out, when the truth is she hasn't the faintest idea. For once she has no action plan, no short-term, intermediate or long-term proposals or costing exercises to support them. And it feels right.

She says nothing. Instead she reaches across as they step outside and takes his hand – the gloved hand. As she does so, she hears the loud exhaust of a car turning into Church Lane. She frowns as she watches a dark blue shape draw to a halt opposite the main entrance, where the hearse and funeral cars are waiting in a line. She can't see the driver from here but there's something about the way he sits hunched over the wheel that sets her teeth on edge and sends her thoughts racing back to that first afternoon in Oakham, when she stood with Liam Sharp outside Primrose Cottage, watching the dark blue Escort disappear down the High Street and for a moment ... just for a moment ...

Then the driver gets out of the car and reaches across to retrieve something from the back seat. He emerges with a little girl and they cross the road hand in hand, heading for one of the cottages opposite the church.

Ellen realises she's been squeezing his hand more tightly than she might and wonders if she's hurt it. She looks at him and smiles as reassuringly as she can.

'We'll think of something,' she says.

ACKNOWLEDGEMENTS

Until recent months I never really gave much thought to the support structures that have to be in place for an author to produce a novel. Now I know better. So, with humble apologies to anyone whose name I have inadvertently omitted, my gratitude goes to:

- My parents for those Saturday-morning trips to the library which fostered my love of books in the first place, and to my family as a whole for constant support and morale boosts whenever I needed them. There were plenty of times when the events of the last few months must have seemed like wishful thinking
- The staff of the Creative Writing MA course at the University of Chichester, especially Stephanie Norgate, Dave Swann, Karen Stevens and Alison Macleod, for helping me to understand the difference between being a writer and being someone who writes
- My fellow students on the course, especially Jill Campbell and Ellie Piddington for feedback of the highest quality on the earlier parts of the novel
- Baden Prince Junior for his perceptive advice and the enthusiastic way he embraced the novel in its early stages

- Friends who have always taken an interest in my writing over the years, in particular Elaine, Sue, Carrie and Gemma, whose willingness to drop everything so that I can have instant feedback is appreciated more than I can say
- David and the Headship team at The Angmering School for enlightened and sympathetic leadership which has enabled me to chase a pipe dream
- Everyone at The Ampersand Agency, The Buckman Agency, whitefox, Midas PR, Bonnier and Twenty7 for all their help and expertise

Grateful as I am to the above however, particular thanks must go to:

- Peter Buckman, agent sans pareil, who opened the doors of The Ampersand Agency to me and made this all possible
- Mark Smith, CEO of Bonnier Zaffre in London, for falling in love with the manuscript and taking a chance on me in the first place
- Joel Richardson, for guiding me through the entire editorial process with intelligence, acuity and no little sensitivity towards my feelings
- My fellow debut authors at Twenty7 who have kept me entertained and offered unbelievable support throughout the bewildering process of getting published
- A handful of dedicated bloggers and reviewers who picked up the eBook of *The Hidden Legacy* at a very early stage and sang its praises loud and clear – you know who you are!
- Gemma, Alex and Leah ... the best.

Watch out for GJ Minett's new book

LIE IN WAIT

Coming in eBook August 2016 and paperback February 2017

For more information go to
@BonnierZaffre @GJMinett